# The Perfect Hope

## By Nora Roberts

*Homeport*
*The Reef*
*River's End*
*Carolina Moon*
*The Villa*
*Midnight Bayou*
*Three Fates*
*Birthright*
*Northern Lights*
*Blue Smoke*
*Montana Sky*
*Angels Fall*
*High Noon*
*Divine Evil*
*Tribute*
*Sanctuary*
*Black Hills*
*The Search*
*Chasing Fire*
*The Witness*

## Nora Roberts also writes the In Death series using the pseudonym J. D. Robb

*Naked in Death*
*Glory in Death*
*Immortal in Death*
*Rapture in Death*
*Ceremony in Death*
*Vengeance in Death*
*Holiday in Death*
*Conspiracy in Death*
*Loyalty in Death*
*Witness in Death*
*Judgement in Death*
*Betrayal in Death*
*Seduction in Death*
*Reunion in Death*
*Purity in Death*
*Portrait in Death*
*Imitation in Death*
*Divided in Death*
*Visions in Death*
*Survivor in Death*
*Origin in Death*
*Memory in Death*
*Born in Death*
*Innocent in Death*
*Creation in Death*
*Strangers in Death*
*Salvation in Death*
*Promises in Death*
*Kindred in Death*
*Fantasy in Death*
*Indulgence in Death*
*Treachery in Death*
*New York to Dallas*
*Celebrity in Death*
*Delusion in Death*

# NORA ROBERTS

## The Perfect Hope

piatkus

PIATKUS

First published in Great Britain in 2012 by Piatkus
First published in the US in 2012 by The Berkley Publishing Group, a division of Penguin Group
(USA) Inc., New York

A CIP catalogue record for this book
is available from the British Library.

C ISBN 978-0-7499-5566-3
HB ISBN 978-0-7499-5561-8

Printed and bound in Great Britain by CPI Group (UK) Ltd, Croydon, CR0 4YY

Papers used by Piatkus are from well-managed forests
and other responsible sources.

MIX
Paper from
responsible sources
FSC
www.fsc.org
FSC® C104740

Piatkus
An imprint of
Little, Brown Book Group
100 Victoria Embankment
London EC4Y 0DY

An Hachette UK Company
www.hachette.co.uk

www.piatkus.co.uk

*For Suzanne,*
*the perfect innkeeper*

To improve is to change;
To be perfect is to change often.

—WINSTON CHURCHILL

# CHAPTER ONE

WITH A FEW GROANS AND SIGHS, THE OLD BUILDING settled down for the night. Under the star-washed sky its stone walls glowed, rising up over Boonsboro's Square as they had for more than two centuries. Even the crossroads held quiet now, stretching out in pools of shadows and light. All the windows and storefronts along Main Street seemed to sleep, content to doze away in the balm of the summer night.

She should do the same, Hope thought. Settle down, stretch out. Sleep.

That would be the sensible thing to do, and she considered herself a sensible woman. But the long day had left her restless, and—she reminded herself—Carolee would arrive bright and early to start breakfast.

The innkeeper could sleep in.

In any case, it was barely midnight. When she'd lived and worked in Georgetown, she'd rarely managed to settle in for the night this early. Of course, then she'd been managing the Wickham, and if she hadn't been dealing with some small crisis or handling a guest request, she'd been enjoying the nightlife.

The town of Boonsboro, tucked into the foothills of Maryland's Blue Ridge Mountains, might have a rich and storied history, it certainly had its charms—among which she counted the revitalized inn she now managed—but it wasn't famed for its nightlife.

That would change a bit when her friend Avery opened her restaurant and tap house. And wouldn't it be fun to see what the energetic Avery MacTavish did with her new enterprise right next door—and just across The Square from Avery's pizzeria.

Before summer ended, Avery would juggle the running of two restaurants, Hope thought.

And people called *her* an overachiever.

She looked around the kitchen—clean, shiny, warm, and welcoming. She'd already sliced fruit, checked the supplies, restocked the refrigerator. So everything sat ready for Carolee to prepare breakfast for the guests currently tucked in their rooms.

She'd finished her paperwork, checked all the doors, and made her rounds checking for dishes—or anything else out of place. Duties done, she told herself, and still she wasn't ready to tuck her own self in her third-floor apartment.

Instead, she poured an indulgent glass of wine and did a last circle through The Lobby, switching off the chandelier over the central table with its showy summer flowers.

She moved through the arch, gave the front door one last check before she turned toward the stairs. Her fingers trailed lightly over the iron banister.

She'd already checked The Library, but she checked again. It wasn't anal, she told herself. A guest might have slipped in for a glass of Irish or a book. But the room was quiet, settled like the rest.

She glanced back. She had guests on this floor. Mr. and Mrs.

Vargas—Donna and Max—married twenty-seven years. The night at the inn, in Nick and Nora, had been a birthday gift for Donna from their daughter. And wasn't that sweet?

Her other guests, a floor up in Westley and Buttercup, chose the inn for their wedding night. She liked to think the newlyweds, April and Troy, would take lovely, lasting memories with them.

She checked the door to the second-level porch, then on impulse unlocked it and stepped out into the night.

With her wine, she crossed the wide wood deck, leaned on the rail. Across The Square, the apartment above Vesta sat dark—and empty now that Avery had moved in with Owen Montgomery. She could admit—to herself anyway—she missed looking over and knowing her friend was right there, just across Main.

But Avery was exactly where she belonged, Hope decided, with Owen—her first and, as it turned out, her last boyfriend.

Talk about sweet.

And she'd help plan a wedding—May bride, May flowers—right there in The Courtyard, just as Clare's had been this past spring.

Thinking of it, Hope looked down Main toward the bookstore. Clare's Turn The Page had been a risk for a young widow with two children and another on the way. But she'd made it work. Clare had a knack for making things work. Now she was Clare Montgomery, Beckett's wife. And when winter came again, they'd welcome a new baby to the mix.

Odd, wasn't it, that her two friends had lived right in Boonsboro for so long, and she'd relocated only the year—not even a full year yet—before. The new kid in town.

Now, of the three of them, she was the only one still right here, right in the heart of town.

Silly to miss them when she saw them nearly every day, but on restless nights she could wish, just a little, they were still close.

So much had changed, for all of them, in this past year.

She'd been perfectly content in Georgetown, with her home, her work, her routine. With Jonathan, the cheating bastard.

She'd had good, solid plans, no rush, no hurry, but solid plans. The Wickham had been her place. She'd known its rhythm, its tones, its needs. And she'd done a hell of a job for the Wickhams, and their cheating bastard son, Jonathan.

She'd planned to marry him. No, there'd been no formal engagement, no concrete promises, but marriage and future had been on the table.

She wasn't a moron.

And all the time—or at least in the last several months—they'd been together, with him sharing her bed, or her sharing his, he'd been seeing someone else. Someone of his more elevated social strata you could say, she mused, with lingering bitterness. Someone who wouldn't work ten- and twelve-hour days, and often more—to manage the exclusive hotel, but who'd stay there, in its most elaborate suite, of course.

No, she wasn't a moron, but she'd been far too trusting and humiliatingly shocked when Jonathan told her he would be announcing his engagement—to someone else—the next day.

Humiliatingly shocked, she thought again, particularly as they'd been naked and in her bed at the time.

Then again, he'd been shocked, too, when she'd ordered him to get the hell out. He genuinely hadn't understood why anything between them should change.

That single moment ushered in a lot of change.

Now she was Inn BoonsBoro's innkeeper, living in a small town in Western Maryland, a good clip from the bright lights of the big city.

She didn't spend what free time she had planning clever little dinner parties, or shopping in the boutiques for the perfect shoes for the perfect dress for the next event.

Did she miss all that? Her go-to boutique, her favorite lunch spot, the lovely high ceilings and flower-framed little patio of her own town house? Or the pressure and excitement of preparing the hotel for visits from dignitaries, celebrities, business moguls?

Sometimes, she admitted. But not as often as she'd expected to, and not as much as she'd assumed she would.

Because she had been content in her personal life, challenged in her professional one, and the Wickham had been her place. But she'd discovered something in the last few months. Here, she wasn't just content, but happy. The inn wasn't just her place, it was *home*.

She had her friends to thank for that, and the Montgomery brothers along with their mother. Justine Montgomery had hired her on the spot. At the time Hope hadn't known Justine well enough to be surprised by her quick offer. But she did know herself, and continued to be surprised at her own fast, impulsive acceptance.

Zero to sixty? More like zero to ninety and still going.

She didn't regret the impulse, the decision, the move.

Fresh starts hadn't been in the plan, but she was good at adjusting plans. Thanks to the Montgomerys, the lovingly—and effortfully—restored inn was her home and her career.

She wandered the porch, checking the hanging planters, adjusting—minutely—the angle of a bistro chair.

"And I love every square inch of it," she murmured.

One of the porch doors leading out from Elizabeth and Darcy opened. The scent of honeysuckle drifted on the night air.

Someone else was restless, Hope thought. Then again, she didn't know if ghosts slept. She doubted if the spirit Beckett had named Elizabeth for the room she favored would tell her if she asked. Thus far, Lizzy hadn't deigned to speak to her inn-mate.

Hope smiled at the term, sipped her wine.

"Lovely night. I was just thinking how different my life is now, and all things considered, how glad I am it is." She spoke in an easy, friendly way. After all, the research she and Owen had done so far on their permanent guest had proven Lizzy—or Eliza Ford when she'd lived—was one of Hope's ancestors.

Family, to Hope's mind, ought to be easy and friendly.

"We have newlyweds in W&B. They look so happy, so fresh and new somehow. The couple in N&N are here celebrating her fifty-eighth birthday. They don't look new, but they do look happy, and so nice and comfortable. I like giving them a special place to stay, a special experience. It's what I'm good at."

Silence held, but Hope could *feel* the presence. Companionable, she realized. Oddly companionable. Just a couple of women up late, looking out at the night.

"Carolee will be here early. She's doing breakfast tomorrow, and I have the morning off. So." She lifted her glass. "Some wine, some introspection, some feeling sorry for myself circling around to realizing I have nothing to feel sorry for myself for." With a smile, Hope sipped again. "So, a good glass of wine.

"Now that I've accomplished all that, I should get to bed."

Still she lingered a little longer in the quiet summer night, with the scent of honeysuckle drifting around her.

WHEN HOPE CAME down in the morning, the scent was fresh coffee, grilled bacon—and, if her nose didn't deceive her, Carolee's apple-cinnamon pancakes. She heard easy conversation in The Dining Room. Donna and Max, talking about poking around town before driving home.

Hope went down the hall, circled to the kitchen to see if Carolee needed a hand. Justine's sister had her bright blond hair clipped short for summer, with the addition of flirty bangs over her cheerful hazel eyes. They beamed at Hope even as she wagged a finger.

"What are you doing down here, young lady?"

"It's nearly ten."

"And your morning off."

"Which I spent—so far—sleeping until eight, doing yoga, and putzing." She helped herself to a mug of coffee, closed her own deep brown eyes as she sipped. "My first cup of the day. Why is it always the best?"

"I wish I knew. I'm still trying to switch to tea. My Darla's on a health kick and doing her best to drag me along." Carolee spoke of her daughter with affection laced with exasperation. "I really like our Titania and Oberon blend. But . . . it's not coffee."

"Nothing is but coffee."

"You said it. She can't wait for the new gym to open. She says if I don't sign up for yoga classes, she's signing me up and carting me over there."

"You'll love yoga." Hope laughed at the doubt—and anxiety—on Carolee's face. "Honest."

"Hmm." Carolee lifted the dishcloth again, went back to polishing the granite countertop. "The Vargases loved the room, and as usual the bathroom—starring the magic toilet—got raves. I haven't heard a peep out of the newlyweds yet."

"I'd be disappointed in them if you had." Hope brushed at her hair. Unlike Carolee, she was experimenting with letting it grow out of the short, sharp wedge she'd sported the last two years. The dark, glossy ends hit her jaw now, just in between enough to be annoying.

"I'm going to go check on Donna and Max, see if they want anything."

"Let me do it," Hope said. "I want to say good morning anyway, and I think I'll run down to TTP, say hi to Clare while it's still my morning off."

"I saw her last night at the book club. She's got the cutest baby bump. Oh, I've got plenty of batter if the newlyweds want more pancakes."

"I'll let them know."

She slipped into The Dining Room, chatted with the guests while she subtly checked to be sure there was still plenty of fresh summer berries, coffee, juice.

Once she'd satisfied herself her guests were happy, she started back upstairs to grab her purse—and ran into the newlyweds as they entered from the rear porch.

"Good morning."

"Oh, good morning." The new bride carried the afterglow of a honeymoon morning well spent. "That's the most beautiful room. I love everything about it. I felt like a princess bride."

"As you wish," Hope said and made them both laugh.

"It's so clever the way each room's named and decorated for romantic couples."

"Couples with happy endings," Troy reminded her, and got a slow, dreamy smile from his bride.

"Like us. We want to thank you so much for making our wedding night so special. It was everything I wanted. Just perfect."

"That's what we do here."

"But . . . we wondered. We know we're supposed to check out soon. . . ."

"If you'd like a later checkout, I can arrange it . . ." Hope began.

"Well, actually . . ."

"We're hoping we can stay another night." Troy slid his arm around April's shoulders, drew her close. "We really love it here. We were going to drive down into Virginia, just pick our spots as we went, but . . . we really like it right here. We'll take any room that's available, if there is one."

"We'd love to have you, and your room's open tonight."

"Really?" April bounced on her toes. "Oh, this is better than perfect. Thank you."

"It's our pleasure. I'm glad you're enjoying your stay."

Happy guests made for happy innkeepers, Hope thought as she dashed upstairs for her bag. She dashed back down again, into her office to change the reservation, and with the scents and voices behind her, hurried out the back through Reception.

She skirted the side of the building, glancing across the street at Vesta. She knew Avery's and Clare's schedules nearly as well as her own. Avery would be prepping for opening this morning, and Clare should be back from her early doctor's appointment.

The sonogram. With luck, they'd know by now if Clare was carrying the girl she hoped for.

As she waited for the walk light at the corner, she looked down Main Street. There Ryder Montgomery stood in front of the building Montgomery Family Contractors was currently rehabbing. Nearly done, she thought, and soon the town would have a bakery again.

He wore jeans torn at the left knee and splattered with drips of paint or drywall compound or whatever else splattered on job sites. His tool belt hung low, like an old-time sheriff's gun belt—at least to her eye. Dark hair curled shaggily from under his ball cap. Sunglasses covered eyes she knew to be a gold-flecked green.

He consulted with a couple of his crew, pointed up, circling a finger, shaking his head, all while he stood in that hip-shot way of his.

Since a dull wash of primer currently covered the front of the building, she assumed they discussed the finish colors.

One of the crew let out a bray of laughter, and Ryder responded with a flash of grin and a shrug.

The shrug, like the stance, was another habit of his, she mused.

The Montgomery brothers were an attractive breed, but in her opinion, her two friends had plucked the pick of the crop. She found Ryder a little surly, marginally unsociable.

And, okay, sexy—in a primitive, rough-edged sort of way.

Not her type, not remotely.

As she started across the street, a long, exaggerated wolf whistle shrilled out. Knowing it to be a joke, she tipped her face back toward the bakery, added a smoldering smile—then a wave to Jake, one of the painters. He and the laborer beside him waved back.

But not Ryder Montgomery, of course, she thought. He simply hooked his thumb in his pocket, watched her. Unsociable, she thought again. He couldn't even stir himself for a casual wave.

She accepted the slow kindling in her belly as the natural reaction of a healthy woman to a long, shaded stare delivered by a sexy—if surly—man.

Particularly a woman who hadn't had any serious male contact in—God—a year. A little more than a year. But who's counting?

Her own fault, her own choice, so why think about it?

She reached the other side of Main Street, turned right toward the bookstore just as Clare stepped out onto its pretty covered porch.

She waved again as Clare stood a moment, one hand on the baby bump under her breezy summer dress. Clare had her long sunny hair pulled back in a tail, with blue-framed sunglasses softening the glare of the bold morning sun.

"I was just coming over to check on you," Hope called out.

Clare held up her phone. "I was just texting you." She slipped the phone back in her pocket, left her hand there a moment as she came down the steps to the sidewalk.

"Well?" Hope scanned her friend's face. "Everything good?"

"Yeah. Good. We got back just a few minutes ago. Beckett . . ." She glanced over her shoulder. "He's driving around to the back of the bakery. He's got his tools."

"Okay." Mildly concerned, Hope laid a hand on Clare's arm. "Honey, you had the sonogram, right?"

"Yeah."

"And?"

"Oh. Let's walk up to Vesta. I'll tell you and Avery at the same time. Beckett's going to call his mother, tell his brothers. I need to call my parents."

"The baby's all right?"

"Absolutely." She patted her purse as they walked. "I have pictures."

"I have to see!"

"I'll be showing them off for days. Weeks. It's amazing."

Avery popped out the front door of the restaurant, a white bib apron covering capris and a T-shirt. She bounced on purple Crocs. The sun speared into her Scot's warrior-queen hair, sent the short ends to glimmering.

"Are we thinking pink?"

"Are you opening alone?" Clare countered.

"Yeah, it's just me. Fran's not due in for twenty. Are you okay? Is everything okay?"

"Everything's absolutely perfectly wonderfully okay. But I want to sit down."

With her friends exchanging looks behind her back, Clare walked in and went straight to the counter, then dropped onto a stool. Sighed. "It's the first time I've been pregnant with three boys fresh out of school for the summer. It's challenging."

"You're a little pale," Avery commented.

"Just tired."

"Want something cold?"

"With my entire being."

As Avery went to the cooler, Hope sat down, narrowed her eyes at Clare's face. "You're stalling. If nothing's wrong—"

"Nothing's wrong, and maybe I'm stalling a little. It's a big announcement." She laughed to herself, took the chilled ginger ale Avery offered.

"So here I am, with my two closest friends, in Avery's pretty restaurant that already smells of pizza sauce."

"You'll have this in a pizzeria." Avery passed Hope a bottle of water. Then she crossed her arms, scanned Clare's face. "It's a girl. Ballet shoes and hair ribbons!"

Clare shook her head. "I appear to specialize in boys. Make that baseball gloves and action figures."

"A boy?" Hope leaned over, touched Avery's hand. "Are you disappointed?"

"Not even the tiniest bit." She opened her purse. "Want to see?"

"Are you kidding?" Avery made a grab, but Clare snatched the envelope out of reach. "Does he look like you? Like Beck? Like a fish? No offense, but they always look like a fish to me."

"Which one?"

"Which one what?"

"There are two."

"Two?" Hope nearly bobbled the water. "Twins? You're having twins?"

"Two?" Avery echoed. "You have two fish?"

"Two boys. Look at my beautiful boys." Clare pulled out the sonogram printout, then burst into tears. "Good tears," she managed. "Hormones, but good ones. Oh, God. Look at my babies!"

"They're gorgeous!"

Clare swiped at tears as she grinned at Avery. "You don't see them."

"No, but they're gorgeous. Twins. That's five. You did the math, right? You're going to have five boys."

"We did the math, but it's still sinking in. We didn't expect—we never thought—maybe I should have. I'm bigger than I've ever been this early. But when the doctor told us . . . Beckett went white."

She laughed, even as tears poured. "Sheet white. I thought he was going to pass out. Then we just stared at each other. And then we started to laugh. We laughed like lunatics. I think maybe we were both a little hysterical. Five. Oh, sweet Jesus. *Five* boys."

"You'll be great. All of you," Hope told her.

"We will. I know it. I'm so dazzled, so happy, so stunned. I don't know how Beckett drove home. I couldn't tell you if we drove back from Hagerstown or from California. I was in some sort of shock, I think. Twins."

She laid her hands on her belly. "Do you know how there are moments in your life when you think, this is it. I'll never be happier or more excited. I'll never *feel* more than I do right now. Just exactly now. This is one of those moments for me."

Hope folded her into a hug, and Avery folded them both.

"I'm so happy for you," Hope murmured. "Happy, dazzled, and excited right along with you."

"The kids are going to get such a kick out of this." Avery drew back. "Right?"

"Yeah. And since Liam already made it clear if I had a girl he wouldn't stoop so low as to play with her, I think he'll be especially pleased."

"What about your due date?" Hope asked. "Earlier with twins?"

"A little. They told me November twenty-first. So, Thanksgiving babies instead of Christmas, New Year's."

"Gobble, gobble," Avery said and made Clare laugh again.

"You have to let us help set up the nursery," Hope began. Planning was in her blood.

"I'm counting on it. I don't have a thing. I gave away all the baby things after Murphy. I never thought I'd fall in love again, or marry again, or have more children."

"Can we say baby shower? A double-the-fun theme," Hope decided. "Or what comes in pairs, sets of two. Something like that. I'll work on it. We should schedule it in early October, just to be safe."

"Baby shower." Clare sighed. "More and more real. I need to call my parents, and I need to tell the girls," she added, referring to her bookstore staff. She levered herself up. "November babies," she said again. "I should have shed the baby weight by May and the wedding."

"Oh yeah, I'm getting married." Avery held out her hand, admired the diamond that replaced the bubble-gum-machine ring Owen had put on her finger. Twice.

"Getting married, *and* opening a second restaurant, and helping plan a baby shower, and redecorating the current single guy's master suite into a couple's master suite." Hope poked Avery in the arm. "We have a lot of planning to do."

"I can take some time tomorrow."

"Good." Hope took a moment to flip through her mental list, rearrange tasks, gauge the timing. "One o'clock. I can clear the time. Can you make that?" she asked Clare. "I can fix us a little lunch and we can get some of the planning worked out before I have check-ins."

"One o'clock tomorrow." Clare patted her belly. "We'll be there."

"I'll be over," Avery promised. "If I'm a little later, we had a good lunch rush. But I'll get over."

Hope walked out with Clare, grabbed another hug before separating. And imagined Clare telling her parents the happy news. Imagined, too, Avery texting Owen. And Beckett slipping off to check on Clare during the day, or just stealing a few minutes to bask with her.

For a moment she wished she had someone to call or text, or slip away to, someone to share the lovely news with.

Instead she went around the back of the inn, up the outside stairs. She let herself in on the third floor, listening as she walked down to her apartment.

Yes, she thought, she could just hear Carolee's voice, and the excitement in it. No doubt Justine Montgomery had already called her sister to share the news about the twins.

Hope closed herself into her apartment. She'd spend a couple hours in the quiet, she decided, researching their resident ghost, and the man named Billy she waited for.

# CHAPTER TWO

H IS MOTHER WAS DRIVING HIM CRAZY. IF SHE POPPED UP
with another project before he finished one of the half dozen
currently on his plate, he might just take his dog and move to Barbados.

He could build himself a nice little beach house. Maybe a lanai.
He had the skills.

Ryder pulled his truck into the lot behind the inn, major project,
finished—thank God—but never really done because there was
always something. The inn shared that lot with what would be, according to the ever-plotting Justine Montgomery, a pretty, clever, state-of-
the-art fitness center.

Right now it was an ugly, green, flat-roofed, leaky lump. And that
was just the outside. Inside currently boasted a rabbit warren of rooms,
a basement full of water, staircases out of a horror movie, and falling-
down ceilings. Not to mention the abysmal state of the wiring and
plumbing, which he wouldn't since they'd just gut the whole fucking
mess.

Part of him wanted to sneak in some night on a giant machine and bulldoze the whole fugly building. But he knew better, and could admit he enjoyed a challenge.

He had one.

Still, as the always reliable Owen had texted him the demo permit was in, at least they could start tearing in.

Ryder sat a moment with his homely and sweet-natured dog, Dumbass, beside him while Lady Gaga seduced the edge of glory. Chick was pretty weird, Ryder thought, but she sure had the pipes.

Together Ryder and his dog studied the ugly green lump. He liked demo. Beating the shit out of walls never failed to satisfy. So that was something. And the work, transforming the ugly bastard, would be interesting.

A fitness center. He didn't understand people who plugged them-selves into a machine and went nowhere. Why not do something constructive that made you sweat? A gym, yeah, he could see a gym with speed bags, a sparring ring, some serious weights. But fitness center said girly to him. Yoga and that Pilates stuff.

And women in those snug little outfits, he reminded himself. Yeah, there was that. Like demo, who wouldn't enjoy that?

No point brooding about it anyway, he decided. It was a done deal.

He got out of the truck, and D.A. hopped out faithfully beside him.

He couldn't figure out why he was in such a broody mood any-way. The bakery project was down to punch-out and paint, Avery's MacT's was coming right along—and he looked forward to sitting down on a bar stool in her new pub and having a beer.

He had a kitchen remodel all but wrapped, and Owen was handling some built-ins for another client. A lot of work was better than no work. He could build a beach house in Barbados when he was old.

Still, he felt edgy and annoyed, and couldn't quite figure out why. Until he glanced over at the inn.

Hope Beaumont. Yeah, that might account for some edgy.

She did a good job, no question about that. The fact that she was anal, obsessively organized, and a chewer of details didn't bother him especially. He'd lived and worked with that type all his life, in the form of his brother Owen.

Just something about her got under his skin, and tended to burn there from time to time since they'd locked lips on New Year's Eve.

It had been an accident, he told himself. An impulse. An accidental impulse. He didn't intend to repeat it.

But he could wish she was a plump, homely, middle-aged woman with a couple of grandkids and a knitting hobby.

"One day she could be," he muttered to D.A., who obligingly thumped his tail.

With a shrug, he walked down, crossed over, and opened the door of the future MacT's Restaurant and Tap House for the crew.

He liked the space, liked it particularly now that they'd rejoined the two buildings, opening the wall between with a wide doorway so the restaurant and bar patrons, and the staff, could move from one side to the other.

Avery knew what she wanted, and how to make it happen, so he knew MacT's would be a good place to eat and drink, to socialize if socializing was your thing. Good dining for grown-ups she called it, as opposed to the casual family style of Vesta.

He had a soft spot for Vesta—and a softer one for their Warrior's Pizza, but as Avery had been trying out recipes on them for months, he figured he'd be able to choke down a meal or two in her new place.

He crossed over to the opening, studied the bar space. A lot of work yet, he judged, but he could envision it finished, with the long bar he and his brothers were building in place. Dark woods, strong colors, some brick on the walls. And all those beers on tap.

Yeah, it wouldn't hurt his feelings to spend some time there, and hoist a beer in satisfaction of a job well done.

When it was done.

He heard voices, crossed back over.

Once he got the crew going, he walked down to the bakery to check on the men there. If he'd had a choice, he'd have strapped on his tool belt, gotten to the real work.

But he had a morning meeting scheduled back at the new job site, and he was already running late.

He started back around, saw both of his brothers' trucks in the lot. He assumed Owen had picked up coffee and donuts as well as the demo permit. You could count on Owen in the everyday and in a nuclear holocaust.

He thought of Beckett, married to Clare the Fair, instant father of three, and now the expectant father of twins.

Jesus, twins.

But maybe the thrill of upcoming twins would distract their mother from thinking up a new project.

Probably not.

He went through the open doors on St. Paul, smelled the coffee.

Yeah, you could count on Owen.

He plucked out the single go-cup left, the one with an *R* written with a Sharpie by his anal brother. Glugged even as he flipped up the lid on the donuts.

His dog's tail immediately sent out a tattoo on the floor.

He heard his brothers' voices, somewhere in the rabbit warren, but took his coffee and, after tossing D.A. a chunk of his jelly-filled donut, walked over to the plans spread out on the plywood and sawhorses.

He'd seen them before, of course, but they knocked him out. Beckett's concept gave their mother everything she wanted, and more. Yeah, he thought, better than bulldozing it. Better to gut what needed gutting and build on what could be built on.

It didn't look like a gym to Ryder—at least not the speed-bag, sweat-soaked locker room–type he might frequent, but it was a beauty.

And enough work, enough complications to make him curse Beckett's name for weeks, months. Possibly years.

And still . . .

Lifting and pitching the roof was practical as well as aesthetically pleasing. Taking the flat-roofed jut off the parking lot side and making it into a deck, also smart. Plenty of glass for plenty of light with new windows and doors. God knew the place needed them, even if it meant cutting into the cinder-block walls.

Fancy locker rooms with steam rooms and saunas. His keep-it-basic mind balked at that, but he had to admit, he liked a good, long steam.

He ate his donut, tossing bits to the tail-thumping D.A., while he studied the first floor, the second floor, the mechanicals.

Beautiful work, he thought. Beckett had the talent and the vision, even if invariably some of the vision was a pain in the ass on a practical work level.

He washed down the donut with coffee as his brothers walked out of the maze.

"Demo permit."

"Check," Owen said. "Good morning to you, too." His sunglasses hung from the neck of his spotless white T-shirt. Since Beckett intended for him to join in the demo, the spotless wouldn't last long.

"You press those jeans, Sally?"

"No." Owen's quiet blue eyes flicked toward the donuts before he broke a cruller in half. "They're just clean. I have a couple meetings later."

"Uh-huh. Hey, Big Daddy."

Beckett grinned, raked fingers through his mop of chestnut brown hair. "The boys want to name them Logan and Luke."

"Wolverine and Skywalker." Amused, Ryder considered. "Melding X-Men and Star Wars. Interesting choice."

"I like it. Clare laughed it off at first, then the idea got a hook in. They're good names."

"Good enough for Wolverine and Skywalker."

"I think we're going with them, which is cool. My ears keep ringing though. You know, like they do after an explosion."

"Two's just one more than one," Owen pointed out. "It's about planning and scheduling."

"Because you have so much experience with rug rats," Ryder said with a snort.

"Everything's about planning and scheduling," Owen countered. "Speaking of which, let's check the plans and schedules." He pulled his phone off his belt.

Ryder decided on another donut, let the sugar and fat soothe him through the volley of details. Inspections, permits, material orders and deliveries, rough-ins, finals, shop work, site work.

Ryder kept it all in his head as well, just maybe not as precisely columned and tallied as Owen. But he knew what had to be done and when, which men to assign to which job, and how long the steps should take. On the inside, and—given the vagaries of construction— the outside.

"Mom's looking at equipment," Beckett put in when Owen paused. "You know, treadmills and cross-trainers and all that happy shit."

"I'm not going to think about that." Ryder looked around. Crap walls, he thought, crap floors. Just crap. Cross-trainers and dumbbells and freaking yoga mats were a hell of a long way off.

"We may want to think about the parking lot."

Now Ryder's eyes narrowed on Owen. "What about the parking lot?"

"Now that we've got it all, instead of patching we should tear the bitch up, level it, add drains, resurface."

"Hell." He wanted to object, just on general principles, but they needed the damn drainage. "Fine. But I'm not thinking about that now either."

"What are you thinking about?"

Rather than answer, Ryder just walked out.

"Is he bitchier than usual?" Owen wondered.

"Hard to tell." Beckett looked down at the drawings again. "It's going to be a pain in the ass—and mostly in his—but it's going to work."

"Ugliest building in town."

"Yeah, it wins that prize. The good news is anything we do's an improvement. As soon as the Dumpster gets here, we can—"

He broke off as Ryder came in with a sledgehammer and a crowbar.

"Get your own," Ryder told them and, setting the crowbar aside, chose a wall at random. Swung away. The hard, undeniably satisfying *thwack* send drywall chips flying.

"The Dumpster . . . " Owen began.

"It's on its way isn't it?" Putting his back into it, Ryder swung again. "According to the holy word of your sacred schedule."

"We should bring in some of the crew," Beckett considered.

"Why should they have all the fun?" When the sledgehammer arced again, D.A. crawled under the sawhorses for a nap.

"He's got a point." Beckett glanced at Owen, got a shrug and grin. "We ought to start on the second floor."

"This one's not load-bearing." Another couple swings and Ryder had the flimsy interior wall in rubble. "But yeah." He leaned on the hammer, grinned back at his brothers. "Let's gut this bitch."

AFTER A FEW days of listening to bangs and crashes, Hope's curiosity won. With Carolee on duty—the honeymooners were now into their fourth day of their wedding-night stay—she crossed the lot toward the newest Montgomery family project. She had a legitimate reason for seeking them out, but could admit her primary motive was curiosity.

She'd heard plenty of banging throughout the day, and every glance out the window showed her some grubby guy hauling debris out, and into a huge green Dumpster.

A text from Avery netted her the intel that demolition had begun on the projected fitness center.

She wanted to see for herself.

The banging booms increased as she approached, and she heard a burst of manic male laughter through the open windows. Grinding, guitar-heavy rock rolled out with it.

She walked up to the side entrance—what was left of it— peeked in.

Her eyes widened.

She'd never been in the building, but she'd looked in the windows, and she was pretty sure there'd been walls, and ceilings.

Now barely a skeleton remained, along with the tangled wire intestines and massive amounts of gray dust.

Cautious now as the thuds, thumps, and bangs seemed to shake the entire structure, she went around to the front.

The door stood open. To air it out? she wondered. Who knew?

Another door, one that led up to what had been second-level apartments, stood open as well. Music, men, bangs echoed down.

She considered the narrow stairs, the grimy stairwell, the noise. Not that curious, she decided, and backed away.

As she circled back around, two men—coated with gray dust, all but anonymous in their safety goggles, work gloves, and grimy faces, hauled out another load of what must have once been a wall. It landed in the Dumpster with a muffled *thump*.

"Excuse me," she began.

She recognized Ryder by the way he turned his head, angled his body.

He shoved up his goggles, aimed one of his mildly annoyed stares with those impatient green eyes. "You're going to want to stay back."

"I can see that. It looks like you're taking the building down to the shell."

"That's about it. You need to stay clear."

"Yes, so you said."

"Need something?"

"Actually, yes. I'm having a problem with some of the lights—the wall sconces. I thought if your electrician was here, he could—"

"He left." Ryder gave his helper a head jerk to send him back inside, then dragged off his safety goggles.

Now he looked a little like a reverse raccoon, Hope thought, and couldn't quite hold back the smile. "It's dirty work."

"And a lot of it," Ryder replied. "What kind of problem?"

"They won't stay on. They—"

"Have you changed the bulbs?"

She just stared at him. "Gee, why didn't I think of that?"

"Okay. Somebody will come check it out. Is that it?"

"For the moment."

He gave her a nod, boosted himself back through the opening, and disappeared.

"Thanks so much," Hope muttered to empty air, and walked back to the inn.

It usually lifted her mood, just walking inside. The way it looked, the way it smelled—especially now as Carolee's chocolate chip cookies sweetened the air. But she strode straight into the kitchen, irked everywhere.

"*What* is that man's problem?"

Carolee, face flushed from baking, slid a batch of cookies in the wall oven. "Which man, honey?"

"Ryder Montgomery. Is rudeness his religion?"

"He can be a little abrupt, especially when he's working. Which is, I guess, almost always. What did he do?"

"Nothing. He was just himself. You know how we've had those sconces keep burning out, or not coming on? I went over to tell him—or one of them, and drew him. He actually asked if I'd changed the bulbs. Do I look like a moron?"

With a smile, Carolee held out a cookie. "No, but they did actually have a tenant once that reported a problem, and Ry went all the way over to find out the problem with the light was a burned-out bulb. The woman, and I guess she was a moron, was stunned to realize she had to change the lightbulb."

"Hmm." Hope bit into the cookie. "Still."

"So what's going on over there?"

"Banging and crashing and a lot of crazed laughing."

"Demo. It's fun."

"I suppose. I didn't realize they were taking the whole place down to the bones. No great loss, but I didn't realize." And she fretted a little how the noise factor would affect her guests.

"You should see the plans. I got a peek at them. It's going to be wonderful."

"I don't doubt it. They do good work."

"Justine's already started looking at light fixtures and sinks."

The cookie, and Carolee, shifted Hope's mood. "She's in heaven."

"She's going all modern and sleek and shiny. Lots of chrome, she said. It's one look, you know, rather than a lot of them like here, but it's still a lot to figure out. It'll be fun to watch it all come together."

"It will." Yes, it would, she realized. She hadn't been in on the renovations here from the start. Now she'd see another building done from beginning to end. "I'm going to get some work done before check-in."

"I'm going to run to the market when the cookies are done. Anything you want to add to the list?"

"I think we covered it. Thanks, Carolee."

"I love my job."

So did she, Hope thought as she settled into her office. One difficult Montgomery couldn't spoil it.

She checked her email, smiled at the thank-you note from a previous guest, wrote a memo to fulfill an upcoming guest's request for a bottle of champagne to surprise his parents on their visit.

She checked reservations—a full house for the weekend—reviewed her own personal calendar.

When the florist arrived, she took the fresh arrangements upstairs to Titania and Oberon. Though she'd already done so, she did a last check of the room to make certain everything was perfect for the new guests.

Following habit and routine, she went into The Library, checked the lights—her daily list included checking all lights and lamps for burned-out bulbs, thank you, Ryder Montgomery. Using her phone, she emailed herself when she found one, added a directive to bring up more coffee disks for The Library's machine.

She continued downstairs to run the same check on The Lounge, The Lobby, The Dining Room. Then she turned into the kitchen, and had to bite back a yelp when she spotted Ryder in the kitchen helping himself to the cookies.

"I didn't hear you come in." How did he move that quietly in those big, clunky boots?

"I just got here. Good cookies."

"Carolee just baked them. She must still be at the market."

"Okay."

He just stood, eating his cookie, staring at her with his dog at his feet, grinning. The doggie grin led her to conclude he'd also enjoyed a cookie.

The man had cleaned up—mostly. At least he hadn't tracked demolition dust in with him.

"Well. There's one on two, and another on three." She turned away, assuming he'd follow.

"Anybody in the place?"

"We have guests in W&B, but they're out, and we have guests coming in for T&O. See, now it's on." She gestured toward the second wall sconce when they topped the stairs. "I was just up here, and it wasn't."

"Uh-huh."

"Look, you can ask Carolee if you don't believe me."

"I didn't say I didn't believe you."

"You act like you don't." Fuming a little, she walked up to three. "There! It's off, as you can see for yourself."

"Yeah, I can see that." He went over, lifted off the globe, unscrewed the bulb. "Got a fresh one?"

"I keep some in my apartment, but it's *not* the bulb."

She pulled out a key, unlocked her apartment door.

Ryder put a hand on it before it could close in his face. He stayed out of her space, but hey, he was right here. So he pushed the door all the way open, took a look inside.

Neat and tidy, like the rest of the place. Smelled good, too—like the rest of the place. No clutter. Not a lot of girly fuss either, and he'd expected that. A lot of pillows on the sofa, but he knew few women who wouldn't load a couch and bed with pillows. Strong colors, a couple of plants in pots, fat candles.

She swung out of her kitchen, stopped short so he knew he'd given her another jolt. Then she held out the new bulb.

He strolled down, screwed it in. It burned bright.

"It's *not* the bulb," Hope insisted. "I put the other in this morning."

"Okay."

D.A. sat by Ryder's feet, eyes on The Penthouse door. His tail wagged.

"Don't okay me. I'm telling you, it's—There!" Her voice held a note of triumph as the bulb went dark. "It did it again. There has to be a short, or something wrong with the wiring."

"No."

"What do you mean, no? You just saw for yourself." As she spoke, the door to The Penthouse eased open.

Hope barely glanced back. Then it hit her. She smelled the honeysuckle, of course, but she'd gotten so used to it. "Why would she play with the lights?"

"How would I know?" His shoulders lifted as his thumbs hooked in his front pockets. "Maybe she's bored. She's been dead awhile. Or maybe she's pissed at you."

"She is not. There's no reason." Hope started to close The Penthouse door, pushed it open instead. "There's water running."

She clipped down the short hall into the big elaborate bathroom. Water ran into the double vessel sinks on the counter, in the generous jet tub, from the shower and body jets.

"Oh, for God's sake."

"Does this happen often?"

"It's a first. Come on, Lizzy," she muttered, turning off the sink faucets. "I have guests coming."

Ryder opened the glass door, turned off the showerhead, the body jets.

"I'm doing the research." Impatient now, Hope turned off the tub. "I know Owen is, too, but it's not exactly a snap to find someone named Billy who lived, we assume, during the nineteenth century."

"If your ghost is acting up, I can't do anything about it." Ryder swiped his wet hand on his jeans.

"She's not *my* ghost. It's your building."

"She's your ancestor." With his habitual shrug, he went out, walked to the parlor door. He tried the knob, glanced back. "How about telling your great-great-whatever to cut it out."

"Cut what out?"

He jiggled the knob again.

"That's just—" She nudged him aside, tried the knob herself. "This is ridiculous." Out of patience entirely, Hope continued to rattle the knob. Then she threw up her hands, jabbed a finger at it. "Do something."

"Like what?"

"Take off the knob, or the whole door."

"With what?"

She frowned, glanced down. "You don't have your tools? Why don't you have your tools? You always have your tools."

"It was a lightbulb."

Temper merged with just a touch of panic. "It *wasn't* a lightbulb. I told you it wasn't a lightbulb. What are you doing?"

"I'm going to sit down a minute."

"No!"

At her near-shout, D.A. moseyed to a corner and curled into it. Out of the line of fire.

"Don't you dare sit on that chair. You're not clean."

"Oh, for Christ's sake." But he went around the chair, opened the window. And considered the logistics of the roof.

"Don't go out there! What am I supposed to do when you fall?"

"Call nine-one-one."

"No. Seriously, Ryder. Call one of your brothers, or the fire department, or——"

"I'm not calling the fire department because the damn door won't open."

She held up her hands, took a breath. Then sat down herself. "I'm just going to calm down."

"Good start."

"There's no call to be snotty with me." She pushed at her hair—and yes, the in-between length definitely annoyed. "I didn't jam the door."

"Snotty?" It might've been a smirk, might've been a sneer, but it hit just between the two. "I'm being snotty?"

"You take snotty to a new level. You don't have to like me, and I keep out of your way as much as possible. But I run this inn, and damn well. Our paths have to cross occasionally. You could at least pretend to be polite."

Now he leaned back against the door. "I don't pretend to be anything, and who says I don't like you?"

"You do. Every time you're snotty."

"Maybe that's my response to snooty."

"Snooty!" Sincerely insulted, she goggled at him. "I'm not snooty."

"You've got it down to a science. But that's your deal." He moved over, looked out the window again.

"You've been rude to me since the first minute I met you. Right in this room, before it was a room."

She remembered the moment perfectly, the dizziness, the powerful surge inside her body, the way the light had seemed to burst around him.

She didn't want to think about it.

Irritated, he turned around. "Maybe it had something to do with you looking at me like I'd punched you in the face."

"I did not. I just had a momentary . . . I don't know."

"Maybe because you charge around on stilts."

"Seriously? Now you're criticizing my shoes?"

"Just commenting."

She made a sound in her throat that struck him as feral, leaped up, and banged a fist on the door. "Open this damn door!"

"She'll open it when she's ready. You're just going to hurt yourself."

"Don't tell me what to do." She couldn't say why his matter-of-fact reaction increased her own temper, and that hint of panic. "You—you don't even use my name. It's like you don't know it."

"I know your name. Stop banging on the door. Hope. See, I know your name. Stop it."

He reached up, covered her fisted hand with his.

And she felt it again, that surge, that strange dizziness. Cautiously, she braced against the door, turned her head to look at him.

Close again, as they'd been on New Year's. Close enough to see those gold flecks scattered across the green of his eyes. Close enough to see the heat, and the consideration in them.

She didn't think about leaning in, but her body did. To stop it, she pressed a hand on his chest. Was his heart a little unsteady? She thought it might be. Maybe she only hoped it, so she wouldn't be alone.

"She trapped Owen and Avery in E&D," Hope remembered. "She wanted them to . . ." Kiss. To discover each other. "She's a romantic."

Ryder stepped back, and the moment broke like glass. "Right now she's a nuisance."

The window he'd opened closed quietly on its own.

"I'd say she's making a statement." Calmer now, steadier as he seemed less so, Hope pushed at her hair. "Oh for God's sake, Ryder, just kiss me. It won't kill you, and then she'll let us out of here."

"Maybe I don't like having women—dead ones or live ones— maneuver me."

"Believe me, kissing you isn't going to be the highlight of my day, but I have guests arriving any minute. Or." She pulled out her phone. "I'm calling Owen."

"You're not calling Owen."

She got him now. Having one of his brothers come over to let them out? Mortifying. Kissing her, she calculated, was the lesser of two evils. Amused, she smiled at him. "You can close your eyes and think of England."

"Funny." He stepped over, braced a hand on either side of her head. "This is because I've wasted enough time, and I want a cold beer."

"Fine."

He leaned down, hovered a moment, a breath from her lips.

Don't think, she ordered herself. Don't react. It's nothing.

It's nothing.

It was heat and light, and oh, that surge again from the soles of her feet to the crown of her head. He didn't touch her, but for that mouth against mouth, and she had to curl her hands at her sides to stop herself from reaching out. Grabbing on, dragging him in.

She let herself slide, couldn't resist it, as the kiss spun out.

He'd meant to do no more than brush his lips to hers. As he might to a friend, an aunt, a plump middle-aged woman with a couple of grandkids.

But he sank into it, too deep. The taste of her, the scent, the feel of her lips yielding to his.

Not sweet, not sharp, but something mysteriously between. Something uniquely Hope.

It—she—stirred him more than it should. More than he wanted.

Stepping back from her cost brutal effort.

He stared back at her for a beat, for two. Then she let out a breath, uncurled her hand, tried the knob.

"There." She opened the door. "It worked."

"Get moving before she changes her mind."

The minute they were in the hall, he walked straight to the now cheerfully burning light, lifted the globe from the floor, fixed it on.

"Done." He stood where he was, gave her another long look.

She started to speak, and the doorbell pealed.

"My guests are here. I need to—"

"I'll go out the back."

She nodded, hurried downstairs.

He listened to the clip of her heels on wood, let himself take a breath.

"Don't pull that crap again," he said. With his dog faithfully at his heels, Ryder walked away, out of the scent of honeysuckle and Hope.

# CHAPTER THREE

GRABBING PRIVATE TIME PRESENTED A CHALLENGE, BUT a woman needed the ear and input of her female friends. Hope grabbed what she could the next day in the window after preparing breakfast for guests and before Vesta opened.

She dashed across Main Street a few minutes after ten, and straight into the restaurant. Clare and Avery already sat at a table, studying Avery's potential wedding dress, again, on the iPad.

"I brought muffins." Hope dropped the little basket on the table, tossed back the cheerful red napkin. "Blueberry, still warm from the oven. Thanks for being here."

"You made it sound urgent." Avery took a sniff, went *mmm*, grabbed a muffin.

"It's not urgent. It's just a thing. I know you're busy."

"Never too busy. Sit down," Clare told her. "You look frazzled, and you never do."

"I'm not. Exactly. Just . . ." With a shake of her head, Hope sat. "I've been having trouble with a couple of the lights," she began, and ran them through the story.

"It's like what she did with Owen and me. It's kind of sweet, in a weird way."

"It's not sweet. It's infuriating. And he actually opened the window, considered climbing out."

"Of course he did."

Hope goggled at Clare. "*Of course?*"

"Not of course that was the answer, but of course he considered it. It's a guy thing." Amused, but supportive, Clare patted Hope's arm. "I have three sons, I know guy things."

"She really does," Avery confirmed.

"It's just stupid, especially since we both had our phones. I wanted to call Owen or Beckett, or the fire department."

"Which is sensible, and a girl thing—and a last resort, probably when starvation threatened, for a guy."

"Well, it's just stupid," Hope repeated. "Anyway, I'd just had it, and I gave him a piece of my mind."

"Now it's getting good." Avery rubbed her hands together.

"He's rude and surly, never uses my actual name. He treats me like I'm a pain in his ass, and I'm *not*."

"Of course you're not," Clare soothed.

"I do my job and keep out of his way. And what do I get? A curled lip and insults, when he bothers to acknowledge I exist."

"Maybe he's got a thing for you," Avery suggested. "So he gives you grief or ignores you."

"Oh." Hope sat back, nodded. "That could be it. If we were *eight*. I said he was snotty, which he is—to me. And he said I was snooty. I am not snooty."

"You're anything but. But . . ."

Hope narrowed her eyes at Clare. "But?"

"I think some people, wrongly, assume really beautiful women are. Snooty."

"That's snotty *and* snobby. But thanks. Oh! *And* he snarked on my shoes."

"Dangerous territory," Avery murmured.

"It sounds like you needed to clear the air," Clare began.

"Well, we didn't clear it, unless you equate that with both of us knowing just where we stand."

"How did you get out?" Avery wondered.

"That's the rest." Hope pointed a finger. "I thought of just what you said before. How she pulled this on you and Owen. So I said he should kiss me, and he got snotty about *that*. I mean, honestly, what's the big deal? He did it before and managed to survive, so—"

"Wait a minute, wait." Avery twirled her fingers in the air. "Rewind. Ryder kissed you?"

"It was nothing."

"We'll be the judge of that. When did this happen?"

"It was just a . . . nothing. New Year's Eve. We happened to run into each other in Owen's kitchen right at the countdown. It was awkward, and I guess we both felt it would be more awkward if we didn't. So we did. It was nothing."

"You keep saying it was nothing." Clare considered. "Which makes it sound like something. Especially since you didn't tell us before."

"Because it was no—" Hope caught herself. "It didn't matter. I forgot about it. My point is, it was just a device, like New Year's Eve. We're dealing with a romantically inclined ghost, which sounds enormously silly, but it is what it is. So we did, and the door opened. Then the bell rang, I had guests arriving. I went down, he went out."

"I must repeat. Rewind. You kissed Ryder, again."

"I might have murdered him if we hadn't gotten out of that room. Kissing seemed less bloody."

"So how was it?"

Hope pushed up, circled around. "He's got skills. And I'm in a dry spell. I'm in a desert. I'm fine with the desert, but it's a desert none-theless."

"You felt something for him," Clare prompted.

"I felt something," Hope qualified. "He's good at it, and the desert is dry. Now I've kissed him, twice. We can barely have a civil conversation—scratch that—we can't have one, and I've kissed him twice. So now it's a situation. Isn't it?"

"I'm going to let Clare take this one," Avery decided, "except for saying the only situation I see is two healthy, unencumbered adults who are both more attractive than they have a right to be engaging in a little enjoyable physical contact."

"But we don't even like each other. And he's one of my employers."

"You'd like each other fine if you'd give each other a chance. And he's not your boss. Justine's your boss. And I still say you're edgy around each other *because* you're attracted to each other."

Clare poked Avery in the arm. "I thought you were going to let me take this one."

"Oh yeah. Take it away."

"Thank you." Clare looked over at Hope. "Ditto. More or less."

Hope sat again. "I agree Justine's my boss, but don't you think Ryder considers himself my boss, too?"

"No, and I think he'd be annoyed if you did."

Avery furrowed her brow, gruffed up her voice. *"I've got enough to deal with, for Christ's sake, without being the boss of you. You're my mother's problem."*

Hope laughed, felt the tension at the back of her neck dissolve. "That sounds just like him, in content anyway. So what am I worried about? It wasn't a way *into* a situation. It was a way *out* of a situation."

"Let's focus on that a minute." Avery wiggled down in her chair. "During the way out of the situation, were tongues involved?"

"Avery." Laughing, Clare shook her head, then reconsidered. "Actually . . . were there?"

With a cat-in-the-cream smile, Hope tucked her hair behind her ear. "You've both known me long enough to know if I'm going to do something, I do it right."

"I admire that about you," Avery said. "Where were his hands?"

"On the door, he kept them off me. I was against the door, so—"

"Mmmmm. Don't you love against the door?" Avery asked Clare.

"A personal favorite. Too bad about the hands, though. I bet he's got good ones. I think it runs in the family."

Hope let out a sigh. "Despite your mutual obsession with tongues and hands, I feel better. Thanks."

"Anytime." Grinning, Avery gave Hope's hand a squeeze. "And I do mean anytime. Ry's going to be working on two sides of you for the next however. The odds of further situations are excellent."

The tension settled into the back of her neck again. "I'm not looking for further situations."

"That doesn't mean you won't walk into one."

"Or open the door and let one in," Clare added.

"The two of you think that way because your current life punch is spiked with weddings and babies. Mine is a crystal-clear bowl of career."

"We've got careers," Avery pointed out.

"And excellent ones. We should all get back to them."

Even as she started to rise, the door opened. Justine Montgomery walked in.

Her appealing wild mass of dark brown hair tumbled out of a messy tail. She pulled off sunglasses with vivid green frames and grinned. "Hello, girls."

Nothing to feel guilty about, Hope reminded herself. Nothing at all.

"Powwow?"

"We were just catching up," Clare began.

Justine walked over, laid a hand on Clare's shoulder. "How are we doing?"

In answer, Clare rubbed a hand over her belly. "We're doing good."

"I was going to run down to see you, and see if I can steal the boys from the sitter later today. I've got a yen for a picnic."

"They'd love it."

"Then it's a date. And you." She pointed at Avery. "I'm hoping we can do another walk-through of the new space, and snag a little time for wedding talk."

"I'm all over it. I ordered the lights from the site you sent me. They're perfect. I can go over as soon as Dave gets here."

"Works for me. Actually, Hope, I came by to see you. I found some furniture for the upper porch I think will work." Justine opened her huge bag, as vivid a green as her frames, fished out a cut sheet. "What do you think?"

"Perfect. Casual, looks comfortable, and the tones and textures are right."

"I thought so. Go ahead and order. And I want to hook up with you at some point about how we're going to handle the guest passes for the gym, and what we could include in a package for guests. It's a ways off, but—"

"It's never too soon to plan," Hope finished.

"Exactly. Staff's going to be key, and I'll need to find a good manager. I've got some feelers out."

"Speaking of managers, I was thinking we might start having a managers' meeting, maybe every four to six weeks. Just to coordinate events, ideas, marketing plans."

Justine beamed at Hope. "I like it."

"I'll send an email out to everyone then, so we can work out the best time. If we go with early afternoons, we can use The Dining Room at the inn. And I should get back."

"I don't want to break up the party."

"We're caught up." Hope got to her feet.

"Then I'll walk over with you, before I go harass my boys. I'll see the two of you later. What do you say to a nice soft, slatey blue to replace that green on the fitness center?" she asked Hope as they walked to the door.

"I say you're my hero."

Avery waited until the door closed. "There's a thing going on."

Content, Clare folded her hands on her belly. "Oh yes, there's a definite thing going on."

"How do we feel about that?"

"They're not each other's usual type. Not even close."

"Absolutely not," Avery agreed.

"Maybe that's why I feel so good about it."

"Me, too!" Avery popped up, grabbed a Coke and a ginger ale out of the cooler. "Part of it could be we're in love with two of the brothers. There's one of us, and one of them left."

"It's the kind of symmetry Hope would appreciate. If she wasn't so annoyed and resistant. But it's not the big part of why. We love them, so we want them to be happy. To have someone in their lives who makes them happy."

"Ryder dates a lot, but . . ."

"He's never involved," Clare finished. "And Hope's not dating at all. Hasn't dated since—"

"Jonathan," Avery said with loathing.

"He hurt her more than she'll admit, even to herself. And over and above that, she's pushed herself into this mind-set that she doesn't want or need to date or have a relationship."

"You had the same mind-set," Avery pointed out.

"That was different, and I did date a little."

"Very little."

"Very little. But I had three children to think of, and a business to run. Plus, and most important, there wasn't anyone until Beckett."

Clare sipped slowly. "And there's another thing, and it sounds a little crazy."

"I'm okay with crazy."

"Lizzy. She, in a way, gave Beckett and me, and you and Owen, that little push—that springboard, so to speak. And look at us."

Avery turned her hand, palm up to Clare. "Married, pregnant with twins."

Clare mirrored the gesture. "Wedding planning. Do you think she, somehow, knows something, or sees something, senses something we don't? About feelings or potential feelings?"

"Maybe. And that's no crazier than having her in residence at the inn while she waits for somebody named Billy."

"I guess it's not. I wish we could find out who he was, what he was to her."

"I'm banking on Hope and Owen. It may take a while, but they'll dig it out." Avery smiled at Clare over her soda. "So, how much about all this do we tell Owen and Beckett?"

"Oh, everything."

"Good. They'll rag on him, which will piss Ryder off. There's a better chance of further situations if he's a little pissed off. And, you know, after that asshole Jonathan, Hope could use somebody a little more real."

"Ryder's real." Clare broke out with a grin. "She called him snotty."

"I *know*." Delighted, Avery tipped back and howled with laughter. "And he comes back with snooty. Snotty and snooty. It's probably wrong, but I love it."

"If it's wrong, I'm right there with you." She lifted her can, tapped Avery's. "Here's to the promise of an interesting summer."

SHE MANAGED TO avoid him for the better part of a week. She saw him—not that she was looking—but it was hard to miss Ryder

Montgomery swaggering from one job site to another in a town the
size of Boonsboro.

Into MacT's, down to the bakery, around to Fit. She'd catch sight
of him chatting with Dick the barber outside of Sherry's, or stopping
for a word with one of the Crawfords.

Here, there, everywhere, she thought with some resentment. And
to avoid running into him she'd all but put herself under house arrest.

It was ridiculous.

Not that she hadn't been busy. The inn proved popular for its first
summer. She'd tended to two out-of-town authors Clare hosted for
a book signing. Then there'd been the sweet couple who'd come into
the area for their fiftieth high school reunion—and the young couple
who'd gotten engaged in Titania and Oberon, and already talked of
spending their wedding night in the same room.

So far she'd had charming guests, strange guests, demanding
guests, and delightful guests. Probably everything in between, she
mused as she hauled out the hose to water the flowers and shrubs.

At the moment she had six rooms booked—two sisters, their
mother, and the three daughters they had between them. They'd had
a fun—and rowdy—time the night before. She expected they'd sleep
in before they headed out for their facials and massages.

She'd definitely plan a Girls' Night of her own. Clare and Avery,
Justine and Carolee, Clare's mom, Carolee's daughter. She'd have her
own mother and sister come down from Philadelphia.

Some fun food, some wine, plenty of wedding and baby talk.

Just what she needed.

She soaked the mulch, pleased the Knock-Out Roses bloomed and
the arching wisteria showed so prettily green. Its flowers had sweetened the air in May—and she imagined them blooming for Avery's
wedding the next spring.

She hummed to herself, soothed by the homey task, ignoring
the banging and sawing from the building across the lot. In her mind

she flipped through her list of morning chores, into the afternoon, the evening, and ended her day's plans with a little research on Billy.

Perfect.

The sound behind her made her jump, spin around.

"Hey!" was all Ryder managed before reflex had her jerking the spray of water up from his crotch. She hit him square in the face.

"Oh God." She shot the spray to the side, fumbled it off.

Slowly, very slowly, he pulled off his sunglasses. He stood, hair and clothes dripping, eyes steaming.

D.A. obligingly lapped at the pool of water on the pavers.

"What the fuck?"

"Shh!" Instinctively, she glanced up at the porch. "I have guests. A lot of female guests."

"So you're hosing down any male who comes on the property?"

"I didn't mean . . . I'm sorry. So sorry. You startled me, and I just . . ."

"You think it's funny?" he demanded as a choked laugh snuck out of her throat.

"No. Yes. Yes, it's funny, but that doesn't mean I'm not sorry. Really sorry," she added, whipping the hose behind her back as he stepped forward. "You shouldn't sneak up on a woman with a loaded hose."

"I wasn't sneaking anywhere. I was walking." He shoved the dripping hair out of his face. "Let me see that hose."

"Absolutely not. It was an accident. What you'd do with it would be deliberate. If you wait here I'll get you a towel."

"I don't want a towel. I want some damn coffee, which was why I was walking—like a normal person—from the job site there, to the kitchen there."

"I'll get you coffee, and a towel." Wary, she gave him a wide berth—turned off the hose at the source—then dashed inside.

She giggled, snickered, chuckled her way to the laundry room, grabbed a towel from the shelf, hurried back to the kitchen to pour coffee into a go-cup. Added the two sugars she knew he used, fit on the top.

She put a chocolate chip muffin in a napkin to sweeten the deal, and dug out a dog biscuit from her supply.

She dashed back through The Lobby, but paused to look out, make certain he wasn't armed. She had a brother, knew how it worked.

Composed, with her features in contrite lines, she stepped out.

And tried not to notice the man looked damn good wet.

"Sorry."

"Yeah, you said." Still watching her, he took the towel, scrubbed it roughly over his dark, wet, unruly hair.

Because she wanted, badly, to laugh again, she pumped a little more contrite into her voice. "I brought you a muffin."

He eyed it, the towel slung over his shoulder. "What kind of muffin?"

"Chocolate chip."

"Okay." He took it, and the coffee while she gave the dog his treat. "Is there a reason you're watering that stuff, and me, at seven thirty in the morning?"

"It hasn't rained in a few days, and I have guests so I need to start breakfast soon. They're family, and they were up late, so they'll sleep in a bit. I had some time, so—" She broke off, wondering why she felt compelled to explain everything. "Is there a reason you're coming here for coffee at seven thirty in the morning?"

"I forgot Owen wasn't coming in till later. He gets the coffee. I figured Carolee was dealing with the kitchen stuff. I need her key so I can get into her place and check her kitchen sink. It's not draining right."

She couldn't claim he wasn't a good nephew—or son, or brother. "She'll be here by eight. You can wait if you want. I could . . . throw your clothes in the dryer."

"Your female guests wouldn't have a problem with a naked man hanging around?"

With this group? she thought. Probably not. "They might consider it a nice perk, but no one's in M&P. You could wait in there."

Naked, she thought. Surly and naked and built.

Oh, the desert was so damn dry.

"I haven't got time to wait around. I've got work." He took an enormous bite of muffin. "Not bad." D.A.'s tail thumped. He fielded the piece Ryder broke off and tossed without moving anything but his head.

"Thank you very much."

He studied her over the next bite. "Any more trouble with the lights?"

"No. But I had a couple in two nights ago. He proposed to her in T&O. They thanked me for scattering rose petals over their bed. I didn't."

She glanced toward the inn. "It was a nice touch. I wish I had thought of it."

"I guess you've got an assistant."

"I guess I do. Is it a problem if I go by Avery's new place later, see how it's looking?"

He kept his eyes on her face—a long, steady stare—then shielded them with his sunglasses. "Why would it be a problem?"

"All right." Out of pique, she supposed, she denied herself that little pleasure. And had no one to blame but herself. "If you're done with the towel . . ."

"Yeah." He passed it to her. "Thanks for the coffee. And the shower."

Unsure, she manfully swallowed the laugh. "You're welcome."

He walked off. D.A. gave her his happy doggy grin before he trotted after his master.

"Who was that?"

The voice from above made Hope jolt again. She thought it was a damn good thing she didn't still have the hose. She looked up, saw the woman in the bathrobe leaning lazily on the rail of the second-story porch. Hope flipped through her mental files.

Courtney, middle sister.

"Good morning. That was one of the owners."

"Yummy." She smiled sleepily down at Hope. "My ex is tall, dark, and handsome. I guess I've got a weakness for the type."

Hope smiled back. "Who doesn't?"

"You've got that right. Is it okay if I come downstairs in the robe? I don't think I've been this relaxed in six months, and I don't want it to end."

"Absolutely. There's fresh coffee in the kitchen. I'll be right in to start breakfast."

Courtney heaved a dreamy sigh. "I love this place."

So do I, Hope thought as she walked over to put away the hose.

And I feel a lot more relaxed myself, she realized. She'd had an actual conversation with Ryder without either one of them snapping at each other.

All she'd had to do was soak him to the skin first.

Laughing, she walked back into the inn to see to her guest.

# CHAPTER FOUR

RYDER GRABBED A DRY, AND REASONABLY CLEAN, T-SHIRT out of his truck, dug out his emergency jeans. He thought getting blasted with a garden hose qualified.

He carted them over to MacT's.

"Women," was all he said, and D.A. gave him a look that might be interpreted as male solidarity. They walked into the job music— country on the radio, as he hadn't been there to switch it to rock—the whirl of drills, the *whoosh, thud* of nail guns.

He walked through the restaurant, past plumbers working in the restrooms, and into the kitchen.

Beckett stood at a prep counter consulting his plans.

"Hey. I thought since we were going down to a single door in here, we should . . ." Beckett glanced up, lifted his brows as Ryder tossed clothes beside the big grill. "Run into a sudden storm?"

With a grunt Ryder bent to unlace his boots. "Innkeeper with a garden hose."

Beckett's laugh blasted out as Ryder fought, cursing, with sodden boot laces. "Dude. She hosed you down."

"Shut up, Beck."

"What did you do, make another grab?"

"No. I never made a grab in the first place." Straightening, Ryder pulled off his shirt, tossed it down with a sodden splat.

Standing hip-shot, Beckett grinned. "That's not what I heard."

Ryder sent his brother a fulminating stare as he whipped off his belt. "I already told you there wasn't any grabbing, and it was her idea. Shut up."

"Man, she *soaked* you. What did you do, chase her around The Courtyard?"

She'd soaked him, all right, right through to the boxers. Since he didn't carry an extra pair in his truck, he'd go commando.

He stripped down to the skin while Beckett grinned at him.

"If your wife wasn't pregnant I'd kick your ass."

"Looks like your ass is the one with the target on it."

"I don't need a target to boot yours." Cautious, Ryder tucked his sensitive parts away before he zipped. "She's out watering the damn flowers, not watching what she's doing. Plus, she's jumpy."

"Maybe because you jumped her."

Keeping his eyes on Beckett, Ryder slid on his belt, one slow loop at a time. "Finished yet?"

"I can probably think of more. Put away wet, that sort of thing."

Ryder shot up both middle fingers as he dragged on his shirt.

"Maybe next time she'll give you a shave with the shower. Okay, that should do it for now."

"I set Chad up in the apartments over the bakery, finishing up the lock sets, the switch plates because Owen wants it all pretty before he shows them today. Carolee's sink's acting up, so she asks if I can take a look. I'm just walking over from the bakery to the inn to get the key and some goddamn coffee, and she whips around and blasts me. Hits the crotch first, sure, then all the way up."

"Did she do it on purpose? 'Cause we can wait for Owen. The three of us should be able to take her."

"Funny." Ryder gave his wet clothes a kick. "I got coffee and a muffin out of it."

"What kind of muffin?"

"Mine. I'm putting the painters up on the manlift. It's supposed to stay dry the next couple days, so they can start the next exterior coat."

"Good. We've already had a morning shower. What am I supposed to do?" Beckett spread his hands as his eyes danced with humor. "It's right there."

"Next time there's a call from the inn, I'm sending Deke to handle it. He can kiss her."

Beckett thought of the laborer—good worker, sunny disposition. And a face only a myopic mother could love. "Harsh, man."

"If your ghost wants to play games, she can play them with some-body else."

"She's not my ghost. And I doubt Lizzy's interested in hooking Hope up with Deke."

"Nobody hooks me up, and if I wanted to be hooked up with the perfect Hope, I would be."

"If you say so."

They heard young voices carry back, and the scramble of feet. Ryder watched his brother's face light up as three boys piled into the big kitchen.

Murphy, the youngest at six, scooted around his brothers and zeroed in on Beckett. He held up a decapitated Captain America action figure. "His head came off. You can fix it. Okay? 'Cause he needs it."

"Let's see." Beckett crouched down. "How'd this happen?"

"I was checking if he could see behind his back, 'cause bad guys sneak up behind you. And his head came off." He offered the head to Beckett. "But you can fix him."

"We can bury him." Liam, the middle boy, grinned. "We have the coffins you made. You can make another, just for his head." He turned that wicked grin up to Ryder. "If your head comes off, you're dead."

"You ever see a chicken after its head's cut off? The rest of it keeps running around, like it's looking for it."

"No way!" The eldest, Harry, cackled and his voice pitched with disgusted delight as Liam gaped.

"Oh, way, young Jedi. In fact, it's—Hey, it's Clare the fair."

"Sorry. We had checkups—all good. They really wanted to stop by and see everything before we go to the bookstore."

"I can stay and work." Harry shot Beckett a pleading look. "I can help."

"If Harry gets to stay, me, too." Liam tugged on Ryder's jeans. "Me, too."

"Me, too," Murphy echoed, and lifted his arms to Beckett. "Okay?"

"We had a deal," Clare began.

"We're just asking." Knowing his targets, Harry changed the pleading look to one of innocent reason. "They can say no."

"We could use some slaves," Ryder considered, and was gifted with Harry's angel smile.

"Ryder, I don't want to saddle you with—"

"This one's a little stringy." He lifted Liam's arm, pinched the biceps. "But he's got potential."

"We'll need to split them up." Beckett handed Murphy the repaired superhero.

"I knew you could fix it." After giving Beckett a fierce hug, Murphy smiled at his mother. "Please, can we be slaves?"

"Who am I against five handsome men? I promised them Vesta for lunch, but—"

"We'll meet you there." Setting Murphy down, Beckett crossed to her. He brushed a hand over her cheek, then his lips over hers. "Around noon?"

"That's fine. Call if you need reinforcements. Boys." Maternal warning vibrated in the single word. "Do what you're told. I'll know if you misbehave—even if they don't tell me. I'm right down the street," she said to Beckett.

"How come she knows even when she's not there?" Murphy demanded when Clare left. "'Cause she does."

"The mysterious power of mother," Beckett told him.

"Anyway, if you screw around we'll just drill you to the wall by your shoes. Upside down," Ryder added. "You got the runt?"

"Yeah." Beckett laid a hand on Murphy's head.

"I'll take pb and j over to the apartments. He can help with lock set."

"How come I'm pb and j?" Liam demanded.

"Because you're the middle."

"I won't be the middle when the babies come. Murphy will."

"He did the math," Beckett said, stupidly proud.

"Another math geek? We'll set Owen up as his keeper when he gets here. I'll take this one." He put Harry in a headlock that thrilled the boy to his toes. "He's not as short as the others. We'll head over to the gym. I'll dump the temporary middle over the bakery on the way."

"Great. Thanks." As Ryder left with two boys in tow, Beckett turned to Murphy. "We'd better get our tools."

Murphy smiled, angel sweet. "Our tools."

Since both men working in the apartment had kids, Ryder figured they wouldn't let Liam do anything overly stupid. Still, he hung around several minutes, setting the boy up with light switch covers, a small screwdriver.

The kid was about eight, he thought, and had good hands. He also—maybe that middle child thing—had the most devious mind of the three, and the quickest temper.

"You get a buck an hour if you don't screw up. Screw up," Ryder told him, "you get zilch."

"How much is zilch?"

"Nothing."

"I don't want zilch," Liam protested.

"Nobody does, so don't screw up. He gives you grief," Ryder told his men, "take him to Beck. Let's go, Harry Caray."

"I should get more than Liam, because I'm older."

"A buck an hour," Ryder repeated as they went down the outside steps. "That's the deal across the board."

"I could get a bonus."

Amused, and a little fascinated, Ryder studied Harry as they walked. "What the hell do you know?"

"Mom gives people bonuses at Christmas because they work hard."

"Okay, talk to me at Christmas."

"Am I going to get to use one of those guns that shoots nails?"

"Sure. In about five years."

"Gran says you're making a place where people come to exercise and have fun getting healthy."

"That's the plan."

"We have to eat broccoli 'cause it's healthy, except when we have Man Night, and we don't."

"The beauty of Man Night is broccoli is never on the menu."

"Am I going to measure stuff? I have a tape measure at home Beckett gave me, but I didn't bring it."

"We've got some spares."

When they stepped in, Harry stood, all eyes.

With demo complete, they had exterior walls, a crap roof, and a space big as a barn. Saws buzzed, hammers banged, nail guns thwacked as the crew worked.

"It's big," Harry said. "I didn't think it was big, but it is. How come there's nothing in it?"

Ryder answered simply. "Because what was here was no good. We'll build what is."

"You just build it? The whole thing? How do you know?"

Realizing the kid meant it literally, Ryder walked him over to the plans.

"Beckett made them. I saw him. The roof part doesn't look like that."

Okay, Ryder thought, the kid not only had a lot of questions—which struck him as sensible—but he paid attention. Maybe they were making the next generation of contractors.

"It will. We're going to take the old roof off."

"What if it rains?"

"We'll get wet."

Harry grinned up at him. "Can I build something?"

"Yeah. Let's get you a hammer."

HE ENJOYED HIMSELF. The kid was bright and eager, with that willingness to do anything that came from never doing it before. And funny, often deliberately. Ryder had helped wrangle the kids and tools a few times when they'd finished Beckett's house, so he knew Harry was reasonably careful. He liked to learn; he liked to build.

And teaching the boy a few basics took Ryder back to his own childhood where he'd learned his craft from his father.

There would be no Montgomery Family Contractors if Tom Montgomery hadn't had the skills, the drive, and the patience to build—and hadn't married a woman with vision and energy.

Ryder found he missed his father more at the beginning of a job, like this one, where the potential rolled out like an endless carpet.

He'd have gotten a kick out of this, Ryder thought as he guided Harry into measuring and marking the next stud. The big, empty space echoing with noise, the smell of sweat and sawdust.

And he'd have loved the boy, have loved the potential of the boy, too. Nine, closing in on ten, Ryder remembered. Gangling frame and sharp elbows and feet too big for the rest of him.

And now two more on the way. Yeah, his father would've gotten one hell of a large charge out of the Brewster/Montgomery brood.

The kid engaged the crew. He fetched and carried tirelessly. That wouldn't last, Ryder calculated, but the novelty of the day equaled that slave labor—and made the boy feel like a man. Like part of the team.

He stepped back, took a swig of Gatorade from the bottle. Harry mimicked him, and stood, as Ryder did, studying the work.

"Well, kid, you built your first wall. Here." He pulled a carpenter's pencil from his belt. "Write your name on it."

"Really?"

"Sure. It'll be covered up with insulation, drywall, and paint, but you'll know it's there."

Delighted, Harry took the pencil, and on the raw stud wrote his name in careful cursive.

He glanced over at the sound of whoops, watched Liam scramble in.

"They kick you out?" Ryder called.

"Nuh-uh! I did a million switch plates, and I did a doorknob, too. Chad showed me how. Then Beckett came to get me so we can have pizza."

As he spoke, Beckett came in with Murphy.

"I built a wall! Look. Me and Ryder built a wall."

Liam frowned at it. "How's it a wall when you can walk through. See." He demonstrated.

"It's a stud wall," Harry said importantly.

Instantly, Liam's face shifted into mutinous lines. "I wanna build a stud wall."

"Next time." Beckett collared him. "Watch yourself. Construction site rules."

"I builded a platform. You can stand on it," Murphy explained. "Now it's lunch break, and we get pizza."

He'd lost track of time, Ryder realized.

"I'm going to get them cleaned up," Beckett said.

"And we get to play video games first. I got *three* dollars." Liam waved the bills in the air.

"Yeah, yeah." Ryder reached for his wallet at Harry's quiet look. "You earned it."

"Thanks! Are you going to have lunch with us?"

"I'll be over in a while. I've got a couple things to finish up."

"Owen's over at the new restaurant, running some things with Avery. He said twenty."

"That works."

"Okay, troops, let's go clean up."

Hope caught sight of them from the kitchen window, Beckett and his little men. Sweet, she thought. Heading to Vesta for lunch, she imagined.

She should probably grab something soon herself, she decided, before her guests came back and she didn't have a chance. She'd already done her room checks, gathering up glasses and cups and other assorted debris. And she needed to order more coasters, and guest towels for The Lobby restroom. More mugs, she reminded herself, as guests tended to walk off with them.

But right now, the inn was quiet and empty, with all the women off getting pampered and Carolee off with Justine looking at tiles and flooring—and whatever else they thought of—for the fitness center.

The cleaning crew would be along in an hour to turn and clean the guest rooms. Then she'd do her recheck. So she'd just finish making this pitcher of iced tea, restock the refrigerator with water and soft drinks. Then take a quick break before doing her orders and filing.

But even as she set the pitcher on the island beside a bowl of fat purple grapes, the Reception bell rang.

No deliveries on the schedule, she thought, but occasionally a guest forgot their key—or someone came by hoping they could wander through.

She started around, her innkeeper's smile in place.

It faded completely when she saw the man through the glass of the door.

He wore a suit, of course, pearl gray for summer. The tie, with its perfect Windsor knot echoed the exact same shade and a contrasting stripe in rich crimson.

He was bronzed and gold, tall and lean, classically, glossily handsome.

And completely unwelcome.

With reluctance, Hope unlocked the door, opened it. "Jonathan. This is unexpected."

"Hope." He smiled at her, all easy charm—as if hardly more than a year before he hadn't dumped her like last year's fashion. "You look wonderful. A new hairstyle, and it suits you."

He reached out, as if to embrace her. She stepped back in firm rejection.

"What are you doing here?"

"At the moment, wondering why you don't ask me in. It's odd to find the door locked on a hotel in the middle of the day."

"It's policy, and we're a B&B. Our guests enjoy their privacy."

"Of course. It looks like a charming place. I'd like to see more of it." He waited a beat, then pumped up the smile. "Professional courtesy?"

Slamming the door in his face would be satisfying, but childish. In any case he might interpret it to mean he mattered.

"Most of our guest rooms are occupied, but I can show you the common areas if you're interested."

"I am. Very."

She couldn't see why. "Again, Jonathan, what are you doing here?"

"I wanted to see you. My parents send you their best."

"And you can take mine back to them." She took a breath. All right, she thought, what the hell. "This is our reception area."

"On the small side, but it's cozy and has character."

"Yes, we think so."

"Is that the original brick?"

She glanced toward the long, exposed brick wall. "Yes, and those are old photographs showing the inn and Main Street."

"Mmm-hmm. The fireplace must be welcome in the winter."

She struggled with the resentment of having him here, having him make observations about *her* place.

"Yes, it's a favorite spot. We have an open kitchen," Hope began, leading the way—and wishing she'd had five minutes to freshen her makeup and hair. Just on pride points. "Guests are free to help themselves."

He scanned the bold iron lights, the stainless steel appliances, the rich granite counter. "Honor system?"

"We don't charge. All food and drink is included. We want our guests to feel at home. The central lobby is this way."

He paused at her office, gave her that smile again. "As tidy and efficient as always. You're missed, Hope."

"Am I?"

"Very much."

She considered various responses, but none qualified as polite. And she was determined to be.

"We're especially proud of the tile work throughout the inn. Here you can see the details of the tile rug under the main table. The flowers are done by our local florist to reflect and celebrate not only the season, but the style and tone of the room."

"Lovely, and yes, beautiful details. I—"

"As is the woodwork." She plowed right over him. Politely. "The framing of the old archways. The Montgomery family designed, rehabbed, and decorated the inn. It's the oldest stone building in

Boonsboro, and was originally an inn. The Lounge, just down here, was once the carriageway.

"Hope." He trailed a fingertip down her arm before she could shift away. "Let me take you to lunch after the tour. It's been much too long."

Not long enough. "Jonathan, I'm working."

"Your employers must give you a reasonable lunch break. Where would you recommend?"

She didn't have to dig for the cold. Her tone simply reflected every sensibility. He expected her to agree, she realized. More, he expected her to be delighted, flattered, maybe a little flustered.

She was happy to disappoint him on all counts.

"If you're hungry, you can try Vesta, right across the street. But I'm not interested in having lunch with you. You might want to see The Courtyard before the rest of the main floor." She opened The Lobby doors, stepped out. "It's a lovely place, especially in good weather, to sit and have a drink."

"The view's lacking," he commented, looking over the pretty garden wall and across the lot to the green building.

"It won't be. That building's currently being rehabbed by the Montgomery family."

"A busy bunch. At least sit down for a moment. I wouldn't mind that drink."

Hospitality, Hope reminded herself. No matter who. "All right. I'll be back in a minute."

She walked back inside, deliberately unclenched her jaw. He could send business to the inn, she reminded herself. Guests and clients looking for an out-of-the-way place, well-run, beautifully appointed.

Whatever her personal feelings, she couldn't deny Jonathan knew the hospitality business.

She'd do her job and be gracious.

She poured him tea over ice, added a small plate of cookies. And because it was gracious, poured a glass for herself.

He was seated at one of the umbrella tables when she carried the tray out.

"I'm surprised you didn't bring your wife. I hope she's well." There, Hope congratulated herself. That didn't choke her.

"Very, thanks. She had a committee meeting today, and some shopping to do. You must miss Georgetown—the shops, the nightlife. You can't find that here."

"Actually, I'm very at home here. Very happy here."

He gave her a smile, with just a hint of sympathy. One that said clearly he believed she lied to save face.

She imagined herself flicking her fingers in *his* face to erase it. But that wouldn't be gracious.

"It's hard to believe, a woman with your drive, your tastes, settling into a little country town. And running a little B&B, however charming, after managing the Wickham. I assume you live right here, on the property."

"Yes, I have an apartment on the third floor."

"When I think of your beautiful town house . . ." He shook his head, and there was that trace of sympathy again. "I feel partially responsible for all these changes you've been through. Looking back, I realize I could have—and should have—handled things better than I did."

Graciousness had its limits. She'd reached hers. "Do you mean sleeping with me, allowing me to believe we were in a long-term monogamous relationship, then announcing your engagement to someone else? Oh, and telling me of that someone else just after we'd had sex?" She took a sip of tea. "Yes, you should have handled that better."

"If we're honest, I never made promises."

"No, you implied them, so that interpretation is on me. I accept it." Under the shade of the umbrella, she studied him. Yes, he looked the same. Smooth, polished, confident. His confidence had once been so appealing to her. Now it struck as arrogance and appealed not at all.

"Is this why you came here, Jonathan? To settle accounts with me?"

"To, I hope, make it right." Sincerity lived in his eyes as he laid a hand over hers. "We parted at odds, Hope, and that bothers me, a lot."

"Don't give it a thought."

"I do, and I'm here to bridge that gap between us. And to offer you your position back. My father's prepared to make you a very generous offer. As I said, Hope, you're missed."

Eyes level, she slid her hand away. "I have a position."

"A very generous offer," Jonathan repeated. "Back where we all know you belong. We'd like to schedule a meeting with you, at your convenience, to work out the details. You could come back, Hope, to Georgetown, to the Wickham, to your life. And, to me."

He put his hand over hers again when she said nothing. "My marriage is what it is, and will continue to be. But you and I . . . I miss what we had. We can have it again. I'd take very good care of you."

"You'd take care of me." Each word dropped from her lips like a stone.

"You wouldn't want for anything."

He continued, oh, that confidence—proving he didn't know her at all. And never had.

"You'd have the work that fulfills you, a home of your choosing. There's a charming property on Q Street I know you'd love. I think we should take a short holiday before you resume your position so we can get reacquainted, so to speak." He leaned toward her, intimately. "It's been a long year, Hope, for both of us. I'll take you anywhere you like. How about a week in Paris?"

"A week in Paris, a home in Georgetown. I'm assuming some spending money to furnish it, and to outfit myself, of course, for my return to the Wickham—and you."

He lifted her hand to his lips—a habit she'd once loved—smiled at her over it. "As I said, I'll take care of you."

"And what does your wife think about *your* generous offer?"

"Don't worry about Sheridan. We'll be discreet, and she'll adjust."

She watched him shrug marriage, vows, fidelity away in a smooth and careless gesture. "You can't be happy here, Hope. I'll make sure you're happy."

She took a moment, almost surprised she had room for the enormity of the insult. Then equally surprised her voice stayed calm and level when the insult clawed at her to shriek.

"Let me explain something to you. I'm responsible for my own happiness. I don't need you, or your incredibly insulting—to me and your wife—offer. I don't need your father or the Wickham. I have a life. Do you think I put that life on hold because you used me and discarded me?"

"I think you're settling for less than you can have, less than you deserve. I apologize, sincerely, for hurting you, but—"

"Hurting me? You *freed* me." She shoved to her feet. Calm and level were done. "You gave me a hell of a rude shove, you bastard, but you pushed me hard enough to make me reevaluate. I was settling, for you. Now this is my home." She threw a hand up toward the porches— thought for a moment she saw a shadow of a woman. "A home I love, can be proud of. I have a community I enjoy, friends I treasure. Come back to you? To *you* when I have—"

She couldn't say what made her do it. Impulse, unspeakable fury, pride. But she saw Ryder crossing the lot, and went with it.

"Him. Ryder!" She dashed through the arch of wisteria when he stopped, frowned at her. She imagined the smile on her face showed edges of insanity. She didn't care.

"Go with me on this," she muttered as she rushed to him, "and I'll owe you big."

"What—"

She threw her arms around him, pressed her lips to his as D.A. wagged and tried to nose between them to get in on the action. "Go with me," she said against him mouth. "Please!"

She didn't leave him a lot of room for otherwise as she was

plastered against him like a second skin. So he went with her. He fisted his hand in her hair, and went.

She lost track of the point for a moment. He smelled of sawdust, tasted like candy. Hot, melted candy. A little unsteady on her feet, she pulled back.

"Just follow my lead."

"Wasn't I?"

"Ryder." She took his hand in hers, squeezed it as she turned. "Ryder Montgomery, I'd like you to meet Jonathan Wickham. Jonathan's family owns the hotel in Georgetown where I used to work."

"Oh, yeah." Okay, now he got it. Sure, he could play the part, no problem. He slid an arm around Hope's waist, felt her tremble. "How's it going?"

"Well, thank you." Jonathan gave the dog a single cautious glance. "Hope was showing me around your inn."

"It's as much hers as ours. Your loss, right? Our gain."

"Apparently." His gaze skimmed over Ryder's work clothes. "I take it you do the construction work yourself."

"That's right. We're hands-on." He grinned when he said it, tugged Hope a little closer. "Looking for a room?"

"No." Annoyance sparked in Jonathan's eyes even as he smiled— tightly. "Just visiting an old friend. It's good to see you again, Hope. If you change your mind about the offer, you know how to reach me."

"I won't. My best to your parents, and your wife."

"Montgomery," he said with a nod, and walked to his Mercedes.

Hope kept the smile on her face until he'd pulled out, driven away.

"Oh God. Oh God." She broke away, strode back into The Courtyard, circled around it. "Oh my God."

Ryder thought of Vesta—homey smells, happy kids, no problems, no drama. He cast his eyes at the sky and followed her into The Courtyard.

# CHAPTER FIVE

H E KNEW BETTER THAN TO TELL HER TO SIT DOWN OR calm down. No man really understood women, but he thought he had a reasonable handle on the species.

So he sat, figuring it might take a while while she circled the pavers. Since she wore one of those thin summer dresses, he couldn't fault the view.

And he sat while his dog crawled under the table as if seeking cover from the fallout. But it was freaking hot, and added to it she had enough steam pumping off her to boil a bucket of lobsters.

Might as well get her started on it, Ryder decided.

"Okay, what's the deal?"

"The deal?"

When she swung around, the skirt of the dress floated up and around long, bare legs.

No, he couldn't fault the view.

"The deal?" she repeated, with those dark chocolate eyes of hers shooting out bullets of fury. "Oh, he wanted to make me a deal all right, the slimy bastard."

Ryder eyed the glasses of iced tea. He wouldn't mind some, but he wasn't sure whose glass was whose, and didn't particularly want to drink after a slimy bastard.

"That"—she waved a hand toward the parking lot—"was Jonathan."

"Yeah, we met."

"We used to be—" What? she wondered. Just what did it used to be?

"I got that. You were hooked up, and he flipped on you for somebody else." He shrugged when she stopped walking off the mad long enough to look at him. "Word gets around."

"The word's inadequate. *I* was the other woman. I didn't know I was the other woman until he told me he was engaged—a bomb he dropped shortly after we had sex. I thought we were in a relationship, an exclusive relationship, but he was *juggling* me. Stupid, stupid, stupid."

She had smoky looks, a smoky voice—and when she was seriously pissed, he thought, you caught the fire under the smoke.

"Okay, he's a slimy bastard and you were stupid. You got smart and kicked him to the curb. Is this glass yours?"

"Yes, and of course I ended it. And I gave my notice. He actually assumed everything would go on the way it was. Me working for his family while he had me on the side."

"Then he was stupid."

"You're damn right!" Fully appreciating the comment, Hope slapped Ryder's shoulder as she started pacing and circling again. "He got married in May—a lavish event, naturally, at the Wickham with a three-week honeymoon in Europe."

"Keeping tabs?"

She stopped. Her chin jutted out. "I read the Style section of the

*Post.* And, all right, yes, I wanted to see—it's human nature. You'd have done the same."

He considered, then shook his head. "Not so much. When something's done, it's done. What was he doing here, because visiting an old friend was bullshit."

"What was he doing here? I'll tell you what he was doing here. He *said* he wanted to tell me he felt partially responsible for my relocation and so on—partially. He *said* he wanted to see the inn, and take me to lunch. He said I was missed, and his father designated him to make me a *generous offer.* Generous offer, my ass!"

He'd never seen her seriously worked up, he realized. Irked, annoyed, somewhat pissed, but not full-throttle. It was probably wrong to sit there thinking it looked good on her.

"Trying to poach our innkeeper." He kept his voice mild in contrast to hers. "Not cool."

"Oh, that wasn't all. Oh no, obviously I'm not suited for this job. According to him I can't be happy and fulfilled unless I'm back in Georgetown, and managing the Wickham—and sleeping with him."

"Huh. You look happy enough to me. Usually."

"Oh, but how could I be, here in this little country town, managing this little country inn. And not being at his fucking beck?"

At a loss, Ryder scratched the back of his neck. "Well . . ."

"So, he made me a secondary generous offer. I'd be the other woman, with full knowledge this time around, and he'd take very good care of me. A little trip to Paris to renew our acquaintance, a home of my choosing—apparently he already has the property in mind—and a generous stipend to be determined. Does he really think I'd be a part of his cheating on his wife? That I'd be his *whore?* I'd just jump right back for a job, for money, and a goddamn spree on the Rue du Faubourg Saint-Honoré?"

Ryder didn't know what the hell rue whatever was, but he

considered the whole. "He said if you came back, were his side piece, he'd set you up?"

"In a nutshell."

If he'd known the whole before the slimy bastard had driven off, the asshole would currently be bleeding and unconscious in the parking lot.

"And you didn't punch him in the face?"

"Oh, oh, I thought about it." A violence Ryder admired and respected flashed in those deep, dark eyes. "I *imagined* it. Vividly. Except I was just going to throw my iced tea in his face and ruin his goddamn Versace suit. Then I saw you, and I just went with instinct. He thinks I'm sitting around waiting for *him*? Arrogant, conceited, immoral bastard. He thinks I can be had for money, for a house, for a trip to goddamn Paris?"

"Hope." It might've been the first time he'd said her name, certainly in just that way—with patience—but neither of them noticed. "He's a fucking entitled, bat-blind idiot. And he doesn't get you."

"Oh he is, and no, he doesn't. So I humiliated him by kissing you in front of him, letting him think we were involved."

"You didn't punch him in the face; you kicked him in the balls."

"Yes." She let out a breath. "And thank you for the assist."

"No problem."

"No, really. Thank you. My pride took a hell of a hit over Jonathan. It meant a lot to be able to have some payback. I owe you."

"Yeah, so you said."

They stared at each other for one throbbing moment with something dangerous and *interesting* sizzling around the edges.

"Okay. Name your price."

He could think of any number of dangerous and interesting things. She'd expect something like that, something that involved dimly lit rooms. He figured her for a woman who usually got just what she expected.

"I like pie."

"Excuse me?"

"Pie. I like it. It's a good time of year for cherry pie. Anyway, I gotta go." He got to his feet; so did his dog. "You know, sometimes what goes around comes around; sometimes it doesn't, and a good kick in the balls has to be enough."

Maybe it was, she thought as he left, but why didn't it feel like enough?

Now that her mad was over, and she was left alone, everything connected to her life that involved Jonathan seemed hollow. All the years she'd dedicated to his family's businesses, to him, to being the perfect employee, companion, hostess felt flat and false. Felt horrible.

Not only had she given the Wickhams and Jonathan her best, but in the end, her best fell short. Worse, so much worse, they'd used her. There was no question his parents had known. They'd entertained her in their home, as their son's . . . companion. They'd met her family.

They'd betrayed her. They'd made her a fool.

No. She pushed herself to her feet, put the glasses back on the tray. She'd done that to herself. She was responsible for her own actions, her own decisions, just as she was for her own happiness.

She carried the tray inside to the kitchen, calmly poured the remaining tea down the sink. Yes, her mad had fizzled, she thought as she loaded the glasses in the dishwasher. Now she felt sad, sad and shamed.

Tears burned her eyes, so she let them come. Why not? She was alone, wasn't she? Dutifully she went into the basement, carried up bottles of water, cans of soft drinks.

She restocked the refrigerator, then just rested her forehead on the door.

And smelled the fresh, warm scent of honeysuckle, felt a hand stroke her hair.

She squeezed her eyes shut. Not alone after all.

"I'll be all right. I'll be fine. I just have to get through this little pity party."

*Don't cry over him.*

Hope wasn't sure if she heard the words, or if they played in her mind.

"I'm not. Not over him, not for him. For me. For the three years I gave myself to him thinking it mattered. It's hard to know it never did. Hard to realize, to really understand he thought of me as an accessory he could buy, use, set aside, and, worse, pick up again whenever he wanted."

She took a breath. "That's done. I'm done."

She turned, slowly, saw only the empty kitchen. "I guess you're not ready to let me see you. Maybe I'm not ready either. But it helps, having another woman around."

Better, she went into her office for the cosmetic bag she kept there. Once she'd freshened her makeup, she made a shopping list.

She had a pie to bake.

As she wrote, she heard The Lobby door open. Even as she rose, assuming her guests had returned, she heard Avery call out.

"Right here."

She stepped out.

"What's going on?" Avery demanded. "Are you all right?"

"Yes. Why?"

"Ryder said Jonathan was here, and you were upset."

"He said that?"

"Well, he said your ex-asshole came by and stirred you up. I figured it out. What the hell was that dickhead doing here?"

"He—" She broke off when she heard the front door open, and the voices pour in. "I can't explain now." She pulled Avery out The Lobby door. "My guests are here. I'll tell you later."

"I'm off at five. I'll get Clare and——"

"I can't, not with guests here. And these ladies like to party." But this took face-to-face, she thought. Texting or emailing wouldn't cut it. "Tomorrow, after they check out."

"Give me a clue," Avery insisted.

"He thought I should move back to Georgetown, take my job back, and be his mistress."

"Big buckets of shit!"

"At least. I can't talk now." She glanced over her shoulder.

"Do you have check-ins tomorrow?"

"No, actually, I don't have guests tomorrow night."

"Now you do. Clare and I are coming, and we're staying. I'll bring food for a roast-Jonathan's-shriveled-little-balls party."

"Yes." The worst edge of her mood flew away as she threw her arms around Avery. "That's exactly what I need. Just exactly. I need to go in."

"You call if you need me before tomorrow."

"I will, but I'm better—much."

A woman could always count on her girl pals, Hope thought as she turned to the door. They never let you down.

But she hadn't realized Ryder had the insight to understand she'd needed them.

Maybe she should have.

THAT NIGHT, WHEN the inn was quiet again—though she wondered if the echoes of six happily tipsy women playing Rock Band would swirl through the rooms for days—Hope settled down with her laptop.

Carolee had the breakfast shift, she thought, so she could sleep late if she needed to. She wanted to give the search for Lizzy's Billy an hour before bed.

She remembered the sensation of a hand stroking her hair when she'd been low. Women friends didn't let you down, she mused, and she supposed she and Lizzy were friends—of a sort.

She brought up the website of the Liberty House School. Her ancestor Catherine Darby—whom she'd discovered was Eliza Ford's sister—their Lizzy's sister—had founded it. Hope had attended it herself, as had her siblings, her mother, her grandmother.

Maybe that connection would bear fruit.

She found the email address for the head librarian and composed a letter. Maybe there was some sort of documentation, old letters, something. She'd already mined her family, but according to everyone she'd spoken to, all the papers relating to Catherine Ford Darby had been turned over to the school long ago.

"Just a name," she murmured. "We just need a name."

The sisters might have written each other when Eliza left New York for Maryland, for Billy. If not, surely Catherine had written a friend or a family member *about* her sister.

Next she wrote a distant cousin, one she'd never met. Family sources claimed the cousin was writing a biography on Catherine Ford Darby. If true, the cousin might be a source of information. You could hardly write about Catherine without writing about her sister, the sister who'd died young, and so far from home.

With the emails sent, she brought up the site listing all the Civil War soldiers buried in the National Cemetery in Sharpsburg.

They suspected Billy had been a soldier, either from the area or who had fought at Antietam. Perhaps both. But the data they'd uncovered on Lizzy had her arriving at the inn right before the battle, and dying while it raged.

Everything indicated she'd given up her wealthy, well-positioned family in New York and traveled to Boonsboro—young and alone. For Billy.

Every instinct told Hope that Lizzy had come for him, for love.

An elopement? An assignation? Had they found each other, however briefly, before she'd contracted the fever that took her life?

She hoped so, but everything pointed to Eliza Ford dying alone, without friends or family beside her.

So many boys died, too, Hope thought. She picked up the sad task of reading names. So many, and William was a common name.

Still, she stuck with it, making notes until her head began to throb and her eyes blur.

"That's all I can do tonight."

She shut down the laptop, walked through the apartment, checking lights and the door.

When she crawled into bed, she reviewed her to-do list for the next day. But fell asleep with the memory of that kiss in the parking lot. Ryder's hand fisted in her hair.

The smell of honeysuckle drifted over her. But this time she didn't feel the hand stroke her hair.

WHEN THE CREW knocked off the next afternoon, Ryder took advantage of the quiet to run through his checklist, make adjustments to the work assignments for the next day.

Dumbass snored under the plywood spanning the sawhorses, letting out occasional yips as he dreamed of chasing whatever dogs chased in dreams.

Long day, he thought. Long week. He wanted a cold beer and a hot shower, in that order.

He'd get the first at Vesta, with his brothers for company since their women were having a hen party at the inn. They'd go over progress, and he'd be pleased to report to Owen he could schedule the final on the bakery building. It looked like their new tenant could start loading in her equipment and furnishings over the weekend.

Another few weeks—maybe middle of August—and Avery could start planning her grand opening.

Then he could focus in on this place, he mused, looking around at the raw walls. If things went right—and he really wanted them to go right—they'd tear off that mother of a tar roof next week and start framing the pitch.

He knew his mother was already looking at tile and paint fans, and put that right out of his mind. He had to deal with the right now, and the right now included bringing in steel beams, cutting through cinder block, and installing a shitload of new windows.

No, he corrected, that was tomorrow and into next week. The right now was that cold beer.

He toed the dog awake with his boot. "You can sleep in the truck, you lazy bastard."

The dog stirred himself to yawn, sit up. And plop his head in Ryder's lap.

"No beer for you." Ryder scratched at the dog's ears, gave the homely face a rub. "You can't handle it. Remember last time? All you did was lap up half a spilled beer before I caught you, and what happened? You walked into walls and puked. You're a lousy drunk, Dumbass."

"My grandmother had a cat who drank brandy."

This time she gave him a jolt. He shifted, watching Hope as she came in the St. Paul Street door. For a moment the light framed around her, caught at the ends of her hair.

She took a man's breath away, he thought. It just wasn't right.

"Is that so?"

"It is. Her name was Penelope, and she had a taste for Azteca de Oro. She had a thimbleful every night, and died at the age of twenty-two. The cat who wouldn't die."

"D.A. likes toilet water."

"Yes, I'm aware." She walked over, set the pie dish on the plywood. "Payment in full."

She'd done the fancy latticework for the top crust, he noted. He stuck a finger in a space between, ignoring her appalled, "Don't! Oh, really." Scooping some out, he sampled.

It hit that perfect note between tart and sweet. He should've figured it. "It's good."

"It would be even better on a plate, with a fork."

"Maybe. I'll try that out later."

"Don't," she repeated, and this time slapped his hand. Reaching in her pocket, she took out a Milk Bone for the dog. "He may drink out of the toilet, but by and large he has better manners than you do." She gave D.A.'s head a pat. "Is it all right if I take some pictures in here tomorrow?"

"Why?"

"I thought I'd update the inn's Facebook page, include some of what's happening. This, Avery's, the bakery. We're going to offer guests free day passes, so some who're thinking about booking might be interested in the progress. Especially if I can add a projected opening date."

He circled a finger in the air. "Look around. Does it look like I can give you an opening date?"

"Projected."

"No. Take pictures if you want. You can put up the bakery's opening soon."

"How soon?"

"Ask the baker. We should get the final and U&O tomorrow, then it's up to her."

"That's great. I'll touch base with her." She hesitated. "It was nice of you to tell Avery I was upset yesterday."

"You'd moved out of pissed off to broody. I figure that's girl territory."

Yes, she thought, more insightful than she'd given him credit for. And kinder.

"Close enough. I should get back. We don't have any guests tonight, so she and Clare are coming over."

"I got the bulletin." He got up, hefted the pie. "I'm going for a beer."

"I got that bulletin." She stepped out, and since it seemed polite, waited for him to lock up. "What color are you going to paint this place?"

"Something else."

"Already an improvement. Your mother's talking about a slatey blue, chrome accents, white trim, gray stonework along the base."

"That's her deal."

"She's good at it. Have you seen Avery's logo for the new place?"

"The pug pulling the tap. Funny."

"And charming. She and Owen are getting one this weekend—a pug, and apparently a Lab since they couldn't come to a full agreement."

He'd heard that, too. Owen had lists. "They're going to chew shoes, boots, furniture, and pee on the floor, and make Owen crazy. I'm all for it."

He put the dog in the cab, windows half down and—knowing D.A.—set the pie in the bed of the truck.

"Well," she began, "have a—"

She didn't manage more as he yanked her against him, lifted her up to her toes, and swooped in for a kiss that shot the rest of the words out of the top of her head. She managed to grab his waist for balance though she couldn't have fallen if the earth had quaked, not with his hands fisted—one in her hair, one on the back of her shirt.

Heat rocketed down her arms, up her legs, into her center, sharp as lightning bolts. Then her hands slid up his back, gripped his shirt in turn as she rode that lightning.

She didn't pull back, didn't gasp in shock or protest. He'd have released her if she had. But he was tired of looking the other way, or trying to. Ignoring her—or trying to. She'd stirred it up. He could give himself that excuse. In The Penthouse, then again here in the damn parking lot.

He'd had samples. Now he wanted a good, healthy bite.

She smelled of summer. Warm breezes, sun-drenched flowers with exotic names. She tasted like the pie, the perfect meeting of tart and sweet. And she met the demands of the kiss without hesitation. Need for need.

When he let her go she rocked a little. Those sultry eyes of hers were heavy and aware. She rubbed her lips together lightly, as if to hold the flavor—and stirred him again.

"What was that for?" she asked him.

"I just wanted it to be my idea this time." He cocked his head. "You want a pie now?"

He surprised a laugh out of her. "That's all right. I made two. One question. Do you consider yourself my boss?"

"Hell no." He looked not only stunned but irritated. "My mother's your boss. I don't have time to boss you. I've got enough to do."

"All right."

"Listen, if you think that was anything like that asshole you were tangled with—"

"Not in the least." She saw irritation edge up toward fury, laid a calming hand on his arm. "Not in the least. It's just a detail I wanted to confirm, for both of us. Then we're clear on that detail in case either of us get any more ideas. Enjoy your pie," she told him, and walked back to the inn.

"She's going to take some more figuring out," he muttered, then turned to the dog. "Take a nap. I'll be back."

He left his truck where it was and walked over to meet his brothers.

HOPE SET UP wine and cheese, herbed crackers, and some summer berries—along with a pitcher of fresh lemonade for the expectant mother. She was fussing with little details when she heard Clare come in. "In here!" she called out.

She poured lemonade in a tall glass over ice, offered it when Clare came in. "Welcome to Inn BoonsBoro and our first official Girls' Night."

"It got me through the day. Are you all right?"

"Oh, I am, but have much to tell. Where's Avery?"

"She's finishing up something at Vesta. Hope, you should've called the minute Jonathan stepped his stupid Gucci loafers in this place."

"Actually, they were Ferragamos. And it caught me off guard, I admit, but I was handling it."

"Avery told me he actually suggested you move back to Georgetown and start up with him again." Clare, her hair spread around her shoulders like sunlight, dropped down on the couch, snarled. "I never liked him, then I hated him. But now? I want to hurt him. I want to beat him unconscious with a shovel, then tattoo *I'm a cheating dickhead* on his ass."

"I love you."

"I love you, too."

"Have a snack."

"All I do is snack." Clare heaved a sigh. "I eat all day long. I can't seem to stop."

"You're eating for three."

"At this rate I'm going to weigh three hundred pounds. I don't care. Sit down, and you eat something, too, so I don't feel like a big pregnant pig."

"I can't sit yet." Not when she was still carrying the sexual buzz from that kiss. But she spread some cheese on a cracker, poured herself a glass of wine.

And hearing Avery, poured a second.

"God! It's always something." Avery grabbed the wine, slugged some down. "Okay, let's get this ball-roasting started. Oooh, raspberries." She popped two, plopped beside Clare on the butter yellow leather sofa, pulled the clip from her hair, shook it out. "Tell us all."

Hope did just that, starting with Jonathan's appearance at the door.

"He's wrong, and he's stupid," Clare interrupted. "Saying you can't be happy here. You are happy here."

"I am, but you know what? Having him say that made me understand just how happy. I'm exactly where I want to be, doing exactly what I want to do. And bonus. I have both of you."

"Smarmy sleaze," Avery muttered. "He's a smeaze."

"He's a smeaze," Hope agreed, then continued. When she got to Jonathan's "offer," Avery sprang up, shook her fists. "He thinks he can call you a whore—because that's *just* what he did. He needs to be punished. He needs to pay."

"He needs to be ignored," Hope corrected. "He'll suffer more. But I gave him what Ryder called a kick in the balls."

"I wish you meant literally," Clare murmured.

"Pregnancy makes her violent," Hope told Avery. "I was telling him what I thought of his offer—as in 'stuff it'—when I saw Ryder coming across the lot. I just went with impulse. I called him and went over and laid a hot one on him."

"On Ryder?" Clare qualified. "You kissed Ryder?"

"In front of Jonathan—I get it." Folding her arms, Avery nodded in approval. "It's 'up yours, asshole. Look at this sexy bite of man candy I've got now.'"

"Exactly. I asked Ryder to go along, and he got it, and he did. Jonathan looked like he'd swallowed a whole lemon—a whole rotten lemon. It was very satisfying. Then." She flicked her fingers. "He left. Done."

"Are you sure?" Clare gripped her hands in her lap. "He could come back. He could try something. I thought Sam was just a nuisance, but—"

"Honey. Honey," Hope repeated and moved to the couch to flank Clare, take her hand. "It's not like that. Sam's a sick, obsessed man. He stalked you, and you were never involved with him. You never gave him reason. I was involved with Jonathan. He's arrogant, his morals are skewed, and he's a major asshole, but it's not like that at all. He's too full of pride and vanity to come back. He'll assume I'll change my mind, and when I don't, he'll move on to someone else."

"You need to be careful. You have to promise me."

"I will, I do. I know him. He thought I'd jump at the offer to come back to work, come back to him. He'd see it as legitimate, no problem. I made my opinion clear. I don't mean enough to him for him to try anything. I know now I never really did."

"I'm sorry. I'm glad, but I'm sorry."

"I'm not. My pride's still a little tender, but I'm not sorry. He showed me I'd wasted myself on him, and what he did ended up bringing me here. Exactly where I want to be."

"I'd've liked it better if Ryder had pounded on him," Avery said. "I'm not pregnant, just naturally violent."

"Speaking of Ryder, he was very considerate, and he listened to me rant about it after Jonathan left. He waited until I'd calmed down. Actually," she corrected, "he helped me calm down."

"He can do that," Avery confirmed. "It's not his usual mode, but he's patted my head—metaphorically—a few times over the years."

"I didn't expect that from him. I didn't expect him to listen, much less say the right things. Say things I needed to hear. I guess I've made a habit of misjudging certain men. I told him I owed him, and you know what he wanted in payment?"

"Hot damn, this is getting good." Avery poured more wine.

"A pie."

"Is that code?"

"No, it's a pie."

"He's sweeter than you know, under it," Clare told her.

"I don't know about sweet, but he was kind, and levelheaded, and funny. I made him a pie, which brings us to the latest. We had another actual conversation. We've broken records here. We walked out of the fitness center together, and when we got to his truck, he grabbed me. And he laid a hot one on *me*."

"It *is* getting good." Delighted, Avery tapped her glass to Hope's. "What happened then?"

"Then I came back here, and he went over to Vesta."

"Come on!"

"No, it was exactly right. Enough." Content, Hope lifted her glass, sipped. "I don't know if I want to take it anywhere else or not. Tempting, but as I explained before, the desert is dry. Not as dry with all these hot ones, but still . . . It's an interesting possibility. Complicated, but interesting."

"It doesn't have to be complicated," Clare protested.

"I think he's a complicated man to begin with, and our situation is complicated. I work for his mother."

"So?" Avery demanded.

"The so is what I need to work out and resolve. I thought the two of you could tell me a little more about him, just give me a clearer picture."

"We can, but can we do that while we eat dinner?" Clare rubbed her swollen belly. "I could eat a side of beef."

"How about a field green salad, lasagna, garlic bread?"

"And cherry pie," Hope added to Avery's rundown.

"I say bring it on." Clare levered herself up. "All of it."

# CHAPTER SIX

MAN NIGHT. RYDER HADN'T INTENDED TO GET ROPED into spending the evening with kids and dogs. It just sort of happened.

Plus, Beckett sprang for the manly meal of spaghetti and meatballs, apparently a Man Night tradition.

Anyway, the kids were appealing, and along with Yoda and Ben, their young Lab mixes, generated enough energy to power the whole damn county.

Dumbass was in dog heaven.

Ryder didn't know what rules applied when the lady of the house was in residence, but Man Night equaled a free-for-all. The kids ran around like demons, ate like wolves, fought like mortal enemies, and laughed like loons.

It reminded him of his own childhood.

The house was made for kids and dogs, he mused. Big, sprawling, open, colorful. He knew Beckett had added on to the plans for the then-unfinished house once he and Clare got together, and had redesigned it with their family at the center. Now the kids had a big boy-style play-room with built-in shelves and cabinets for kid debris. He knew because he'd helped build it, and because Murphy dragged him up to see it.

Then proceeded to haul down every action figure known to man.

Ryder had a collection of his own boxed away. Some things were sacred to a man.

"Yoda ate Green Goblin."

"Kid, they're not even in the same universe."

"Not the *real* Yoda. Our Yoda. He chewed him up, but he was just a puppy. He doesn't eat action figures anymore. And Santa brought me a new Green Goblin for Christmas. He left it in my stocking. And he brought me Gambit."

"You've got Gambit?"

"Uh-huh." Delighted with the interest, Murphy dug into the colorful bodies, pulled it out. "Sometimes he and Wolverine fight, but mostly they fight the bad guys together."

Ryder had always had a soft spot for Gambit.

"We should have a war now. See, we can use the Bat Cave and the Millennium Falcon for bases, and the Green Goblin and Magneto and the Joker, and like that they are planning the attack in the garage. See, you can put cars in it, but bad guys, too."

What the hell, Ryder decided, and helped the kid set it up.

The war proved vicious, bloody, and, like all wars, involved cowardice, heroism, and numerous casualties. Collateral damage included a one-legged T-Rex, three Storm Troopers, and a ratty teddy bear.

"Teddy took it in the gut!" Murphy shouted.

"War's hell, kid."

"War's hell," Murphy repeated since it was Man Night, and giggled insanely.

Owen walked in as the allied Avengers, X-Men, and Power Rangers blew up the enemy base.

"We defeated them." Murphy leaped up to do his victory dance and exchange high fives with Ryder. "But Iron Man's wounded bad. He's in the hospital."

"He's Iron Man," Owen said. "He'll pull through. You've got to take Harry on in Wii Boxing," he told Ryder. "He beat the crap out of me."

"Let Beckett fight him."

"He beat the crap out of Beckett, too. And Liam. You're our last hope."

"Fine. You've got to help the runt clean this up."

"I wasn't in the war," Owen protested. "I was Sweden."

Ryder considered. The room resembled a battlefield—that had been hit by a tornado. Bribery worked. "I've got pie in the truck."

"Where'd you get pie?"

"Cherry pie. You want any, help the runt. I'm going to take the other kid down."

"I like cherry pie." Murphy hit Ryder with his beautiful angel smile.

"Clean it up, and you'll get some."

Pretty good deal, Ryder decided as he headed toward the family room. Skate out of cleanup, and prevent himself from eating a whole pie—which he would have, and no doubt he'd have felt sick after.

He walked in, rolled his shoulders, did a little boxer's dance in place. "You're going down, Harry Caray. Down and out."

Harry raised his arms over his head. "Undefeated. World Champ. I knocked Owen out! He had X's in his eyes."

"Glass-Jaw Owen," Ryder scoffed, tapped his own jaw with his fist. "Big whoop." He went to the fridge under the bar, got a beer. "Say your prayers."

"I'll say some for you," Beckett offered his brother. "The kid's merciless."

"Save 'em. I've got a cherry pie out in the bed of the truck. Why don't you go get it?"

"Pie?" Liam jumped up from the floor where he'd been rolling with the dogs. "I want pie."

"Then pie you shall have, grasshopper." Beckett shoved out of the big leather chair.

"Okay, current and soon-to-be ass-kicked champ. Set it up."

Harry brought up Ryder's Mii—dark hair, eerily green eyes, scowling face—offered the controller.

The crowd went wild.

The kid beat the crap out of him.

He dropped down with his beer while Harry circled the room, pumping fists in the air.

"What do you do, play this twenty-four/seven?"

"I've got natural talent."

"My butt."

"Granddad said so. I beat him, too. But he's kind of old."

"I want to play!" Murphy came tearing in.

"It's my turn." Liam braced to defend his rights. "Beckett said we could do PlayStation next, and I got to pick. WWF."

First boxing, Ryder thought, now wrestling. Beckett must sleep like the dead every night.

"I'm going for pie." Ryder pushed up. Young desire turned on a dime as they stampeded into the kitchen.

NOT A CRUMB of pie remained, a fact Ryder regretted a little. They wrestled, chased thieves, outwitted assassins. Liam was the first to give it up, passing out in the pile of dogs. Beckett plucked him up, carted him up to bed.

By the time he got back, Harry was sprawled facedown on the sofa. While Beckett repeated the process, Murphy sat cross-legged and wide awake on the floor, guiding Owen through some Mario Brothers game.

"Doesn't he ever conk?" Ryder asked, jerking a thumb at Murphy.

"Kid's like a vampire. He'd stay up till sunrise if you let him. Time to call it, Murph."

"But I'm not tired. There's no school. I wanna—"

"You can watch a movie up in my bed."

"Okay! Can I watch two movies?"

"Let's start with one." Beckett hauled him up, tossed Murphy over his shoulder to make the boy laugh.

As Beckett carried Murphy out, Owen stretched out on the couch. "Two more?"

"Yeah. But Beck seems to have the dad thing down. Plus, he'll have his own basketball team, if the runt ever gets some inches on him."

"Avery and I figure on two."

"Nice even number." Absently, Ryder dug a hand into a partially mangled bag of barbecue potato chips. "Have you got the date of conception, birth, college graduation mapped out?"

Used to it, Owen merely shrugged.

"Jesus, you do."

"Just ballparking. Anyway, we're starting with dogs."

"I'm not sure a pug is a dog. They're more cat-sized."

"They're dogs, and they're good with kids. Gotta think ahead. When we started researching breeds—"

"When *you* started researching."

"Anyway, Avery fell pretty hard for the pug idea. Then she talked to Mom, and Mom put her onto the rescue idea. So we're getting a year-old pug named Tyrone who's deaf in one ear."

"A half dog—not the deaf part, the size. He's half a dog, so you'll have a dog and a half with the Lab."

"Bingo." Owen shook his head. "What kind of sadist names a dog Bingo? He's only four months old, so we'll change that. Give him some dignity."

Beckett came back in, went straight for a beer. "Jesus, I've been at this, more or less, for almost a year, and sometimes I still wonder how Clare did it all on her own."

He shoved Owen's legs off the couch, dropped down. "It's the first time she's been away all night. It's kind of weird."

"You've already knocked her up," Ryder pointed out. "She can use the rest."

"She wants to start fooling with the nursery. She's talking bassinets and changing tables."

"Nervous?"

"Maybe, but mostly it's bassinets. It sounds girly."

"What the hell is it?" Ryder wondered.

"It's like a basket on a stand."

"You're going to put your kids in a basket."

"A fancy baby basket. The one she showed me has this frilly white skirt with blue bows on it." Needing support, Beckett gave his brothers a pleading look. "You can't put a boy in a basket with a frilly white skirt. It's not right."

"So put on your pants and man up," Ryder suggested.

"She's pregnant."

"Which is why you're sitting there talking about frilly white skirts. It's embarrassing."

"Eat me." Beckett looked down the couch at Owen. "I'm thinking we could build something. Well, two somethings. A kind of cradle, but raised on a stand so you don't have to bend down to get the kid. A little fancy work to make Clare happy, and enough so she won't want to cover it up with a damn skirt."

"We could do that. Make them so they'd rock."

"Carve their names into them."

Intrigued, Beckett looked back at Ryder. "Their names."

"Makes them unique, and it'll keep you from mixing them up. Better come up with something for the three you've already got so they don't get their noses out of joint."

"I'm going to build them a tree house. I haven't gotten past the design stage yet. Too much going on."

"Nothing like a tree house," Owen said. "Man, we spent hours in ours. Stockpiled candy, comic books. Remember," he said to Ryder, "you bought that skin mag off Denny. I saw my first porn in that tree house. Good times."

"I got laid the first time up there. Tiffany Carvell. Excellent times."

"Christ." Beckett closed his eyes. "Don't mention porn or getting laid to Clare. She'll never let me build it."

"Pussy."

Beckett sneered right back at Ryder. "Say that to me again when you're married."

"The two of you can drive that train for a while. The women of the world need at least one Montgomery brother free and clear."

"I'm going to like being married," Owen commented.

"You might as well be already."

"Yeah. And I like it. I like knowing she'll be there when I get home, or she'll be coming home. And it is weird," he said to Beckett, "that she won't be tonight."

"They must be having a good time. Clare only called in once to check on the boys. And she said Hope needed some girl time. Speaking of which, what's the deal with this Wickham guy? Clare didn't have the whole story."

"He thought he could poach her."

"Fucker."

"Fucker in a five-thousand-dollar suit."

"He dumped her, right?" Owen lazily sipped at his beer. "For some blonde. Pretty hot blonde if you like the type. Avery showed me her picture in the Style section of the *Post*."

"The Style section?" Ryder snorted. "Seriously?"

"Kiss ass. Avery found it, showed me. So, he dumps her for the blonde, has his big, splashy society wedding, *then* he comes up here to our place and tries to poach our innkeeper? Makes you want to kick his ass and mess up his five-thousand-dollar suit."

"He added a perk. She'd hook back up with him and he'd set her up."

Owen sat up now. "What the fuck did you say?"

"You heard me. He'd set her up as his side piece. Buy her a house, toss in some spending money and a trip to Paris or some shit."

"And yet he lives," Beckett murmured. "Why didn't you beat the shit out of him?"

"Because I didn't know about it until he'd left. Besides, she handled it, handled him. She was telling him to stick it when I walked by. And check this." He dug for more chips. "She sashays right up, tells me to go with it, and plants a long, steamy one on me."

"I didn't hear about that." Owen looked from one brother to the other. "Why didn't I hear about that? I hear about everything."

"It was just yesterday, and we've been busy since. Word's probably inching along the grapevine now, which I figure she didn't think about at the time."

"You went with it?" Beckett asked.

"Sure. Why not? I got the picture, and I didn't like the look of him. Or his suit. I figured she just wanted to give him the business, make him jealous. No skin off mine. Then after he left . . . She was shaking."

"Goddamn it," Beckett muttered.

"Most of it was mad. She was plenty mad. Insulted. But she was shaken up, too."

Owen pulled out his phone. "Did you see his car?"

"This year's Mercedes C63 sedan, black." Ryder rattled off the license plate. "I don't think he'll be back—she hit him where it hurts—but it doesn't hurt to keep an eye out."

"Exactly. Son of a bitch just got married and he's trying to make Hope his . . . He did her a favor when he dumped her."

"Yeah, she seems to get that."

Beckett shot out a finger. "She made you the pie."

Ryder grinned. "Good pie. She wanted to even the score, I guess. So I took it, then I put a move back on her. I like to be ahead in the game."

"You kissed her again?" Owen demanded.

"The other times she started it. I was starting to feel cheap and used."

When Beckett laughed, Owen punched his arm. "Hey."

"It may not be funny. Are you starting a thing with Hope?"

Ryder took a lazy slug of beer. "That would come under the heading of none of your damn business."

"She's the innkeeper."

"Avery's a tenant. It didn't stop you."

"Yeah, but . . ." While Owen tried to work that out, Ryder shrugged.

"Relax. Jesus. Kissing a woman—an available, willing woman— is a man's God-given right. It doesn't mean I'm looking at bassinets. Plus, she kissed me first."

"And she's smokin'," Beckett added.

"Married, father of three with two in the oven," Ryder pointed out.

"I could be the father of twenty, I'd still have eyes. She's smart, smokin'—former beauty queen, remember—and bakes pies. Nice job."

"She's got nice moves, too."

Owen put his head in his hands and made Beckett laugh again. "He's just got to worry about something."

"She's the innkeeper. She's Avery's and Clare's best friend. She got dumped by the son of her boss."

"You don't want to put me in the same class as Wickham, bro."

"I'm not. I'm just stating facts. Add one more. Mom's crazy about her. So if you want to have sex with her, and she wants to have sex with you, great. Just don't screw things up."

"You're starting to piss me off," Ryder said mildly—always a dangerous sign. "Why don't you give me the name of a woman I've screwed things up with?"

"She's not just a woman. She's Hope. And I feel sort of—"

"You've got a thing for her?" Ryder asked.

"Oh, just suck me," Owen snapped back. "I've spent more time with her than either of you, dealing with the setup of the inn, and researching for our resident ghost. She's sort of like a sister."

"You're sort of like my brother."

"Yeah, so it's weird. And Avery's given me the down and dirty on the Wickham thing. He really did a number on her, Ry. The whole frigging family did. So, she's, you know, maybe still a little tender."

"What do you mean, the whole frigging family?"

"They knew. Wickham's old man, his mother. He's got a sister, too. They all knew he was stringing her, and whether they thought it was okay or not, they let it slide. She was managing their hotel, and she handled a lot of their personal event planning. They had her over to their house for dinner, had her up to their place in the Hamptons. Avery said they treated her like one of the family, so she felt like one of the family. So it was like getting dumped by the whole damn family and getting screwed over by Wickham, *and* being used by her employers. They fucked her over good."

It spelled things out, clearly. Ryder decided the whole Wickham clan could go to hell. "I don't fuck women over. Neither does my family."

"No, you don't. We don't. But now you've got a better picture."

"Yeah, I got the picture. If anything moves between us, and I'm not saying it will, I'll be sure she's got a clear one of her own. Satisfied?"

"Yeah."

"And don't go running to Mom."

"Jesus, why would I? I'm no tattletale."

"You told her I broke her cut-glass vase throwing the ball in the house, and hid the pieces," Beckett reminded him.

"I was eight!" Genuine grief and insult vibrated in Owen's voice. "How long are you going to hold that over me?"

"Forever. She took TV privileges away from me for three days—for hiding the pieces, and another day for throwing the ball in the house. I missed *Teenage Mutant Ninja Turtles*."

"Grow up and buy the DVD."

"I did. Doesn't clear you, dude. The Silence of Brotherhood is sacred."

"I was eight."

Since Owen's mind was on something besides his potential sex life, Ryder pushed to his feet. "You girls work this out now, like ladies. I'm going home, get some rack time."

"Material's coming at eight," Owen told him.

"I know it. I'll be there."

"I'm going to work in the shop on the panels for the bar. Text me if you need me to come in."

"I can make it through one day without seeing your pretty face. You I can use." He pointed at Beckett. "Seven a.m."

"It's going to be eight, eight thirty. Clare's mom wants the boys tomorrow. I have to get them up, dressed, fed, and over there. Clare's at the inn, remember."

"Just get there. Let's go, Dumbass." He started out. "And don't throw the ball in the house."

He remembered the pie plate at the last minute, backtracked to grab it. With D.A. he drove the short distance home, winding out of the woods, down the road, back into the woods where his house sat tucked away.

He liked it tucked away, and private. Liked having his own space—and a lot of it. He'd hired a landscaping crew to do the grounds. His mother had tried to make a gardener out of him, but it just hadn't stuck. He was fine digging a hole for a tree, the occasional shrub, but when it came to planting posies? He hired it out.

He liked the look of them, the different heights, textures, shadows in the walkway and deck lights.

Since Beckett had washed it, Ryder left the pie plate in the truck so he wouldn't forget it. He let D.A. sniff and wander and do what a dog had to do while he stood in the quiet, under a sky full of stars.

He couldn't imagine living anywhere else, or wanting to. Not because he'd grown up here, though he imagined that played a role. But because this place—this air, these quiet night sounds—had a hold on him. And always had.

He'd chosen this spot, well back from the main road, to put down his own roots, to build his own place. He'd walked and wandered these woods all his life. He'd known his spot long before he'd become a man.

He went in through the mudroom, into the kitchen, flipped on the light. He'd designed the space, with Beckett's help. Clean lines, simple, and roomy enough for a table. He put the cell phone he'd finally stopped resenting on the charger, grabbed a bottle of water.

He'd get that hot shower now, a hell of a lot later than planned.

The dog trotted upstairs with him, went directly to the big square of pillow he used as a bed. Circled once, twice, a third time, then with a huge sigh curled up with the ratty stuffed cat he loved. Still he watched Ryder, tail thumping contentedly as Ryder emptied his pockets, pulled off his belt.

He stripped down, tossed the clothes in the direction of the hamper, and walked naked into the big indulgent master bath.

A man who worked with his hands, with his back, deserved the king of showers. Especially if he was a contractor and knew how to get it done.

It rivaled the baths they'd put in the inn—the tile work, in his case, in tones of stone gray, the long white counter, the stainless steel vessels. He turned the rainhead and body jets on full, and plenty hot, and let them beat the muscles tight from a long day of work, and play.

And as they loosened, he thought of Hope.

He wasn't going to screw with her. And he sure as hell wasn't responsible for her history with assholes.

She'd started it. He reminded himself of that because it was damn well the simple truth. He'd kept his distance, until recently. He'd kept it because there'd been something right from the jump. He hadn't wanted something, not with a sloe-eyed, sharp-cheekboned beauty queen who probably paid more for a single pair of those stilts she wore than he had for every shoe in his closet combined.

Maybe the stilts made her legs go on forever, but that wasn't the point.

She wasn't his type, and he sure as hell wasn't hers. Hers wore designer suits and ties, probably went to art openings and galas. And liked it. Maybe even the opera. Yeah, the asshole had looked like the opera sort.

She'd started it, and if they finished it, he'd make sure they both laid their cards on the table first. He played fair. And since maybe Owen had a few valid points, he'd think about it awhile before deciding either way.

And if the time came when they both gave the nod, well, he'd play extra fair. No problem.

He shut the shower off, grabbed a towel to scrub his hair dry. It made him think of Hope and her garden hose, and made him smile. Maybe it hadn't struck him funny at the time, but it did now.

She wasn't always perfect. She made mistakes, took missteps. He liked it better that way. Perfect? It could be boring, intimidating, or just outright annoying. He liked the chinks, and wondered if—*if*— things moved forward, he'd find a few more.

Taking time on it, he thought. He had enough on his mind, enough on his plate without adding her right now, straight off.

He walked naked back into the bedroom, pulled down the sheet he'd pulled up that morning—his method of making the bed.

His dog was already snoring, and his windows open to the night breeze, the night sounds. He didn't bother to set the alarm. There was one in his head, and if it didn't go off, D.A. would.

He thought about switching on the TV, winding the rest of the way down. He thought of Hope again, saw in his mind's eye that look on her face—that post-kiss look.

And thinking of Hope, fell straight into sleep.

# CHAPTER SEVEN

R YDER UNLOCKED THE DOOR OF THE INN JUST BEFORE
seven a.m., while the early sun slanted over roses tumbling
around the garden wall. He'd started the crew early, before the heat
of the late June day drummed down on them. Already the sounds of
hammers, saws, drills, echoed from the open windows across the lot.

The inn sat silent, which didn't surprise him. He figured women
who had the whole place to themselves with nothing to do but whatever women who hung out on their own all night did would sleep in.

He vaguely remembered what it was like to sleep in.

He went into the kitchen. Whatever women did on their own all
night, they left the kitchen tidy, he noted. He set the empty pie plate
on the counter, started to walk out again.

Turned back.

He'd been raised better, so opened a couple drawers hunting for
something to write with and on. He hit on the third drawer, came
up with sticky notes and a pen.

*Good pie. We're square.*

He stuck it to the lip of the pan, then eyed the coffeemaker. Considered.

As he considered, Clare shuffled in, and let out a gurgling yelp.

"Easy." In case the baby weight overbalanced her, he started around the island to grab hold of her arm. But she waved him off.

"You *scared* me." She laughed when she said it, leaned back against the refrigerator, a hand resting on the mound of her belly as pregnant women seemed compelled to do. "I didn't think I'd run into anyone this early."

"I just brought this dish back." Her hair tumbled like the roses, and her face held a quiet glow. Being knocked-up looked good on her, he decided. "What are you doing up? I figured you'd all be down for the count after a night of female debauchery."

"Habit, I guess. My body clock hasn't switched to summer hours. Even with that, the boys are usually up by now." She rubbed her belly. "These two are."

The idea of a couple of entities rolling around in there made Ryder vaguely uneasy. "You should sit down."

"Coffee first. Wonderful, warm, brain-clearing caffeine. I'm allowed one stingy cup a day."

He tried to imagine getting through the day on one cup of coffee. It didn't bear thinking about. "So sit. I'll make it. I was thinking I'd grab some to take with me."

Enjoying the idea of being served, she boosted onto one of the stools. "Thanks. It was nice of you and Owen to hang out with Beckett and the boys last night."

"I got a meal out of it." He glanced back at her as he started the coffee—Clare of the sunny hair, and the love of his brother's life. "Your firstborn's a killer at boxing."

"And lets everyone know it. They love their Man Nights. Usually we coordinate them with book club night. When the twins are born I'll take them with me, I think, so the tradition can continue until they're old enough to join in."

"Don't trust Beck to ride herd on five?"

"He's never started from the ground up. It's a lot."

"He'll figure it out."

"I know. He's a wonderful father, just so natural and easy. He changed my life. I guess we changed each other's." She smiled as Ryder got a mug for her, a go-cup for himself. "The pie was good, wasn't it?"

"Yeah. It went fast."

"Hope filled us in on Jonathan's visit. I'm not naive. I know there are selfish, nasty people in the world. But it still surprises me he could treat her the way he has. The way he did."

To Ryder's mind, the giving and good-hearted were often out-numbered by the selfish and nasty. "He's used to getting what he wants just by wanting it. That's my take anyway."

"I think you're right. Hope deserves better. She always did."

"Not a fan?"

"No. I mean, I barely know him, really, but I never liked him very much. Hope says it's not like Sam."

He thought of rushing into the bedroom of Clare's little house down on Main Street, just after Beckett. Of seeing her, pale, dazed, swaying after that bastard Sam Freemont had been after her. And of Beckett pounding Sam's face—after Clare had clocked him with the only weapon at hand: a damn hairbrush.

"Honey, it's not. It's not like that. Freemont's a sick son of a bitch. Wickham?" He remembered Hope's term. "He's just a slimy bastard."

"She convinced me, mostly. But, after you really understand how far some people will go, how obsessed they can be . . . Will you keep an eye out anyway?"

"It's already done."

She took the coffee he handed her. "Then I feel better." And drew in the scent. "A lot better."

"I've got to get going. Are you all right on your own?"

Her smile warmed as she patted her belly. "We're fine."

He went out, let D.A. out of the truck, and they walked over to MacT's together. He might rag on Beckett about the husband and daddy deal, but he knew his brother had hit the jackpot with Clare. Ryder considered her one in a million.

They'd changed each other's lives, as she'd said, but things were supposed to change. Change meant progress, improvements, the occasional happy surprise.

Like when they'd opened the wall between the restaurant side and bar side and discovered the old wood siding complete with two old windows.

Owen hit it big with Avery as well, Ryder mused. She'd taken one look at the old siding and instead of asking them to cover it up again, embraced it, appreciated the character and what it added to the building.

He imagined within a handful of years, Owen would be juggling kids and work and life. Owen might write up schedules, but wasn't so stupid or rigid he wouldn't adjust.

Change, he mused as he got another day's work started, he was in the business of it.

He put in time with his tools, interrupted three times by the phone, which he started hating again. He crossed over to the fitness center to deal with a problem there, then back to the restaurant, where he found Beckett picking up where he'd left off.

"Owen met with the inspector," Beckett told him. "Bakery's good to go."

"I heard."

"He's meeting with Lacy now," Beckett said, referring to the baker.

"Then he'll go ahead and pick up the U&O. That's a big check mark off the list."

"Plenty left to go. Things are under control here." Ryder looked around to be certain. "You can come with me."

"Where?"

"We're going to tear off that bastard roof."

"We had that for midweek."

"We've got a dry day, and it's supposed to stay under ninety. Let's get it done."

It wasn't the first tar roof they'd ripped off, but it would be the biggest. And Beckett remembered, not at all fondly, just how laborious, filthy, and downright nasty the job was.

"You don't want to wait for Owen?"

Ryder just sneered at him. "Afraid of a little sweat, sweetheart?"

"Sunstroke maybe."

"Find your balls, and let's go get it done."

IT WASN'T AS bad as Beckett remembered. It was worse.

Slathered in sweat and sunscreen, he huffed through his breathing mask as he hacked with the tear-off shovel. His muscles burned as if covered with simmering hot coals. Laborers hauled away the waste in wheelbarrows and carts, or hauled up replacement coolers of ice water.

They drank like camels, and never quite kept up with the thirst as every ounce of fluid poured out in more sweat.

"How many son-of-a-bitching layers of this shit is on here?" Beckett shouted.

"It's a miracle the whole goddamn thing didn't fall in last winter." As he broke up another section with a roof cutter, Ryder looked over and grinned. "She's going now."

"If she doesn't kill us first. What are you grinning at?"

"I like the view."

Beckett paused, swiping at sweat and looked out. The copper roof of the inn gleamed and glinted in the sun. He could see The Square, and the traffic passing, people walking into Vesta's for lunch, and shifting, he looked down Main to Turn The Page.

"I'd rather look at the view from a shady porch, with a beer in one hand and my woman in the other."

"Use your imagination." Ryder stripped off his saturated mask, glugged down water. Since he couldn't waste the jug, he imagined pouring that cold water over his head.

As he took a moment to roll his aching shoulders, he saw Hope come out onto the second-floor porch. She paused a moment, looking over and up, studying the work and workers. He knew the instant her gaze reached him; he'd have sworn he felt it like an arrow to the loins.

She stood for a beat, as he did, then unlocked the door to J&R and disappeared inside.

"Must have someone coming in," Beckett commented.

"Huh?"

"Caught ya looking."

Ryder picked up a fresh mask. "No law against it."

"Not yet. Why don't you ask her out?"

"Why don't you put that shovel to work?"

"A little dinner, some conversation. Hell, she baked you a pie."

"You had as much of it as I did. You take her to dinner and talk to her."

"I have. Or Clare and I've had her over. You need a buffer, bro? We can have the two of you over, smooth the way."

"Blow me," Ryder suggested, and hacked away.

IT DIDN'T HURT to look, Hope told herself. She went inside, unlocked Eve and Roarke. There she could open the blinds, just enough to see through, and across to the roof. Or what she imagined was left of it.

She'd had no idea how they'd intended to remove it. It seemed to involve a lot of sharp-bladed shovels, heavy bars, and some sort of saw. Along with a great deal of noise.

She imagined it miserable work, but it provided her with an interesting perspective.

Most of the men had stripped off their shirts. She hoped they'd made liberal and repeated use of sunscreen or they'd be hurting tonight.

She debated with herself a moment, thought, what the hell?

She hurried up to her apartment, grabbed her opera glasses, and jogged down again.

Definitely miserable work, she concluded as she brought that perspective close through the glasses. And oh my, my, the man was seriously built.

She'd seen it, when he had a shirt on, felt it the few times she'd been pressed against him. But . . . there was nothing quite like a full-on view of a sweaty man with muscles rippling.

No woman alive could deny a little buzz, even if the sweaty, ripply-muscle sort wasn't her usual type.

She saw him glance over, pull down the mask to call out something to one of the other men. He had a damn good face, too—a little scruffy and unshaven over those strong bones, but damn good. And when he laughed, as he did now, another buzz zipped along inside her.

She made a little humming sound.

"Hope? I wasn't sure what you wanted to do with . . ."

Hope turned. She nearly whipped the opera glasses behind her back, but she wasn't quite that bad off. Instead she grinned, maybe a little sheepishly, as Carolee stopped at the door.

"I'm spying on the neighbors."

"Really?" Wiggling her eyebrows, Carolee walked over. "What's—

Oh, the roof. God, they have to be hot and sweaty and—" She broke off, laughed. "And that's the whole point. Let me have a look."

She took the glasses, peered out through the slats of the blinds. "They are pretty, aren't they? I only see two of the boys—Justine's boys. Owen must've figured a way out. Horrible work. We should make them some lemonade."

"Oh, well, I don't know if—"

"Absolutely." Beaming, Carolee handed the glasses back to Hope. "We'll fill a couple of coolers, an ice bucket, take some plastic glasses. We have that folding table downstairs. It's a good deed."

"And I should pay for the show?"

Carolee gave her a little pat. "I wouldn't say that. Come on, it won't take much time. We've got a couple hours before check-in."

She couldn't say no to Carolee, especially since she'd been caught ogling the woman's nephew. So together they made vats of lemonade. They carted out the folding table, coolers, ice, cups. Carolee called one of the men by name, hailed him over. That started a rotation of men from the roof, from inside.

She got a lot of "thanks, Hope," or in a few cases "Miss Hope."

"You're a lifesaver." Beckett downed a cup, winked at his aunt.

"You be careful up there."

"You bet. We're almost done. We're cutting through to the damn rubber now. Your timing's good. We're going to break for lunch, finish it up after."

"Sweep that area over there for nails," Ryder ordered someone, then grabbed a cup, gulped down the contents. "Thanks."

"I'm going to call in the lunch order," Beckett announced, and stepped away with his phone.

"Here, Ryder, have another. Your mama's coming by later."

"What for?"

"Because I told her you were tearing off that roof, and she wants to see. I'm going to make another batch so y'all can have more with lunch."

"And she's going to want to see the restaurant, and the bakery," Ryder muttered. "Where the hell is Owen?"

"Here." Hope poured him another cup herself. "Cool off."

"There isn't enough lemonade in the world." But he drank it. "We'll have gotten that bitch off before it gets too hot, so that's something."

Hearing his master's voice, D.A. wandered out, rubbed up against Ryder's legs. Hope took a dog biscuit out of her pocket.

"He's going to start expecting a cookie every time he sees you."

"You got lemonade."

"He hasn't been ripping off a tar-and-gravel roof and sweating off ten pounds."

She bent to pet the dog, tipped her face up so her eyes glinted through a dark curtain of hair. "Maybe I should get my garden hose."

"I might just use it at the end of the day." He hesitated. "Have you got people coming in?"

"Yes. Three rooms, one staying through the weekend."

"Okay."

"Any particular reason you asked?"

"No."

Back to one-word responses, she thought, and tried another avenue. "I hear you shared your pie on Man Night."

"The kids were like vultures. I underestimated them."

"I've got half of one left. You can have it."

"I'll take it."

"Pick it up before you leave. I have to get back to work."

"We'll bring the table and stuff back. We appreciate it."

"All right. Oh, and I'm sure I can make time if you want me to hose you off."

She had the satisfaction of seeing his eyes narrow in speculation before she turned and walked away.

Hope considered herself a pretty good judge, and in her judgment she and Ryder Montgomery were having a serious flirtation.

They'd see where it went from there.

❧

OWEN SHOWED UP as Ryder climbed down from the roof for the last time of the day. He could've bitched, but he noted Owen showed some sweat and dirt, and still wore his tool belt.

But what the hell, a little bitching between brothers was just another sign of affection.

"Figured you'd show up when the hard work was over."

"Somebody had to run the other crew since you got a wild hair to go off schedule. Those fugly tiles are gone over there, and wasn't that fun?"

Anything but, Ryder thought, and couldn't help but be glad he didn't have to do it.

"If you get material in here tomorrow, we can start the new roof."

"It'll be here at eight." Owen gave Ryder an up-and-down study. "Looks like you've earned a beer."

"I earned a fucking six-pack."

"Avery's closing tonight, so I'm going to go over, hang awhile. It's Beckett's turn to buy."

"Beckett's going home," Beckett announced. "And taking a five-hour shower. I may eat and sleep in the shower."

"Looks like you and me, Ry."

"Looks like you," Ryder corrected. "I'm doing what Beckett's doing, and so's my dog."

"Fair enough, considering how the two of you smell. We'll rain check it until tomorrow. We need to go over some things, both sites. We can do it before the crew gets here in the morning, or after we knock off."

"After," Ryder said, definitely.

"Friday night?" Beckett arched his brows. "No hot date?"

"My hot dates don't start that early, they go until early." But he didn't have one, and hadn't thought about it. Maybe after he'd showered off three or four inches of grime, he'd give it more thought.

"See you tomorrow then." As Owen strolled off, Beckett looked back at the building. He and Ryder stood together like a couple of refugees from hell. "Flip you for who does the final check and locks up."

Mostly because he remembered early-morning coffee in the kitchen with Clare, Ryder shrugged. "Go on home to the wife and kids. I'll do it."

"I'm already gone."

Ryder went back in, grabbed his clipboard. He wanted to note a couple things down, after he could stand to be around himself again. He checked the door facing St. Paul, got his cooler.

Thought of lemonade.

No time for that, he told himself. And though he wouldn't mind the pie, he wasn't going into the inn in his current state. He'd have to rain check that, too.

He started out just as a truck pulled in.

Willy B's, he noted, with his mother riding shotgun. He tried not to think of the fact that Avery's father was sleeping with his mother. He'd rather just continue to think of Willy B as he always had: an old family friend—a hell of a nice guy who'd been Tommy Montgomery's best pal since childhood.

If he thought of big, red-bearded Willy B as his mom's lover, it just got sticky.

Justine hopped out. She wore those pants that stopped inches above the ankle and some sort of girly T-shirt with fancy work around the neck.

She'd fussed with herself some—the hair and face stuff—and looked damn pretty.

"Don't get too close." He held up a hand. "I'm not fit for close."

"I've seen you worse, but this is a new shirt. So." She blew him a kiss.

"Back atcha. How's it going, Willy B?"

"Going good." He stood six and a half feet. A big man with a big heart, and a full head of wild red hair that matched the beard he sported. He stood, thumbs tucked in pockets, eyeing the building. "Took the roof clean off."

"There wasn't anything clean about it. I guess you want to take a look inside."

"Wouldn't mind it. If you want to get on, I can lock it up for you."

"It's okay." He led the way.

Willy B ducked in, swiveled his head side to side, up and down as he walked the space. "Justine, you got some imagination."

"It's going to be fabulous. My boys won't settle for less."

"She doesn't give us a choice. We got material coming first thing in the morning so we can start on the new roof."

He talked roofs and windows with Willy B, then let Justine drag Willy B around, pointing to the rough spaces that would be locker rooms, a little classroom, reception space.

"I expect you to join up."

"Oh now, Justine."

"Don't 'oh now' me." She wagged a finger, then patted Willy B's arm. "I'm going to give you a discount since we're going to be in-laws."

He grinned at that. "That's something, isn't it? My girl and your boy. Wouldn't Tommy do a dance over it?"

And that was it, Ryder thought. What made Willy B Willy B. He would think of his friend, always.

"He really would. And he'd've told me I was crazy for buying this place. Then he'd have strapped on his tools. Oh, I tell you we're going to have such a pretty place here, nothing like it around. I've got big plans for the locker rooms."

"Your mom mentioned the lockers and such," Willy B said to Ryder. "I know a guy, they do good work there."

"Owen's been looking into it some. Maybe you can give him the name."

"I'll do that. We're going over to Vesta in a bit. I'll give it to Avery."

"Owen's there."

"Perfect." Justine nodded. "We want to go through the new restaurant space before we get some dinner."

"Owen's got the key. He'll take you through."

"Buy you a beer," Willy B offered. "And pizza if you want."

"Not like this." Ryder spread his hands. "The Health Department might shut her down. But thanks."

"When this place is finished, you can take a shower and a steam." Justine smiled at him. "I hear you're hitting on our innkeeper."

"Oh now, Justine," Willy B murmured as Ryder scowled.

"I am not."

"Was it someone who just looked like you kissing her out in the lot yesterday?"

"That was just . . . nothing."

"It looked like something to Mina Bowers, who was driving by, and who told Carolee, who told me."

He'd known it would get around, but he hadn't expected it to get around to his mother so quickly. "People should mind their own business."

"Well, that never happens," Justine said cheerfully. "And oddly enough I heard firsthand from Chrissy Abbot, who was walking her dog, the two of you had another 'just nothing' earlier. A little digging and I found out the man in the fancy suit who was here at the time was that Jonathan Wickham."

"Yeah, he came by to try to steal her back for his hotel, and try to talk her into sleeping with him again."

"I thought he got married," Willy B began.

"Oh, Willy B, don't be so naive. That bastard," Justine said, with considerable heat. "Why do I hear about you kissing Hope and not knocking that bastard on his ass?"

Ryder's smile covered his face, and came straight from the heart. "I love you, Mom. Seriously."

"That's not an answer."

"Because I didn't know until he was out of range. She set him straight."

"I'd expect no less. If that son of a bitch shows his face around here again, I want you to kick him right off our property. Or call me and I'll do it myself. I'd like to do it. I should go in and talk to her."

"She's got people in there."

"I'll talk to her tomorrow then." She took two long breaths to calm down. "If you want to hit on her and not have people talk about it, do it in private."

"I'm not hitting on her."

"If you're not, I'm disappointed in you. Meanwhile, you go on and clean up, get some rest. I'll talk to you later. And, Ry, it's good work here. You can see it already."

She could, he thought as they left. She always could see. Sometimes more than was comfortable.

"Hitting on her. Jesus. Disappointed if I'm not. You just can't figure women, even mothers. Maybe especially mothers. Come on, Dumbass, let's go take a shower."

He knew the word, wiggled in anticipation, trotting out as Ryder followed.

After he locked up, he turned and saw Hope, with another pie plate, crossing to his truck.

Why the hell were they always meeting up in the damn parking lot?

"You just missed my mother and Willy B."

"Oh. I wish they'd come in."

"I thought you had people in there."

"I do." She gestured at the two cars in the lot beside hers and Carolee's. "And I bet they'd have loved to meet her. Your pie."

"Appreciate it."

"Carolee's serving wine and cheese to the guests, but I should get back in and help. I wanted to ask you something first."

"Okay."

"Are you considering the idea of having sex with me?"

"What the hell am I supposed to say to that?"

"The truth would work. I'm very big on honesty in any sort of relationship, however casual. I've lived and learned on that one. So I'd like to know if you are while I'm considering it. Straightforward," she continued, as he stood, scowling and speechless. "No strings, no complications. If you're not, no problem. I'd just like to be on the same page."

Talk about putting the cards on the table. "The same page. I don't know what the hell page I'm on."

He was tired, filthy, and she was hitting on *him* in the damn parking lot. Had he thought she needed more figuring out? Hell, there *was* no figuring her out.

"All right. When you do, just let me know."

"Just let you know," he repeated. "Yes or no."

"It's simpler, isn't it? You look tired," she observed. "You'll feel better after you clean up and get something to eat. I have to go in. Good night."

"Yeah." He opened the door to let the dog jump in. After a debate, he decided to drive with the pie on his lap. D.A. wouldn't be able to hold back from sticking his whole face in it otherwise.

He got behind the wheel, just sat there.

"No, you can't figure women, Dumbass. You just can't figure them."

# CHAPTER EIGHT

WITH HER GUESTS OUT AND ABOUT, THE ROOMS TURNED, and Carolee doing a market run, Hope carved out some office time. She had payroll and invoices to deal with, the home page, the Facebook page, emails, reservations—and a space of quiet time to get it done.

Then there were lists, the routine tasks and chores that needed doing on a continuous loop. Guests commented on how fresh, pretty, and clean the inn was—and it took steady work to keep it that way.

With the payroll out of the way, she uploaded a few new pictures to the Facebook page, added a brief, chatty post, then moved on to emails.

She clicked Send on the last one just as the Reception bell rang. As good a time for a break as any, she thought. She started to rise when the idea of Jonathan flipped through her mind. If she found him at the door, fine. Even good. This time she'd finish giving him that piece of her mind.

She geared up for it, almost looked forward to it, but found Justine at the door.

"Hi! I thought you had a key."

"I do, but I don't like using it." She glanced back over her shoulder where workers hammered and sawed on the skeleton of a roof. "I hope the noise isn't a problem."

"It's not bad, and the view improves every day. We've got a lot of excitement and interest in the idea of a fitness center right in town."

"That's what I want to hear."

"I'm sorry I missed you and Willy B yesterday."

"I'm making up for it. It always smells so good in here." Justine strolled into the kitchen, helped herself to a Diet Pepsi out of the refrigerator. "It gives me a lift every time I come in. Oh, did you see Lacy's getting equipment installed? Icing Bakery should be up, running, and open to the public in about ten days."

"We can't wait. It's nice to have a neighbor, too—one I'm told makes amazing sticky buns."

"Avery says we'll all be in heaven. We've also rented the two apartments over the bakery. So you'll have more neighbors. Got time to sit?"

"Sure." Adjusting mental lists, she joined Justine at the kitchen island.

"Guests in the house?"

"We've got the cutest couple staying the weekend in J&R. He's a huge Civil War buff. In fact they hit TTP before closing yesterday and he scooped up some books by local authors he didn't have. You'd have thought he found gold. Now they're touring the battlefield. They booked the Historical Adventure package. But the deal is she goes with him today, and tomorrow he has to go antiquing with her."

"Fair's fair."

"He's full of stories. We had two other couples in last night, and he kept everyone entertained until after midnight. Oh, and he loved the Civil War chess set in The Lounge. He's hoping one of the guests checking in today's a player."

"Tommy and Willy B used to play. Me? I like Monopoly." She let out her big laugh.

"You play it really well. I was going to email you once I have all the details, but we've got someone interested in booking the inn for a bridal party."

"A wedding?"

"No, they've got the venue for the wedding and reception, but they're interested in booking us for the night before. Bride, groom, attendants, parents. And the same for the wedding night. I've blocked it off, for now. They're supposed to confirm by Monday."

"Sounds good. How was your Girls' Night?"

"It was great. I really appreciate being able to do something like that. I'd like to have another down the road, with you and Carolee, maybe Darla joining in. My mother and sister if I can manage it."

"Sounds even better." With a satisfied nod, Justine sat back. "You're happy."

"This is a dream job for me, Justine. I couldn't be happier."

"So, no temptation to take Jonathan Wickham up on his offer?"

Hope winced. "Should I have told you about that?"

"Not necessary." Justine waved the question away. "I hear everything worth hearing eventually."

"I guess you do, and no, not the least bit tempted. This is my home. Jonathan may think I can't exist without Georgetown, the Wickham, and him, but he's wrong. I feel more . . . myself than I have in a very long time."

"I'm glad to hear it. Glad to know you didn't give either of his offers the time of day."

"Oh. Oh! Don't get me started on door number two."

Justine laughed again. "That's exactly why I'm here. To get you started. Men don't give the real details, just a sketchy overview."

"What kind of person was I involved with?" Hope shoved back, got a soda for herself. "I knew he was flawed, everyone has flaws. And I knew there were weak spots, and of course, I assumed I'd shore them up. I know better than that, but—"

"You were used to him. You cared for him."

"I was, I did. Looking back, I see it was the whole package. The place, Jonathan, the people. I considered his sister one of my closest friends. She wasn't. I thought I was where I belonged, and the lifestyle . . . It was a good one. Or it was on the surface. It's hard to admit it was all surface."

"How can you see that when you're in it?"

"By looking." She sighed. "Even realizing, admitting, seeing it all, and him, for what it was, he completely stunned me by suggesting we go back to how it was—with benefits including some sort of *pay* scale."

"Prick."

"Oh, at least. Once I calmed down enough, I called my mother and ranted to her for nearly an hour. He was always so charming to my mother, to my family. That mattered to me. She supported me when it all went to hell, but I know she had this soft spot for him. Until I unloaded on her. She was madder than I was when I'd finished."

"I think your mother and I would get along just fine."

"You would. Coming here in his Versace suit and Hermès tie, with his honeymoon tan still glowing, and telling me I'm unfulfilled here, out of place here, how I should come back to the Wickham—at a substantial raise—and to him. How he'd take care of me. Asshole."

"Asshole's a compliment next to the word I'm thinking."

"I never thought I'd feel sorry for Sheridan—his wife. But I do."

"Hold on. Didn't she rub your face in it? Didn't she, knowing full well he'd been involved with you, come into your office and tell you she wanted you to run point on planning her wedding at the hotel?"

"Yes, she did." Hope's eyes narrowed as she drank. "Yes, she damn well did. Scratch feeling sorry for her. They deserve each other."

"I'd say they do. I'm glad Ryder came along in time for you to do some nose-rubbing of your own."

Hope met Justine's amused eyes, sipped slowly. "You heard about that, too?"

"Ear to the ground, honey. Always."

"I guess I didn't think Ryder would mention it to you. It doesn't seem like the sort of thing he'd bring up."

"I heard it from another source, then poked him in the ribs about it. And about the second rendezvous."

"It wasn't a . . . You heard about that, too."

"Small-town ways. If you kiss a man in a parking lot, somebody's going to catch wind."

And she'd thought she'd rolled into the rhythm of those small-town ways. She supposed she still had a bit to learn. "Obviously. I understand if you'd prefer I don't—or we don't—get involved on that level. I——"

"Why would I prefer that?" Justine arched her eyebrows. "You're both grown-ups."

"He's your son. I'm your employee."

"I love my son. I love him enough to believe he can and should make his own decisions, choose his own way. I love this inn—not as much as my boys, but it's up there. I wouldn't have put anyone in charge of it I didn't believe in, I didn't care about. Anyone I didn't respect and trust to make her own decisions. If you and Ry decide to get involved, on any level, that's your choice."

She paused, her smile blooming. "I've seen the sparks, honey. I've wondered what the hell the two of you were waiting for."

"I wasn't sure we even liked each other. I'm still not entirely sure."

"I'm prejudiced, but I'd say there's a lot to like on both sides. You'll

figure it out. And if it just turns out to be sex, you'll both enjoy your-
selves."

"That's something I didn't expect to hear from an employer, or
the mother of a man."

"I'm Justine first. Now that we've settled that, is there any inn
business we need to go over before I go poke my nose in the bookstore
to make sure Clare's taking care of herself and my new grandbabies?"

"Speaking of that first, would it be all right to have the baby shower
here? I know we wouldn't have it until into the fall, but if that's a go,
I want to set up the date and block it."

"I think that's perfect. You let me know what I can do to help."

"You could stay over. You, Clare, Avery, Clare's mom, Carolee.
There'd be room for three more if Clare wanted."

"A baby shower followed by a Girls' Night? Better than perfect.
Count me in. Just give me the date when you set it up with Clare. We
could do the same with Avery's wedding shower."

"I was hoping you'd say that. God, it's going to be so much fun."

"I think Lizzy wants to make sure she's invited."

"I didn't notice," Hope said as she caught the scent of honeysuckle.
"Sometimes I don't. It's just part of the place. Or she is."

"That means you're comfortable with her."

"I am. I'm waiting for some information from a cousin who's doing
a biography on Catherine Darby. And I've reached out to the school,
to the head librarian, hoping they may have some letters or documents
archived. Trying to find her Billy with so little isn't moving very well."

Frustration eked through. When you had a job, a task, a duty, you
got it done. Finding she couldn't, at least not expediently, left Hope
itchy.

"I wish she'd tell us—one of us—more. The last name, something.
She spoke to Owen. I keep waiting for her to speak to him again."

"Who knows what barriers there are between her plane and ours?
I like to think she'll tell you what she can, when she can."

"Me?"

"You're with her more than any of us, and she's your ancestor," Justine pointed out. "Have any of the guests mentioned anything?"

"I had one woman who said she heard music in the middle of the night, and thought she smelled honeysuckle. She woke up not feeling well, couldn't get back to sleep. So she went to The Library for a book. And when she was in there reading, she heard music."

"Interesting."

"She thought she'd dozed off, dreamed it. I'm not sure she didn't, as music hasn't been part of Lizzy's repertoire before."

"It wouldn't surprise me if she branched out. I need to get out of your way. You get me those dates, and I'll mark them down in indelible ink."

"I will."

Hope rose with her, walked her to the door. They stood a moment, watching the men work across the lot.

"The first time I saw Tommy Montgomery he was up a ladder working, his shirt off. I was starting my brand-new job, and I wanted to be so professional, so dignified. And I saw him, and thought: Oh my God." Laughing a little, Justine laid a hand on her heart. "That was the end and the beginning for me."

"I wish I'd had a chance to meet him. Everyone who speaks of him speaks so well."

"He was a good man. Had his flaws, like any. Made me crazy some of the time, and made me laugh a lot. I wouldn't have had him any different. Not one bit." She put an arm around Hope's shoulder for a hug. "If Ryder doesn't make you laugh, you toss him back. Sex isn't worth it if he doesn't make you laugh. I think I'll go interrupt his day before I go nag at Clare."

Hope watched her walk across the lot in her red sneakers, hailing Ryder as she went. And he straightened, shook his head, and grinned down at his mother.

Who wouldn't want to be Justine when they grew up? Hope thought, and slipped back inside.

SHE DIDN'T HAVE time to think about potential lovers or ghosts, or anything else once the Friday arrivals began to roll in. Hope walked—or jogged—up and down the steps too many times to count. She figured until the fitness center opened, she got plenty of cardio right on the job. She showed guests to their rooms, answered questions, accepted compliments on the decor in the name of her boss, served refreshments, offered advice on dining and shopping.

When her Civil War couple returned, she set them up with wine—on request—in The Courtyard.

Some guests, she knew from experience, wanted a private little getaway where the innkeeper was nearly as invisible as Lizzy. Others wanted her to be a part of their experience, wanted to share with her the adventures of their day.

She listened and chatted when it was called for, vanished when it wasn't. And like Justine with the town, Hope kept her ear to the ground of Inn BoonsBoro.

By five, with a full house, she had guests scattered around The Courtyard and in The Lounge.

"I can stay," Carolee told her. "And that woman in E&D has you running your tail off. She assumed we'd have a wine list," Carolee said, trying for a snooty accent. "And she certainly hopes we have Greek yogurt. It's not that I minded running out to get it, but she could've asked nice—or better, in advance."

"I know, I know. She's a pill." Hope poured out another bowl of bar mix. "It's only two days," she said like a mantra. "It's only two days. And maybe she'll be less of a pill as it goes on."

"That type was born being a pill. She snapped her fingers at you."

She had, Hope remembered, but for some reason it made her laugh.

"Oh, girl, girl—because I'm much too important to be expected to remember or use your name—do you at least have water crackers available? I'd like to give her a water cracker."

Now Carolee laughed. "Oh well, everybody else seems really nice, and ready to relax and enjoy. I can stay," she repeated.

"No, you go home. You have to be back bright and early to help me make breakfast for this crowd. Civil War Bob's bound to keep everybody entertained again."

"He couldn't entertain *that* one if he juggled fireballs naked. You call me if you want me to come back. I can even bunk in your spare room if you need me."

"You're the best." Because she was, Hope drew her into a hug. "I'm on it. Don't worry."

She carried out more bar mix, another bottle of wine, and smiled easily when The Pill asked her for cocktail olives. Since she had some, she put them into a pretty bowl, carted them out. She chatted with those who wanted to chat, went back in to check on the guests in The Lounge.

And made the rounds until she could take a breath and offer up a prayer of thanks when The Pill and her husband went out to dinner.

Civil War Bob—bless him—talked his wife and two of the other couples into pizza delivery and games in The Lounge. She heard the good, satisfying sound of laughter and knew there would be no finger-snapping from that quarter.

She could get a little dinner herself, maybe do a little research while she ate—with that ear to the ground in case she was needed.

But first, she'd do a sweep of The Courtyard to gather up any dishes or napkins.

She stepped out into the balmy evening. Such pretty light, she thought, and quiet now that the Fit crew had knocked off. Next empty night, she'd treat herself to dinner in The Courtyard. She might even fix something fussy, just for herself, have a couple glasses of champagne. A little innkeeper indulgence, she thought as she gathered empty bottles for recycling.

Maybe he'd gotten noisier, or she more attuned, but she looked over just as Ryder stepped under the arch of wisteria.

"Some party," he commented.

"We've got a full house, and some of them took advantage of the nice evening. You're in town late."

"Had some things. Meeting at Vesta."

"All those irons in the fire require meetings."

"So Owen claims."

"He's right." She gestured toward the building under construction. "The roof's looking good. I think I can imagine that part finished. It's going to look so much bigger, and so much better."

He took the tub she used for the bottles. "I'll get it."

"I've got it."

"I'll get it," he repeated, muscling it away. He carried it to the shed, dumped them in the recycling bin. Before she could pick up the bag of trash she'd finished filling, he took that as well.

"Thank you."

He shut the shed door, turned to study her.

"Is there something—"

"Yes."

After silence followed she lifted her eyebrows. "All right, what?"

"Yes," he repeated. "I'm considering the idea."

"You— Oh." Not a conversation she'd expected to have with an inn full of people playing gin rummy.

"That's not accurate. I've finished considering the idea."

"I see. And what's your conclusion?"

He gave her that look—that not exactly a smile, a sneer, a smirk. "What do you think?"

"I'm going to take a leap and say you've concluded in favor."

"Good leap." He reached out; she stepped back.

"I have people inside. Guests inside. I wouldn't call this an optimum time to move forward with that conclusion."

"I wasn't figuring on wrestling you to the ground here and now." But he put his hands in his pockets as the image of doing just that had considerable appeal. "So, what would you call the optimal— Christ, now I'm talking like you. When's good for you?"

"I—"

He pulled his hands free, waved it away. He had smoother moves than that, for God's sake. She just threw him off-stride. "You want dinner or something? That's fine. You've got a night off sometime, or a night without bookings. I can work with that." When she hesitated, he shrugged. "Unless you've changed your mind."

"No." Simple, she reminded herself. Straightforward, no frills. That's what she wanted. Wasn't it? "I haven't changed my mind."

"Okay, then. You've got the schedule in that spreadsheet in your head. I've got a brother who has the same kind of brain."

"Tuesday's good."

"Tuesday works. We can—"

"Damn it. Sorry." She spotted someone crossing The Lobby toward the kitchen. "I've just got to check on the guests."

When she dashed inside, Ryder looked down at his dog. "Wait here. You know how she is about you coming in when people are inside."

D.A. sighed, plopped down, gave his sad look before his face nestled on his paws.

Ryder went in. A burst of laugher exploded from the direction of The Lounge, with a lot of voices in its wake. Another rumble of it rolled out from the direction of the kitchen.

Lively place, he decided. He'd never actually been in it when she had paying customers. It didn't hurt his feelings to know that when she did, they enjoyed themselves. He just wished they'd all go the hell away for a few minutes so they could finish this deal.

Better yet, they could go the hell away for a couple hours, then they'd just seal the deal. He caught the scent of honeysuckle, rolled his eyes. "Stay out of it, sister," he muttered.

Hope came back through with a man wearing what Ryder thought of as dad jeans—though his own had never worn them. He had a beer in each hand while Hope carried two glasses of red wine.

"Got yourself a walk-in, Hope." The man grinned, all affability. "Better make up a cot."

"Ryder. Ah, Bob Mackie, this is Ryder Montgomery. His family owns the inn."

"Sure, sure, you told us about that." Bob hooked the necks of the beer in the fingers of one hand, stuck out the other for an enthusiastic shake. "Pleased to meet you. You did a hell of a job here, hell of a job. My wife and I haven't left yet, and we're already talking about coming back."

"Glad you like it."

"The bathrooms alone," Bob said with another grin. "And the history of the place. I love the old photos you've got back there. I'm into the Civil War. Connie and I spent the day at Antietam. Beautiful place. Just beautiful."

"It is."

"How 'bout a beer?"

"I was just—"

"Come on, a man's always got time for a beer. You gotta meet Connie. And Mike and Deb, and Jake and Casey. They're good people." He thrust a beer into Ryder's hand. "Say, we're in Jane and Rochester. I bet that copper tub was a pain in the ass to get up there."

He all but herded Ryder toward The Lounge like a border collie with a reluctant sheep.

Hope took a moment to compose herself. Ryder, not the most sociable of men in her experience, was about to be Civil War Bobbed.

HE TRIED TO get away. It wasn't that he didn't like the guy; Bob Mackie was as likeable as a puppy. He made an excuse, citing his dog in The Courtyard, but all that accomplished was the unified insistence he bring D.A. inside.

Where his dog was petted and made over like a visiting prince.

Mike, from Baltimore, wanted to talk carpentry. He ended up taking them all around, showing them some of the details, explaining how they'd been done, why, when. They had a million questions. Before he'd finished, four more people came back, and had a million more.

Hope didn't help, not one damn bit. She just smiled, tidied up behind them, or worse, offered another avenue of discussion.

By the time he managed to get out, it was full dark, and his brain felt soft. Not from the beer; he'd been careful there. From the *conversation*.

He hadn't gotten across The Courtyard when The Lobby door opened. He relaxed, a little, when he recognized the click of Hope's heels.

"How do you do that?" he demanded. "All the time?"

"Do what?"

"Talk to total strangers."

"I like it."

"I worry about you."

"They're a very nice group, except for the ones who came in and went straight up to their room. You had a lucky break there. She'd have probably asked you to remodel something in the room on the spot. I call her The Pill—in my head." She smiled, touched a hand to his arm. "You were very polite, even friendly. It has to be gratifying when people—total strangers—so admire your work."

"Yeah, but I don't want to talk to them."

She laughed. "You enjoyed Bob."

"He's okay. But next time I'll know to steer clear when you've got a houseful. Tuesday, right? Nobody."

"Just me. And Lizzy."

"I can handle you and Lizzy," he replied and pulled her in before she could evade.

In the moonlight, with the scent of roses. In the shadows of the inn with stars dazzling above. She wasn't looking for romance, but when it dropped in your lap, what could you do?

She locked her arms around him and took it. The heat, the promise, the quiet splendor of the night.

She fit against him as if she'd been made to. And the scent of her mixed with the perfume of roses. A man could get drunk just on the scent of her.

Better not.

He drew away. "Tuesday. Do you want dinner or not?"

"We'll order in."

His grin flashed. "That works for me. Come on, Dumbass, let's go home."

She wouldn't watch him cross the parking lot, she told herself. That was silly, and not at all what this—whatever this was—was about. But she did glance back once, just once, as she walked back to the inn.

She walked back in, to the voices, the energy, the peals of laughter. Smiling—a woman with a hot little secret—she went into the kitchen to make a plate of cookies for her guests.

## CHAPTER NINE

THE SCREAM SHOT HER STRAIGHT UP IN BED AT TWO IN the morning. Dreaming? she wondered. Had she been—

The next scream sent Hope flying out of bed, rushing for the door. She grabbed her cell phone on the run and bolted into the hallway in her cotton shorts and sleep tank. Heart thudding, she charged downstairs and into considerable hysteria on the second floor.

The Pill loosed one glass-shattering scream after the next while her husband, wearing nothing but boxers, gripped her shoulders and shouted at her to stop. Leading with shouted questions, other guests poured out of rooms in various states of undress.

Calm, Hope ordered herself, someone had to be calm.

"What happened? What's wrong? Mrs. Redman. Mrs. Redman. Lola, *stop!*"

Hope's order cracked out, but she thought it carried less insult than a slap across the face. The woman sucked in her breath. Color flooded into her face.

"Don't you speak to me in that tone."

"I apologize. Are you hurt?"

The color died again, but at least she didn't scream. "There's someone—something—in that room. It—she—was standing right over the bed. She *touched* me!"

"Lola, nobody's in there," her husband began.

"I *saw* her. The door to the porch was open, wide open! She came in through the door."

When everyone began talking at once, Hope raised her hands. "Just give me a minute, please."

She opened the door to Elizabeth and Darcy, thinking, *Damn it, Lizzy,* and switched on the lights. She saw nothing out of place, but she could certainly smell honeysuckle. Mr. Redman came in behind her, with Jake Karlo at his heels. Jake's wife held the door open, her eyes sharp as she tightened the belt of the inn robe she'd thrown on.

"There's nobody in here," Redman began, and checked both porch doors. "These are still locked from the inside."

"Nothing in the bathroom," Jake announced, then got down on all fours to peer under the bed. "All clear."

"Bad dream, that's all," Redman said and scrubbed at his close-cropped gray hair. "She just had a bad dream. I'm sorry for the disturbance."

"Please, Mr. Redman, don't apologize."

"Austin," he said to Hope and scrubbed a hand over his face. "I'm standing here in my underwear. Make it Austin. Sorry about that, too." With a sigh, he stepped over to take one of the robes from the hook in the bathroom.

"We're all pretty casually dressed." Jake stood in jeans so hastily yanked on he'd yet to fasten them. "Is there anything we can do?"

"I'm sure we're fine now," Hope told him, "but thank you."

She stepped out to where Mrs. Redman remained in the hall, her arms crossed tight, hands hugging her elbows. She might have been a pill, but she was shivering, and obviously frightened.

"Austin, maybe your wife would like a robe."

"I don't care if there's no one in there now." Lola jutted up her chin, but it trembled. "I don't care if you say the doors are locked. There *was* someone."

"Lola." With a patience Hope found admirable, Austin laid the robe over his wife's shoulders. "You had a bad dream, that's all. Just a bad dream."

"I saw her. The door was open, and the light shone right through her. I'm not going back in that room. We're leaving. We're leaving now."

"It's two in the morning." Twin edges of irritation and embarrassment jutted through the patience. "We're not leaving now."

"Why don't I go down and make you some tea?" Hope suggested.

"I'd appreciate that," Austin said when his wife remained silent. "Thank you."

"I'll give you a hand."

Jake's wife—Casey, Hope remembered—fell into step beside her. "You don't need to bother."

"I don't mind. I could use a drink myself. If I were you," she continued, lowering her voice as they went down, "I'd add a solid jigger of that whiskey you have in The Library."

Tempting, Hope thought. "I'll suggest it." Hope wound her way to the kitchen, put on the kettle. "What can I get you?"

"I can get it myself. She really put you through the paces tonight. You don't have to say anything," she added. "It's just I know the type. I waitressed all through college."

At home, Casey got an open bottle of wine from the refrigerator, took off the topper. "She's the type who wants to adjust everything she orders, complains about the food, the service, the table, calculates a tip on the wrong side of insulting, and acts like she's doing you a great big favor leaving that."

As she spoke, she got down two glasses, poured both.

"This is a beautiful place, and you went out of your way—way out—to accommodate her, with class. You give some people a canteen in the desert when they're dying of thirst, they'll bitch that the water's not wet enough."

"Unfortunately true." And that, Hope decided, was all she could discreetly say about that. "Still, I'm sorry your night was disturbed."

"It's all right. Excitement's always a plus. And Jake and I weren't asleep yet." She smiled, sipped. "We were just getting there. So, Hope." She slid onto a stool. "Tell me about the ghost."

"I—" Hope broke off when Jake strolled in.

"The other women have Lola in The Library. Austin's having some whiskey with Bob out on the porch. I think she's calming down some."

"Hopefully some tea will finish the job."

"Hope was about to tell me about the ghost."

"Yeah?" He took his wife's wineglass, had a swallow. "What's her deal?"

"Jake's all about ghosts," Casey explained. "Whenever we can get away, we always look for an interesting old hotel or B&B—with potential. Like this one."

"We were out on the porch a couple hours ago," Jake said. "I thought I saw her. Young, in period dress. Maybe nineteenth-century. Just a flash, you know. Like—" He snapped his fingers. "And the air smelled sweet."

"I didn't see her, but he's right about the scent. Sweet and pretty."

"Busy night," Hope murmured, and heated one of her little teapots with hot water.

"She wasn't threatening or scary. But I guess if you're not into it, and you get woken up by a ghost, screaming's a viable option."

"Come on." Casey took her wine back. "She screamed like

somebody's mutt chewed the heel of her Jimmy Choos. She screamed so loud she woke up Bob and Connie, and they're out in that room off the back porch."

"If she hadn't, we'd have missed Bob's Mickey Mouse underwear. That was a perk. Okay," Jake said as Hope poured him his own glass of wine. "What do you know about her? You must know something. You live with her."

Maybe it was the hour, or the easy company after a shocking strain, but Hope found herself telling them. "Her name's Eliza Ford. She came here from New York, and died here in September of 1862. It was honeysuckle you smelled. She favors it."

"That's it! I couldn't place it." Jake grinned at her. "Honeysuckle. This is too cool."

"How did she die?" Casey asked.

"A fever. She was young, and from a wealthy family. She came here to meet or find someone named Billy. She's still waiting for him."

"That's so sad, and romantic. How do you know about this Billy?"

"She told us," Hope said simply, and finished making the tea. "She's loyal, funny, and yes, romantic—and completely benign. She also happens to be one of my ancestors."

"You're kidding!" Casey gaped. "Seriously?"

"Cooler and cooler."

"That's about all I can tell you. I need to get this tea to Mrs. Redman."

"Here, let me carry that for you." Jake took the tray she'd filled. "Eliza should've come to our room. We wouldn't have screamed the house down."

"I don't think Mrs. Redman would be as entertained." And, Hope thought, as they walked upstairs, she didn't think Lizzy had meant to be entertaining.

It was nearly three thirty before Hope had the inn quiet again, and her guests settled down. The whiskey in the tea—Austin had added a generous portion himself—did the trick. When Jake and Casey offered to switch rooms, he'd gratefully led a half-asleep Lola into Titania and Oberon.

Back in her own apartment, Hope let out a long, long sigh.

"Lizzy, what were you thinking?" On a jaw-cracking yawn, she shuffled her way back to her bedroom. "Oh, I know what you were thinking. The woman's rude, demanding, ungrateful, and an all-around pain in the ass. You scared her on purpose, a little occult payback."

She put her phone back on the charger, set her alarm as a precaution before she slid back into bed. "It worked. We may have gotten her back to bed, with the help of a couple shots of Irish, but no way her husband's going to talk her out of leaving tomorrow, a day early. I don't think he wants to—he's had it. Me, too. So I'll adjust their bill and say good-bye to them tomorrow. I don't think they'll be back."

As she reached over to turn off the light, Hope's hand froze.

Lizzy didn't shimmer into existence or ease into form like a photograph in a chemical bath. She was simply just there, her blond hair caught tidily back at the nape, her gray—no blue, blue dress, softly belled. Her lips curved in a smile full of fun.

"Good riddance," she said.

"You're here," Hope managed.

"I don't know how to be anywhere else. But I like it here, especially now that you are."

"You have to tell me more, so I can find him for you, find Billy for you. We all want to find him for you."

"It fades." Lizzy lifted her hands, turned them. Hope saw them go in and out of focus. "I fade. But the love stays. You can find the love. You're my Hope."

"His name. The rest of his name."

"Ryder. Did he come?"

"He was here earlier. He'll come back. Tell me Billy's full name."

"He was here." She crossed her hands over her heart. "Close, but too far. I was ill, and it fades, like an old letter. Rest now."

"Eliza—" But she was gone in that same finger-snap. Hope tossed back the sheets. While it was fresh, she wrote down everything in that brief, surreal conversation.

Never sleep now, she thought, and lay in the dark, watching in case Lizzy reappeared. But the minute she shut her eyes, she dropped away.

SHE DIDN'T EXACTLY crawl out of bed, but it was close to it. She revved her shower on full and hot, then gritting her teeth finished it off with a blast of cold, hoping to wake up both brain and body.

One look at her face had her moaning. The day called for a whole bunch of concealer.

By the time she made it to the kitchen, Carolee was already there, humming away as she mixed waffle batter.

"Sorry. Little late."

"No, you're not. Have some coffee, and tell me how it went last night."

"Oh boy, have I got an earful for you."

"I knew that woman was trouble."

"That's not the half of it." She poured coffee, made herself drink the first cup black. She began to arrange the fruit she'd sliced fresh the night before as she filled Carolee in on the details.

She got a lot of *Oh my God*s, *You're kidding*s, *I can't believe it*s, but finished the entire tale by the time they'd prepared the fruit, bacon, juices, cereals.

"You must be exhausted!"

"It wouldn't be so bad, but this group's full of night owls."

"Didn't Justine make it clear that just because a guest wants to stay up half the night, you don't have to?"

"I know, but I can't settle down until they do. I'll work on it."

"As soon as we get breakfast done, you're going up to take a nap."

"Let's see how it goes. In any case, we're down to seven rooms tonight."

"Good riddance," Carolee muttered, and made Hope smile.

"That's what she said. Lizzy."

"It's so exciting." Carolee's bright hazel eyes danced. "She talked to you. I knew she would sooner or later. And if she'd let me, I'd give her a high five for chasing that woman out of here today."

"We're going to get a lot of rude or high-maintenance guests in the mix. It's part of the hospitality package. But I can't be sorry, either."

"Sit down, have more coffee. I'll get the tables set."

"It's done. I had plenty of time last night. Why don't you fill the coffee urn? I'll do the eggs."

Hope liked the rhythm and routine she and Carolee worked out when they had a full house. And the snatches of conversation they managed between carrying out food, greeting guests for the day.

Despite the late night, several woke early and hungry.

She topped off Lola Redman's coffee herself on a pass through The Dining Room. "How are you feeling?"

"I'm fine, thank you."

She spoke stiffly, but Hope detected more embarrassment than rudeness.

She checked chafing dishes, refilled, brought out refreshed pitchers of juice, chatted with Connie about the best antiquing prospects in the area, and with Mike and his wife about their planned drive to Cunningham Falls.

She gave all her guests high marks for steering talk away from the night's disturbance, and imagined they all discussed it in detail outside of Lola's hearing.

While some guests lingered over coffee and conversation and

others went up to gather what they needed for the day's adventures, Hope sat down to generate the Redmans' bill.

Austin tapped on her open office door. "I'm loading up," he told her. "Your key."

"Thank you. I'm so sorry your stay wasn't as pleasant as you'd hoped."

"No fault of yours. I enjoyed it."

"I hope you did. Do you want to leave the charges on your card?"

"Yes, that's fine."

"Just give me a moment."

"I think I'll grab a couple bottles of water for the road."

"Help yourself."

When she went in, he stood in the kitchen chatting amiably with Carolee. "Thank you, Austin. Have a safe trip."

"You went out of your way." He took her hand, pressed bills into it.

"No, that's not necessary."

"Please. I'd consider it a favor if you'd take it. It was nice meeting both of you. You take care now."

As he left, Hope looked down at the two folded fifties in her hand.

"It's his way of apologizing," Carolee said. "You don't turn away a sincere apology."

"It still wasn't necessary. Here. Your half."

Carolee shook her head. "That's yours, honey."

"Carolee—"

"No." To add emphasis, Carolee shook a finger. "That's yours, and you earned it. Why don't you go on up for a little bit, get some rest?"

"Too much coffee." The combination of fatigue and caffeine made her feel like an exhausted hamster who couldn't stop running on its wheel. "Maybe later. But Avery's opening today. Maybe I'll run over, talk to her."

"You do that."

Time with a friend was as refreshing as a nap, Hope thought as she crossed Main. And she needed opinions, advice, commentary. She rapped on the glass door and waited for Avery, hair clipped back, bib apron in place, to come out of the closed kitchen.

"Hey, what's up? I thought you had a full house."

"Carolee's got it for now. I'm taking a break, and boy, do I have a load to tell you. I wish Clare was around."

"Good stuff? Juicy gossip?"

"All of that and more."

"Come on back and spill it. We had a run on pizzas last night, and I'm prepping more dough."

"I'm grabbing a Coke. I shouldn't have any more caffeine, but I have to function."

"Rough night?"

"All of *that* and more." She walked in the back where Avery stood at the stainless steel worktable cutting dough for the rising pans. "First, there was The Pill."

"Birth control pill?"

"You have a one-track mind. The Pill in the form of one Lola Redman."

"Oh, I know the type," Avery said when Hope elaborated. "We get them. You can't deal with the public and not. Did I tell you about the guy last week who—Sorry, your story time."

"And there's more. I'm trying to decide if I tell it chronologically or in order of impact."

"Impact."

"Even then it's hard to judge. So I'm going with sex."

"You had sex?" Avery fisted flour-covered hands on her hips. "When did you have time for sex since I talked to you last?"

"I didn't have sex. I'm going to have sex. Thank God. Next Tuesday night."

"You've made an appointment for sex." On a pitying look, Avery let out a sigh. "Only you."

"There are logistics involved," Hope pointed out. "We don't have any bookings Tuesday night. I can't have sex when I have guests."

"Why not? You have an apartment with a door and a lock on it. I suspect, call me crazy, some of your guests have sex behind their own closed doors."

"True, but I don't want to risk it the first time. We could have another group who wants to party until one in the morning. I'd like more privacy."

"Are you planning to raise the roof?"

"It's been over a year," she reminded her friend. "The roof may be raised. I need to buy some new underwear. Sexy underwear. I haven't bought sexy underwear in a year either, which is a sad, sad thing. This requires new, doesn't it?"

"Absolutely. Not that Ryder's going to pay much attention to that before he yanks it off you."

"I didn't say I was having sex with Ryder."

"I read the subtext." Avery carried dough pans to the under-counter cooler, stirred the sauce already simmering on the stove. "Are you going out first, like dinner or a movie, or just jumping?"

"I suggested we order in, which got his approval. Then I'll jump him."

"That's so sweet." Avery beamed at her. "Why don't I make you something, a grown-up meal? One of the entrees from MacT's."

"You don't have to do that. Pasta's fine."

"Vesta's pasta's more than fine, but why not bump it up a level? It'll be my contribution to the Hope Finally Gets Laid Event."

"We thank you for your support."

"Leave that to me. You can pay me by calling or texting at the first possible moment to confirm liftoff."

"Done. Should I be worried about complications with this? With Ryder."

"Ryder's not a complicated guy. Him man, you woman. I'm pretty sure he'll be okay with that. I know some of the women he's dated in the past."

"What are they like? Come on," Hope added, "who wouldn't want to know?"

"Hope, he's been dating—and I assume 'dating' "—she gave the word air quotes—"since he was in his teens. It's a variety pack. But I can say he manages to keep it friendly after the 'dating' "—more air quotes—"stops."

"That's all I want. Uncomplicated, friendly sex with a man I like— which is a surprise—and am attracted to, which really isn't. Okay." She swiped her hands in the air. "Settled. Now for the rest of the story. I fell into bed about twelve thirty last night. And woke up just after two, due to the screaming from downstairs."

"Oh my God." Avery stopped stocking her toppings dish. "What happened?"

"Let me tell you," Hope said, and did.

At the point in the telling Avery doubled over with laughter, Hope shook her head. "I should've known you'd think it was funny. You and Lizzy have a lot in common."

"She did it on purpose. You *know* she did. Lizzy likes us, and The Pill was treating you like a mentally challenged servant instead of her gracious and classy host. She deserved a good scare."

"She got one. Everybody's packed into the second-floor hall, in their underwear, robes, or skimpy nightclothes—including me—and she's screaming like somebody jabbed her in the eye with an ice pick. I feel guilty not telling her she actually did see something—or someone, but—"

"She'd have been more freaked."

"Exactly. Judgment call. I did tell Jake and Casey. He'd kind of seen Lizzy earlier on the porch. He's into ghosts, but doesn't seem weird about it. I'm absolutely sure he's going to be wandering around tonight, trying to get her to make another appearance. Anyway, two cups of whiskey-laced tea, and we got Lola settled down again. But in T&O. Jake and Casey switched with them, which, of course, meant I had to change the sheets and towels in both rooms, but it was worth it for the peace."

"What time did you get back to bed?"

"It was going on four."

"God, you must be dead on your feet."

"Caffeine." She held up the Coke. "It's my best friend today—besides you. But that's not the end of the story. I saw her."

"The Pill?"

"Lizzy. Eliza. I was talking to her while I got ready to go back to bed. I do that sometimes, thinking it may ease her into communicating. Boy, did it work."

"She was in your apartment?"

"It's not the first time, but it's the first time she let me see her. Or I could see her. And, Avery, she talked to me."

Eyes wide, Avery reached over to grab Hope's hand. "What did she say? Did you ask her about Billy?"

"The first thing, which showed admirable control and presence of mind, by the way."

"Kudos. What did she tell you?"

"I wrote it all down. I think I got it word for word, so I can share it with Owen. Everybody, but Owen especially." She pulled out the note she'd folded into her pocket, and read it to Avery.

"What's it got to do with Ryder?"

"I don't know. My take is she's got that romantic streak, and she sees me and Ryder matched up."

"She'll be very pleased Tuesday night."

"Maybe so, but we're going to disappoint her with this love angle."

"Maybe not." Avery lifted her shoulders and her hands for peace. "Just saying. It fades—she fades. That's awful. Poor Lizzy. It sounds like she can't remember, or pull it all out. It comes and goes. Do you think that's it? Fades in and out, like she does?"

"I think that might be it."

"It really might. I told you how I got her vibe, smelled her, when I snuck in the building when I was a teenager. And Beckett got that sense of her when they started work on the inn. He'd do walk-throughs at night when he lived over here, talk to her. He named her—that's probably powerful, right? The naming."

"And maybe more so because the name was basically the right one."

"Which just goes to show you."

"What?" Hope asked.

"Something woo-woo." Avery wiggled her fingers at her ears as if that made her point. "Anyway, it—she—seemed to get stronger as they brought the place back."

"Bringing it back helped her come back?"

"In a way, yeah. It's her place, and it wasn't happy. You know? It was sagging and dirty and neglected. Broken windows and rubble and piles of pigeon poop. That's a kind of negative energy, don't you think?"

"I'd give pigeon poop a big negative."

"Then the Montgomerys brought it back, step-by-step. And they put a lot of care, even love, into that. It's more than work."

"And it shows."

"And it *feels*," Avery added. "You and Carolee do the same thing, every day. The care and love, and keeping it beautiful. Owen thinks Lizzy likes having it pretty again, and having people there. So do I. But maybe it's got something to do with energy—positive, this time—too."

Thoughtfully, Hope nodded. "The energy of the place, the people in it helping revitalize the energy of her spirit. It's a theory."

"And you're there. Living there. She's your ancestor," Avery pointed out. "That's got to be more energy."

"And responsibility," Hope added. "I feel that. She's putting so much faith in me, Avery. I don't want to let her down."

"You definitely have to tell Owen, but I think you should talk to

Ryder since she mentioned him. Maybe she'll come back when he's there with you, talk to both of you. Maybe, if it's the two of you, a stronger vibe. I don't know, it's possible, and she'll be able to tell you Billy's whole name."

"It's worth a try. Take this for Owen." She passed Avery the note. "I made another copy."

"Naturally. They're all doing shop work today on my bar and built-ins. You could run over, talk to them."

"I can't leave Carolee when we're so busy."

"I'll go by on my way home. They're planning on putting in some shop time tomorrow. I can let you know."

"Tomorrow afternoon I could manage an hour or two. They work at their mother's, right? In that big building that looks like another house."

"That's it. I'm not working tomorrow, so anytime works for me. I can alert Clare. If she doesn't have anything going on, we can have a full-out ghost meeting."

Other voices, other opinions, other theories. She could use all she could get. "I'll work it out with Carolee. I should get back to her. They'll be turning the rooms soon, and we're going to have a truck-load of sheets and towels."

"I know you don't usually schedule in a nap, but make an exception today. You look tired."

"I have on five pounds of concealer, expertly blended."

"I know you, so concealer can't fool me. Grab a nap, or at least have Carolee run the show tonight."

"Since The Pill's out of the equation, I might do that. She'd have fun with the rest of this group. Give Clare the lowdown. I'll see you tomorrow."

"If Lizzy comes back, call me!"

"I will." Lighter in step, Hope went out, then frowning, checked out the sky.

Clouds slid in over the sun. Rain might not have been in the fore-cast, but she knew a threatening storm when she saw one.

Which meant guests would probably come back early from their plans for the day, or hunker down and not leave at all.

The potential nap, she decided, just got crossed off the list.

# CHAPTER TEN

H OPE WOUND UP THE LANE TOWARD JUSTINE'S LATER than she'd planned on Sunday afternoon. Still, she'd enjoyed the drive in the summer green along the curvy roads with her windows down and the wind lifting her hair.

A day tailor-made for a convertible, she thought. She'd toyed with buying one once, but hadn't been able to justify the purchase with her urban life. And now she couldn't justify it due to the long, often snowy country winters.

It was hell being practical.

She liked the way Justine's house seemed tucked away in the woods and still managed to sprawl. And the gardens, she noted, put on a pretty spectacular show.

She saw why when she spotted Justine yanking weeds with a wide-brimmed straw hat perched on her head, purple gloves on her hands, and a bold red tub beside her.

When Hope pulled up, nosing behind a trio of trucks, a pack of dogs raced up to sniff and wag and dance. Justine's two Labs, Atticus and Finch. Hope counted off as she eased open the car door. Clare's family's Yoda and Ben, Ryder's D.A., and . . . Oh, the puppy!

The sniffing and wagging continued as she scrubbed heads. "Hi there. You must be Spike. Look how cute you are!"

Justine, earbuds dangling, clapped her hands. "All right, boys, back off some." As she spoke, a pug waddled around the big red tub.

"Oh, they're everywhere." Laughing, Hope started forward as Justine hefted the weed-filled tub and walked to meet her.

"Yeah, they are. This one's Tyrone, and a little overwhelmed."

"Everybody else is so big. Hello, Tyrone."

"He's only got one good ear, and he's shy yet. But he's got a sweet nature once he's got his bearings."

The trio of boys raced toward them from the direction of the shop, Murphy pumping hard to bring up the rear. Immediately, the dogs—sans Tyrone—ran to surround them.

"Mom's coming," Harry announced. "We're thirsty."

"She's going to get us drinks. Can we have Specials? Can we, Gran?"

Justine flipped at the brim of Liam's ball cap. She'd started stocking jugs of V-8 Splash, and her Special was a tiny dollop of ginger ale added to the cup. "Okay by me. Take this one with you." She motioned toward the pug. "And see he doesn't poop on my floor."

"Okay!"

Murphy wrapped his arms around Hope's legs, looked up with a face shining with joy. "We got lots of dogs. We got more dogs than anybody else in the universe."

"So I see."

"Wait! Wait for me!" he shouted when his brothers ran off.

"Seems like it was just me and my two dogs for a while," Justine said, carting her weeds to her composter. "Though the boys were always thinking up reasons to come by and check on me. Now I've got those three and a wolf pack."

"And you love it."

"Every second. Clare!" Justine fisted a hand on her hip as Clare walked down the slope from the shop. "I'd've gotten those boys drinks."

"I can use the exercise and an indoor seat. I didn't hear you drive up," she said to Hope. "It's noisy back there."

"It's going to be noisy inside, too," Justine pointed out.

"That I'm used to. They kicked me out of the shop anyway. They're going to start staining and varnishing something, and didn't want me around the fumes."

"I didn't raise idiots. Go on inside. I'm nearly done here so I'll be along to help you ride herd. Hope, why don't you go out there to the shop, get a gauge on when they're going to take a break."

"All right."

She walked toward the shop, and the dogs came tearing after her. Finch was wild-eyed, with a ratty, slobbery ball in his mouth. "I'm not touching that," she told him.

He dropped it at her feet. "Still not touching it."

He repeated the process every few steps, all the way to the shop with its covered porch crowded with old chairs, tables, window frames, and various salvage she couldn't identify. Music banged out the open windows along with male voices raised in what might have been a discussion, debate, or argument.

She poked her head in the door and saw men, a lot of toothy tools, piles of lumber, stacks of paint, shelves jammed with cans and jars, and God knew what else.

Finch hustled right in, dropped the ball at Ryder's feet. Ryder barely glanced down before he kicked the ball through the window.

The dog soared through after it. There was a crash, a thud. As Hope scrambled back to make sure the dog was all right, Finch rolled with the ball clamped in his teeth, raced back into the shop.

"For heaven's sake," she murmured. She walked back, this time going in. And had just enough time to lift her hands in defense and catch the ball before it hit her in the face.

"Good reflexes," Ryder commented.

"Yuck." She heaved the ball outside. A deliriously joyful Finch flew after it.

"And not a bad arm."

"You might look where you're kicking that disgusting thing."

"It would've gone out the window if you hadn't blocked it." He pulled a bandana out of his pocket.

She only eyed it when he offered it, and instead reached in her purse for a mini bottle of antibacterial gel. "No, thanks."

"Hope! Look at my bar." Avery, in cargo shorts, hiking boots, and a wildly green bandana tied around her hair looked more like one of the trekkers who came off the Appalachian Trail than a restaurateur. She negotiated the maze of power tools and lumber to grab Hope's hand and pull her through. "These are the panels that go on the bar. Aren't they gorgeous?"

Hope didn't know much about carpentry, but she thought she saw potential in the unfinished wood, the cleanly defined details.

"All of those? It's going to be bigger than I realized."

"Belly up!" Avery wiggled her butt. "I've nearly decided on what I want for the top. I keep going back and forth. We're going to start staining some of the panels today so I can see how they look."

"There's no *we*," Owen corrected.

"But I—"

"Do I mess around in your kitchen?"

"No, but—"

"Why?"

Avery rolled her eyes. "Because you're too fussy and picky about having everything lining up like soldiers, and won't experiment."

"And you're not. Makes you a good cook. Fussy and picky make me a good carpenter."

He did something Hope never expected to see the fussy and picky Owen do. He licked his thumb, rubbed it on the unstained wood. "Nice," he said as the dampness brought out the deep, rich tone. "Go cook something."

When she bared her teeth at him, he laughed and grabbed her in for a hard kiss and a butt squeeze.

Beckett came in from another area carrying a couple of large cans. "I told you I knew where it was. Hi, Hope."

"If you'd leave it where I put it, you wouldn't have to look for it," Owen began.

"It was in the way, and I knew where it was."

"It's not in the way if it's in the paint, stain, and varnish area."

"Ladies."

Hope turned to Ryder when he spoke. "Not you. I'm talking to them. Open the damn cans," he told his brothers. "I'd like to get these pieces stained sometime this century."

"Let me do just a little of it." Avery put on her best smile. "Just one little corner of one little panel. Then I can say I had a hand in it. Loosen up, Owen."

"Yeah," Beckett agreed. "Loosen up, Owen."

That started another round of arguing.

"Is it always like this?" Hope asked Ryder.

He took a long swig from a bottle of Gatorade. "Like what?"

Before she could answer, Finch came back with the ball. She barely managed to jump back so it didn't plop wet and filthy on her shoe. Ryder just booted it out the window again so the happily crazed dog could leap after it.

"High school football," he said when Hope frowned at him.

"Aren't you afraid he'll hurt himself?"

"He hasn't so far. Do us a favor and get Little Red out of here. Everything takes three times as long with women around."

"Oh really?"

"Unless she picks up some tools and knows how to use them, yeah. If you want to get to your ghost talk before nightfall, move her along."

"If you know Avery, you know she won't leave until she does her corner. When she does, I'll get her out."

"Fine." He picked up a glue gun, ran a bead along an edge of what looked to be some sort of counter with shelves above it.

"What's that going to be?"

"Built-in for the waitress station. If you're just going to be standing there, hand me that clamp."

She looked around on a table scattered with screws, tools, rags, glue tubes and located a clamp. And felt something just above her hair.

"Did you just sniff me?"

"You smell good. If you go to the trouble of smelling good, you should expect to get sniffed." Their eyes met over a wood clamp. "Why don't you come by my place when we're done here?"

"I have guests."

"You've got Carolee."

That surge worked through her, but she shook her head. "Tuesday night." She stepped away before she could change her mind. "Avery, let's get out of the way."

"You did your corner, Red," Ryder added. "Scram. No girls allowed."

"Boys are mean." Avery drilled her finger into Ryder's belly as she passed.

Then when they got outside where kids and dogs ran like the wild in the yard, she hooked her arm through Hope's. "Sizzling-hot sex vibes."

"Stop."

"I know sizzling-hot sex vibes when they're snapping in the air. You know he lives a couple minutes away."

"I have—"

"Guests. Still. Quickies are underrated."

"Again, I say, one-track mind."

"I'm engaged to my boyfriend. I'm supposed to think about sex."

"You're supposed to think about wedding dresses and caterers."

"And sex." Laughing, Avery pulled off the bandana, scooped her fingers through her hair. "I don't want to pick the dress yet. I've been looking at magazines and scoping online to get ideas, to try to find a style that pulls at me. It's like the bar top."

"Avery." With an eye roll for her friend's lack of romantic priorities, Hope sighed. "Your wedding dress is not like the bar top."

"It is because they both have to be exactly right, exactly what looks fabulous and makes me feel excited."

"Okay, your wedding dress is like the bar top."

Avery walked inside, through the kitchen door where Clare sat at the counter peeling carrots. Justine stood, chopping celery with the pug curled at her feet. Something boiled on the stove.

"Avery, your dad's coming over."

"Great. I want to introduce him to the puppies." She bent down to rub and nuzzle Tyrone—currently hiding under Clare's stool.

"We're cooking out," Justine announced. "Ry's been dropping broad hints about the lack of potato salad in his life, so I figured I've got three girls here. We ought to be able to pull that off."

"I'd be happy to help," Hope began, "but I really have to get back in about an hour."

"I called Carolee. She'll hold the fort until you get there."

"Really I should go, let her come, be with the family."

"She's fine," Justine insisted. "Avery, will you make that marinade you do for this chicken? The spicy one. We can handle it—we'll do something mild for Harry and Liam. God knows Murphy can handle the heat. The boy would eat hot peppers like gummy bears if we let him."

"He likes them better than gummy bears," Clare agreed. "Relax," she told Hope. "This will give us more time to brainstorm about Lizzy."

True enough, Hope thought. But if she'd known she'd have extra time, she might've taken Ryder up on that visit to his house.

Now who was thinking about sex?

"I'd love a cookout," she said, smiling at Justine. "How can I help?"

Justine just handed her a potato peeler.

RYDER WALKED IN with his brothers, a herd of kids, and a pack of dogs. Chaos immediately ensued. Rolling, running, wrestling, demands for food, drinks. His mother, as expected, ignored it or rolled with it. Avery added to it—also expected. Clare handled the boys' insanity with a look that cut it almost in half—that mom thing—while Beckett grabbed cups to deal with claims of death by thirst.

None of that surprised him.

Hope did.

She hauled the runt onto her lap, listening with appropriate responses of shock and awe as he bombarded her with every detail of his past hour.

The women had gotten into the wine, but he didn't think that was responsibile for her equanimity. In his observations, she just handled what came.

"Can we have a snack?" Liam tugged at Justine. "We're *starving*."

"We're going to eat as soon as you wash up and Willy B gets here."

"That could be forever."

"I think it'll be sooner. In fact, I hear Willy B's truck coming up right now."

So did the dogs, who immediately ran out the door—except for Tyrone, who stuck by Justine as if Velcroed. "Go on, wash your hands. We're going to eat out on the deck."

Ryder opened the fridge for a beer, spotted the bowl of potato salad. Grinned. "Keep your fingers out of that," Justine ordered, anticipating him. "Wash your hands."

So Hope ate grilled chicken and potato salad on the deck in the early summer evening, hip to hip with Ryder, with dogs wandering mournfully in the yard hoping for handouts.

Except for Tyrone. He sat—despite Justine's protests—in Willy B's lap, gazing up with shining love.

"This sure is good."

Justine arched her eyebrows. "How much are you sneaking to that dog?"

"Oh now, Justine, I'm not. He's a good boy—aren't you a good boy? He's not even begging." Tyrone planted his front paws on Willy B's massive chest and wiggled in ecstasy as he licked Willy B's bearded face.

Then the dog laid his head on Willy B's shoulder.

"That's it." Avery shook her head. "Dad, that's your dog."

The same shining love beamed out of Willy B and he stroked the dog's back. "He's my first granddog."

"No, he's *your* dog. You're taking him."

"Avery, I'm not taking your pup!"

"That dog's yours. I know love at first sight when I see it, and I'm looking at it. He likes me, and he'll love me eventually. But he's *in* love with you. And you're in love with him. You're taking him."

"She's right," Owen agreed. "You're made for each other."

The little dog snuggled into the big man's arms.

"I wouldn't feel right taking . . ." Tyrone turned his head, stared at Willy B with his dark, bulging eyes. "Are you sure?"

"You come by on the way home, get his things. You just got an extra Father's Day present."

"Best one ever. But if you change your mind—"

"Dad." Avery reached over, gave Tyrone's back an affectionate scratch. "Love's love."

Yes, it was, Hope thought. And there was plenty of it to go around on an early summer evening.

When the food was cleared they managed to interest the boys in the toys Justine had started stockpiling in a spare room. The room she now thought of as the boys' room.

They sat outside as Hope related the details of her eventful Friday night.

"Before we talk about what all of this might mean, and so on, I wanted to ask you, Justine, if we should have any sort of a policy. Do you want me to tell people about Lizzy, or not tell them?"

"I think a policy is too limiting. You should handle it just the way you are. You judge, guest by guest, what to say, how much to say. This is the first time she's ever disturbed anyone," Justine considered. "And it seems like she did it on purpose. She didn't like seeing someone being rude to you."

"Ought to have better manners," Willy B commented and gave Tyrone a tickle under the chin. Tyrone grumbled happily in his throat.

"Well, manners aren't requirements for paying guests. They're a nice benefit. I've certainly dealt with ruder."

"But we're not talking about Ry," Beckett pointed out, and grinned when Ryder sneered at him.

"I think Lizzy makes certain allowances," Hope continued. "I mentioned broadening those allowances to her."

"You talked to her again?" Owen asked.

"Not exactly. I talk to her now and then. She doesn't talk back. Except for Friday night."

"It's heartbreaking," Clare murmured. "What she said about fading."

"And yet she rarely seems sad. She's got hope." Beckett smiled at Hope. "She had it even before you. I can't figure why she mentioned Ryder. He had less to do with her than me and Owen."

"How do you know?" Ryder demanded.

"I don't remember you saying much about her until she played games with you and Hope in The Penthouse."

"We all spent plenty of time in that place, together, separately. I got along with her. We gave each other space."

"Did you ever see her?" Owen asked him.

"You don't have to see her to know she's there. She didn't like Shawn—you know the carpenter we hired on right after we got started?"

"Nobody liked Shawn after we found out he was skimming materials for side jobs," Owen pointed out.

"And hitting on Denny's wife. What kind of idiot makes a play for the wife of a town cop, especially when the town cop's a friend of his bosses—*and* the woman's not interested?"

"Before we didn't like him, and fired him—Lizzy didn't like him. She used to hide his tools, his lunch bucket, his gloves, like that. At first I thought he was just being careless, then I found some of his things down in the old basement, where he hadn't been. All stacked up neat and tidy—and smelling like honeysuckle."

"A better judge of character than we were in that case," Owen decided.

"Sounds like. She'd spook some of the crew now and then, but sort of playful. And . . ."

"Uh-oh." Beckett pointed at him. "You've been holding back."

"It didn't seem relevant. But since we're getting in deeper." Ryder shrugged. "That time with Hope wasn't the first time she'd stuck me in The Penthouse. Right after Hope showed up, and Mom hired her. On the spot."

"Proving I'm a good judge of character."

"Well, okay, yeah. Anyway, maybe I was a little irritated about hiring somebody so fast, without talking it over."

"You were rude," his mother reminded him. "Rude and pigheaded."

"It's not pigheaded to express an opinion. Rude, okay. I apologized," he pointed out. "Maybe I was still a little steamed. I went back up to do a little more work. The door slammed shut behind me, and wouldn't open. We didn't have the lock sets on yet, but that damn door wouldn't open."

"She gave you the smackdown," Avery said.

"Who's telling the story? I could smell her in there, and that just pissed me off more. Windows won't budge, door won't budge. She fucking grounded me." Then he laughed, quick and easy. "You've gotta respect that. Then she wrote your name on the window glass, inside a little heart."

Hope blinked in surprise. "My name?"

"Inside the heart. I got the picture. She liked you, she wanted you around, and I'd better fall in line. Pissed me off more, but it's hard to argue with a ghost."

"Which you resolved by being snotty to me. Tell the innkeeper this, tell the innkeeper that."

Ryder shrugged again. "She was okay with it."

"Hmm."

"Maybe you should try talking to her, Ryder," Clare suggested. "Since she mentioned you specifically. And since you and Hope are . . . friendlier."

"You don't have to use code," Justine told her. "But you've got a point."

"I don't have that much to say to live people."

"It wouldn't hurt to try," Hope insisted. "She has a connection to you, to the three of you," she said to the brothers. "Avery and I talked about this. We think because you brought her place—her home—back to life, there's a connection. Because you and your mother cared enough to bring it back, make it beautiful, give it warmth again, you helped her. She doesn't know how to be anywhere else, she said. So it matters that where she has to be is loved and cared for. Because it is, she's more *there*. All of you had a part in that. But you, Ryder, had the most hands-on in the actual work. Maybe she'll tell you what she can't seem to tell the rest of us."

"Fine. Fine. I'll ask the dead girl."

"With respect," his mother warned.

"Meanwhile," Hope continued, "I heard back from my cousin and from the school. My cousin promises to send me what she can. She doesn't buy the ghost angle for a minute. Her response was very amused and *really* condescending, but she's enthusiastic about her research, and pleased someone else in the family shows an interest. Even if it's about the wrong sister. And the librarian's working through the red tape, but feels due to the family connection, and the family's long-term support of the school, she can cut through it. There are letters. She hopes to scan me copies within the next few weeks."

"Progress." Owen sat back. "Better than I'm doing."

"If they both come through and I end up with piles of documents, I'm dumping half on you."

"Willing and ready."

Angry young voices punched through the open deck door.

"It couldn't last forever," Clare said and started to rise to break up the fight.

"I've got it." Beckett nudged her down again.

"Go with it," Justine told her. "Pregnancy pampering doesn't last forever either. Plus I've got ice cream to bribe them with. Any other takers?"

Hands shot up around the table.

"I appreciate it," Hope said, "but I really need to get back. Carolee's held the fort long enough. Thanks for dinner, for everything. It was just great."

"We'll do it again," Justine promised. "And I'd like to see those letters when you get copies."

"I'll let you know as soon as I do. 'Night."

Ryder tapped a finger on his knee for about twenty seconds, then pushed up from the table. "Be right back."

As he walked to the door Owen made exaggerated kissing noises. Ryder just shot up his middle finger and kept going.

"My boys." Justine sighed. "So damn classy."

He caught her before she got to her car. "Wait a minute."

She turned, hair swinging, settling.

"What time are you clear on Tuesday?"

"Oh. I should be done by five. Maybe four thirty."

"That works, if I can use one of the showers."

"It's your inn."

"It's not about whose inn it is."

"Then yes, you can use one of the showers. Any one you like."

"Okay."

When he said nothing else, simply stood, bringing that surge up with the steady look, she angled her head. "Well? Are you going to kiss me good-bye?"

"Now that you mention it . . ."

He left her breathless and needy, light-headed and trembly. The perfect end, she thought, to an unexpected summer evening.

"That oughta hold ya."

She laughed, shook her head as she slid into her car. "Let's hope it holds *you*. Good night."

"Yeah." He watched her back out, make the turn. She flipped out a wave as she drove down his mother's lane. He continued to stand where he was as D.A. wandered over to sit at his feet, to stare out at nothing as Ryder did.

"Jesus, D.A., what is it about her? What the hell is it?"

A little uneasy he might just find out, he walked his dog back toward the house.

# CHAPTER ELEVEN

E VERYTHING TOOK LONGER THAN HE'D EXPECTED, BUT
that was nothing new. Rehabs ran on their own schedule, and
when you bounced between two major jobs, schedules went to hell.

Unless you were Owen.

Still, one job had a roof ready to shingle, and the other was about
to move into drywall and brick veneer. He glanced back across the
lot, beyond the huge crane to the building. The new roofline changed
everything, the shape, the sense of space and balance. He imagined
even the untrained eye could see the potential now.

Then he put it out of his mind. He didn't want to think about
shingles and drywall. He wanted to think about taking Hope Beaumont to bed.

Actually, he didn't want to think about it. He just wanted to act
on it.

He let himself in Reception, took a quick glance around. Everything in place, as always. For a moment, he imagined himself as a

guest, walking in for the first time. Yeah, he decided, he'd want to stay here, wouldn't have a problem with that.

Even as he walked to the kitchen, she turned out of her office to meet him.

Everything in place there, too, from the short summer dress and the sexy stilts to the thick, shiny swing of her hair.

She pulled up short when his dog wagged his way over to her.

"Where I go, so goes the Dumbass," Ryder told her.

"Oh. Well." She gave the dog an absent pat. "I tried calling your cell."

"I forgot to charge it." And the fact that it hadn't rung a thousand times to interrupt his work didn't hurt his feelings. "If you needed me to bring something, I can go get it, as long as I can get it fast."

"No, it's not that. I—"

But he grabbed her, pulled her in. If she was going to go around looking the way she looked, she had to expect the man she'd agreed to sleep with would want a sample.

Sample hell, he decided in two seconds flat. They should head straight upstairs. If she wanted conversation, they could talk later.

A whole lot later.

"Let's go upstairs. Pick a room. Grab a key."

"Ryder, wait."

"I'll shower first." He remembered belatedly he had a day's worth of sweat and dirt all over him. "Better yet, you can shower with me."

"Oh boy." She let out a breath, holding up a hand as she eased back. "That sounds really good. Exceptionally good. But I have guests."

What language was she speaking? "You have what?"

"Guests. Up in W&B. Walks-ins. They came to the door a couple hours ago. I tried to call you, but—"

"You're not supposed to have anybody here."

"I *know*. We were clear, but they came to the door and wanted a room. I can't turn people away when we have room. You wouldn't want me to turn guests away, would you?"

He stared at her. Short summer dress, endless legs, twist-your-guts-into-knots brown eyes. "Is that a serious question?"

"Ryder, it's my job. Believe me, I wanted to say no, but I can't do that."

"You're awful damn responsible."

"Yes, I am. That's one of the reasons your mother hired me. They eloped, or they're in the process. They're going to the courthouse to get married tomorrow, and they'd been driving for hours."

"What's wrong with a motel? I'll take them to a motel. I'll pay for the room."

"Ryder." Her laugh bubbled out, with frustration around the edges. "He wanted to give her something special since she's not getting a real wedding. He found us on his iPad when they were at a rest stop, but he didn't call ahead because he wanted to surprise her. They booked two nights so they can have what passes for a honeymoon because they both have to go back to work—and face their families."

"Why did they tell you all this?"

"You'd be surprised what people tell the innkeeper. Added to it, they're young, excited, in love, and maybe he was afraid I'd say no without a reservation without some romantic backstory. Even if it wasn't my job, I wouldn't have had the heart. Her father doesn't like him."

"I don't like him either."

"Yes, you do. Or you would. I'm really sorry, but—"

"What is that?" he interrupted, moving back toward the door. "Was that somebody screaming?"

"They're at it again." When he glanced back at her, frowned, she lifted her shoulders. "They *really* wanted a room."

"That's . . . wow." Head tilted, he listened another minute. "We double insulated—floors, ceilings, walls. Do you always get an audio show?"

"No. No! Thank God. It's an anomaly. I think it's the frequency."

"How many times can he bang her in a couple hours?"

"Not that kind of frequency," she began, then saw him grin. "Although, ha-ha, there's that, too. I meant like radio frequency. Plus they have the windows open."

"Yeah?" He moved to the door, stepped out. He listened to the cries, moans, squeals while Hope tugged on his hands.

"Stop!" She struggled with another laugh. "It's rude. It's intrusive. Come back inside."

"I'm not the one banging with the windows open. I deserve to get off vicariously."

"No, you don't. In fact . . ." She managed to get him back inside, then hurried to the counter, turned on her iPod.

"What did you do that for?"

"Eavesdropping Tom."

"Like you didn't listen."

"Only until I realized what it was. And maybe for a short period thereafter. I'm really sorry, Ryder, but—"

"We can work around them."

"Excuse me?"

"They're busy." He jerked a thumb at the ceiling. "Really busy doing what they're doing, so they're not worried about what you're doing."

"I can't. It's not only awkward—and unprofessional—but I have to be available for them. They're going to come out eventually, want food."

"Burning a lot of calories."

"I imagine so. I need to be available when they do come out."

He narrowed his eyes at her. "I bet you were a Girl Scout."

"You'd lose. I didn't have time for scouts. Listen, I have all this food. Avery made this wonderful food so I'd just have to warm it up. You could at least have a drink and a meal."

Damned if he wanted to go home and scrounge something up. "I need a shower."

She smiled at him. "Pick a room—except for W&B."

"I'll just take the one down here—it's the farthest away from . . . guests."

"Good choice. I'll get the key."

"I've got a change of clothes in the truck."

He walked out before she could tell him to take the dog. "Stay right there," she ordered D.A., then went to her office for the key. Hoping the dog listened, she went to Marguerite and Percy, opening the door, turning on the lights, giving the room a quick innkeeper's scan.

When he came back with a small duffle, she offered the key. "You know how everything works?"

"Everything but you, but I'll figure it out."

"It's not that complicated."

They stood together in the doorway a moment. "You know, you could just put out a sign. Leave them Vesta's number and a six-pack."

"Yes, that's the kind of service we pride ourselves on at Inn Boons-Boro." She touched a hand to his arm. "I have tomorrow off. I could be off-campus until nine, maybe ten. I could come to your place."

"That should work. I don't allow walk-in guests."

"Consider this booking a reservation." She stepped back so he could close the door.

He'd taken it better than she'd expected. And, truth be told, better than she had herself initially.

She went back into the kitchen, took out the food Avery had prepared. She'd just put it on low so they could eat whenever it suited him. Then she opened a bottle of wine, let it breathe.

She deserved a glass of wine.

Tomorrow, she promised herself. She'd focus on personal business, including driving over to Ryder's. That was probably better anyway. No chance of interruptions, problems, no ghost who might decide to play games.

Just the two of them. She glanced down to where D.A. snoozed on the floor.

Well, the three of them.

She got two glasses from the cupboard, was about to pour her own when she heard feet on the stairs.

Naturally, she thought, and put the glass down again.

Chip Barrow's sandy hair stood up in mad spikes. Along with his tattered jeans he wore the faded Foo Fighters T-shirt he'd worn for check-in. Only now he wore it inside out. She doubted he realized it.

He gave her a sleepy, sex-drugged smile she envied bitterly.

"Hey." He cleared his throat. "Sorry to bother you."

"You're not. What can I do for you?"

"Me and Marlie were wondering about maybe some dinner. Like I could get takeout so we could just . . ."

"Couldn't be easier." Though there would be one in their room packet, Hope opened a drawer for Vesta's menu. "They're right across the street, and they'll deliver if you like."

"Really? Awesome. Pizza's like just right. It's good, right?"

"It's very good. I'd be happy to call the order in for you when you decide."

"I know what Marlie likes." His face shone as he said it. "We could do a large, with pepperoni and black olives. And some of this dessert here. This Chocolate Decadence. Sounds awesome, too."

"I can tell you it is."

"Um. Can they maybe bring it up to the room? Just like knock on the door?"

"No problem. Would you like a complimentary bottle of wine?"

"Seriously? Yeah, that's great."

"Red or white?"

"Um, why don't you pick? Ah, could we get a couple of Cokes, too?"

"Give me one minute."

She got a tray, an ice bucket, screwed two Cokes into the bed of ice. Added the wine she'd opened for herself, the two glasses.

"This is so cool. Marlie's blown away by the room. We even turned on the fireplace. It got pretty warm, so we opened the windows, but it's, you know, romantic with the fire going."

She bit down on the inside of her cheek. "I'm sure it is. I'll— Oh, Ryder. This is Chip."

"Hey," Chip said.

"How's it going?"

"Awesome."

"Would you like me to take that up for you?" Hope offered.

"No, thanks. I got it. And you'll order the pizza and stuff?"

"Right away. Give it about twenty minutes."

"Cool. Marlie's going to dig on the wine. Thanks."

"You're welcome."

As he carted the tray out, Hope pressed her lips together to hold back the laugh. "Awesome," she murmured.

"What is he, twelve?"

"Twenty-one, both of them. She had her birthday just last week. They looked so young I carded them." She got out another bottle of wine. "Why don't you open that wine while I call this order in? If you'd rather beer, there's some in the fridge."

"Wine's okay." A little change of pace, he decided. Like the woman. He poured a glass for each of them, sampled his own. And decided he could develop a taste for change of pace.

After she'd placed the order, he nodded toward the stove. "What's cooking?"

"Warming, since I can't take credit for the cooking. Beef

medallions, roasted fingerlings, butter-glazed carrots and peas. And there's a little scallop appetizer."

"Sounds good."

She got out the appetizer. "Try it and see."

He took a sample. "It's good. Red Hots has the touch."

"She does. She worked in a pizza joint when we were in college. I always knew when she'd made the pie. It was just that much better."

"She dove right into Vesta, and she makes it work."

"She's the dive-in type." Deciding she might as well go with the first part of her evening plans, she added a dish of olives, slid onto a stool. Appetizers and conversation here, dinner in The Dining Room. Phase Three would have to wait until tomorrow.

The dog bellied under the stools.

"Were you surprised when Avery and Owen got together?"

"Not especially. He's had a thing for her since we were kids."

"And Beckett had one for Clare since high school, and carried that spark all those years."

"He always knew she was with Clint. He never messed with that. Suffered in secret," Ryder added. "Unless you lived with him. He used to write really crappy love-ripped-my-still-beating-heart-out-of-my-chest songs and sing them in his room till Owen and I threatened to beat him with bricks."

"Really?" She laughed, trying to picture it. "That's so sweet. The songwriting, not the bricks. Were you friends with Clint?"

"Yeah, not close, really. We played football together, got drunk together a time or two. Mostly he was centered on Clare, like she was on him, and looking to join the service."

"So young, both of them. Like Chip and Marlie."

"Who?"

"Wesley and Buttercup—the almost newlyweds. I didn't meet Clare until she moved back to Boonsboro and Avery introduced us. After Clint died."

"Hard time for her. She looked——"

"Go on," she said when he broke off. "Tell me."

"Delicate, I guess. Like you could shatter her with a hard look. The two kids, basically babies, the runt still in the oven. But she wasn't. Delicate, I mean; not down into it. Clare's got more spine than anyone I know."

She thought it might be his longest single discourse on any one person since she'd met him. More, the bone-deep affection and admiration came through.

She'd seen that affection and admiration for her friends, but hearing it touched her.

"I'm lucky to have her and Avery in my life. If I didn't, I'd probably be in Chicago now instead of here. That's where I thought my compass would point after Jonathan. Here's better."

"Can't figure what you saw in him."

Hope sipped her wine, studied Ryder. "Do you want to know?"

"We're sitting here."

"All right. I don't want to compare myself to Clint—his service, his sacrifice, but like him, I had a life plan. It runs in my family. My sister wanted to be a vet since she was eight, and my brother always wanted the law. I loved hotels, the drama, the puzzles, the people, the constancy and the flux. All of it. So my life plan was to manage a hotel. The right hotel, in the right spot. That was the Wickham. Jonathan was part of the Wickham, and as classy—so I thought—and elegant as it is."

"That'd be your type."

"Classy and elegant has its pull," she qualified. "And he was charming, believe me. He knew art and music and wine and fashion. I learned, and I wanted to. He pursued me, and that was flattering and exciting. His family opened the doors for me, and that was heady. My life plan expanded. I'd manage the Wickham, marry Jonathan. We'd be one of D.C.'s power couples. I'd entertain, brilliantly, manage the hotel, again brilliantly, eventually have two children we'd both adore, and so on . . . I know exactly how shallow all that sounds."

"I don't know about that. It's a plan."

"I thought I loved him, so that's a factor. But I didn't." Realizing that had been both comfort and pain. "He didn't break my heart, and he should have. He broke my spirit, and that's lowering. He shattered my pride, and that's hard to come back from. But he didn't break my heart, so in some ways I understand, now, I used him, too."

"Bullshit."

His instant and terse opinion surprised her. "Really?"

"Really. He pursued you, your term. His family went right along with it. You had reason to believe things were going according to that plan. And you thought you loved him. Maybe you were stupid, but you didn't use him."

She considered. "I think I like the idea of using him more than being stupid."

"It's finished anyway."

"Yes, it is. So. You. You have two brothers who hold long-term affection from a young age. Any torches held?"

"Me?" The idea amused him a little. "No. I leave that to Owen and Beck."

"No broken hearts or spirits?"

"Cameron Diaz. She doesn't know I exist. It's tough to take."

He made her laugh again. "I have that same problem with Bradley Cooper. What's wrong with them?"

"Got me. We're as hot as they are."

"Absolutely. Plus, you probably look more natural in a tool belt than Bradley. Tool belts are also hot," she explained. "They're like gun belts—Old West cowboy gun belts. When a man's wearing one—naturally—a woman knows he can handle himself."

"That's a lot for a tool belt."

She pointed at him. "You like my shoes."

"The stilts?"

"Yes, the stilts. You mention them, often, which tells me you notice. And you notice what they do for my legs." She shot one out, turned her foot at the ankle. "They're good legs." She angled her head and her smile. "Maybe not as long as Cameron's, but they're good legs."

"You're not lying." He gripped her calf, swiveled her toward him. When his hand started its slide up, she swiveled back, rose quickly.

"We should eat. I thought I'd set up in The Dining Room."

He simply reached around her, turned off the oven. Then pressed her back, moved in.

Not just his mouth this time, but his hands, quick, impatient, just on the edge of rough. Desire, never far below the surface when he was near, punched through and made her knees weak.

Some sane part of her thought of the impropriety if one of the guests walked in. But that part simply wasn't loud enough, strong enough to drown out the primal pull.

"Stay there," he ordered the dog, who sighed and settled again.

Hope was still reeling when he grabbed her hand, dragging her out of the room. "Ryder—"

"They've got wine, pizza, and sex. It'll be a miracle if they come out before morning." He paused briefly at her office. Not M&P, he thought, not with those two doubles. "Not down here. We're going to need a bigger bed."

"I can't just—"

"Wanna bet?"

And not her apartment. Damned if he was hauling her up to the third floor. He grabbed the key to T&O, pulled her out and toward the stairs.

"But if they need something—"

"They've got what they need. It's time we did."

He turned her on the stairs, pressed her back to the wall, and kissed her until even the idea of protest seemed not only impossible but absurd.

If she didn't have him, and now, she might just blow apart. Then nobody would have an innkeeper.

"Hurry," she managed, and began pulling him.

Breathless from much more than a dash up a flight of stairs, she clung to him when they reached the second floor. Now her hands rushed and took, riding over his hips, up his back as they stumbled their way to the door.

"Hurry, hurry, hurry." She chanted it, and fixed her teeth on his shoulder as he fought with the key.

His hand shook. He'd have thought it mortifying if he could think at all. He could only want, and want. When the key shot home, he pushed her into the room, barely had the presence of mind to lock the door behind them before they fell on the bed, into the canopied bower.

"Leave the stilts on," he told her.

She managed a laugh, started to pull him to her. The laugh tumbled into a grateful gasp as he yanked the thin dress down to her waist.

His mouth, his hands, his weight, his scent. Everything she wanted, everything she so desperately needed. She wanted the thrust of him, hard, strong, *crazed* inside her more than she wanted to breathe.

"Yes. Yes." She turned her face into his throat. "Anything, everything, everywhere."

The tidal wave swarmed over her, roared through her, at last. The heat, the pleasure, the quick spikes of panic and madness. Hard hands on her flesh; a hungry mouth on her breast. Taking, feeding, destroying.

More. More. More.

He felt her hands on his belt, working, tugging, and her breath hot on his throat, against his ear. Everything blurred, the feel of her—smooth as silk and soft as water, and hot as lava. Her voice on a cry of release when he shoved up her dress and found her. Movement, all movement, her hips, her hands, her legs.

Her mouth found his, fixed greedily as her hips rose, ground to him. Knives of need tore through his body when she shoved his jeans down and closed her hand around him.

And her legs locked around his waist. They took each other in a kind of madness, all speed and desperation breaking on pleasure so keen it sliced.

She clung to him while her body quaked, while the glory of those aftershocks trembled and shook. Then weak, her hands slid away. Spent, he collapsed onto her, and lay there waiting for his mind and body to make a connection.

She'd . . . annihilated him, he realized. And that was a first.

He understood, dimly, he still wore his boots, and his jeans were somewhere down around his ankles while her dress was a fragile bunch at her waist.

Not exactly the way he'd planned it. And a far, far cry from what he'd expected of her.

At length she let out something between a moan and a sigh. "God. God. Thank God."

"Are you praying or thanking me?"

"Both."

He managed to roll off her so they lay side by side as they were, still mostly dressed, dazed, and utterly satisfied.

"I was in a hurry," she said.

"Tell me about it."

She sighed again, closed her eyes. "I've been in the desert where sex is concerned. It's been more than a year."

"A year? Jesus, I'm lucky to be alive."

A laugh sounded low in her throat. "Believe me, you are. I can't believe I spent all this money on new underwear. Neither one of us appreciated it."

No, he thought, nothing like what he'd expected of her. On every level, a whole hell of a lot better. "Were you wearing underwear?"

"See? And I still am. Just not where it's meant to be worn."

Still flat on his back, he reached over, down, skimmed his fingers over the lace-edged bra bunched with the dress around her waist.

"You can put it back where it goes. Then I'll appreciate it later before I peel it off you. We'll go for full naked next time."

"I could use some full naked. You've got a really nice body, but—well, in a hurry . . ."

She turned her head, studied his profile—those strong bones, those hard curves. After a moment, he turned his so they stared into each other's eyes.

So damn beautiful, he thought. It ought to be against the law to look like that. It messed up a man's head.

"We must look ridiculous," she murmured.

"Don't look."

"I won't if you won't. Are you hungry?"

"That's a loaded question, considering."

She smiled as she worked her bra back into place. "Why don't we go down and eat, pretend we're civilized adults."

"Too late for the second part."

"It's never too late to be civilized."

"You're starting to think about the kids in W&B."

"Avery made us a beautiful meal, and we should eat it. And it gives me the opportunity to be available in case. Then we can bring the wine—should there be any left—back up here. You can appreciate my new underwear."

"It's a good plan." He levered up enough to pull up his shorts, his jeans. "And maybe next time I'll manage to get my boots off before you jump me."

She wiggled back into her dress, smiled. "No promises."

# CHAPTER TWELVE

R YDER COULDN'T QUITE DEFINE THE SITUATION WITH
Hope. They weren't exactly dating. They weren't exactly
friends. They weren't exactly what his aunt Carolee called An Item.

But however he angled to consider the situation, he liked it.

Maybe it included a few elements of strange, the way he parked
his truck behind Vesta or over by the fitness center job site rather than
right behind the inn.

It wasn't as if someone couldn't figure out what was going on if
they paid attention. Someone always paid attention. Still, it didn't sit
right with him to be blatant about it.

And maybe it added more strange the way he went up The Courtyard stairs to the third floor, and into the building that way.

Some evenings he heard voices from below, and just let himself
and D.A. into her place until she knocked off for the night.

And maybe he found himself taking more of an interest in the

workings of the inn than he'd expected to, but he was in it more than
he'd imagined, so that followed.

And those workings struck him as pretty well oiled. No surprise,
since in a lot of ways she was Owen in a skirt.

She emailed herself, doing room checks with her phone, using the
phone to email herself notes she turned into lists on her office desktop.
Fresh batteries for the remote in N&N, more TP in W&B, fresh room
packets or menus or lightbulbs wherever. Saved steps, he imagined,
as she'd be up and down countless times a day—stocking the coffee
supply in The Library, hauling up wine, sodas, water from the basement storage.

She lived and died by lists, to his way of thinking. And, again like
his brother, by the sticky note.

He'd invariably find a few whenever he'd go into her place while
she handled guests. *Beer in the fridge*—stuck on the fridge door as if
he couldn't open it and see for himself. *Leftover pasta on warm if you're
hungry*—stuck on the oven, as if ditto.

But he had to admit it was nice to have her bother.

He supposed he'd figured she'd be rigid—live and die by the schedule as much as her lists and sticky notes. But she flexed, and plenty,
when things called for it, giving here, adjusting there, shoring up or
letting go.

He could admit he'd expected her to start laying down rules or
making demands about their . . . situation. Instead she rolled with
it—and rolled plenty with him, he thought as he set the next replacement window in the fitness center.

Even as he thought of her she came out, helping the laundry service
haul away a load of linens and towels.

She looked so damn fresh and pretty. He'd seen her mussed now—
and done the mussing up himself—but she still managed to grab a
man by the throat and the balls.

She turned as someone came out of The Lobby doors. She had a houseful, he knew, for the July Fourth weekend. He couldn't hear her, but he could *see* her laugh and engage fully with the three women who came out.

"Problem with the window?"

"Huh?" He glanced around as Beckett came up behind him.

"Oh yeah, nice view. Clare said she's got sixteen people in there, through the weekend."

"It's a holiday," Ryder said and went back to installing the window.

"Yeah, the boys can't wait to hit the park tomorrow. We're going early so they can eat and run off some steam before the fireworks. And we can claim enough territory for everybody. It's too bad Hope can't make it."

"She'll be able to see the fireworks from the top porch of the inn." But it was a pisser, he admitted. He couldn't think of the last time he'd hung out on the Fourth without a date. Not that he couldn't ask somebody else—technically.

"Don't you have something to do?" Ryder asked him.

"I've been doing it. You're on the last windows. Roofers are on the shingles; looking good, too. Owen texted from MacT's. The steel's on its way here. Looks like we're getting those beams up today."

"Place'll be full of subs next week." Finished, Ryder stepped back from the window. "You sit on Mom until she picks out the style and finish of the rails for this place."

"Why do I have to sit on her?"

"Because I thought of it first." He checked the time. Close enough to lunch to take the break, but he didn't want to leave the site if the steel was en route.

"And you can go get us some lunch."

"I can?"

"I've got too much going on to leave, and I want to go over a couple things on the plans with you."

Beckett's jaw set. "Changes, you mean."

"Don't get your panties in a bunch, sweetheart. Just some adjustments, some clarification. If we're going to have the bones of this place in, I want to nail down the lighting."

"We'll do it now. I'll call in an order. What do you want?"

"Food." When one of the men hailed him, Ryder left Beckett to figure it out.

They used a back corner, what would eventually be the circuit-training area, to bargain over the plans. Ryder always wanted changes, Beckett knew, just as Ryder knew Beckett only held the line against them if they messed with the vision or didn't make architectural sense.

"I'm making Mom a list," Beckett began. "Number of lights, types, areas. She knows the look she wants."

"Don't let her order until you check the wattage."

"It's not my first rodeo, Ry." He pulled out his phone as it signaled. "Owen's in The Courtyard with food."

"What's he doing over there?"

"You want to eat, let's find out."

He did want to eat, and he'd be within sight if the steel arrived. And since the plans were burned in his brain, he didn't need the blueprints to bug Beckett about them.

"About the bamboo floors," he began as they started out.

"Mom's set on bamboo; so am I for that matter. Don't even go there."

"It would save time and money, and look fine if we ran the padded gym flooring throughout."

"It'd look boring and pedestrian. Bamboo's got a nice give to it for the classroom, the interior steps and hallways."

"The steps are going to be a pain in my ass if we use wood."

"Not budging on it," Beckett told him. "And you can bet your ass, pain or not, Mom's not either."

They stepped into The Courtyard where Owen sat under a cheerful umbrella with three take-out containers and a stack of papers.

"Hope caught me as I was going by and said to eat out here. Nice."

"What'd I get?" Ryder flipped back the lid of the container, nodded at the panini and fries. "That works."

"I've been going over the paint system for the exterior of the fitness center. It's a lot of steps, a big process, to get those cinder blocks looking like anything but cinder blocks."

"Don't you start," Beckett warned, and grabbed his own panini. "No way we're just slapping on some paint and calling it a day. It'll still be ugly."

"It's already less ugly," Ryder pointed out. "But I'm on your side of this one."

"Who said I'm not?" Owen stretched out his legs, circled his tired neck. "I'm saying we could do it, but we should go ahead and hire a sub who knows how to do it. It'd take us too long, and there's too much room for screwups."

Before Ryder could argue about that, Hope came out with a tray. A big pitcher, glasses, and a plate of cookies.

"Iced tea," she announced. "And there's more where that came from. I swear, the calendar turned over to July, and the furnace revved up. They're calling for triple digits by Sunday."

"Thanks. You didn't have to bother," Owen told her. "Avery said you're slammed this weekend."

"Boy, are we. All the guests are off doing something right now, so I've got a minute. There's a lot of interest in the fitness center and the new restaurant. Everybody wants opening dates."

"Everybody's going to have to wait," Ryder muttered.

"I'm telling them to watch Facebook and the web pages. Let me know if you want anything else."

Ryder downed half a glass of tea when she went inside. "Be right back," he said, and followed her.

"Does he know he's hooked?" Owen wondered.

"Ry? Hell no."

"That was a rhetorical question. Mid-August for MacT's," Owen added with his mouth full. "It's moving good, and I know how Ry is about deadlines, but it's not going to be a problem. I figure it'll take about the same time for him to realize he's hooked."

Hope started to turn into her office when she heard the door open and close. Walking back toward the kitchen, she smiled as she saw Ryder.

"I told Owen you could eat inside where it's cool. If you want I can—"

He grabbed—he always seemed to be grabbing her as if she might get away. And the kiss was hot as July.

"Just wanted to get that done," he told her. "Now, I won't be so distracted."

"Funny, it works just the opposite on me."

"Well, everybody's out, so—"

"No." She laughed, nudged him back. "Appealing, but no. I'm swamped."

"Carolee—"

"Is getting a root canal."

His wince was knee-jerk and heartfelt. "I didn't hear about that."

"She just went in this morning because I nagged her. She was going to pump Advil and tough it out until Monday. Laurie from the book-store's going to come over and give me a hand later."

"You need any help until? I can spare Beck."

"No, I should be fine."

He had an idea now just what went into her day—and a weekend with sixteen guests meant that day would be jam-packed. "You could probably use a vacation, a long weekend. Something."

"I think I'll have a couple days clear in September. I intend to be a sloth."

"Block it out. Mom would be okay with it."

"I'll think about that." She gestured back as her office phone rang. "But we're a popular place."

"Block it out," he repeated, and left her to work.

Ryder dropped back into his chair, picked up his sandwich. "Carolee's getting a root canal, and we're overworking the innkeeper."

"You can call her Hope," Owen pointed out. "You're sleeping with her."

"Root canal?" As his brother had, Beckett winced. "Does she need more help? Hope?"

"I don't know. Not my area. But when she doesn't have people in there, she's doing stuff to get ready for having people in there, or that marketing crap. Whatever. She needs some time off."

"There wouldn't be any self-interest wound through there?" Owen suggested.

"Sex isn't the problem. If she runs herself into the ground, we're in trouble."

"Okay, that's a point. Plus, none of us wants her overworked. So——"

Owen broke off as she burst out the door. "I've got documents," she announced. "My cousin came through. There's a load of them. I don't know when I'm going to get to them, but——"

"Forward them to me," Owen told her. "I'll start combing through."

"I will, and I'll carve out time to do the same. It feels like progress." Unconsciously, she laid a hand on Ryder's shoulder as she spoke. "I have to believe we'll find something."

"Why don't you sit down a minute?" Before she could respond, Ryder just pulled her down on his lap. When she tried to push away, he grinned at his brothers and tightened his hold. "Screws with her dignity."

"My dignity remains unbowed. You're sweaty."

"It's hot. Eat some fries."

"I just had a yogurt, so—"

"Then you definitely need some fries."

She knew full well he'd keep her pinned in his lap until she did. She plucked one out of his container. "There. Now—"

"Wash it down." He picked up his glass, put it in her hand.

"Fine, fine." She drank, put the glass down again.

"Ry was saying you could use more help," Owen began.

Her back went stiff as a two-by-four. "Have there been complaints?"

"No, but—"

"Have *I* complained? No," she answered for herself. "I know what I can handle and what I can't. Keep that in mind," she told Ryder, poking her elbow into his gut and pushing to her feet. "I need to get back to work."

"You've got a big fucking mouth, Owen."

"You just said she—"

"A big fucking mouth. There's the steel." He took his sandwich with him as he walked away.

"Definitely hooked," Beckett observed.

"He's the one who said she was overworked."

"Yeah, 'cause he's the one who's hooked."

HE SENT HER flowers. Ryder's working theory had always been if a woman was pissed off, no matter the cause or the blame, a guy sent flowers. Mostly that smoothed things out again. Then he forgot it in the sweat and effort of work until he was locking up for the night and she walked over.

"The flowers are beautiful. Thank you."

"You're welcome."

"I've only got a minute, which doesn't mean I'm overworked. It means I'm working."

Damn Owen, he thought. "Okay."

"I don't want you telling your family I can't handle this job."

"I didn't."

"If I need more help, I'll talk to Justine. I can speak for myself."

"Got it."

A man could always hope that would cap that, but as he expected she—like most women—gnawed on it.

"Ryder, I appreciate your concern. It's nice, and it's unexpected. Sometimes there's a lot of stress and pressure involved. I'm sure it's the same with your work."

"Can't argue there."

"You could probably use a vacation, a long weekend or something."

He laughed at having his own words tossed at him. "Yeah, probably. The thing is, I've got the next two days off."

"How much time will you spend in the shop, or working out next week's plan of attack, or talking to your mother about this job?"

She had him there. "Some."

D.A. waddled over, nudged his nose at her hand. "He thinks I'm mad at you. I'm not."

"Good to know."

She stepped up, kissed his cheek. "Maybe you could come by after the fireworks tomorrow."

"I can do that."

"I'll see you tomorrow, then."

"Hey," he called when she walked away. "You want to go to the movies? Not tonight," he added at the puzzled look on her face. "Next week, your night off."

"Ah . . . I can make that work. Sure. I'd like that."

"Set it up. Let me know."

"All right." She smiled, but the puzzled look stayed in her eyes. "Do you buy a ticket for your dog?"

"I would, but they won't let him in."

"Do you have a DVD player?"

"Sure."

"A microwave?"

"How else would I cook?"

"Then why don't I come over to your place? We can watch a movie there—all three of us."

It was his turn to be puzzled. "Okay. If that's what you want."

"Wednesday night?"

"Fine. You want dinner?"

"Not if you're cooking it in the microwave."

"I can toss something on the grill."

"Then yes. I'll come by about six, give you a hand. I have to get back. Laurie's on her own."

"See you later."

Ryder stuffed his hands in his pockets, watched her walk away. "Every time I think I get her," he said to D.A., "I don't."

THE NEXT NIGHT, as the sun lowered, Ryder gave the second half of his second steamer to Murphy.

"You're a bottomless pit."

"They're good. And they ran out of ice cream."

"Ought to be illegal."

"We can put them in jail." With a smile and steamer-sticky hands, Murphy climbed into Ryder's lap. "Mom says we can go by the Creamery if they're still open when we get there. You wanna come?"

A hot July night. Ice cream. "Maybe."

"Mom says Hope couldn't come 'cause she has to work." Devouring the sandwich, Murphy licked steamer juice off the heels of his hands. "Is Hope your girlfriend?"

"No." Was she? Jesus.

"How come? She's really pretty, and she mostly always has cookies."

Considering, Ryder thought the combination was as much a no-brainer as ice cream on a hot night in July.

"Those are excellent points."

"My girlfriend's pretty. Her name's India."

God, the kid just killed him. "What kind of a name is India?"

"It's India's name. She has blue eyes, and she likes Captain America." He pulled Ryder's head down, whispered. "I kissed her, on the mouth. It was good. You kissed Hope on the mouth, so she's your girlfriend."

"I'm going to kiss you on the mouth in a minute if it'll shut it up."

Murphy's gut laugh rolled out, dragged a smile out of Ryder.

"They're gonna start soon, right? Right?"

"As soon as it's dark."

"It takes forever to get dark, except when you don't want it to."

"You're wise, young Jedi."

"I'm going to play with my light saber." He wriggled down, grabbed up the toy light-up sword Beckett had bought him, swished it through the air.

His brothers immediately launched an attack.

"That used to be you," Justine told him.

"Which one?"

"All three of them. Why don't you go on up to the inn? You can see the fireworks from there."

Ryder stretched out in his sling chair. "Montgomery family tradition."

"I'm giving you dispensation."

He laid a hand over hers. "It's okay. She's busy."

"Liam! If you don't stop I'll take that thing away from you."

Justine glanced over at Clare, sighed. "And that used to be me. It goes by, Ryder." She turned her hand under his, laid the other over Willy B's, who sat at her other side with Tyrone on his lap. "It pays to grab what's good and right when you can."

"Don't tell me you've bought something else."

"You know what I'm talking about. It's starting," she murmured as a trail of light streaked skyward. "There's nothing like the start of something big."

FROM THE PORCH of the inn, Hope watched the sky explode. Around her the guests applauded, oohed, ahhed. She'd made margaritas on request, enjoyed one herself while she watched the color and light.

And thought of Ryder, down in the park with his family.

Flowers, she mused. Such a surprise. She liked surprises, but she also liked to know what they meant. An apology in this case, she concluded. Though it hadn't been necessary.

Then there was the movie business. Where had that come from? Straight out of the blue, as far as she could tell.

Silly, she told herself. A movie was just a movie.

But it was the first time he suggested going anywhere—a date?—since they'd started sleeping together.

Were they dating now? Dating was different from sleeping together. Dating had a kind of structure and a set of rules—loose ones, depending, but rules and structure.

Should she start thinking about that—about rules, and structure?

And why was she complicating what was absolutely simple? They enjoyed each other in bed, and bonus, liked and enjoyed each other out of it.

And, both of them were sensible, straightforward people with busy lives.

Enjoy the moment, she ordered herself. Enjoy the fireworks.

A hand closed over hers, so she turned. No one touched her; everyone's eyes were trained on the sky.

"All right, Lizzy," she murmured. "We'll enjoy them together."

When the last boom echoed, she went down to make a fresh batch of drinks. It pleased her, a great deal, to know her guests had a good holiday experience, and were even now talking about the show, the feel, the local color.

It pleased her, too, to realize Lizzy wanted her companionship.

She fixed more chips and salsa, plated the pretty mini cupcakes topped with American flags she'd gotten from the bakery. She left some on the counter for those who came down, trayed the rest to carry up for those who wanted more time out in the summer night.

She carried up the tray. Belatedly thought Ryder might like something if and when he came by. She slipped out and down, plated a few more cupcakes. She had beer in her personal refrigerator now.

And what did *that* mean?

Just that she often had the company of a man who preferred it to wine, she told herself as she once again climbed the steps.

And stopped short when Ryder came down from the third floor.

"I didn't know you were here."

"I put D.A. in your place. The kids wiped him out. Did you make those?"

"No, the bakery—"

He grabbed two, ate the first in one bite. "Good."

"Yes, they are. I was taking them upstairs in case you made it by and wanted some."

"Good thinking. I do." He ate the second, then held out some sort of plastic wand with a star on the top. "I got you a present."

"You— What is it?"

"What does it look like? It's like a magic wand or a fairy stick. They sell these light-up toys down at the park. The boys got light sabers and ray guns. This is girly."

"It's girly."

"They're fun." He pressed a couple buttons, had it singing and shooting off light.

Laughing, she took it, gave it a little wag through the air. "You're right. They're fun. Thanks."

"Did you see the show?"

"Yes, it was great. We had chips and salsa and margaritas on the porch."

"It's not Cinco de Mayo."

"The guests are always right. And they're excellent margaritas. Do you want to come out and have one?"

"Really don't. I've had my quota of people today. The park was jammed with them."

"Here. Take the cupcakes. I'll be up as soon as I can."

"Am I supposed to save any of these?"

"Yes."

"Always a catch."

"Beer's in the fridge," she said, and went out to her guests.

IT WAS LATER than she'd hoped, but they made their own fireworks. With too little sleep, she climbed out of bed to work with Carolee on breakfast. By the time she managed a minute to go back up, he and his dog were already gone.

See? Simple. Straightforward.

Then she picked up the silly wand, turned it on.

And felt her heart melt a bit—more, she realized, than it had with flowers.

She laid it down again to go and begin the process of reordering her inn after the long weekend.

As she hauled bags of linens into the laundry room to store till pickup, Avery poked her head in.

"Take a break."

"I used to know what that meant. What are you doing in town?"

"Dragging you away. Come look at the new place. You haven't been in for more than a week."

"I wanted to, but—"

"I know. Now everybody's gone. Take a break."

"We have to turn all the rooms—and I have to order more supplies. We have a couple checking in later."

"That's later. Come on. Clare's coming. She just had to check something at the bookstore. You can take twenty minutes."

"You're right. And I could use it. Just let me tell Carolee."

"I already did." Avery grabbed her hand. "Come let me show off."

"I saw the sign. It's great. Charming and cute and fun."

"We're going to be full of charming and fun, and really good food." She pulled Hope along by the hand. "Owen says mid-August, and I'm so excited about that—but the way it's going, maybe sooner. I mean they'd be finished sooner and I'd have longer to set up and perfect."

"You'd have had sixteen people Saturday night, I can tell you that. I'm plugging you big-time."

"Appreciated." As they crossed the street, Avery dug out her keys. "Prepare to be wowed."

"Prepared."

Avery threw open the door.

The old dark tile was gone. Hardwood replaced it, deep and rich and protected by tarps and cardboard sheets, but Hope saw enough to be wowed. Stamped copper gleamed from the ceiling, and the walls were smooth, primed and waiting for paint.

"Avery, it's going to be even better than I imagined."

"You ain't seen nothing yet. They tiled the bathrooms."

She kept dragging Hope, here, there—to see the tile, the fresh walls in the kitchen, through the now framed opening to the bar side.

"Oh, they've restored the siding. It's fabulous!"

"Isn't it?" Avery ran her fingers over the smooth wood. "This was the best surprise, and see my brick wall—it's just right. They're going to paint, and put in the lights, the bathroom fixtures, the kitchen . . . then the bar goes in. I may cry when the bar goes in."

"I'll bring tissues. Oh, here's Clare. And look at the raised platform; the kids helped build it. I may cry now. Honey," she said when she got a good look at Clare, "are you okay? You're a little green."

"It's July," Clare reminded her, and took slow little sips from her water bottle. "And it's twins."

"There's a step stool in the kitchen. Stay right there."

"I'm fine," Clare began, but Avery was on the dash. "But I could sit."

"You shouldn't be out in this heat."

"I'm not going to be for long. But pregnant or not, I have to live. Beckett's dealing with the boys, the dogs, and the super-duper sprinkler."

"You hit the jackpot there."

"And I know it." She didn't argue when Avery came back with the stool, but sank onto it. "Thanks. It really looks good in here, Avery. Everything's coming together just the way you imagined it."

"Even better. There's a fan back there. I'm going to get it."

"Avery, stop. I'm fine. It's a lot cooler in here than it is out there. I just got a little queasy. It's passed."

"I'm walking you to your car when you go, and if you're not a hundred percent, I'm driving you home."

"Deal. Now relax. There's a lot of summer yet to get through. And don't say anything to Beckett. I mean it." Clare added a pointed finger. "He hasn't been through this before. I have. I'd know if anything was off with myself or the twins. It's just normal pregnant in high summer."

"Times two," Hope added.

"Boy, tell me. I'm getting huge and I've got months yet. They're kicking," she announced, pressing a hand to one side, then the other. "I swear I think they're wrestling around already."

"I have to feel," Avery and Hope said together.

"Wow. Bump, bump, bump," Hope said.

"It's great, isn't it? So lively. It's worth going a little green. So, mid-August for your first baby," she said to Avery.

"That's the word, currently. I'm going to throw the best friends and family night, probably closer to September when I have it all perfect. Just wait."

"Ryder sent me flowers."

Avery blinked. "Sorry?"

"No, I'm sorry." Surprised at herself, Hope tapped her temple. "Where did that come from? It's working on my head."

"Is there a problem with getting flowers from a man you're involved with?" Clare wondered.

"No. I love getting flowers. It was sweet. He's not usually sweet."

"He is, under it," Avery corrected.

"It was an apology, for the most part. Poking in about my work schedule."

"Ah. Men will do this when it interferes with their sex."

"No." She shook her head at Avery, laughed a little. "It wasn't that, because it's really not. I guess I'm still making up for lost time, because I'm just fine for that even after a brutal day. Anyway, he sent me flowers. We didn't even have an argument, not really."

"Flowers to women are his thing," Avery told her. "I don't mean that in a bad way. I mean it's his go-to. His mom loves flowers, so it's his go-to."

"That's simple then. But . . . there are some other things. I want other takes."

"I have a take. Avery has a take."

"Always."

"Okay. When I thanked him for the flowers, he suggested we go out to the movies."

"Oh my God." Staggering, Avery clutched at her heart. "This is awful. What next? Will he suggest going out to dinner? Perhaps live theater. Run away. Go now."

"Shut up. He hasn't suggested going out before, not like that. We stay in. We get takeout or I throw something together—more often than not he just comes over after dinner. Late, when there are guests. And we have sex. What does it mean, a movie? Flowers? And he bought me a magic wand."

"A what?" Clare said.

"One of those things they sell over by the park with the fireworks. It's one of the light-up, singing wands, with a star on it."

"Aww," was Avery's response.

"Yes. It's adorable. Why would he buy me a magic wand?"

"Because it's adorable," Clare suggested. "And you couldn't come down with the rest of us. It's sweet."

"There's that word again. I don't know what it means, if anything. We're not dating."

"Yes, you are," Clare disagreed with a smile that came from sympathy and amusement. "Didn't you get the memo? You're in a relationship with Ryder."

"We're not. I mean, we are, of course, because we're sleeping together. But . . ."

"People who sleep together fall into specific categories." Avery began to tick off her fingers. "One-night stands, which doesn't apply. Friends with benefits, which doesn't fit either because you weren't all that friendly before the benefits. Pay to play, and that's out. Or two people who like each other, care about each other, who have sex with each other. That fits, and that's a relationship. Deal with it."

"I'm *trying* to deal with it. I have to understand it, and I'm not sure I do. I'm not going to go into this with expectations. I've done that."

"You shouldn't compare him to Jonathan," Clare advised.

"I'm not. Not at all. It's me. I have to take some responsibility for what happened with Jonathan. I built up expectations, and—"

"Hold it right there." Avery threw up a hand. "Did Jonathan tell you he loved you?"

"Yes."

"Did he talk to you about a future, the potential of one?"

"Yes, he did."

"He's a lying, scumbag dickhead. Ryder's not. If he ever tells you he loves you, you can take it to the bank. I told you I know women he's dated. He's easy, he doesn't commit—or hasn't—but he doesn't lie, cheat, or evade. My take? He cares about you. He's being decent, and yeah, sweet. He *is* decent and sweet. He's also cranky and abrupt. He has layers. Start peeling them if you want to understand."

"What she said. And," Clare added, "he brought you a silly toy because he was thinking about you. He asked you out because he wants to spend time with you, and give you time away from your workplace. If you don't think about him or want to spend time with him outside sex, make it clear."

"I would. I'd never do to anyone what Jonathan did to me. I do think about him. I'm just not sure what it means. Maybe I worry about what it could mean. I don't know. I thought it would all be simple."

"It's never simple." Avery slid an arm around Hope's waist. "It shouldn't be. Because being with someone should matter enough to be at least a little bit complicated. Are you going to the movies?"

"Actually, I suggested dinner and a movie at his place. Maybe I shouldn't have."

"Stop second-guessing him and yourself." Clare pushed to her feet. "Enjoy him, and yourself. Let it happen."

"I'm lousy at that."

"Try it. You may be better at it than you think."

"If I'm lousy at it, I'm blaming you. I need to get back. Avery, I love this place."

"Me, too. Come on, Clare, I'm walking you to your car, then giving my judgment."

They parted ways outside. Clare took Avery's hand as they crossed Main. "She's falling for him."

"Oh yeah, she is. We know you can't resist a Montgomery man for long."

"He bought her a magic wand, Avery. I'd say the falling's mutual."

"It's going to be fun to watch."

## CHAPTER THIRTEEN

A FTER A LONG, BRUTALLY HOT DAY THAT INCLUDED A
go-round with an inspector he'd considered strangling with a
bungee cord, a key crew member who had to be rushed to the ER for
twelve stitches, and a screwup on a materials delivery, Ryder wondered why he didn't end the day having a beer and take-out Warrior's
Pizza in his underwear.

But a deal was a deal, so he grabbed a quick shower, and took the
time to shave.

He remembered to make the bed, a chore he rarely bothered with.
Then, rolling his eyes, muttering curses in a way that had D.A. bel-
lying into his own bed, Ryder unmade the bed by stripping off the
sheets.

The least a man could do was provide fresh sheets if he planned
on tossing a woman into them.

He knew the rules. And they included clean sheets, fresh bathroom
towels, and a scrubbed-out sink. Women were fussy, and a woman

like Hope—as he'd spent considerable time at her place and seen for himself—was fussier than most.

Fair enough.

Satisfied the bedroom would pass, he went downstairs, picked up a few things on the way through. He wasn't a slob, he told himself. And he had Betts, his cleaning lady, in every other week. But between work and his time with Hope, things had gotten a little messy.

He wound through to the kitchen and tossed what he'd picked up into the utility room to be dealt with later. No problem with the kitchen, he mused. He kept that squared away because if his mother dropped by—and she did—she wouldn't say a word. Oh no. She didn't have to when she had that *look* if he had piles of dirty dishes or trash and recyclables around.

He got out the bottle of Cab he'd picked up, dug up a wineglass. Then muttering again, got out another. He didn't mind wine, and drinking it with her was more sociable.

He knew the damn rules.

He had a clean house, pretty much. He had wine and decent glasses for it. He had a couple of steaks. He didn't cook. He grilled and he nuked. So he'd grill the steak, nuke the potatoes, and dump the salad mix he'd picked up into a bowl.

If she didn't like it, she should go to some other guy's house for dinner.

Why was he acting nervous? He wasn't nervous. That was ridiculous. He'd had women in his place before. Usually it was after they'd gone out somewhere, but he'd done the grill-and-nuke for women before.

They were fine with it. She'd be fine with it.

He dumped the bag of salad in a bowl and considered it a job well done. He scrubbed a couple of potatoes, opened the wine. He caught himself fiddling—turning on music, letting the dog out, letting the dog in.

Relief flooded when he heard the knock on the front door. He was better at doing than thinking about doing.

She looked amazing. Every time he saw her was another kick in the gut. "You cut your hair."

"Yeah." She lifted her hand to the short cap with long, spiky bangs. "I had some time, and it was driving me crazy. What do you think?"

"It looks good on you." Everything did. It set off those smoky eyes that matched the smoky voice. She wore a dress, the kind that made him wish summer would never end. It bared her shoulders, and a lot of leg, and when she stepped in, he noted it bared a lot of back.

"Here you go."

He hadn't even noticed the flowers in her hand, and now just frowned down at them.

"Hasn't anyone ever brought you flowers?"

"Can't say they have."

"Let me be the first. And I picked this up at the bakery. Have you had their brookies?"

"No. What are they?"

"Orgasmic."

"I figured we'd be taking care of that ourselves."

"Why stop there? Believe me, you're in for a treat. I'll put the flowers in water for you. Do you have a vase?"

"Ah . . . I don't think so."

"I'll find something. And I didn't forget you," she said to D.A. while he rubbed against her legs. She opened her purse, produced a massive rawhide bone.

"What, did you take down a mastodon?"

Laughing, she pointed until D.A. managed to sit on his wagging tail. "It was a bitter battle, but I won."

D.A. clamped it in his teeth, pranced over into the living room to collapse and gnaw.

Hope smiled up at Ryder. "So?"

"I've got some wine in the kitchen."

"Just what I need after defeating a mastodon."

She glanced around—discreetly—as she went back to the kitchen with him. She'd been in his home once, but hadn't seen much more than the bedroom.

She liked his space, his use of color and comfort, and the detailing of the wood. She knew he and his brothers had built it, as they'd built Owen's and Beckett's.

If she ever found herself in the market for a house, she'd make sure it was a Montgomery Family Contractors project.

She loved his kitchen, the easy efficiency, the clean lines—dark woods, open shelving, glass-fronted cabinets.

"Is it all right if I look for something to put the flowers in?"

"Sure. I've probably got a jug or something."

He poured the wine while she hunted. "I heard there was a glitch with the inspector at MacT's."

"Picking nits is all. We'll deal with it."

"I saw it the other day. God, it's going to be fabulous."

She found a clear pitcher, filled it with water.

"First round's on Red Hots."

"You can count on it," Hope said as she arranged the flowers. "I love your house. It's very you—and your brothers. Your mother, too, I'm betting with the landscaping. All the Montgomery family touches."

"Nothing gets done that everybody doesn't have a hand in."

"It's nice. We're not very handy, my family. With the practical things, I mean. My mother's creative and artistic, and my father can discuss any book or movie ever written or made, but neither of them can handle anything more complex than a screwdriver."

"It's people like that who keep us in business."

"They have their repair people on speed dial. Personally, I like being able to do minor repairs myself." She caught the smirk, narrowed her eyes. "I can and do make minor repairs. Do you think I call you or your brothers over every time something needs a hammer or screwdriver? I have my own tools."

"Are they those pretty ones with flower handles?"

Now she drilled a hand into his stomach. "They are not." She picked up her wine, touched to see it was her usual brand. "What can I do?"

"About what?"

"Dinner. How can I help?"

"Nothing much to do. We can go outside, and I'll start the grill."

He led the way through a dining room he currently used as an office. Here Hope's innate organizational soul shivered. Papers unfiled, supplies jumbled, a desk all but trembling under the weight of undone tasks.

"Don't start," he said, seeing her look.

"Some of us handle tools, others handle office space. I can say, proudly, I'm reasonably adept with the first and a genius with the second. I could help you with this."

"I—"

"Know where everything is," she finished. "That's what they all say."

She stepped out onto a wide deck, breathed deep. His mother, she had no doubt, had spearheaded the charming country-cheer garden, the planters spilling with color. It all flowed into the green spread of woods and the rise of hill.

"This is wonderful. I'd want my coffee out here every morning."

"There's never much time for that in the morning." He opened an enormous, shiny silver grill that struck her as intimidating. "I wouldn't think the house in the woods would be your style."

"I don't know, maybe I've never had a chance to find out. From the 'burbs to the city, from the city to small town. I've liked all of it. I think I'd like the house in the woods, too. Which way is Clare? And which way is Avery?"

After he'd switched on the grill, he walked to her, stepped behind her. Lifting her arm with his, he pointed in one direction. "Avery." Then angled her arm again. "Clare. And." He turned her, pointed again. "My mother."

"It's nice to be close. But not too close."

"I can see their house lights when the leaves fall. It's close enough."

She looked over her shoulder to smile, and found herself turned into him, pressed again him. His mouth took hers, hot and urgent. A surprise, as he'd seemed so casual. A wonderful surprise, she thought, as his need stirred her own.

He took her wine, set it aside. "We'll eat after." And grabbing her hand pulled her back into the house.

She scrambled to keep up. "All right."

He made it to the stairs before he pushed her against the wall, tortured himself with her lips, her body. "Just let me . . ."

He found the short zipper that started halfway down her back, yanked it down. She barely had time to gasp before she was naked but for a thong, her heels, and a pair of dangling earrings.

"Christ. Damn it." He'd sworn he'd keep his hands off her until after dinner—until after the movie, or at least until during. But the way she looked, smelled, sounded . . . It was too much. Just too much.

He filled his hands with her breasts, ravaged her mouth.

And she gave back—as eager, as desperate as he. She tugged his shirt up and off, tossed it away, scraped her nails up his bare back, and tied his guts into knots.

When he lifted her off her feet, she melted against him, hot, fragrant wax.

She felt weightless. He carried her up the stairs as if she were. She'd never been carried up the stairs before, and certainly not with her dress in a heap behind her.

Glorious.

She fed herself on his neck, his face, feasted on his mouth as he moved through the bedroom door.

"I can't keep my hands off you."

"Don't." She wrapped tight as they fell on the bed. "Don't keep your hands off me."

He wanted that warm, smooth flesh, the long, slim lines and curves. And the taste of her filling him as he worked his way down her body. She arched up, crying out.

He knew he was rough, tried to slow, tried to gentle, even a little. Tried to remember her delicacy and the hardness of his own hands. He brought his mouth back to hers, softer now, deep and lingering. The revving engine of her body went to purr.

Something turned inside her, a slow, liquid spin, and another, another, that left her dizzy, left her weak.

She breathed out his name as his lips slid over her, featherlight now. A drug seeping into her blood.

She reached for him again, her own hands stroking lightly, dreaming as sensations fell over her like tissue paper.

Now to savor rather than devour, to seduce rather than ravish, they moved together in the quieting light.

When she cupped his face in her hands, when their eyes met, she felt joy merged with desire.

He saw her lips curve before he lowered his to brush them. Felt her fingers thread through his hair. And now when she arched to him, when she opened, welcomed, he slid into her, into velvet heat.

Her breath caught, released, caught again. And those eyes held his as they rose and fell together. Deep, dazzled eyes that went dark and blind as he urged her up and up, and over.

Her body held, taut as a bow, and held quivering until it went slack with release.

He pressed his face into the curve of her throat, and took his own.

Dreaming still, she turned her head, brushed her lips over his hair as her hand trailed up and down his back, while they lay quiet. When he shifted, she curled against his side. His arm came around to wrap. Drifting, he didn't make the connection that affection had tangled with heat, on both sides.

"I guess I should put those steaks on."

"I could eat. But I think I'll need my dress."

"You look good without it, but it's a nice dress. I'll get it."

"And my purse?"

"What for?"

"I need to make a few repairs."

He frowned at her. "What for?" he repeated. "You look good."

"It'll take me five minutes to look better."

She could already wring every beat out of a man's heart, but he shrugged and went downstairs. The dress smelled like her, he thought, sniffing at it as he hunted down her bag in the kitchen.

D.A., the rawhide—worse for wear—still clamped in his teeth, gave him a look that said: I know what you've been doing.

"You're just jealous." He carted the dress and purse upstairs where she sat on the bed, knees drawn in. When she smiled, he wanted to jump her again.

"Thanks. I'll be right down, give you a hand."

"Okay, but it's no big deal."

He left her alone before he broke and climbed on her again.

True to her word, she was done in five. "I don't see any difference except for the dress."

"Good. You're not supposed to."

"How do you like your steak?"

"Rare."

"That makes it simple." He tossed a couple of enormous potatoes in the microwave, punched buttons, then pulled the salad out of the fridge.

"Would you like me to dress that?"

"I got a bottle of Italian and a bottle of blue cheese."

Considering, she poked her head in the fridge, took stock. "I can do better, if you've got olive oil."

"Yeah. Up there." He pointed to a cabinet.

She opened the cabinet, found a couple other things that met with her approval and took them out. "Little bowl, a whisk?"

"I got the bowl."

"That and a fork then."

She went to work, smooth and quick, and looked nothing like a woman who'd fogged his brain only minutes before. He left her to throw the steaks on. When he stepped back in, she was tossing the salad. "I couldn't find your salad set."

"I don't have one. I use forks."

"Well then." She angled the forks she'd used in the bowl.

"I thought we'd eat out on the deck."

"Perfect." She carried out the salad, went back for plates, flatware. By the time he pulled the steaks off the grill, she'd set the table—with the flowers—topped off their wine. She'd managed to find his butter, sour cream, salt, pepper. And plated the potatoes.

He had to admit, the table looked just a little classier than it would have left to him. "What was your talent in that beauty pageant? Magic tricks?"

She only smiled as he slid her steak on her plate. "This looks great."

She served his salad, then served herself before lifting her glass, tapping it to his. "To long summer nights. My favorite."

"I'm a fan. What was your talent?" he repeated. "That's part of the deal, right? I bet you tossed flaming batons."

"You'd be wrong."

She sipped her wine, picked up her fork.

"Give it up, princess. I'll just get Owen to find out. He's better at searching the Internet than I am."

"I sang."

"You can sing?"

She lifted her shoulders as she ate. "I didn't win the talent portion."

"You can't sing."

"I can sing," she countered with some force. "I can also play the piano, and tap. But I wanted to focus on one element." She smiled as she ate her salad. "And the girl who tapped while tossing flaming batons won the talent."

"You're making that up."

"You could search the Internet for it."

"How'd you win if you lost the talent?"

"By sweeping the rest. I *killed* the interview."

"I bet you killed the swimsuit deal."

She smiled again, that slow, sultry look. "You could say so. Anyway, long time ago."

"I bet you still have the crown."

"My mother has it. More important, I got the scholarship. That was the goal. I didn't like the idea of putting myself and my parents into debt. They already had two children going to college, and moving to grad school. Winning made a big difference, and I earned it. Those pageants are brutal. Still, I earned and I learned."

"Sing something."

"No." Flustered and amused, she shook her head. "I'm eating. The steak's perfect, by the way. Hey!" she made a grab, but he was fast, and pulled her plate up and out of reach.

"Sing for your supper."

"You're being ridiculous."

"I want to hear you, judge for myself."

"Fine, fine." She thought a moment, then gave him a couple bars of Adele's "Rolling in the Deep," since it had played in her car on the drive over.

Throaty, sexy, rich. He wondered why he was surprised. "You can sing. Keep going."

"I'm hungry."

"I don't have a piano." He set her plate in front of her again. "But you're definitely going to tap-dance after dinner."

Her eyes narrowed when he tossed a bite of steak to the dog. "Your mother taught you better than that."

"She's not here. What else can you do?"

Hope shook her head again. "No. Your turn. What can you do besides what I already know?"

"I can kick."

"I saw you kick for your mother's dog."

"That's nothing. I kicked the game-winning field goal my senior year—championship win." Long time ago, too, he thought, but still. "Sixty-three yards."

"I'm guessing that's impressive. The yardage."

"Sugar, as far as I know, the longest ever kicked in high school ball's seventy yards."

"I'm impressed then. Did you keep it up in college?"

"The scholarship helped. There were three of us, too. College wasn't my thing, but I gave it a shot."

"Did you ever consider going pro?"

"No." No passion for it, he thought now. No gut-deep drive. "It was a game. I liked it. But I wanted what I've got."

"It's nice when that works out. When you get what you want. We're both lucky there."

"So far."

The light softened toward dusk as they finished the meal, lingered over wine. She rose to clear as the first fireflies winked in the green shadows.

"I'll get them in the morning," he told her.

"I'll get them now. I can't relax if things like dishes aren't done."

"Maybe you need therapy."

"When things are in their place, the world's in balance. When they're done, you can take me to the movies. What are we watching?"

"We'll find something." For now he liked just watching her. "You want popcorn?"

"There's that balance again," she said as she loaded the dishwasher. "Movies. Popcorn. One without the other is just wrong."

"Butter and salt?"

She started to refuse, then gave in. "What the hell. It's my night off. And I'm going to have a fitness center in my backyard before too much longer."

"Do you have any of those little outfits?"

She slanted him a look from under her long, spiky bangs. "I do. But the opening will give me an excuse to buy new. Right now nobody sees them but me when I find time to put on a workout DVD."

He put the bag of popcorn in the microwave, glanced at her. "You're going to want the corn in a bowl, aren't you?"

"Yes, I am. And a plate for the brookies."

"Just more dishes to deal with."

"It's a process, Ryder. Maybe I should check in with Carolee before we settle into movies and popcorn."

"Does she know where you are?"

"Yes, of course."

"She's got the number if she needs anything. Put it away."

"I've been doing that very well. I just had a tiny relapse."

He smiled at her. "You're good for the inn."

"Thanks. You didn't think I would be."

"I didn't know you."

Her eyebrows arched under the bangs. "You thought, city girl in a fancy suit with fancy city ideas."

His mouth opened, shut again.

"You did!" She poked at him. "Snob."

"I figured you for the snob."

"You figured wrong."

"It happens." He ran a hand over her hair, surprising both of them. "I like the hair," he said and barely resisted stuffing the hand in his pocket. "Shorter than mine."

"You need a haircut."

"I haven't had time."

"I could cut it for you."

He laughed. "No, you fucking won't."

"I'm good at it."

He pulled the popcorn out, dumped it in a bowl. "Let's go watch a movie."

"I even have the right tools."

"No. Do you want more wine? I've got another bottle."

"I've got to drive, so no. I'll switch to water."

"Grab those chocolate things. Big-ass TV's downstairs."

She followed him down, gaped, grinned.

"This is wonderful!"

"I like it."

She supposed he thought of it as a man cave, but there was nothing cavelike here. Glass doors opened to the outside, giving it a sense of more space. He'd used color again, sharply, nothing soft, nothing pale, mated it with dark glossy wood, a lot of leather.

Delighted, she wandered, studied the alcove where he kept weights, an old-fashioned water bubbler, the punching bag boxers used—what was it? Speed bag, she remembered.

She peeked around and into the small, Deco-inspired black and white bath.

He had games—the Montgomery brothers seemed to love them. Pinball machine, an Xbox, even one of those touch-screen games Avery had at Vesta.

But the best was the bar—carved and compact, and the retro refrigerator, the glass shelves with old bottles.

"Is this a reproduction or the real thing?" she asked.

"It's the real thing. I like old things." He opened the old Frigidaire, gave her a bottle of water.

"It's like the fifties meet the now. It's great." She admired the antique poker table, the old-style pinball machine.

"You must have great parties."

"That's Owen's deal more than mine."

"I should say you *could* have great parties." Her party-planning brain already organized themes, menus, decorations. "And that is, without question, the biggest TV I've ever seen."

"Might as well have big. That cabinet's for the DVDs. You can pick what you want to see."

"I get to pick? That's very considerate."

"There's nothing in there I won't watch, so you can pick."

She laughed and, before she did, walked over, wrapped her arms around his waist. "See, you didn't have to say that. I'd've believed you were considerate."

"It is what it is."

"I like what it is."

"So do I. Ah, what's that thing called before the movie?"

"Previews?"

"No, the old-fashioned thing. Before they played the movie."

"The overture?"

"Yeah, that's it." He scooped her off her feet. "It's time for the overture."

She laughed as he rolled them both onto his black leather couch.

# CHAPTER FOURTEEN

W HEN THE WOMAN YOU HOOKED UP WITH WORKED
long, weird hours, you started living that way. He didn't
mind. It freed up his own off-time, left him choices. Work, TV sports,
a long easy spell over a beer. He could mooch dinner off his mother
or one of his brothers.

Or, like tonight, he could enjoy a night at the ballpark with his
brothers and nephews.

Nothing hit the bell, to Ryder's way of thinking, like minor league
baseball. Sure, a trip to Camden Yards to watch the O's play in the
colorful cathedral of ball equaled a hell of an experience.

But minor league offered the intimacy, the drama and the simplic-
ity of what the summer game was about. And when you added three
young boys to the mix, it genuinely kicked ass.

He sat, munching a loaded dog, drinking a cold beer—since he
and Owen had voted Beckett the designated driver—and enjoying
the hell out of himself.

The crowd booed, cheered, catcalled the pitchers—including their own. The Hagerstown Suns, down two runs in the fifth, took the field. The mid-July heat that had steamed through the afternoon calmed with the hint of a breeze as the sun dropped west.

Ryder watched the pitcher fan the first batter, glanced over where Harry devoured the action, elbows on his knees, body tipped forward, face intent the way only a devout baseball fan could understand.

"Picking up some pointers, Houdini?"

Harry grinned over as the next batter stepped up to the plate. "I'm pitching Saturday, Coach said."

"I heard." He'd make time to be there, to watch the kid strut his stuff.

"I'm practicing my curveball. Beckett showed me how."

"He's got a pretty good one."

Ryder settled back to watch the next pitch. At the crack of the bat, he moved instinctively, hauling Liam up, shooting the boy's gloved hand in the air. He angled, and felt, as Liam did, the ball smack the sweet spot of the glove.

"I caught it!" Dumbfounded, thrilled beyond measure, Liam gaped down at the ball in his glove. "I caught the ball."

"Nice." Beckett sent Liam and his brother a mile-wide smile. "Pretty damn nice."

"Mr. Hoover sucks it up. Let's see it," Owen demanded, and six males examined the ball as miners might a vein of gold.

"I want to catch one." Murphy held out his glove. "Can you help me catch one?"

"They have to hit it this way. We had a high-flying foul that time." Ryder knew better than to add they'd gotten lucky. "Keep your eyes peeled and your glove hot."

"Ry! I thought that was you."

The pretty blonde owned a sexy river of hair and generous curves snugged into tiny shorts and a tight T-shirt. She squeezed in beside him.

Hooking her arms around his neck she gave him a loud, cheerful kiss.

"Jen. How's it going?"

"It's going great. I hear the buzz about what you're all doing in Boonsboro. I keep meaning to get down your way, see for myself. Hey, Owen, Beck. Who you got here?" She smiled at the boys.

"Beck's and Clare's," Ryder told her. "Harry, Liam, Murphy."

"Well, hi! I heard you and Clare got married. How's she doing?"

"She's good. It's nice to see you, Jen," Beckett said.

"My mom's got two more brothers in her tummy," Murphy announced.

"Two—seriously? Well, wow! Congratulations. And didn't I hear you and Avery got engaged, Owen?"

"Yeah, we did."

"I've really got to catch up with her, get into her place, grab some pizza. And I'm going to check out her new place when it's open. Lot of buzz there. Two out of three of the Montgomery boys off the market," she continued, as Harry shifted to see around her. "You're prime real estate now, Ry." She let out her quick, up-the-scale and down again laugh. "Hey, I'm just here with a couple of friends. Why don't you drive me home after the game, we can catch up?"

"I'm kind of . . ." He spread his hands to encompass his group.

"Oh, sure. Well, call me! I'll get down to Boonsboro and you can buy me a pizza at Vesta. You tell Avery I'm coming down to see her, Owen."

"Will do."

"I'm going to get on back." She gave Ryder another squeeze, whispered, "Call me," in his ear.

As she walked away both his brothers slid their gazes in his direction.

"Cut it out," he muttered. After an uncomfortable internal debate, he pushed up. "Be right back."

"Get me a beer," Owen called out.

"Can I get nachos?" Murphy demanded. "Can I?"

Ryder just waved his hands and kept walking. He caught up with Jen as the second baseman fielded a line drive, and the side retired.

"I've got to hit concessions," he told her. "I'll buy you a beer."

"Sounds good. So much going on with you. I'm dying to see that inn of yours. I saw the article in the paper last winter, and it looks awesome. And Beckett having twins, Owen getting married—and to Avery!"

She chatted all the way. He'd never minded that about her because she was so damn happy to babble, and never cared if he didn't respond. Or listen all that close.

They'd known each other since high school, had dated on and off—more off than on, since she'd gotten married at one point. Divorced at another. They'd stayed friends—friendly—with nothing more serious than occasional sex when it worked out for both of them.

It was pretty damn obvious it would've worked out for her now.

He bought her beer, Owen's, his own, nachos for the runt, then set them down at one of the high tables while he tried to work out how to handle it.

"I almost didn't come tonight. I've been swamped with work, too. I'm glad I let Cherie and Angie talk me into it. You remember Cherie."

"Yeah." Probably.

"She got divorced about a year ago. It was a rough time for her."

"Sorry to hear that."

"She's dating one of the players. The center fielder, so we came to keep her company for the game."

"Nice."

"Listen, what are you up to this weekend? I could come down. You could give me a tour of the inn." She offered her sparkly-eyed smile. "Maybe we could book a room."

"I'm seeing somebody." He didn't know the words were there until they fell out of his mouth.

"Well, that's not news, you're always . . . Oh." Those sparkly eyes widened. "You mean *seeing* seeing. Wow. Did you and your brothers all drink from the same bottle?"

"I'm not—we're not—I'm just seeing somebody."

"Good for you, and her. So who is she? Tell me all. Do I know her?"

"No. I don't think so. She's the innkeeper."

"Really? Now I have to get down there and see the place."

"Come on, Jen."

"Come on, Ry," she tossed back at him. "How long have we known each other? I'd never mess you up."

"No." He let out a breath. "You wouldn't."

"And I'm happy for you. A little sorry for myself," she admitted, "but happy for you. I've been having shit-all luck with men lately."

"Then the men you're looking at are stupid."

"There's a lot of that going around. I'm still coming down, catching up with Avery, taking a look at what you've got going on."

"That'd be good."

"I'd better get back before my friends send out a search party. Thanks for the beer."

"Anytime."

"What's her name?"

"Hope."

"Nice. Is she pretty?"

"She's the most beautiful woman I've ever seen." And again, he hadn't known the words were there.

"Aw." Jen leaned forward, kissed his cheek. "Good luck, sweetie."

"Yeah. The same."

And that, Ryder thought as he gathered up the food, had been just plain weird. He started back, paused, balancing nachos and beer to watch the Sun's batter knock a solid left field double, bringing in a run, and putting men at second and third.

Looking up, he decided, and worked his way back.

"Did you see?" Harry demanded.

"Yeah, nice hit." Ryder dumped the tray of nachos in Murphy's lap, passed Owen the beer.

"So?" Owen said.

"So what?"

"So what did you tell Jen?"

"That I was seeing somebody. Jesus, Owen, I don't mess with women that way."

"He doesn't mess with women that way," Murphy echoed soberly. "Jesus, Owen."

As Ryder roared with laughter, Beckett winced. And the Suns knocked in the tying run.

RYDER FULLY INTENDED to go home and stay there, work out for an hour—considering dogs, nachos, beer—then maybe stretch out with his dog and watch another game on TV.

Fifteen minutes after Beckett dropped him off, he walked back out of the house with his dog. Annoyed with himself, he climbed in his truck and drove into Boonsboro.

They'd just straighten this deal out, he thought. Cards on the table. He didn't like weird situations. He didn't like situations period, so they'd deal with it, get it done.

He noted the two cars in the lot with Hope's. He'd known she had guests. No big, he decided. He'd just go up and wait for her, then they'd deal.

And that would give him time to figure out how to deal.

The exterior lights gleamed in the dark, turned The Courtyard into an elegant dream stirred with the fragrance of roses madly blooming above the stone wall.

Beckett had called that, he remembered. The wall, the flowers, the center weeping redbud. It made such an appealing space he wondered why none of the current guests were taking advantage of it.

He went up the outside steps to the third floor, let himself in. Quiet lay comfortably over the inn so he deduced the guests had settled into The Lounge with a movie or a hot game of Scrabble.

He unlocked Hope's apartment, walked in with D.A. At home, he got a Coke out of the fridge and considered how the hell to pass the time until she came up.

He should probably let her know he was here, but damned if he wanted to go all the way down, then up again. He'd just text her after he stretched out on her bed with the ball game.

He stepped into her bedroom, and there she was, sitting cross-legged on the bed in sleep shorts and a tank, earbuds connecting her to her iPod as she studied the screen of her laptop.

She stopped his heart. It was humiliating the way she could do that without even trying. Without even knowing.

A delighted D.A. trotted right over, planted his front paws on the side of the bed.

She screamed as if someone plunged a knife in her belly.

"Hey, hey." He moved forward as she lunged up to her knees, clamped a hand over her heart.

"You scared the *hell* out of me." Dragging her fingers through her hair, she dropped back on her heels. "I wasn't expecting you tonight."

"Yeah, well . . . I figured you were downstairs with people. I'd've knocked."

"Both sets of guests settled in fairly early." She rubbed at her heart again, then laughed. "God, I live with a ghost. You wouldn't think I'd scare that easy. Did I scare you back?" she purred to the dog, scrubbing at his head. "I was taking advantage of the downtime, looking into all these documents and letters for Lizzy."

"Getting anywhere?"

"I'm not sure. But I'm getting to know her a little better. I know her father ruled with an iron fist, and her mother often took to her bed with 'the headache,' which I'm interpreting at this point as a way of evading conflict more than suffering from migraines. Her father was wealthy and had considerable social standing, political influence, and—"

"I'm not sleeping with anybody else. Right now," he added belatedly.

She stared at him for a moment. "That's . . . good to know."

"If you're thinking about seeing or sleeping with somebody else, I want to know about it."

"That's fair. I'm not. Right now."

"Okay." Ryder glanced over, saw that D.A. had already settled into the bed Hope had bought him, with his paws over the squeaky hamburger she'd added as a toy. "We can get out of your way if you want to keep going with that."

"I think I'd rather you stay and tell me what brought this on."

"There's no this. Just avoiding this—avoiding a situation."

"I see."

What was it with some women? he wondered. The ones, like his mother, who could use silence as effectively as a veteran cop sweating a witness. "I just ran into a friend at the ball game. That's all."

"Oh?" She kept her voice casual, absolutely pleasant. "And how was the game?"

"Good. Suns pulled it out, took it four to three. Liam caught a foul ball."

"He did!" She smiled, added quick applause. "He must be thrilled."

"Yeah, it'll stay with him awhile."

"It's great the boys had a night out with all of you." With her eyes direct, she let silence hang.

"I've known her since high school."

Hope merely angled her head, said nothing.

"Look. Hell. We hook up sometimes. Nothing serious. Christ, what's your problem?" he demanded when she remained silent.

"I don't have a problem. I'm waiting for you to finish."

"Fine. I ran into her, that's all, and she talked about getting together. Seeing the inn, and, you know, maybe we could rent a room."

"Oh." Hope folded her hands neatly. "That must have been awkward, as you're currently sleeping with the innkeeper."

With his scowl, his eyes held a fulminating green. "*Awkward*'s a stupid word. It's a girl word. It was weird. I had to tell her I was seeing somebody because I didn't want it to be weird."

"Was she angry?"

"No. She's not like that. We're friends."

All reason, Hope nodded. "It's good, even commendable, you can stay friends with someone you've slept with. It says something about you."

"It's not about that." Something about her calm, goddamn *reasonable* responses put his back up. "It's about being clear. I'm not sleeping with anyone else, so you're not sleeping with anyone else. That's clear."

"It absolutely is."

"I'm not like that asshole you were tangled up with."

"You're nothing like that asshole," she agreed. "And, just as important to me, I'm not the same person I was when I was tangled up with that asshole. Isn't it handy we are who we are, and maybe better, can be who we are with each other?"

"I guess it is." He hissed out a breath, and finally most of the frustration. "You throw me off," he admitted.

"How?"

"You don't ask questions."

"I ask plenty of questions. Otherwise I wouldn't know you got that scar on your butt taking a tumble sledding when you were eight. Or you lost your virginity in the tree house your father built you— fortunately some years later. Or—"

"About where we're going," he interrupted. "Women always ask where we're going."

"I'm enjoying where we are so I don't need to know where we might be. I like being here. I'm happy being with you, and that's enough."

Relieved, he sat on the side of the bed, shifted to face her. "I've never known anybody like you. And I can't figure you out."

She lifted a hand to his cheek. "It's the same for me. I like that you'd come here tonight, to tell me all this. That it bothered you enough you'd need to tell me."

"Some women can't handle a guy being friends with another woman, or having a conversation with one he's had sex with."

"I'm not the jealous type. Maybe if I had been, if I'd been less trusting, I wouldn't have been betrayed, but I'm not made that way. If I can't trust the man I'm with, I shouldn't be with him. I trusted Jonathan, and I was wrong. I trust you, and I know I'm right. You don't lie, and that matters to me. I won't lie to you, and we'll be fine."

"I've got more friends."

Laughing, she linked her hands around his neck. "I bet you do." She kissed him lightly, then lingered over it. "Are you going to stay?"

"Might as well."

"Good. Let me put this work away."

HE PUT EXTRA time in most evenings, sometimes alone, sometimes with one brother or with both. If she didn't have guests, they had dinner together, or went out somewhere, then stayed at his place.

She never left anything at his house, which he found strange. Women were always leaving little bits of themselves behind. But not Hope.

So maybe he picked up a bottle of the shower gel stuff she used to keep at his place. Hell, he liked the way she smelled, didn't he? And he sprang for a couple new towels since his were heading toward ratty.

It wasn't like he'd filled his place with flowers and smelly candles.

She stocked his beer, he stocked her shower stuff, and yeah, the wine she liked. No big deal. She didn't make an issue out of it.

She didn't bitch about the dog, and he'd been primed for that one. But she didn't—hell, she'd bought Dumbass a bed and a toy so he'd be at home when they stayed over in her apartment.

He thought about that more than he should—more than he liked—that she didn't do what he assumed she would.

The constant surprise of her kept him off-balance in a way he'd come to appreciate.

And he sure as hell appreciated she wasn't the type who whined when work kept him tied up, as it did now.

He glanced around the bar side of MacT's, pleased with the lay of the land, the gleam of the hardwood, the symmetry of the lights.

"When we get this bastard done," he began as he and his brothers worked to finish the bar, "I want a Warrior's Pizza. It's Beckett's turn to buy."

"Can't do it." Beckett paused, swiped at his sweaty face. "I need to get home, give Clare a hand. She's so freaking tired by the end of the day."

"It's Ry's turn anyway," Owen said. "And I could eat. Avery's closing tonight, so it works out."

"How'd it get to be my turn?"

"That's how turns work. God, this bitch is big. And beautiful."

With the last piece in place, they stepped back, admired the dark, lush gleam of mahogany, the detail of the panels they'd built and installed.

It still lacked the rail, the top—and the taps—but Ryder saw it as damn good work.

Owen ran his fingers over the side. "The way this is moving, we'll have this place punched out in a week, week and a half, tops. It's handy Ry's stuck on the innkeeper and has to keep himself busy right here."

"It's looking good," Beckett agreed. "Only downside is between all this work, and Ry keeping Hope so damn busy, we haven't gotten as far on finding Billy as we thought we would."

"It's a lot to get through," Owen reminded him. "We're getting there. Lizzy's old man managed to expunge a hell of a lot from official records. There are gaps. Jesus, what kind of father basically tries to erase his own kid?"

"The kind kids run away from," Ryder said. "Like she did."

"Owen? Are you in here? I saw the lights when . . ." Avery walked through the opening from restaurant to bar side, stopped dead. "Oh! Oh! The bar. You finished the bar. You made my bar! You didn't tell me."

"If you hadn't been so nosy you'd have been surprised tomorrow. The top's going on tomorrow. The counter guys are scheduled to do the insert in the morning."

"It's beautiful. Just beautiful." She rushed in, ran her hands over it. "It feels beautiful." Then she spun around, grabbed Owen, danced, spun to Beckett, then to Ryder. "Thank you, thank you! I have to see the back."

She scurried around, made happy noises. "As beautiful from this side as the front. Oh, I wish Clare and Hope could see, right now! I can text Hope, tell her to come over."

"She's got people," Ryder told her.

"It'll only take a minute. I need a girl here. I can't believe you got this done in here without me knowing," she continued as she pulled out her phone.

"It wasn't easy," Owen admitted.

"But it was really sweet. She says she'll be right here. It's really happening. I have so much to do. Let me take a picture of the three of you in front of the bar."

"I'll take one of you and Owen in front of it," Ryder said.

"The three of you first, you built it. Then one of me and Owen."

They obliged her, with Owen going behind the bar as if tending.

"One more," she murmured, and snapped.

"Now you, Red Hots." Ryder picked her up, sat her on the front lip. "Don't lean back or you'll fall in."

"I won't." In fact she leaned forward, resting an elbow on Owen's shoulder as he came out to stand beside her.

"I'm going to put these up on Facebook right away. I want everybody to see— Owen."

She held out her arms, wrapping around him as he helped her down.

"Jesus, if you need a room there's a few of them right across the street."

Ryder glanced over just as Hope lifted a hand to knock.

"I was about to come over before Avery texted me," she began when he let her in. "I've got— Oh. You've finished the bar."

"Isn't it beautiful?" Avery stroked its side as she might a beloved pet. "My boyfriend and his brothers built it for me."

"It's a piece of art. Really. It's wonderful. It's wonderful in here. I love the colors, Avery, and the lights. The floor. Everything. You're going to have an enormous hit."

She stepped up, stood in the opening to study the restaurant side. "And you got the waitress station in. I couldn't really visualize, but—"

"It's in! I didn't even see." Avery leaped up, dashed through.

"You made her night," Hope told Ryder.

"You're revved about something else," Ryder observed.

"It shows? I am revved. I found something in one of Catherine's letters to a cousin. It was long, and full of family chat, comments about the war, a book she'd read that she'd hid from her father. And mixed in, I found this passage about Eliza."

"Something new?" Owen asked.

"It talks about being worried because their father was arranging for Eliza to marry the son of a state senator. And Eliza was bucking him. It's clear bucking wasn't something her father tolerated. More, it talks about Eliza sneaking out at night to meet one of the stone-masons their father hired to build walls on the property."

"A stonemason," Owen considered. "Beneath her station, right? Daddy wouldn't approve."

"Catherine writes she's afraid of what will happen if Eliza's caught, but she won't listen. She claims she's in love."

"Is there a name? Did she write his name?" Beckett demanded.

"No, at least I haven't found it yet. But this has to be Billy. It has to be. She was in love, risking her father's considerable wrath. They both were. The letter was written in May of 1862, just months before Lizzy came here. Months before Antietam. If we could just find some records of who worked on the estate, or find the names of stonemasons from this area . . ."

"If she came here, he was here," Avery agreed. "Either lived here, or joined the fight and was sent here. It's a good lead, Hope."

"It's the best we've had in weeks. Months, really. You can see it unfold, at least parts of it. Her father was strict and fierce, and women—daughters—were to do what they were told, marry who they were told to marry. She fell in love with someone he'd never approve of. She ran away, ran to him. Came here to wait for Billy. And died waiting."

"It was a long way to come back then—New York to Maryland," Beckett said, "and in wartime. She risked a lot."

"She loved," Hope said simply. "Enough to give up her family, her lifestyle, risk her safety. She's been so quiet lately. I wonder if I tell her what I found, if she'd be able or willing to tell us more."

"Worth a shot," Owen agreed.

"Let's go over now. Right now," Avery insisted.

"I have guests, and one couple in E&D. I think this wouldn't be the best time. Tomorrow. After checkout. I'll try then."

"I'll come over. Eleven thirty?"

"Yes, good. I really think we've turned a corner. We're closer to finding him. I have to get back."

"I'll walk you over."

"All right."

"Stay here," Ryder told the dog.

"You didn't have much to say," Hope pointed out as they left.

"Thinking. Okay, you're probably right, and he's the stonemason she was messing around with. But without a name, it's still a crap-shoot."

"We'll get a name." She wouldn't give up until they did. "I have more letters, more papers to go through, and so does Owen. We'll find it." She turned to him at the door of Reception. "Try being positive."

"It goes against the grain."

"Don't I know it."

"Have you had dinner?"

"Not yet. I had a little time, so I started looking at the letters."

"I can bring you something. Guests figure you eat."

"All right, thanks. A dinner salad would be great. The Palace."

"That's it?"

"They're huge." She kissed him lightly. "Thanks. And the bar does look beautiful."

"It'll look better when they pull the tap and draw me a beer. I'll bring your pitiful definition of dinner by in about an hour."

"I'll be here. Oh, and if you're interested, I'm getting sticky buns from the bakery for breakfast."

"I'll be here, too."

# CHAPTER FIFTEEN

HOPE BID GOOD-BYE TO THE LAST OF HER GUESTS. A midnight storm had brought welcome rain the night before and left behind a sodden blanket of heat and humidity. She stood in it just a minute, looking across the lot, through the herd of trucks. She needed to find twenty minutes to get over there, update pictures of the fitness center's progress for the website.

But this morning held other priorities.

She walked back in, to the kitchen where Carolee polished the granite island.

"We need supplies," Carolee told her. "I know it's on your to-do list, but I thought I might go ahead and get them now. She might be more comfortable with less people around."

"I don't know what I'd do without you."

"You just try to find out. I'll take the list and load us up. Justine'll be around later, so you can fill us both in. Hope, what do you think'll happen when you find Billy for her?"

"I don't know. If she . . . passes over, well, I'm going to miss her."

"I know what you mean. I like being able to talk out loud and not feel like I'm talking to myself. And feeling her around. You know what I mean."

"I really do."

"I won't be too long." Carolee got her purse, put the supply list inside. "Oh, where's my head? When you started telling me about that letter this morning, I forgot to tell you the news. Justine's hired the manager *and* the assistant manager for Fit."

"She found someone? That's great news. Did she find someone local?"

"Local as they come, and with plenty of experience, and according to Justine, with energy to spare."

"That sounds like just what you'd want in a fitness center manager."

"She's got a way, Justine does"—Carolee gave Hope a one-armed hug—"of finding the perfect person for the right job. I'll see you in a few hours."

Alone, she took a breath. As she'd decided after considering all morning, she started for the stairs. Best to try this at Ground Zero.

Two steps past her office, the phone rang. She nearly let the machine pick up, then backtracked to answer.

"Good morning. Inn BoonsBoro."

Twenty minutes later, she tried again. And Avery rushed in the door.

"I got hung up. Have you tried talking to her yet?"

"No, I got hung up myself. Do you know Myra Grimm?"

"Maybe. I know Brent Grimm. He works at Thompson's, and he's a regular at Vesta. I think Myra's his older sister. Why?"

"She wants to book the inn for a small second-time-around wedding. I can tell you she divorced Mickey Shoebaker sixteen years ago, took her maiden name back, lives a couple miles outside of town and works at Bast Funeral Home."

"Fortunately I haven't needed to do business with her."

"She met her future husband there three years ago when he buried his wife."

"Huh. You wouldn't think of funeral homes as hook-up parlors."

"Love finds a way," Hope said with a laugh. "Anyway, he popped the question, as she put it, and they want to get married here next month."

"Moving fast."

"They aren't getting any younger, she tells me. Just a small wedding, maybe twenty or twenty-five people. In the afternoon. Details to follow."

"A small second-time-around afternoon wedding," Avery considered. "I could do some simple food, and Icing could do a cake."

"I suggested both. She's going to talk to her fiancé, but again, as she tells me, he's fine with whatever she wants to do."

"Handy for her."

"She sounded giddy. It was sweet. Well." She looked toward the stairs, then turned as Clare rapped on The Lobby door.

"I wanted to be here, if it's all right. She helped me, and I thought maybe having us all together would help."

"Good idea. Let's go on up. E&D's her favorite place, so we'll try there."

"It's strange, isn't it?" Avery brought up the rear behind Clare. "But not spooky strange. It's kind of like going to talk to a friend. One you don't know all that well, really, but care about."

"I'm learning more every day. She led such a restricted life. Not just because of the times, the culture, but her father was so stern, so hard-line. Do you know I haven't found a single letter from Eliza in her sister's things? There should have been. People wrote letters routinely back then."

"The email of the nineteenth century," Avery commented.

"Sisters would have written each other," Clare agreed. "But if the father was so rigid, he may have destroyed any letters Lizzy wrote."

"I think that may be it. There's plenty of subtext in the letters I have read," Hope continued. "Catherine feared him. It's horrible, really, to imagine being afraid of your own father. And I think Catherine founded the school, once she was married and out from her father's thumb, because of the way she and her sister were restricted. Catherine loved to read, and discovered a love of medicine during the war. She wanted to study, but that was out of the question."

"So she founded a school so other girls could study." Clare's eyes went damp. "So other girls could pursue their dreams."

"And Lizzy?" Hope added. "All she really wanted was to fall in love, get married, make a home, and raise a family. Everything her father expected of her, except for the first step because love didn't enter into his plans for his daughters."

She slipped the key in the lock, opened the door. "We had guests in here last night. The room hasn't been serviced yet."

"I think we're okay with an unmade bed. Sit down, Clare," Avery ordered.

"I'm fine."

"Pregnant women should never turn down the opportunity to sit."

"You're right." Clare lowered into the purple velvet chair. "Does she stay in here, do you think, when you have guests like last night?"

"It depends. Sometimes I feel her up in my apartment. Or in The Library if I go in to refill the whiskey decanter or restock the coffeemaker."

"She spends time with you," Avery added. "Tell us about the letter."

"I told you."

"Tell us again, and maybe you'll be telling her, too."

"There are hundreds of letters. My cousin and the school archivist made enormous efforts to find letters written to and by Catherine.

The bulk of what they have and what I've had access to were written to her. Letters from friends, relatives, the governess she had as a child, her music master, and so on."

Avery nodded, sat on the edge of the bed.

"There are letters from James Darby, the man she married, and several from her to him. They've been my favorites so far. In them you can see the evolution of their feelings for each other, the affection, the humor, the respect. He fell in love first, I think, and I think his loving her, understanding her, helped her discover herself."

"Lucky for her," Clare stated. "She married someone she loved, and who loved her."

"I think they had a really good life," Hope said. "He not only financed the bulk of the school she wanted to build, but came to share that vision with her. He was from a good family, financially and socially solid, so her father approved. But they loved each other. She was able to have a full life with the man she loved. It wasn't a marriage based on fear or duty or convenience."

When she caught the scent of honeysuckle, Hope eased down beside Avery. "Love opened her life. She loved her sister, but she was young, afraid, and didn't know yet what it was to be in love. She kept her sister's secret, as far as I can tell. And my sense of her, from the letters, is loyalty. I don't believe she would have betrayed you. She wrote to your cousin Sarah Ellen. They were close to the same age, and she shared her heart, her thoughts, her joys and worries with her. She feared for you, if your father learned you were slipping away to meet Billy. He was a stonemason, working on your father's estate. Is that right? You need to tell us if that's right, so I can keep looking."

She appeared in front of the door leading to the porch.

"He carved our initials into a stone. He showed me. Initials inside a heart in the stone. He put it into the wall, so it would last forever, and no one would know but the two of us."

"What was his name?" Hope asked.

"He's Billy. My Billy. I was riding, and went past where I was permitted, alone. Down to the stream, and he was there, fishing on a Sunday afternoon. He should not have been, and I should not have been. A brisk March afternoon, and the water in the stream pushing through the thawing ice."

Lizzy closed her eyes as if looking back. "I could smell spring trying to break through winter, yet snow still lay in the shadows. The sky was winter gray, and the wind still bitter."

Opening her eyes, she smiled. "But he was there, and it was no longer cold. I should never have spoken to him, nor he to me. But we knew as if we had always known. A look, a word, and hearts opened. Like in the novels Cathy would read me, and I would laugh at love at first sight."

Hope wanted to speak, to interrupt. His name, just his name. But didn't have the heart.

"We met when I could get away, and loved the rest of that cold March, into the blooming spring and to the lushness of summer."

She held out a hand toward Hope. "You know. All of you know what it is to feel so strongly for someone. He worked with his hands, not with wood, as your loves do, but stone. This alone would make him unworthy in my father's eyes. We knew it."

"Did your father find out?" Hope asked.

"He would never believe or suspect I would defy him in such a way. He chose a husband for me, and I refused when I had never refused him. At first, it was as if I hadn't spoken. He simply continued with his plans for the marriage. I continued to refuse, but, in truth, I would have had no choice. And the war . . ."

She turned to Clare. "You understand what war does to those who fight it, and to those who are left behind to wait and fear. He said he must fight, must go, or have no honor. I begged, but in this he would not be swayed. We would leave together, marry, and I would stay with his family until he came back for me."

"Where was his family?" Avery prompted.

"Here?" Lizzy's fingers worked at the high collar of her dress as she looked around. "Near? It fades. His face is clear, his voice, his touch. Hard hands. Hard and strong. Ryder."

"Yes," Hope murmured. "Strong, hard hands. You eloped with Billy?"

"I could not. That very night my father signed my marriage contract. I should have remained silent, but I shouted at him, I raged. I thought of Billy going to war, and I raged at my father. I would never marry but for love. He could beat me, lock me away, throw me away, and still I would not do what he demanded of me. So he did lock me away, in my room. He struck me."

As if that memory remained all too fresh, Lizzy touched her cheek. "My mother took to her bed, and he struck me again, and dragged me to my room, locked me in. I could not get out, could not get away. Three days and nights, my father kept me locked in my room with only bread and water. I did what I should have done before. I told him I would obey. I asked his forgiveness. I lied and lied, and I waited for my chance. I left that house and my family, my sister whom I loved, so much, in the dead of night with what I could carry. I took the train to Philadelphia. So afraid, so excited. Going to Billy. I traveled by coach. So hot. Such a hot summer. I was ill. I wrote . . . to his mother. I think. It fades. I wrote, and I came here. He was here."

"Billy came here?" Hope asked her.

"Near. He was coming. I could hear the cannon fire, but I was so ill. He was coming. He promised. I'm waiting."

"Eliza, I need his name. His full formal name." Hope got to her feet. "He was William."

"No. He was Billy, but Joseph William. He would build us a house, with his own hands. Will your Ryder build you a house?"

"He has a house. Eliza—"

"And a dog. We would have dogs. I left my dogs and my home and my family. But we would have dogs and a home and make a family. I think I was with child."

"Oh God," Avery murmured.

"I think . . . Women know. Is that true?" she asked Clare.

"I think it is."

"I never told him. I only began to know when I came here. Then the heat, and the sickness. And it fades. It's too long." She held out a hand they could see through. "It all fades."

"Oh, don't—" Hope began, but Lizzy faded away like her hand.

"Pregnant and alone and sick, while the man she loved went off to war." Avery rose to crouch by Clare's chair, lean her cheek on Clare's hand.

"It wasn't like that for me. I was never alone. I had family who loved me. But yes, I can understand how frightened she must have been, and God, how determined. To leave everything with only what she could carry, to come to a strange place—and to realize she was carrying a child."

"Then to lie in bed, sick and dying, listening to cannon fire. He fought at Antietam," Hope said. "I'm sure of it. He was near, and he was a soldier."

"His family was near, too," Avery reminded her. "And we're not looking for a William, but a Joseph William. Maybe Williams? Would they have called him Billy?"

"I don't know, but having a potential first and middle name, or a potential first and last, is going to help."

"The longer she talked, or tried to, the less she was *here*. She was less and less defined as she talked to us."

Hope nodded at Clare. "That happened before. It must have something to do with energy. Who the hell knows? I could start researching paranormal activities, hauntings, and so on, but that would take time away from trying to find Billy. That's the priority."

"I'll let Owen know, and he'll dive in, too. But she talked to us."

Avery took Clare's hand as she straightened, reached for Hope's. "She talked to all of us. She hasn't had anyone she could tell her story to, all this time. All she wanted was Billy, a home, a family, a damn dog. I wish her father would make an appearance. I don't know if you can punch a ghost, but I'd like to try."

"For now, this is her home." Hope sighed. "And we're her family."

"Beckett brought her out. I really believe that," Avery said to Clare. "Something about him let her reach out. Maybe he reminded her of Billy. Maybe they all do—Owen and Ryder, too. She trusts them, cares about them. There's a connection there, and maybe it's more than how they rebuilt this place."

"Yeah." Hope frowned. "You're right. There's something—" She broke off when she heard the door open downstairs, and voices carry up. "Cleaning crew."

"I need to get back to the store." Clare levered herself up. "We should write all this down. I can do that. Maybe if it's all written down, we'll see something we missed in the telling."

"I'll start the search for Joseph William—or Williams—as soon as I can." Hope led the way down.

"We should have a meeting. The six of us—and Justine if she wants."

"I'm open tomorrow night. Can you get a sitter?"

"I'll take care of it," she told Hope. "Can we get together here? It may jump-start something."

They stopped in The Lobby, chatted with the cleaning crew. When the phone rang, Hope waved her friends off.

With plans for the meeting working through her head, she braved the heat to go outside and weed. She thought better if her hands stayed busy.

They'd had a breakthrough, she was certain of it. Momentum would carry them the rest of the way.

And what then? she wondered. When they found Billy—discovered where he'd lived and died, how he'd died and when—what would that mean to Lizzy?

She'd never had a chance, Hope thought, not really. And just as she'd believed her life would begin, it had ended. Yet her spirit remained faithful, compassionate, had humor and affection.

And love, she thought. The love just shone in her.

They'd have had a good life together, she mused. That stone house, that family, those dogs. However young she'd been, however tragic, she'd known what she wanted, and she'd grabbed for it.

And what do you want? Hope asked herself.

Her hands stilled as her own question surprised her. She had what she wanted. Didn't she?

A job she loved, friends she treasured, family she could count on whenever she needed it. A lover she cared for and enjoyed.

It was enough, just as she'd told Ryder. It was more than enough.

Yet something niggled at her, something inside her that wanted to stretch for more.

Don't spoil it, she warned herself. Don't start piling on expectations. Take it all as it comes, and be happy *now*.

She stepped back as Carolee pulled in, and went through the arch to meet her at her car.

"I'm loaded!" Carolee announced.

"And I'm here to help."

"So's she." Carolee gestured as Justine pulled in. "She's been behind me the last mile and a half. Good timing," Carolee called out. "Grab a bag and haul it in."

Justine, wearing sandals with rainbows for straps and sugary pink sunglasses, flexed her biceps. "I've got the power. Jesus please us, it's freaking *hot*."

"I'd hoped that storm last night would cool things off." Carolee reached in, pulled out a skid of toilet paper. "No such luck."

"Took down a branch as big and wide as Willy B and dropped it across my lane. I had to get the damn chain saw."

"You ran a chain saw." Hope gaped at her.

"Honey, I can run a chain saw, a wood splitter, and whatever else you toss at me. If I have to. One of the boys would've done it, but I wasn't calling them away from work when I could do it myself."

"I can run a Weedwacker." Carolee laughed as they hauled supplies inside. "But I've lived in town for decades and Justine in the woods. Remember how Mama thought Tommy was all but taking you to a foreign country when he bought up that land?"

"Mama figured I'd become a hillbilly. Tommy used to tease her that he was putting in a still."

"She didn't approve of him?" Hope wondered.

"Oh, she loved him. Crazy about him. She just didn't love the idea of him plopping me down in the middle of the wilderness, which was how she saw anything more than three miles outside of town. My father grew up on a farm not far from here, and he couldn't wait to get some town on him. They were made for each other."

"Everyone's got their place," Carolee said.

"And mine's in the wilderness. I'm lucky my boys feel the same so I can have them close."

"No, sit," Hope said when Justine turned to go out again. "I can get the rest. You have something cold, and I'll give you the latest Lizzy update when we've got everything in."

"I'll do just that, and watch my sister put all this away."

"You always did boss me."

"You always needed it."

Amused, Hope left them to it, went out to get the last of the supplies from Carolee's car.

As she did, a red BMW Roadster pulled into the lot. She didn't recognize the car—that was new—but she recognized the woman behind the wheel.

Her jaw tightened; her shoulders tensed. She didn't bother to fake a smile as Sheridan Massey Wickham slid out of the car and onto gorgeous—damn it—Louboutin stiletto sandals.

Her hair fell in such perfect, shiny waves Hope was certain Sheridan had stopped five minutes down the road to freshen it and her makeup. She wore a watercolor-print sheath—Akris, Hope guessed—drop earrings of platinum, and a sparkling wedding set that could have put someone's eye out.

Just my luck, Hope thought, when I'm sweaty, wearing weed-the-garden clothes and haven't freshened my lip gloss since I put it on this morning.

Just perfect.

"Sheridan." She left the greeting at that.

Sheridan whipped off sunglasses, tossed them into her candy pink leather purse. "I'm going to give you one warning, and that's all you'll get. Stay away from Jonathan."

Hope recognized fury when it shot into her face, but couldn't judge the cause. "I don't see him anywhere in the vicinity."

"You're going to lie to my face now? I know he's been here, don't deny it. I know he's been with you. I know exactly what you're trying to pull."

"I don't intend to lie to your face or behind your back, nor have I got anything worth lying about. You can consider your unnecessary warning received. Now, I'm working, so have a nice drive back."

"Listen to me, you *bitch*!" Sheridan grabbed Hope's arm, clamped her fingers tight. "I know he was here. He stopped for gas. I saw the receipt. I'm not an idiot."

Yes, Hope thought, jealous types would paw through receipts, emails, search pockets. What a sad way to live.

"You should be talking to him about this. But I'll tell you he was here, once, earlier this summer to tell me his father wanted to make me an offer to come back to work at the Wickham."

"You're a liar, and a slut."

"I'm neither." Hope wrenched her arm away.

"If his father wanted you back, I'd know about it. And you'd have jumped at the chance."

"Obviously you're wrong on both counts."

Only more furious, Sheridan pitched her voice to a shout. "You won't get away with the games you played before. I'm his wife now. I'm his wife, and you're *nothing*."

Hope resisted the urge to rub her arm. Sheridan had used her nails as well as her fingers in the grip. "I never played any games."

"You slept your way up to manager, and you tried to sleep your way into marriage. And I know you're trying it again. You think I don't know who he's sneaking off to see when he says he has a business trip, or a late meeting."

Hope might have felt pity if her own temper left room for it. Instead she used every ounce of control to keep from shouting back. "Sheridan, get this into your head. I couldn't be less interested in Jonathan. If you think I'd give him the time of day much less sex after what he pulled on me, you *are* an idiot."

"Lying bitch!"

The crack of Sheridan's hand across her face stunned her, and came forcefully enough to knock her back a full step.

"You tell me the truth! I want the truth right now, or—"

"You're going to want to back off." Ryder pulled Sheridan back. "And a long way off."

"You take your hands off me or I'll call the police."

"Do that. In fact, I can call them for you."

"Ryder—"

"Go inside, Hope."

"Yes, go run away." With a toss of that beautiful hair, Sheridan sneered. "The way you did when Jonathan told you he was through with you."

"I'm not going anywhere, but I suggest you do."

"I'll go. I'll go straight to your employer. You'd better start looking for another place to land because you're going to be done here when I tell him what you're up to."

"Why don't you tell me now?" Justine suggested as she stepped forward. "This is my place. Hope's my innkeeper. So make it good. Otherwise I'm going to tell my son to go right ahead and call the police so they can escort you off my property."

"She's just using you, the way she uses everyone. Jonathan told me how she called him, begging him to come here to talk to her, and how she begged him to take her back."

"Girl, if you've got problems like this so early in your marriage, you're in trouble. Coming here and going after Hope isn't going to fix them."

"I've seen Jonathan once since I left D.C.," Hope began. "I've never called him. I've never slept with him. I don't want him, Sheridan. And right now, I wonder why you do."

As Sheridan lunged forward, Ryder merely shifted to stand between her and Hope. "Put your hands on her again, I can promise you'll regret it."

Sheridan's eyes narrowed. "So that's it. Reverting to type, Hope? Sleeping with the boss's son. How pathetic."

"Lady, there's a dozen men over there who saw you give Hope that bitch slap. Every one of them will go to court and say so when she has you charged with assault."

"I—"

"Shut up, Hope." He snapped it out at her interruption. "You get in your car and you get the hell out of here. You don't come back. If I hear you do, and in a small town word gets around, I'll have you arrested. I bet the Wickhams will love having their name smeared all over the *Washington Post*."

"She's just using you." But there were tears in Sheridan's eyes now, and the quaver of them in her voice. "She's using you and trying to wreck my marriage. You're the one who'll be sorry when she tosses you away for a bigger catch."

"Sheridan?" Justine spoke with surprising gentleness. "You're making a fool out of yourself now. Go on home."

"I'm going. It's impossible to try to reason with a couple of hicks anyway."

Justine's grin spread wide as Sheridan swung back to her car. "Yee-haw." As the BMW peeled out, Justine put her arm around Hope's shoulders. "Oh, honey, don't let that pitiful fool upset you so."

"I'm sorry. I'm so sorry."

Ryder turned back—he'd wanted to be sure the Roadster kept going. And saw tears spilled down Hope's cheeks. "Cut that out. Just stop it."

"I'm sorry."

"You've got nothing to be sorry about. Come on inside," Justine urged. "We'll put some ice on that cheek. She really clocked you one, didn't she?"

"I'm sorry," Hope repeated, couldn't seem to say anything else. "I need to . . ."

She shook free, rushed for the door, past a stunned Carolee, and straight up to her apartment.

"Ryder, you go after her."

"No. No, ma'am."

Justine whirled on him, eyes hot, hands fisted on hips. "You go after her right this minute. What the hell's wrong with you?"

"She's crying. I don't do that. You do that. You go. Come on, Mom, you go."

"Christ on a broken crutch." Justine rapped one of those fists on his chest. "What kind of man did I raise who won't go see to his woman when she's crying?"

"My kind. Please. I'll talk to her when she stops. You'll know what to say to her, what to do."

Justine huffed out a furious breath. "Fine then. You do what you do and go buy her some goddamn fucking flowers." After giving him a second, harder rap, Justine turned on her heel and marched inside.

Wincing, Ryder rubbed his chest, pulled out his phone to call the local florist.

# CHAPTER SIXTEEN

JUSTINE CONSIDERED GETTING THE SPARE KEY TO THE innkeeper's apartment, but thought Hope's privacy had been compromised enough for one day. Instead she climbed up to the third floor, her mind brewing dark thoughts about foolish women who blamed other people for a bad marriage, and men who couldn't strap on the balls to deal with tears.

She raised her hand to knock on Hope's apartment door. And it opened, quickly, smoothly.

Hope instantly sprang up from where she sat weeping on the couch.

"I didn't open it." Justine lifted her hands to show them empty. "Someone's looking out for you."

"I just need a few minutes to settle down."

"What you need is a shoulder, and if it weren't so early in the day, a good three fingers of whiskey. We'll settle for the shoulder and the tea I'm going to make—in a minute."

She walked straight over, put her arms around Hope, and pulled her in tight.

"Oh God. God!" Hope managed, helpless against the unquestioning support. "It was horrible."

Soothing, soothing, Justine rocked a little from side to side. "Well, on a scale of one to ten, one being a paper cut and ten being, say, slicing your hand off with a machete, it only ranked about three. But that's bad enough."

"I'm so—"

"Don't you apologize to me again for someone else's bad behavior." Though her voice was stern and brisk, Justine rubbed a comforting hand up and down Hope's back.

"I wasn't with Jonathan because of my career. And Ryder. . . Please don't think that."

"Let's sit down here while I explain to you why those are unnecessary things to say to me. Honey . . ." Justine's lips tightened when she studied the red streak still marring Hope's cheek. "Let me get that ice for you first."

"It's all right." Instinctively Hope lifted a hand to the dull but steady throbbing. "I'm all right."

"Caught you right on the cheekbone. You've got such good ones, but it makes an easy target. Now, you sit."

Justine walked into the little kitchen, poked in the freezer. "No frozen peas. I always kept frozen peas when the boys were around—still do. God knows they're always banging themselves up." She found baggies, filled one with ice. "This'll do. You hold that on your cheek for a few minutes," she ordered and passed the makeshift ice pack to Hope.

"Where was I?"

"Justine—"

"Oh, that's right. You and that worthless prick Jonathan Dickham."

The deliberate mispronunciation surprised a half laugh out of Hope.

"Every woman's entitled to a mistake. I had my own worthless prick when I was sixteen and crazy about Mike Truman. He cheated on me with a majorette with big boobs. He's been divorced twice, and is looking like he's heading into his third. Goes to show you."

She babbled, they both knew, to give Hope time to settle.

"What happened to the majorette?" Hope asked her.

"She got fat. It's petty of me to be smug and superior about that, but every woman's entitled to a little petty here and there."

Hope couldn't defeat the sigh—part upset, part humor. "Oh, Justine."

"Sweetheart, you just put your faith and your emotions into the wrong hands, and he didn't respect either. Apparently he's not respecting his wife's, but that shouldn't be your problem. That stupid woman—with fabulous shoes and desperate eyes—wants to make it your problem so she can blame you for the obvious fact that her husband's now her worthless prick."

"I know it. I know it, but, Justine, it's such an awful ugly mess."

"Hers, not yours. You could have told her he'd come here and proposed you and he have an affair."

"I didn't see the point. She wouldn't have believed me."

"Oh, some part of her would have. Some part of her already knows how it stands." As she spoke, Justine rose, found tissues. When she sat again, she dabbed at Hope's cheeks herself.

"Pisses her off, embarrasses her. So she embarrassed you. That's the part I'm sorry about. As for Ryder, why would I think you're with him for some kind of career advantage? You're already the innkeeper, and I don't plan on opening a chain of them. Added to that, Ry has his flaws, God knows, but he's a good man. He's a pleasure to look at, and I expect he knows what to do and how to do it, and well, in bed."

"Oh God."

"That embarrasses you, but, sweetie, if you and Ry aren't having a hell of a good time in bed at this point in your relationship, that would be a damn shame. That aside, you've got integrity and pride. If you didn't, you'd be with the worthless prick when he snuck out on that stupid woman, and use sex as a lever to get what you wanted out of him."

"Why won't they just stay away from me? I've left them alone."

"You're going to be a hook in her craw as long as she's with him. Which I predict won't be more than a year—two at the outside. And you're always going to be one in his. You walked away," Justine said simply. "He'll never understand that, and never comprehend he has himself to blame. I don't think either of them will be back or bother you again. But if they do, I want to know about it. I want you to tell me. That's not negotiable."

"All right."

"Here, let me see that now." Justine took the ice bag, gave Hope's cheek a study. "That ought to do it."

"It's fine. Really. It was just such a shock. And I just stood there. You'd have slapped her back."

"Oh, honey, I'd have knocked her on her skinny ass. But that's me. You're made different. I'm going to make that tea now."

"Thank you."

"Part of the package." Back in the kitchen she put the kettle on, poked around until she found Hope's collection of tea. She chose jasmine, a personal favorite.

"Now I'm going to apologize."

"You?" Hope swiped at a few lingering tears. "Why?"

"For my son. He should have been the one to come up here, give you a shoulder, listen, lecture, and make you tea."

The smile came as a welcome relief. "He'd have hated it."

"So what? Women have men leaving the toilet seat up, or not

watching their aim after one too many beers. We deal with it. He retreats from tears, and always has. The other two handle them okay, but not Ry. If you slice your finger off, he's your man. But cry about it, he's gone."

"I don't hold it against him."

"Me, I like a man who'll sop up a few tears, as long as the woman doesn't blubber every time she gets that paper cut. I'm not going to ask if you want my advice. You'd say yes even though nobody really wants advice. So I'm just going to give it to you. See that he listens to you. Feelings need to be expressed, Hope. They aren't always under- stood the way people like to assume."

She poured hot water over the tea bag in the cup. "He's a good man, like I said. A clever one. Smart, hardworking, and he tells the truth whether you like it or not. If he's not going to tell the truth, he doesn't say anything. He's got a sweet side that doesn't always show, and a surly one that too often does."

She brought the tea to Hope, angled her head. "And he's never been serious about a woman in his life. He respects them, enjoys them, appreciates them, and he's always been careful to keep his feet right under him. He's slipping some with you, in case you haven't noticed."

"No, I'm not . . . Do you think so?"

"I do. He's going to send you flowers, and he's going to hope the storm's passed by the time he comes around." She bent down, kissed the top of Hope's head. "Don't let him get away with it. Now you drink that tea, take a little time for yourself."

"Thanks. Thank you, Justine."

"All in a day's work. I'm going to go see what my boys have been up to. You call me if you need to."

"I will."

As Justine started for the door, it opened. She let out a baffled laugh. "It's hard to get used to. Well, it looks like she'll keep you company awhile."

WHILE HIS MOTHER sat with Hope, Ryder tried to work off his mad. The more he worked, the madder he got.

Subcontractors surrounded him, crisscrossing each other, full of noise and questions. Getting in his damn way, and he was fucking sick of it. Sick of needing to know the answers, sick of making decisions, sick of finishing up every goddamn day covered with sweat and dirt.

The next son of a bitch who got in his face was going to—

"Hey, Ry, I need you to—"

He whirled on an unsuspecting Beckett. "Fuck off."

"If something's crawled up your butt, you'd better clench. I've got—"

"I don't give a shit what you've got. I said fuck off. I'm busy."

Several members of the crew slid a safe distance away.

"So am I, so suck it up." Beckett's eyes narrowed, fired as hot as his brother's. "If you swing at me, bro, I'm swinging back, but at least I won't walk off the job." He turned, pitched his voice to a shout. "Take lunch. Now. Everybody."

"I run the crew. I say when they break."

"You want to do this with an audience? Fine by me."

Ryder ground his teeth. "Lunch. Now. Clear out. Whatever's going on at MacT's," he told Beckett, "deal with it yourself. I'm up to my ass here."

"I don't give a single happy fuck what you're up to. Knock off. Go the hell home. Go beat hell out of your speed bag or whatever."

"I don't take orders from you."

"And I don't take shit from you. If you've got a problem with the work, or you had some fight with Hope, just suck it, Ry. Yelling at me in front of the men makes you look like a dick."

"I don't have a problem. I didn't have a fight with Hope, for fuck's sake. Get off my back."

Beckett walked over to the cooler, flipped up the lid. He took out a bottle of water, threw it at his brother. "Cool off," he suggested when Ryder snagged it an inch from his face.

Ryder considered heaving it back, then stewed as he twisted the top, gulped water. "Stupid blond bitch comes shoving her way up here, piling on Hope. Slapped her."

"Say what? Who? Hope slapped some blonde?"

"Other way." Ryder rubbed the cold bottle over the back of his neck. He wondered that steam didn't rise off his skin.

"What the hell's going on?" Owen came in, still wearing his tool belt. "I had two of the crew come into MacT's and tell me there was a catfight in the parking lot, and the two of you were going at it in here."

"Does it look like we're going at it?"

Owen studied his brothers. "It looks like you want to. What the hell's going on?"

"Ry was just telling me. Some blonde slapped Hope."

"Jesus Christ. A guest hit her?"

"Not a guest." And, Ryder realized, he was making a mess out of this. "Wickham's new wife, the blond bitch. I came out to talk with the rep for the exterior paint system, and I see Hope talking to this fancy blonde, over by Carolee's car. It looks tense, full of drama. Sounds like it because the blonde's yelling her goddamn head off. I'm not getting into that, and the next thing I know, the blonde's hauling off and slapping Hope. You could hear the fucking crack across the lot."

"For God's sake," Beckett muttered.

"By the time I got over there, it looked like the blonde might take another shot. She's yelling all manner of shit about how Hope's having sex with that asshole, how she slept with him to make manager, and other loads of bullshit."

"Sounds like the asshole deserves the blond bitch," was Owen's opinion.

"That may be, but she kept going after Hope, threatened to go to her boss and say how she was banging Wickham to get back down to D.C. That's when Mom got into it."

"Mom was there." For the first time Beckett smiled, showed his teeth. "I didn't hear any ambulance."

"She must've walked out during, I didn't see her, but she told the blonde to get gone and make it fast. There was more in there. Threats to call the cops."

"Mom said she'd call the cops?" Owen wanted to know.

"The blonde. And I said we could do just that. Anyway, she left. It was a fucking mess." He drank again. "She left."

"Okay." Beckett took off his cap, dragged his hands through his hair. "Harsh, ugly, and done."

"She made Hope cry."

"Goddamn it." Beckett leaned back against a wall. There was done, in his mind, and there was *done*. "It sounds like we need to take a little road trip, have a discussion with Wickham."

"And after I bail the two of you out of jail, what then?" Owen demanded. "Beating the living shit out of Wickham doesn't help Hope. It won't make her feel better."

"We'll feel better," Beckett said, and Owen was forced to nod.

"Yeah, we would. Hell. I'll drive."

"I'll handle it," Ryder told him. But knowing his brothers had his back defused the time bomb of temper.

"Somebody's got to post your bail," Owen reminded him.

"I'm not going to pound on anybody. Probably. I've got a better idea. I've gotta go. The two of you will just have to pick up the slack for the rest of the day. And keep my dog."

"What are you going to do?" Beckett demanded.

"I'm not going to hit him in the face. I'm going to hit him in the wallet and the pride. I figure that's something he'll understand."

"Call if you need backup," Owen said as Ryder stripped off his tool belt.

"I won't."

THE DRIVE TO D.C. gave him time to think. He really couldn't afford the time, but saw no choice. Somewhere during the rise of temper and the fall of it, he'd figured where all this could, and likely would, go. The blonde, all pissed off and worked up, goes after Wickham about Hope. Dragging her into it again. She'd probably have plenty to say, too, at the hair salon, the nail place, the freaking country club.

Tossing her personal brand of shit all over Hope's name and rep.

That damn well wasn't going to happen.

The whole load of bull could make Wickham decide Hope might be more willing to take his offer, since she was being accused of it anyway. He might get it into his head to make another trip to Boonsboro, or call her, freaking email her, and get her twisted up again.

That wasn't going to happen either.

He could warn Wickham off, but that would give the fucker too much attention, too much punch. He and his crazy wife humiliated Hope, and did it on her home turf.

Let them feel a little of the same.

As he got into the city, he followed his GPS directions, and cursed the traffic, the stupid one-way streets, the circles, the incompetence of other drivers.

He hated coming down here, avoided it like the plague. Just buildings and roads and people and construction detours, all of them crowded together in a way that made no sense to him.

He couldn't wait to drive out of it again.

But a job was a job, he told himself when he finally managed to park. Heat and humidity bounced off the sidewalk, slathered him as he walked toward the pristine entrance of the Wickham. Colonial elegance with rivers of summer flowers, windows that tossed sunlight, and a doorman liveried in dignified gray with red trim.

Dignified enough he didn't blink at opening the door for some guy in work clothes.

The lobby spread, white marble floors veined with black, huge-ass urns of flowers—forests of them. Dark oak paneling, crystal chandeliers, velvet sofas all worked together to say, clearly: high-class. And a gleaming front desk manned by a woman in black who could've made a living on any catwalk.

"Welcome to the Wickham. How can I help you today?"

"I need to see the owner. Wickham. Senior."

"I'm sorry, sir, Mr. Wickham is unavailable. If you'd like to speak with our manager?"

"Wickham. Tell him Ryder Montgomery needs to speak with him. Don't bother to call the manager," he said, anticipating her. "Or security. Just tell Wickham I'm here to discuss the charges against his daughter-in-law for assault."

"I'm sorry?"

"You heard me. If he's okay with that, I'll go on home and make that happen. If he's not, he'll talk to me." Ryder just shrugged as she lost her composure enough to goggle at him. "I'll wait."

He stepped back, glanced around. Looked like a hell of a nice bar off the lobby, he noted. He'd have liked to go in—not for a beer, he was driving in this goddamn traffic again shortly—but to see how it was put together.

He could see Hope here, easily. In her excellent suit and her fancy stilts. She'd fit right in with the marble and crystal, with the shine and elegance and flowers so damn big he suspected steroids.

"Mr. Montgomery."

He turned, studied the man in the dark suit. "Security? No need to toss me out. I'll just see Mr. Wickham in court."

"I'll escort you to Mr. Wickham's office. And remain."

"Works for me."

They walked up a curving staircase, along a mezzanine, then through a set of oak doors into a small secondary lobby.

Security knocked on another set of doors.

"Come!"

"Mr. Montgomery, sir." The security guard stepped back, stood at parade rest.

Wickham remained seated at a heavily carved desk that might have suited a president or the king of some small country. He had a shock of white hair, hard blue eyes, and a smooth golden tan.

"I don't allow people to threaten my family."

"No?" Ryder hooked his thumbs in his front pockets. "Me either. Let me lay this out for you, and when I have you can say what you want to say, and we'll be done. My family owns Inn BoonsBoro. Hope Beaumont is our innkeeper."

"I'm aware."

"Good, saves time with the setup. I'm not going to get into what went on with Hope and your son, your part in it or anyone else's. I wasn't around, and that was then anyway. This is now."

"My family has nothing to do with yours, Mr. Montgomery. And I take threats against my son's wife very seriously."

"Good, you should, because they're damn serious. As to your family having nothing to do with mine? You're going to need to reevaluate that when I'm done. A couple of months ago your son showed up at our inn. He told Hope you had an offer for her, a big fat one to lure her back. That's your business, and I can't blame you for trying. She's damn good at what she does. Then he made her a side offer. She comes back to him, too, and he'll take care of her. He'll set her up, make it worth her while."

A red flush—temper or embarrassment—rose onto Wickham's cheeks. "If you think you can come in here—"

"I'm going to finish, Mr. Wickham. She turned him down. If you knew her at all you're not surprised by that. She left here because he'd lied to her, cheated on her, used her. And when she learned he was going to marry someone else, she got out of the way. But that's not enough for some."

"What was, or is, between your employee and my son is their business."

"There's no *is*, and you know it." Ryder could see it. "He, and his crazy wife, made it my business. Today, this morning, your son's wife made the trip to Boonsboro, to our inn. She drives a red BMW Roadster, this year's model. She had on mile-high shoes with red soles and one of those sleeveless jobs that looked like someone painted a garden on it. You could probably check on her wardrobe choice this morning if you need to verify. She caused a scene on our property. I witnessed this myself, as did a number of others. She yelled accusations, threats. She thinks Hope's sleeping with your son again, which I can guarantee she's not—but he's sure as hell sleeping with somebody not his wife. Women know. She topped it off by physically assaulting Hope, and wouldn't stop or leave until we threatened to call the cops."

A visible heaviness settled over Wickham, and sounded in his voice when he spoke. "Sit down, Mr. Montgomery."

"No thanks."

"Jerald." Wickham waved to the security guard, who slipped quietly out of the room.

Wickham himself rose, turned to the window overlooking the back garden and patio of his hotel. "I'm not comfortable discussing my family with you. I'll only say I have no reason not to believe you."

"That saves time, too."

"Were the police called? Have charges been filed?"

"Not yet."

"What do you want?"

"I want five minutes alone with your son, and for your daughter-in-law to spend thirty days in a cell. But I'll settle for neither of them coming near Hope or our place, neither one of them contacting her in any way, for any reason. And if I hear they're spreading lies that damage her reputation, I'll do a lot worse to theirs, and by proxy yours and your hotel. Make that happen, and we're square."

"You have my word." He turned back, face grim, and Ryder saw the kindling of disgust in his eyes. "Neither my son nor his wife will trouble Hope again, in any way. I regret, deeply, they've already done so."

"All right. I'll trust your word; you'll trust mine. But I'm going to warn you, Mr. Wickham, if they don't keep your word, I'm going to cause them a whole shitload of trouble."

"I understand." He picked up a card from the desk, wrote something on the back. "If you would contact me—this is my private line—should either of them break the word I'm giving you. Trust me, Mr. Montgomery, I can and will cause them both more trouble than you. And I will."

"Fair enough." Ryder pocketed the card.

"I'll have Jerald show you out."

"I know the way. Let's hope we don't speak again."

RYDER FOUGHT THE miserable traffic toward home, and felt some of the tension dissolve when he caught his first sight of the mountains as he traveled north.

He'd done what seemed right—not as personally satisfying as kicking in Jonathan Wickham's balls—but it wasn't about personal satisfaction.

He trusted Wickham would make good on his word. God knew

what kind of wrath and pressure he'd bring to bear, but Ryder imagined it would be fierce and plentiful.

It hadn't just been anger and embarrassment he'd seen on Wickham's face at the end. There'd been regret, too.

He turned off the highway, took the winding, blissfully familiar road that wound through those mountains, into and out of Middletown, and straight into Boonsboro.

He turned at The Square, spotted Beckett's truck—but not his dog as he pulled in beside it.

He did catch a glimpse of Hope in one of her floaty dresses, serving drinks to some guests in The Courtyard.

He needed to check on what had been done at Fit in his absence, and at MacT's, needed to find his dog and an ice-cold beer.

But even as he climbed out of the truck, Hope stepped around The Courtyard wall.

He didn't see any signs of tears—thank Christ—and didn't think she'd let guests see any.

"How're you doing?"

"I'm fine. I'd like to speak with you. Privately."

"Okay."

"In there." She pointed to the fitness center. "Carolee's here."

Without waiting for an answer, she started across the lot.

Okay, he thought, she was a little pissed that he hadn't patted her hand while she cried. Maybe the flowers hadn't come through yet.

He unlocked the door, took a quick scan. Progress on the rough electric and plumbing on this level, and signs the HVAC was moving. He needed to get upstairs, check it out up there. Maybe they'd—

"Ryder, I'd appreciate it if you'd pay attention."

"Okay. What?"

"You had no business confronting Jonathan behind my back. You had no right to take this situation out of my hands, or to do *anything* at all without so much as a discussion with me. It's *my* business. Did you think I wouldn't hear what you were doing, where you went?"

"Didn't give that much thought. And I didn't bother with your ex-asshole. I went to the power source, it's usually the best way. I talked to his father."

"You—" She went pale first, then righteous fury bloomed in her cheeks. "How could you do that? Why would you do that? This is my mess, it's my business."

He'd just spent over three hours on the road into and out of what he considered a man-made hell. And she was ragging on him?

"You're my goddamn business. Do you really think I'd let some bitch of a blonde come around here and slap you around and do dick about it?"

"I got slapped. She's stuck with Jonathan. I'd say she's got the worst of the deal."

"You got that right. She doesn't get away with it. She doesn't get to walk away after hitting you, after making you cry. That's it."

"I wasn't crying because she hurt me. I was humiliated. Beyond humiliated. I don't even have the word. That your mother would have to see that, hear that."

"She can handle it."

"And your crew, all those men who saw it. Everybody in town knows what happened by now, or some variation of it."

"So the fuck what?" Jesus, he was tired, and getting a damn headache, and she stood there bitching at him for doing what needed doing. "It's how it goes, and she's the one who comes off the idiot, not you. And don't, don't, for God's sake, don't start crying again."

"I'm not crying!" But one tear trickled through. "And I'm allowed to cry. People cry! Deal with it."

"Here." He grabbed a hammer out of the tool belt he'd discarded earlier. "Hit me in the head with it. That I can deal with."

"Stop. Just stop." She spoke to herself as much as him, gripping her hands in her hair as she turned. "None of that matters. None of that is the *point*! You took it on yourself, without a word to me, to drive to the Wickham, to tell Jonathan's father all this *sordid* mess."

"That's right. I talked to him, and it's handled."

"You talk to him, but you don't talk to me. You couldn't spend five minutes talking to me, but you'd spend close to four hours driving round-trip to Georgetown and talking to Baxter Wickham. I don't expect you to dry my tears, Ryder, or kiss it better, but I damn well expect you to talk to me, to take my thoughts, feelings, needs into account. And until you do, I'm done talking to you."

"Wait a damn minute," he said when she strode to the door.

She looked back. "I waited four hours. It's your turn to wait. And thanks for the goddamn flowers."

She sailed out, leaving him baffled and pissed off all over again.

# CHAPTER SEVENTEEN

CLIMBING UP AND DOWN HER STEPLADDER TO REMOVE, wash, and replace every vent filter in the inn kept Hope's mind from wandering—very often—in Ryder's direction. With that seemingly endless task accomplished, she dived into paperwork.

They'd made a mistake, obviously, believing they could maintain any sort of relationship with too much passion and too little common ground.

They didn't think alike; their makeup diverged too sharply.

She couldn't be involved with someone who didn't respect her feelings, her needs, her capabilities.

It was best they'd taken a big step back before things became impossibly tangled.

Her work kept her busy and fulfilled enough. And if she finished everything on her list, she could put some time into Lizzy/Billy research that night. As she had the night before, and the night before that as Ryder continued to keep his distance.

Nice trick, she thought, when he worked every day within spitting distance.

She left her office to take delivery from the florist for the rooms booked that day, and happily carried the fresh arrangements upstairs. She came down just as Avery stepped in The Lobby door.

"I knocked first." Avery pocketed her key.

"I was up in The Penthouse. It's booked tonight."

"Swank. Are you all clear now? Have you got a minute?"

"I have several if you need them. Is something up with MacT's?"

"Not that. It's still on to open two weeks from Thursday—or we'll have our friends and family night then. Official opening that Friday." Avery pressed a hand to her belly. "I feel a little sick when I say that, but not in a bad way. But today's breaking news? I think I found my wedding dress."

"Where? When?"

"Online. This morning when I was poking around before coming in."

"Online? But—"

"I know, I know, but with the new place moving so fast, and Vesta busy, Clare starting to waddle—don't tell her I said that—and you tied up here, there's not a lot of chances to hit the shops. And, well, I was just poking, trying to get an idea of the style I might want, what I thought would work, and there it was."

Hope held up a hand. She did plenty of shopping online, primarily for the inn, and respected the convenience. But there were limits. "You ordered your wedding dress online?"

"Not yet! What do you take me for? I wouldn't order a wedding cracker—if I wanted one—without showing you and Clare first. I just went down to TTP and showed Clare." She waved the iPad she carried. "Now I want to show you. I couldn't send links, because I want firsthand—*honest*—reaction."

"Okay. Hit me."

"I've got it bookmarked on my iPad."

"Let's go sit."

"You can tell me if you don't like it," Avery began as they walked into the kitchen.

"What did Clare say?"

"Uh-uh. You're going into this without prejudice." Avery sat, sucked in a breath, and brought the image up on her tablet.

In silence, Hope took a long, careful study. "Well, it's beautiful."

"Beautiful's not hard in a wedding dress. Your eyes could bleed from beauty when you're scrolling through them online. It's the lines and details that pulled me toward this. I've got a small build, so I can't carry the big princess dress, which is sad for me. But I've got good arms and shoulders, so I can carry strapless. But the ruching on the bodice helps with the fact I don't have much boobage."

"Your boobage is lovely."

"Aw, thanks. But there's not a lot of it. And see it's more Empire style, which should help me look taller, and the detailing, the beading . . ." Avery enlarged the beadwork on the flow of skirt. "It's all small scale."

"Like you."

"Yeah. The skirt's got some flare and flow, but no poof." She sighed a little. "I'd love the poof. If you can't have poof on your wedding day, when? I asked myself that, and concluded, for me, never. And I'm too white to wear white so the ivory will warm me up. I'm going to skip the veil, just go for a sparkly tiara type deal. That's my princess thing. I want something princessy."

"You'll look like one in this," Hope decided, taking the tablet to move, shift, enlarge, shrink the image for her own judgment. "A fairy princess. You're right to go with flow instead of poof, the higher waistline, the smaller, more delicate details. I think you'll look gorgeous."

"You've got a 'but' buried in there."

"It's just if you order it this way, you can't try it on, compare it with others, feel the material."

"I can try it on when it gets here, feel the material. And if it doesn't make the grade, I can send it back."

Hope thought of the thrill, the one-time excitement, of surrounding yourself with wedding gowns, the silk, the tulle, the subtle shades of white.

And realized that was her thrill much more than Avery's.

"That's all true."

"I'll model it for you and Clare. And Justine. There's plenty of time if it doesn't work to look for another."

After one last study—of the dress and her friend—Hope handed the tablet back. "You love it."

"I love the picture. I want to see if I love it when I'm wearing it."

"Then you should order it."

"Good, because I've got it holding in the shopping cart, with everything filled out. All I have to do is . . ." Avery tapped, swiped, gulped, and pressed Order Now. "Oh God, I just bought a wedding dress. Hope."

With a laugh, and damp eyes, Hope leaned over and into the bouncing hug.

"How does it feel?"

"Scary, and good. And exciting to order something that doesn't cook, freeze, or flush, which is what I've been spending money on lately."

"I want to know the minute it comes in."

"Promise. I guess it's a little too soon to check the tracking." Avery grinned, brought the image back up just to look at it. "Which I'll be doing every hour on the hour until it gets here."

"Shoes. You need absolutely fabulous shoes."

"I want mile-high shoes," Avery declared. "Sexy, gorgeous, mile-high shoes. I can change into a lower pair when the dancing gets serious, but I want to feel tall. Sparkly, I think, like the tiara, so I've got sparkle head and foot."

"Excellent idea." Hope narrowed her eyes. "You've got those book-marked, too."

"Actually, I have three pairs bookmarked."

Hope tapped the tablet. "Let's have a look."

They spent the next ten minutes debating pumps, strappy sandals, and peep-toes. Hope nixed the pumps—beautiful but too refined, and on her advice, Avery ordered both other pairs, to have that comparison when she tried on the dress.

"I knew I could count on you for the best shoe advice." Avery laid her fingers on the dress one last time, then set the tablet aside. "So, things with you and Ry? All smoothed out?"

"There's nothing between me and Ryder, apparently. I haven't spoken to him since the day before yesterday."

"God. If I had to choose which one of you is more stubborn, I'd judge it a dead heat."

"I'm not being stubborn. I'm right here if he wants to talk to me."

"And he's right there if you want to talk to him." With a roll of her eyes, Avery jabbed a finger toward the door. "Don't you even want to know what he said to Jonathan's father, and vice versa?"

"It's not relevant." Even if it did drive her a little crazy. "Besides, you know. He'd have told Owen by now."

Avery hissed out a breath. "So instead of having an actual conversation with Ryder, you want to circle around to what he told Owen to what Owen told me?"

"Yes."

"But not stubborn," Avery added.

"Are you going to tell me Ryder had a right to go down there and confront Baxter Wickham without talking to me first?"

Heaving out a breath, Avery rose, got a soda from the fridge. This would take longer than she'd planned, and might be thirsty work.

"You grew up with a sister and a mom as well as a brother and a dad. Me? It was mostly me and my dad, and the surrogate family of the Montgomerys, which was three guys. I have more of a guy perspective about some stuff."

"Which means?"

"I think Ry did exactly what Ry's instincts told him to do—or his secondary instinct, because the first would've been to hunt Jonathan down and turn him into pulp. I like his first instinct, but you wouldn't. His second was civilized."

"Civilized?"

At Hope's appalled tone, Avery lifted her shoulders, spread her hands. "Sorry, that's my take. He drove all the way to D.C., and you should know he hates going down there. Ryder would consider the 270 corridor the seventh circle of Hell. Plus, he would've been pissed at losing a half a day's work. But he did that because nobody was going to screw with you that way and get away with it."

"But—"

"Relationships aren't always rational and balanced, Hope. They're human. And you're in a relationship with a guy who's wired to act rather than talk about it—discuss, debate, weigh alternative options. Harder for you because you're the talk and discuss and weigh-it type. You're not wrong, either of you. You're just dealing with different wiring."

Understanding her closest friend stood on the other side of that line, or at least straddled it, made for a tough swallow. But honesty meant more than lip service.

Usually.

"That's the problem, isn't it? We're too different."

"So are Owen and I. In fact, he's more like you; I'm more like Ry. But I'm not in love with Ryder. I'm not going to marry Ryder in the dress I just bought. I'm messy and impulsive and fly off quicker than most. But Owen doesn't try to change me."

"I'm not trying to change Ryder. That's not what I want to do," she amended when Avery just winged up her eyebrows. "It's my mess, Avery."

"Bullshit. I tied myself up over my mother with the same narrow logic. I was wrong."

"You think I'm wrong now."

"I think you and Ryder need to have a damn conversation instead of sulking. And yes, you are, too."

Despite herself, Hope laughed. "I like to think of it as being thoughtful. Well, damn it, tell me what Ryder said to Baxter Wickham and what Baxter said to Ryder."

"No." Avery rose, nodded firmly. "Ask Ryder."

Disagreement might be a tough swallow, but dissension lodged sticky in the throat. "Avery!"

"No. And I'm leaving now before I cave in. I love you, so I'm not going to help you evade something we both know you need to deal with for yourself. Maybe things won't work with you and Ryder, but the two of you should give each other the courtesy of some damn words."

Sincerely stunned, Hope stared after Avery as her friend snatched up her iPad, marched to the door, flipped the lock and sailed out.

"Well, damn it," she repeated.

Now she *had* to know what had been said or it would drive her crazy. And maybe Avery had a point, a half a point anyway. Still, she could hardly go to Ryder and ask. And she couldn't—wouldn't—apologize for having feelings and a point of view.

She might think about the situation as it stood, consider various solutions. But she wasn't just going to cave.

And that wasn't being stubborn or sulky.

"And so what if it is," she mumbled.

Restless and annoyed, she pulled out the bag of kitchen trash to take out to the shed. Once out, she pulled a few weeds, deadheaded her roses. And yes, she looked over toward Fit to see what was going on.

She didn't spot Ryder, which she told herself was just as well. She'd think about the best route out of this stalemate they were in.

Walking back, she started to let herself in The Lobby door, found it closed and locked when she *knew* she'd left it cracked open for easy reentry. With a shrug, she took her key out of her pocket. It slid in, refused to turn.

"Stop this," she muttered. "Let me back in."

The lever wouldn't budge.

Nor would it budge on the other door, or the second-floor access door.

"For God's sake! You're being ridiculous."

Hope stormed down the steps again. Fine, she'd just go get Avery's key. And if that failed, she'd call Carolee and ask her to come in early.

With a full head of steam, she started down the sidewalk beside the building, and stopped short a foot from Ryder as he came in her direction.

He took one long look at her face. "Problem?"

"No. Yes, damn it. She's locked me out."

"Carolee?"

"No, not Carolee. My key won't work on any of the doors back here."

He simply held out a hand for it, and taking it, walked around to the first door.

The key slid in, turned.

"Works now."

"I can see that."

"What did you do to piss her off?"

"I didn't do anything." She snatched her key out, started to step inside.

The fireplace came on with a whoosh of flame. Every light began to flash and blink. From where she stood, Hope heard the refrigerator door slam repeatedly.

"Looks like pissed off to me." Ryder nudged Hope aside.

The minute he stepped inside, all the activity stopped.

"Did this just start up?"

"Yes, just this minute. I don't know why she's upset. I've put a solid five hours in on the search over the last couple of nights."

"She's settled down now." He started to turn back to the door, and it started again.

He picked up the remote and again switched off the fire. "Cut it out!"

The answer was an audible click of the lock on the door.

"Maybe she's upset you haven't been around the last couple of days," Hope suggested.

Ryder set the remote down. "I got the impression the innkeeper didn't want me around."

"You got the wrong impression. I didn't like you doing something that involved me without talking to me."

"I didn't like seeing you get slapped." He shrugged. "You can't like everything."

"I'm not wrong to want you to talk to me."

"I'm not wrong to stand up for you."

She started to argue, realized she couldn't. And didn't want to. "Tell me I'm not wrong about wanting you to talk to me, and I'll tell you you're not wrong to stand up for me."

"Okay. You first."

Her laugh snuck through about the same time as his quick, cocky grin. "All right. You're not wrong."

"Neither are you. Are we finished with it?"

"No, we're not. I need to know you'll consider how I feel."

Frustration flashed back on his face. "Hope, I considered nothing but. I considered your hurt and your embarrassment. I wasn't going to let it slide."

"If you'd just talked to me first—"

"You wouldn't have talked me out of it. We'd've had the fight sooner than we had it, but I'd've still gone and said what I had to say."

"I wouldn't have talked you out of it," she agreed. "I would have tried, at first. Then I'd have gone with you."

He stopped, frowned. "You'd have gone down there?"

"Yes. In fact, before I knew you had, I'd calmed down enough to think it through. I was going to handle it by letter—a letter listing the details—to Baxter Wickham. Because I realized I couldn't, and shouldn't, let it slide either."

"Face-to-face is better. But I didn't consider that part—the part where you'd have wanted to go. You were crying."

"I stopped. I needed to cry, then I stopped, and I started to think. There were things I needed to say, and I intended to write them down. I admit I would have done several drafts, taken a few days to perfect the tone and language."

"I bet."

"But if you'd told me, and I'd realized I couldn't talk you out of going, I'd have gone, Ryder. I'd have had that face-to-face."

"Okay." His shoulders relaxed as he nodded. "Okay. I can say I'm sorry I cheated you out of that."

"I'm sorry I didn't appreciate you standing up for me the way I should have."

"Good enough. Now are we done with it?"

"No."

"Oh, man."

"I'll get you a cold drink, then you'll tell me what you said to Baxter, and what he said to you. Reverse the situation. You know damn well you'd want to know."

"You want me to replay the back-and-forth?"

"I absolutely do."

"Crap." Details, he thought. Women always wanted them. "Okay, but if I do, I want makeup sex."

She got him a cold Coke from the refrigerator, smiled. "That's a deal."

He could take the time, he calculated as he dropped down on a stool. It felt good to get off his feet for five minutes. It felt good to look at her, up close, to catch her scent, to hear her voice. He could tell her about the deal with Wickham. He didn't see why he needed to tell her they'd run into each other right outside because he'd dropped what he'd been doing with the intention of coming just where he'd ended up—with her—and having it out.

He'd had enough, that's all, enough of giving her time to cool off and the space to do it in. Enough of thinking about her all the god-damn time to the point he'd lost sleep.

He never lost sleep over a woman.

And he'd had enough of trying to figure out what the hell she wanted him to do since his ever-reliable flower gambit had gone down in flames.

So he owed Lizzy a favor for maneuvering things so he was where he wanted to be. Better than, he admitted, because he was sitting down with a cold Coke and Hope was sitting beside him, waiting. Watching.

And there was a bout of makeup sex in his future.

"Well?" she said at length.

"I'm thinking. How long do you figure before the blonde blasts the asshole she married, tossing you in his face?"

"I don't know her that well. Probably not long," Hope admitted.

"And being a gutless asshole, how long would it take him to turn it around so you made the moves, came onto him, that kind of thing."

"Immediately."

"Yeah, I figured. You still have contacts down there, people in the business, or people who like to travel, to stay in nice places, unique places."

"Yes, I do. In your scenario, to protect themselves from someone who doesn't even give a damn, and to protect their pride, they might try to damage my reputation. They might spread lies and gossip about pitiful, scheming Hope who slept her way in and out of a job, and now into another."

"Not good for business."

"So, you were thinking about business."

"It's a factor." Maybe minuscule in the big picture, but a factor. "A bigger one is they—neither of them—deserve any shot of getting off easy. Kicking his ass? Owen's always worried about arrests for assault and criminal trials."

"It's a factor," she said dryly.

"But to my way of thinking, it's mostly worth it, until you think about how bruises and broken bones heal. And some people knee-jerk toward feeling bad for the ass that's been kicked, no matter how it's earned. So I liked the idea of longer-term benefits. The asshole's dickless. Plus, you take one good look at him, and the one he married, you can see what drives them is money and show and status. You've got to have money and opportunities for the show and the status. Old man Wickham's still running things, so he's the power source. He could cut off the money—or channels leading to it, and shut down opportunities."

She'd come to all the same conclusions, but could admit—a little shamefully now—she hadn't given Ryder credit for doing the same. "You thought of all this?"

"It's a long freaking drive down there in a lot of freaking traffic. Plenty of time to work it out. Anyway. It's a good-looking hotel."

"Yes, it is."

"I could see you there."

"Could you?"

"Suits you, all the shine of it."

"It did. Once."

He studied her in silence a moment. "I guess you could say I looked a little out of place, going straight from the job. They were polite, I'll give them that, and probably would've politely booted me out if I hadn't suggested pending charges of assault if Wickham didn't see me."

"Assault?"

"She slapped you."

"Yes, but—"

"It's fucking assault. If I'd've punched the asshole, you can take it to the bank there'd have been cops and lawyers. Maybe we don't handle things around here by running to cops and lawyers over a slap or punch, but I figured those kind do. Owen's got that right."

"You did a lot of thinking in freaking traffic."

"It's that or buy a gun and shoot somebody. He had his security guy bring me up to his office."

"Jerald?"

"Yeah, that's what Wickham called him. Once I started laying it out, Wickham gave Jerald the signal to step out. I figured it was going to take a while, a lot of moves, countermoves, defense, offense. But it didn't, not really."

"What did you tell him, Ryder?"

"That Jonathan came here, uninvited, unexpected, and unwelcome, claimed his father had an offer to make you if you came back to work. And that Jonathan made one of his own, if you'd hook up with him again. And that you weren't interested. He wasn't happy to hear it, Wickham. That's when I got the sense he had some guilt where you were concerned. Some regrets. But when I got to the second act, told him about the blonde coming here—that's when he sent security out of the room," Ryder remembered.

"I imagine so," Hope concurred.

"He got the picture, and we came to terms."

"What terms?"

"He makes sure they leave you the hell alone, and that includes spreading lies. Then we're square. Either of them comes here, takes any kind of hit at you, they'll pay for it. That's it."

"That's it?"

"Yeah. He gave me a card with some private number on it. Asked if I'd let him know if either of them didn't hold the deal."

"Wait." Stupefied, she held up a hand. "Baxter Wickham gave you his private number?"

"Yeah, so? He's not God. He's just some guy, an embarrassed and pissed-off guy who's got an asshole for a son. Now it's done, like I said." He took a long swallow because, *Jesus*, he felt like he'd been talking straight for an hour. "You're the one big on communicating, expressing. Talk, talk, talk. Maybe you should've done some communicating, expressing, talking to him when the asshole showed up here. The old man strikes me as a pretty reasonable guy."

*Reasonable* wasn't the word most used to describe Baxter Wickham, Hope thought. Powerful, private, occasionally pugnacious. "He was my employer for a long time. And I believed he'd be my father-in-law. But you're right. I should've gone to him. I guess I was still carrying some hurt and anger in that area—plus, blood's thicker."

"Maybe, and maybe he'd have shrugged off his son's offer. You were free to say yes or no. But the daughter-in-law bit? No. The dickless asshole may not be able to keep her in line, but Wickham will."

"It shouldn't have gotten this far. And it should never have caused trouble between you and me. I'm sorry it did."

"Makeup sex ought to balance it out."

When she laughed, he reached out without thinking, stroked his fingers down her cheek in a way that stilled the laughter.

"I missed your face," he told her.

Moved, she closed her hand around his wrist. "I missed yours."

He rose, smooth and quick, lifting her from the stool, wrapping her against him. She expected urgency and demand, a prelude to that makeup sex. Instead, the kiss floated over her senses, dreamy and sweet. It shimmered over her heart, then into it before she understood, before she could prepare.

Even when he drew away it held there, beating like a pulse inside her.

His thumb brushed over her cheekbone. Calloused skin; a gentle stroke. "I'll pick up some food and be back later."

"All right. I have—"

"Guests. I know. I keep up. I'll wait." His eyes, green and searching, stayed on hers another moment. "We'll wait," he amended. "D.A. missed you, too."

He walked out, left her weak and wondering.

Is this what she'd thought she'd felt for Jonathan? Stupid, stupid to have mistaken contentment, habit, what had proven to be a foolish affection and loyalty for this overwhelming, undermining, dazzling emotion.

She had to sit, wait to get her breath back, wait for her knees to stop trembling. She hadn't understood, had *never* understood love caused such a staggering physical reaction. She felt feverish, unsteady, and, she had to admit as she closed her eyes, frightened.

She had a *plan*. Falling in love hadn't been part of it.

"Adjust," she ordered herself, and laid her cheek on the cool granite. "Adjust."

Some people never felt what she felt now. Right at the moment she didn't know whether to envy or pity them. But realities had to be faced. She was in love with Ryder Montgomery.

She just had to figure out what the hell to do about it.

"Is this what you felt?" Hope stayed where she was, breathing in honeysuckle, struggling to find her balance. "No wonder you've waited. What else could you do? He loved you, too. You knew. You didn't wonder or worry or doubt. If you'd wait, if you could, so could he. I'll find him."

*Billy.*

Hope heard the joy in the name, the *life* in it.

*Ryder.*

"Yeah." On a long breath, she pushed herself up to sit again. "It looks that way. It looks as if I started moving here, to this, from that first minute. Dizzy, hot, overwhelmed, dazzled, scared. Just like now. It shouldn't be, but it is. It shouldn't have been for you either, considering. It must run in the family."

*Billy. Ryder.*

"And I'll bet Billy had that same cocky nature. It shouldn't be so appealing. Swept you off your feet. I can see it. I can see it now. It didn't matter who your father was, what your station was. He loved you. He saw you, and that was all that mattered. I wonder what that's like. To have someone so strong and confident see you, look at you, and you're all that matters."

She sighed now, got to her feet. "I can't think about that right now. I can't expect that. I need to finish my list, and I should bake some muffins before the guests arrive."

The cupboard door where she kept her baking supplies flew open, slammed shut.

"There's no reason to be annoyed with me. Billy loved you, I understand. He wanted to marry you. Ryder doesn't . . ."

She stepped back instinctively as the door slammed again. She heard the names clearly.

*Billy. Ryder.*

"All right, Eliza. Enough. If I say I wished Ryder felt for me what Billy did for you, will you be satisfied? But Billy and Ryder aren't . . ."

She stopped, braced a hand on the counter as it sprang up in her. "Oh God, is that it? Was it always that simple. Billy Ryder? Joseph William Ryder. Is that it? Is that his name?"

The lights came on in a brilliant glow, pulsed like a heartbeat.

"Billy Ryder. Yours, and apparently mine. His ancestor? Could that be? His, like you're mine. Wait."

She grabbed the kitchen phone, punched in Ryder's cell.

"What?"

She ignored the automatic annoyance. He hated being interrupted, but that was too damn bad. "Ryder's a family name, isn't it?"

"Huh? Jesus. So what?"

She pitched her voice up, compensating for the hammering on his end. "It's your mother's maiden name? Her family name?"

"Yeah, and so what?"

"Billy. It was his family name, too. He's Joseph William Ryder."

"Son of a bitch."

"Do you recognize the name? Is it familiar?"

"Why would it be? He was dead a couple hundred years before I was born. Ask my mother. Ask Carolee. Call Owen. Any one of them would know more than I do."

"All right. Thanks."

"Congratulations."

"I haven't found him yet. But yeah, it's worth a high five. I'll talk to you later."

She hung up before he could, immediately dialed Carolee. No time to bake muffins, she decided. She'd get something from the bakery instead.

Whatever time she had to spare, she'd spend looking for Joseph William Ryder.

# CHAPTER EIGHTEEN

I T TOOK SOME TIME AND SCHEDULE SHUFFLING BEFORE
everyone could get together at one time, in one place. At Justine's
request, they met in her home. There, she felt, everyone could talk
and speculate freely.

And if she had everyone who mattered to her most under one roof,
they might as well make a party out of it.

She knew her men, so she marinated flank steaks, picked up corn
at her favorite roadside stand, harvested tomatoes and peppers fresh
from her garden.

"You don't have to fuss so much." Willy B sat at the counter, snapping beans, his contribution from his own little garden. His pug curled
devotedly under his stool.

"It feels good to fuss some. This summer's flown by, and we've
hardly managed to all get together like this. And it keeps my mind
settled." She sprinkled paprika on a platter of eggs she'd deviled—one
of Owen's favorites. "When I think about it all, Willy B, how I just

had to have that inn, felt that pull in my heart for it. Now it turns out there's this connection. Billy Ryder. All this time."

She sighed. "I never asked questions about my people, or not many. Never bothered to find out much at all."

"You lived your life, Justine. You had Tommy and your boys, and Carolee."

"I know it, and it's always been about the now and the next for me. And still, aren't I the one for buying up these old places? So there's something. Anyway, Carolee doesn't know any more than I do. Daddy, either. When we find out whatever we find, I'm going to make more of an effort to learn about who came before me. You looked into yours. I remember."

"It was kind of interesting to find out." He paused his snapping to scratch through his red beard. "Where they came from in Scotland, how they came here—those who did. And I thought Avery should know. Maybe I thought she didn't have much on her mama's side, so she should have as much as I could give her on mine."

"You're the best daddy there is. Nobody could've done better."

"Well, I had the best girl to work with." He smiled over the beans, then shifted, cleared his throat. "Justine, you don't want to get married or anything, do you?"

"Why, Willy B MacTavish." She fluttered her lashes. The question may have come out of left field, but she knew how to catch. "That's the most romantic proposal ever uttered."

"Oh now, Justine."

She laughed, the sound full of amused affection. "What makes you ask?"

"I don't know, exactly. All this talk about families, I guess, and your boy, my girl—wedding talk. You're here alone, and don't give me that look. I know you can take care of yourself, and whatever else needs it. But we've been . . . you know, for a while now."

"I like 'you know.' You're the sweetest man I know, and if I wanted or needed marriage, I wouldn't look at anyone else. We're good as we are, aren't we, Willy B?"

As answer, he took her hand. "You mean the world to me, Justine. I just want you to know it."

"I do know it, and I'm grateful you'd ask. Maybe, down the road some, I'll ask you."

"Oh now, Justine." He pinked up at the idea, made her laugh again as she came around the counter to hug him hard. "I love you to pieces, Willy B." She eased back enough to plant her lips on his.

And Ryder walked in, D.A. behind him.

"Man." He gave them a wide berth, went straight to the refrigerator for a beer. "Man," he said again and popped the top.

Tyrone leaped up, shivered a little as D.A. walked over to sniff him.

"Oh now, Tyrone, D.A. won't hurt you." But Willy B got off the stool, crouched down to soothe the puppy and scratch D.A.'s ears.

"Where's Hope?" Justine asked him.

"She had stuff. She'll be here." Lightning quick—a man had to be quick in his mother's kitchen—he snagged a deviled egg.

"Has she had any more trouble from down in the city?"

"No, and I don't see that happening. Book's closed."

"Good. Go on and let those dogs outside now. Tyrone's fine with Finch and Cus. He'll be fine with D.A. before long."

Ryder obeyed, nudging the still reluctant pug out with the toe of his boot. "Beckett and his brood just pulled up. Dogs, too."

"Oh, well, maybe I should—"

"Willy B, you let that pug socialize," Justine ordered. "You're going to make a neurotic out of him otherwise."

"Everybody's bigger than he is."

"And you're bigger than anybody else. You don't hurt anyone." She opened a cupboard, took out three bubble-shooting guns she'd already loaded, and took them out to the boys.

Seconds later Clare came in with a bowl.

"Whatcha got?" Ryder asked as he took it from her. "Potato salad? You're my favorite sister-in-law."

"I'm your only, but not for much longer. Avery and Owen are right behind us." She stepped over to kiss Willy B's cheek.

"You sit right down here, get off your feet."

"I'll do that, and snap the rest of these beans."

"Okay then. I'm going to go out and . . ."

Clare lifted her eyebrows as Willy B hurried out the door.

"He's worried the other dogs will traumatize that bug-eyed rat of his."

"They won't, and Tyrone is adorable."

"He looks like a dog from Mars."

"Maybe a little." She snapped beans while boys shouted, dogs barked. Male laughter rolled over it all. "Go on outside. You know you want to. I'm fine here. It's like a small sanity break."

"If you say so."

He did want to go out, especially since he'd stowed the old Super Soaker in the shed for just such an occasion.

When Hope pulled in, a war raged. Kids, dogs, grown men, all soaked to the skin, battled with a variety of water shooting weapons.

She eyed the combatants warily. She could probably trust the boys not to aim in her direction. The dogs simply had to be avoided. But she knew very well grown men could rarely resist a fresh target.

She got out carefully, using the car door as a shield as she reached in the back.

And caught the gleam in Ryder's eye through his dripping hair.

"I have pies!" she called out. "If I get wet, the pies get wet. Think about it."

He lowered his weapon. "What kind—" And, vulnerable, took a shot in the back from the youngest water warrior.

"I got you good!" Murphy shouted, then screamed in hysterical delight as Ryder gave chase.

Hope took advantage of the distraction, and her cherry pie shield, to make a beeline for the house.

"Everyone out there's soaked," Hope announced, then spotted Avery, wineglass in hand, a man's work shirt draped to her knees. "Casualty?"

"I gave as good as I got, but they ganged up on me. Men can't be trusted."

"Now everybody's here." Justine gave Hope a quick hug. "Willy B, why don't you start the grill?"

"Well . . ." The pug curled in his lap, Willy B gave the door a dubious look.

"Oh, I'll fix that. Hope, get yourself a drink." So saying, Justine walked out. Curious, Hope walked over, looked out. Watched Justine turn on her garden hose.

She fired without warning or mercy as cries of *Mom!* and *Gran!* echoed.

"Time for a truce. Y'all dig up some dry clothes and clean up. We're eating in a half hour or so."

WARDROBE MIGHT HAVE leaned toward eccentric, but the food struck a perfect note. There was restaurant talk as Avery was counting down in days now. Construction talk, town talk, baby talk, and wedding talk.

Plates cleared, the kids and dogs raced back for the yard restricted by female decree to bubbles and balls.

"Now then." Justine leaned back. "I'll let you know where things stand on my end. There's an old family Bible." She patted her sister's hand. "Carolee managed to track it down to our uncle. Our father's brother Henry. Uncle Hank. When my daddy's daddy passed, Uncle Hank and his wife loaded up. Some people are just that way. God knows what he wanted with all that stuff, but he filled a damn U-Haul.

Twice. And the Bible was in there. It goes back a ways so if Billy's ours, he'd be listed. All we have to do is get it back."

"He says we can borrow it," Carolee put in. "Once he finds it. Claims it's stored, which probably means it's buried somewhere in the piles."

"He won't be in any rush to dig it out," Justine continued. "But I talked to my cousin, his daughter. We always got along, and she'll nag at him for me. Meanwhile, he doesn't remember a Joseph William Ryder; my father doesn't either. But Daddy thinks he heard stories from his grandfather about a couple of his uncles fighting in the Civil War, and one of them, he thinks, died at Antietam. But I can't swear that's a fact. It might just be Daddy's remembering it that way because I asked that way."

"It's a start," Hope said. A frustratingly slow one. "I can't find any Joseph William Ryder listed as buried at the National Cemetery."

"I've got nothing so far," Owen added. "But there's still a lot to go through."

"Daddy said he knows there was an old Civil War bayonet, and some other things—shells, a uniform cap. Even old cannonballs," Carolee added. "What he didn't know is if they came down in the family or if they just got dug up in the farming. A lot of old stuff gets dug up."

"I barely remember the farm," Justine told them. "It got sold off before you boys were born. Houses planted on it now, and the Park Service bought some of it. But Daddy said—and this he was sure of—there was a little family cemetery."

Hope straightened. "On the farm?"

"People buried their own in the country sometimes rather than in churchyards or cemeteries. He said it was down an old, rutted lane, backed by some trees. It might still be there."

"I can find out," Owen said. "If they exhumed, it takes paperwork to move graves."

"On the old Ryder farm." Frowning, Ryder considered his beer. "There's a pond. A little one."

"Daddy said they had a little swimming hole. How do you know that?"

"I dated a girl who lived in one of the houses they put up. There's a small cemetery, an old one. It's got a low stone wall around it, and a plaque. The Park Service type. I didn't pay much attention. I was more focused on trying to get her naked and into the pond."

"Why didn't you say so before?" his mother demanded.

"I don't usually tell you about girls I'm trying to get naked." And he smiled at her. "Mom, I was like sixteen. She was the first girl I took around after I got my license. What the hell was her name? Angela— Bowers, Boson—something. I didn't get her naked, so it didn't stick. And I didn't think of any of it until now. I do remember thinking, shit, some of those dead people are relatives, then it was back to hoping for naked."

"A guy's attention span's short at sixteen," Beckett put in. "Except for naked girls."

"It's still there," Justine remembered. "We should've known that. It's disrespectful we didn't, Carolee."

"Daddy just wanted off the farm," Carolee reminded her. "He wanted away from everything to do with farming. And he and Grandpa were at odds over that for so long. It's no wonder we didn't know."

"We know now," Owen reminded them. "We'll go take a look."

"All right." Justine rose. "Let's corral the kids and dogs."

"What?" Owen blinked at her. "You want to go now?"

"What's wrong with now?"

"The sun's going to set before long, and—"

"Then we shouldn't waste time."

"If we wait until tomorrow, I can go, take a look, let you know what—"

"Why are you wasting your breath?" Ryder asked him.

After a rush, a pause for debates, much excitement from the boys on what promised to be an adventure, they piled in various cars and trucks. One debate involved dogs, and in the end, they left Ben and Yoda with Cus and Finch—cutting the numbers.

Hope found herself riding shotgun in Ryder's truck, D.A. sprawled on the seat between them.

"Tomorrow would've been more sensible," Hope commented.

"None of this is about sense."

"No, it's not. And I'm glad we're going tonight. He may not be there, or the headstones may have been damaged. It may never have been marked."

"Good. Keep up that positive thinking."

"Just preparing for possibilities."

"There's a possibility you'll find what you're after."

"I guess I'm a little nervous that we won't find anything, and a little nervous that we will."

He took one hand off the wheel, reached over to take one of hers in a gesture that surprised her heart into thudding. "Stop, and relax."

Because the abrupt order struck more in line with what she was used to, she did just that.

"This was all farmland," he told her as he turned onto a winding road with homes spaced wide enough for some decent elbow room, for sloping lawns, shady trees.

"It must've been beautiful. All fields and rolling hills."

"People have to live somewhere. And they didn't crowd them in, so that's something. We got some work out here during the boom. People adding on, remodeling."

She leaned forward. "Is that—"

"Yeah, the old Ryder farmhouse. The developer was smart enough not to tear it down, to put some money into it—and I bet he got plenty out of it."

"It's beautiful, the stonework, the gingerbread. And it's big. Pretty gardens and trees. They must've added on that solarium, but it's well done. It's a nice spot." She looked at him as they drove past, turned again. "Have you ever been inside?"

"We did some work in it about three years ago. Updated the kitchen, two baths, added on a bonus room over the garage. And that sunroom you liked."

"How did it feel?"

"At the time? Like a job. A good one. Now?" He shrugged. "I guess I get what Mom was talking about. Maybe we should've paid more attention to this part of us, had more respect for it. My grandfather pretty much hated the farm, and it was clear he didn't get along with his old man, so I never thought much of it."

He turned yet again, onto a narrow gravel lane.

"Is this private property?"

"Maybe. Might be Park Service. We'll deal with it if we have to."

"They fought here? North and South, boys and men."

"All over hell and back," Ryder confirmed. "See there?"

She saw the little pond he'd spoken of, its water dark and deep in the lowering light. Cattails crowded around it with their brown velvet heads, and ferns green with summer formed a verdant carpet.

Beyond it, before the trees thickened, stood a low stone wall. The sort, she thought, Billy Ryder might have built. Headstones tilted in its center. Hope counted sixteen—small markers, pocked by time and weather, some tipped in the rough ground.

"It looks lonely. Sad and lonely."

"I don't think dead's a party."

He parked, got out with the dog scrambling behind him. When Hope simply sat, he walked around, opened her door as the rest of the family convoy pulled up.

"He's here or he's not. Either way, we are."

She nodded, stepped out beside him.

It felt less lonely with people, with voices. With boys running and dogs sniffing. Still, she felt unsteady enough to reach for Ryder's hand, to be grateful when he linked his fingers with hers.

More than sixteen, she realized as they approached. Some of the markers were hardly more than a stone set flush with the ground.

Not all had names, or if they had once, time had erased them. But she read those she could. Mary Margaret Ryder. Daniel Edward Ryder. And there a tiny one, marking the grave of Susan—just Susan, who'd died in 1853 at the tender age of two months.

Someone tended to the grass here, she mused, so it didn't grow wild. Still, there was that sense of wild. To offset the infant, she found the grave of Catherine Foster Ryder, who'd lived from 1781 to 1874.

"Ninety-three," Justine murmured beside her. "A good, long life. I wish I knew who she was to me."

"You'll get the Bible, then you'll know."

"How come they can't stay at the inn like Lizzy?" Murphy asked her. "How come they have to stay here?"

"Lizzy's special, I guess." Justine lifted him up, pressed her face to his throat as Hope turned.

She'd thought Ryder stood beside her, but saw now he'd walked off, to the right, stood alone by a trio of graves.

She walked toward him, realized her heart began to thud as she did.

"He's the middle one."

"What?" Her hand trembled as she reached out for his again.

"He was born last, died second. They were brothers."

"How can you—I can't make out the names."

"Light's going," he said as she dropped down to her knees to peer closer.

"Oh God. Billy Ryder. They didn't put his formal name on his grave. Just Billy. March 14, 1843, to September 17, 1862."

"And Joshua, earlier that same year. Charlie, twenty-two years after. Three brothers."

"It's Billy." It was all she could think at first. Here. They'd found him. "Is she here?" Hope's head came up. "How could she be here?"

"It's not her." Understanding, Ryder gestured. "Honeysuckle. It's about buried the wall behind these graves."

He turned, looked at his mother. As their eyes met, he didn't have to call out to her, to speak. Hers filled as she started toward him.

"You found him."

"Time's dulled the carving, but you can make out the name. He died the same year as Lizzy. The same month, within the same day."

Owen stepped to his mother, slipped an arm around her waist, kept Avery's hand in his. Then Beckett with Clare, and the boys miraculously quiet. And Willy B, patting Carolee's back when she let out a little sob.

The sun slid into twilight, and the air stirred the thick scent of honeysuckle.

Hope traced the name with her finger, then laid it against her heart.

"We'll bring flowers next time." Justine leaned her head against Owen's arm, touched Beckett's, touched Ryder's. "It's time we remembered them. We're here because they were, so it's time we remembered them."

On impulse, Ryder took out his pocketknife, cut through honey-suckle vines. He laid it down.

"That's something anyway."

Inexpressibly moved by the simple gesture, Hope rose, took his face in her hands. "That's perfect," she said, and kissed him.

"It's cooling off. You're going to get cold," Beckett told Clare. "I'm going to swing by, pick up the dogs, take Clare and the boys home."

"We need to tell her." Clare looked at Hope. "I feel like we should all be there when you tell her."

"It can wait until tomorrow. You get pale when you're tired."

Beckett trailed a finger down her cheek. "And you're pale. It can wait until tomorrow."

"Maybe that's better anyway." Avery lifted her hands. "We can think about how to tell her. I mean we found him, here he is. But what does that mean? It seems almost cruel to tell her he's buried out here, miles away from where she is."

"In the morning," Justine agreed. "Let's say about nine. Yes, it interrupts your day," she said to Ryder before he could speak. "But it's before Clare and Avery open, before Hope and Carolee have any-one checking in."

"Nine's fine."

"Will you come, Willy B?" She turned to the big man with the little dog in his arms. "Can you take the time?"

"If you want me, Justine, I can be there."

"I'd appreciate it. I want to know which of these is their mama. She lost two of her sons, maybe the third, too, before she died. That's a cruel thing." Justine's voice thickened before she breathed deep to steady it. "I want to know her name and remember her."

"It's getting dark." Willy B patted her arm, stroked it. "Let me take you home now, Justine."

"All right. Let's all go home."

But Ryder lingered as the others started away. He made himself step back from the trio of graves when Hope touched his arm.

"Are you all right?"

"Yeah. I don't know. It's weird."

"That there are three of them. Like you and Owen and Beckett?"

"I don't know," he repeated. "It hits home, I guess. He's my moth-er's. He's ours. She's yours. I've got his name—the last of it for my first. And—" He shook his head as he wanted to shake this *feeling* away. "Let's go."

"What? And what?" she insisted as he drew her away.

"Nothing. It's just weird, like I said."

He didn't tell her he'd known, the minute he'd stepped inside the low stone wall, where to find Billy. He'd known where to walk, what he'd find.

Imagining things, he told himself as they got back in his truck. Just that graveyard at dusk deal.

But he'd known something, felt something still, like a shiver just under the skin. As he drove away, his gaze shifted to the rearview mirror. He took another long look at the stone wall, the markers and the madly thriving honeysuckle.

Then he turned his eyes to the road ahead.

# CHAPTER NINETEEN

H E KNEW THIS LAND, THE RISE AND FALL OF IT, THE *spread of the fields, the rough shoulders of rock that jutted out. He knew the stone walls that kept the fat cows grazing on the green. His hands had helped build some of them, with his uncle's patient tutelage to guide him.*

*Though he'd traveled some distance from this land, its rise and fall, he'd always planned to come back to it. To make his home near some bend in the creek that ran over rocks and cooled its water under the shade of the woods.*

*He loved this land as he'd loved no other his feet had trod upon.*

*But today on this September morning, it was a landscape of hell. Today, his sweat soiled his uniform and the ground beneath him. His sweat, but not his blood. Not yet.*

*Today he fought, and lived as he had on other days since some deep-seated need drove him to enlist. And today, he wished with all of his heart, all of his soul, that he had carved out that need and crushed it under his boot.*

*He'd thought he'd find honor, excitement, even adventure. Instead he'd found despair, terror, misery, and questions he couldn't begin to answer.*

*The sky that had dawned beautiful and blue turned to a dirty haze under the sooty smoke of cannon fire. Mini-balls sang on their vicious journey, ending in a crescendo of flying earth, destroyed flesh.*

*Oh, what an insult to the body and soul was war.*

*The sound of men's screams assaulted his ears, his guts, until he heard little else, deaf even to the blast of cannon, the endless screech of shell, the hail-on-tin-roof patter of bullets.*

*He lay a moment, fighting to chase his breath that seemed just out of his reach. The blood on his uniform had been inside the friend he'd made on the march—George, a blacksmith's apprentice, a jokester with hair the color of cornsilk and eyes as blue and happy as summer.*

*Now the cornsilk ran red, and those eyes stared out of his ruined face.*

*He knew this land, Billy thought again as his ears rang and his heart beat like the battle drums. The quiet road that wound through it divided the Piper and Roulette farms. His parents were friendly with the Pipers.*

*He wondered where they were now, now that this meandering border sunken into that rolling land served as a line of blood and death.*

*Hill's Rebels dug into that sunken road, and they used that concealed position to blast off murderous volleys, burning through the advancing troops like a lighted match on dust-dry brush. In that first volley, a musket shell had torn away half of George's face, and laid low the good Lord knew how many more.*

*Artillery thundered, shook the ground.*

*It seemed like hours he lay there, staring through the smoke to the blue of the sky, listening to screams, moans, shouts, and the endless, incessant, world-filling clatter of gun and cannon.*

*Minutes only in reality. Only minutes to breathe, to understand his friend was dead and himself alive by inches.*

*His hand trembled as he reached inside his uniform, carefully took out the photograph. Eliza. Lizzy. His Lizzy with hair like sunlight and a smile that opened his heart. She loved him, despite all. She waited for him, and when this hell was over, they'd marry. He'd build her a house—not so very far from where he lay now. But the house would live with love and joy, with the laughter of their children.*

*When this hell was over, he'd go back for her. He'd had one letter, and only one. Smuggled out of her house, to his mother, and passed on to him. He'd read her despair at being locked in on the night they'd planned to elope, and her unwavering faith that they would find each other again.*

*He'd written her only the night before, carefully forming the words while restless in camp. He'd find a way to get the letter to her. No man could live through hell and not believe in heaven.*

*He'd have his with Eliza. They'd have forever.*

*He heard the shouted orders to regroup, to advance again on that damned sunken road. He closed his eyes, pressed his lips to the image of Eliza, then slipped her carefully away again. Safe, he promised himself. Safe against his heart.*

*He got to his feet. Breathed, breathed. He would do his duty to his country, trust in God, and find his way back to Lizzy.*

*He charged again, the murderous hail of bullets flying from both sides.*

*He lived again as bodies, torn and rent, littered the once quiet farmland. Hours passed like years—and somehow like minutes. Morning into afternoon. He knew by the sun he'd lived another morning. He never wavered in duty, shouldered beside others who'd vowed to serve.*

*He moved forward, climbing fences, through an apple orchard where windfalls scattered over the ground and bees half-drunk buzzed over them. And on the rise looked down at the men in that old road. Finally the high ground served, and they ripped through a gap. He stood near the bend of the road, looked down into horror.*

*So many dead. It seemed impossible; it seemed obscene. They lay stacked on each other like cordwood, and still those who survived fired, fired, determined to hold that bloody ground.*

*For what? For what? For what? he wondered in some grieving part of his brain, but he heard the order to fire and obeyed. He thought of George, and obeyed. Robbing another mother of her son, another woman of her love.*

*Taking another life that, like him, only wanted home.*

*And he thought of Lizzy, pressed against his heart. Lizzy who loved him, despite all. Who waited for him.*

*He thought of his mother weeping over his brother Joshua, dead at Shiloh.*

*He couldn't fire again, could not stop one more heart, drive one more mother to weeping. This was slaughter, he thought. Hundreds dead and hundreds more to die. Farmers and masons and blacksmiths and shopkeepers. Why didn't they surrender? Why would they fight and die in that depressed earth surrounded by their dead brothers?*

*Was this honor? Was this duty? Was this the answer? Exhausted, heartbroken, sickened at the carnage below, he lowered his weapon.*

*He didn't feel the first shell punch into him, or the second. He only felt suddenly and terribly cold, and found himself once more on the ground, looking up at the sky.*

*He thought clouds had rolled over the sun. Everything grayed and flattened. And all the noise, all the hell of it dimmed into an almost peaceful quiet.*

*Was it over? At last, was it over?*

*He reached a hand inside his uniform for Lizzy, drew her photograph out. Stared, stared as blood smeared over her beautiful face.*

*Then he knew.*

*He knew.*

*Pain came in a sudden, shocking flood as blood streamed out of his wounds. He cried out against it, cried out again in a sorrow too deep to bear.*

*He would never build her a pretty stone house near the singing creek with honeysuckle growing wild and wild as he'd promised her. They would never fill that house with love, with children.*

*He had done his duty, and lost his life. He tried to kiss her face one last time, but the photograph fluttered out of his numb fingers.*

*He accepted his death, he had sworn an oath. But he had sworn one to Lizzy as well. He could not accept that he would never see her again, or touch her.*

*He murmured her name as the breath and the blood ran out of him.*

*He thought—his last thought—he heard her call to him. He thought he saw her, her face pale, wet with sweat, her eyes glazed as if with fever. She spoke his name. He spoke hers.*

*Joseph William Ryder, known as Billy to all who loved him, died on the bend of the road above the sunken ground that came to be known as Bloody Lane.*

RYDER WOKE COLD to the bone, with his throat burning dry and his heart at a gallop. Beside the bed, D.A. shoved his nose against Ryder's hand, let out a nervous whine.

"It's okay," he murmured. "I'm okay."

But in fact he didn't know what the hell he was.

Everybody has dreams, he told himself. Good ones, bad ones, weird ones, wet ones.

So he'd dreamed about Billy Ryder. They'd just found the guy's grave. It wasn't such a stretch to dream about him, about dying at Antietam.

A soldier who dies on September 17, 1862? Odds were pretty damn good he'd bought it on the battlefield on that bloodiest day of the war.

Billy Ryder had been on his mind, that's all.

And that was bullshit. Stop being an idiot, he ordered himself.

He'd felt something at that grave site, and he felt it now. Something off, something he couldn't quite get a grasp on.

Sleep hadn't helped, obviously. He glanced at the clock, saw it was still shy of five. He wasn't going to get any more sleep, and wasn't sure he wanted to risk it anyway.

The dream, vivid as life—and death—left him unsteady.

He'd stood on that battlefield. He'd walked the sunken road of Bloody Lane. And though he considered himself a practical, grounded man, he'd felt the pull of the place, the power of it. He'd read books on Antietam—he lived here, after all. He'd studied it in school, taken visiting friends and relations on the tour.

But until tonight he'd never imagined it—no, he corrected, *felt* it so vividly.

The smells of it, the sounds. Stinging smoke, fresh blood, burned flesh, the raging storm of artillery fire that filled the world above the cries of dying men.

If he'd been a fanciful man he'd have said through the dream he'd lived in it, and died in it.

As Billy Ryder had.

Put it away, he told himself. Beside him Hope stirred a little, and the warmth of her layered over that cold he couldn't quite shake. He thought about just rolling over, onto her, clearing his mind with that slim, soft body.

He considered the hour, deemed it pretty damn unfair to wake her before dawn, even though he figured he could make it worth her while.

He rolled out of bed instead, then just walked to the glass doors, pulled them open and stepped out on the bedroom deck.

Maybe he just needed some air.

He liked the quiet of this hour, and the way the slice of moon, not quite finished with the night, showed itself through the trees. He wished fleetingly that he'd gotten water before he'd come out, then just stood pulling in the peace.

All the work, stress, frustrations of the job were worth it for moments like this. Moments of utter quiet and stillness before night ended and day began. Soon, the sun would blur the sky to the east with red, the birds would wake chattering, and the cycle would start again.

He liked the cycle fine, he thought, absently lowering a hand to D.A.'s head when the dog leaned on his leg. He had what he wanted. Good work, a good place, family who not only mattered but who understood him, and if he had to be sentimental, loved him anyway.

He couldn't ask for better. Then why, he wondered, did it feel as if something hadn't quite clicked into place? That something hung up, just slightly out of alignment, and all he had to do was turn it a bit, and it would fall just where it should be.

"What's wrong?"

He turned, saw Hope. Something wanted to click, wanted to shift and fall.

"Ryder?" She stepped out, tying the short little robe he wished she hadn't bothered with.

"Nothing. I'm awake, that's all."

"It's early, even for you." She moved to him, laid her hands on the deck rail as he did. "Listen to the quiet. Country quiet, country dark. You can forget in all the busyness that there are times and places so wonderfully still."

Since he'd been thinking nearly the same, he looked down at her. How could she be so damn perfect? It threw him off.

She smiled back at him, and the look of her, still flushed and soft from sleep, blew right through the center of him.

"I could make coffee. We could sit out here, drink the first cup of the day and watch the sunrise."

"I've got a better idea." He wanted her—too much and too often—but what was the point in fighting it? Not in the bed, he realized, where he'd dreamed of bloody death and bitter loss.

So he took her hand, pulled her toward the steps leading down.

"What are you doing? Ryder, you can't just wander around. You're naked."

"Oh yeah." Quick and clever, he tugged off her robe, tossed it in the direction of a deck chair. "You, too."

Over her protests, he towed her down the stairs.

"Country dark, country quiet, country private. What are you worried about? Nobody's around to see you. Well, there's Dumbass, but he's seen you naked before. Me, too."

"I'm not walking around here without any clothes on."

"I wasn't planning on doing much walking." So saying, he lowered her to the grass, damp and cool with dew.

"Oh, and this isn't nearly as crazy as walking around naked. We can——"

He lowered his mouth to hers, stopped her words with a slow, shimmering kiss.

"I want to touch you while the sun comes up. I want to watch you, to be in you when the day takes over. I just want you," he said and kissed her again.

So with words that touched her heart, he seduced her. With hands thorough and skilled, he aroused her. She gave herself to him, thrilled to be wanted, grateful to want. She opened herself on the dew-laced grass as the last stars guttered out like candle flames, as the moon slid away under the rise of shadowed land. As those first glimmers of red and gold eked through the night-dark woods.

He took what she offered; gave her what he had. With her he ended the night and began the day. The dreams of death and despair faded away. Inside him something turned, just a little. Something clicked and fell.

Here was hope. Here was Hope. And she was perfect.

As he felt her crest, birds woke singing. And the sky bloomed with another dawn.

❧

SHE EXPECTED GUESTS by three, and the family well before. After she picked up her car, drove back to the inn, she spent the time doing her routine room checks.

She needed to be busy, she thought, so she wouldn't be tempted to speak her thoughts aloud. To speak to Eliza.

In Nick and Nora she checked the lights, the TV remote, the room folder, added a bit to the room diffuser before going out and doing the same in Jane and Rochester.

Fresh flowers would arrive early afternoon.

She moved from room to room changing lightbulbs when needed, adjusting room temperatures.

Back in the kitchen she filled a fruit bowl, set out cookies, made a fresh pitcher of iced tea.

In her office, she checked and answered emails, phone messages, busied herself while she wished the time away.

Today, they'd tell Lizzy they'd found her Billy. What would happen then, she couldn't know. But she wanted to.

Just as she wanted to know what had been behind that look in Ryder's eyes in the predawn dark. He'd been too quiet, even for him, since they'd found Billy Ryder's grave.

And there'd been something quietly urgent in his lovemaking. They should have laughed, she thought now. Two people making love on the lawn with a dog for silent company should have laughed, been playful. But he'd been intense, so focused.

And she? She'd been swept away, taken under by his intense, focused need.

She wanted to reach him. She thought she'd begun to, and now? She didn't know, and he wouldn't say.

She remembered Avery's words. You didn't love and try to change. That was true, that was real and right. So she'd wait until he was ready to tell her what was behind that look in his eyes.

She heard Carolee come in, call out. Hope ordered the rest of her work, added to her list, crossed off what she'd done, then walked out to the kitchen.

"I got sticky buns from next door." Carolee offered a slightly shamed smile. "I just wanted to do something."

"I know what you mean."

"Then I thought I'm not sure sticky buns were the right thing to do."

"They always are." Understanding, Hope put an arm around Carolee's shoulders.

"Will this change things, you think? I know it's selfish, but I don't want things to change. I love everything about this place, including Lizzy. I know, some part of me knows, what we're doing is important. Important things so often make change."

"I wish I knew."

"I guess we'll all know soon enough. I left The Lobby door unlocked," she said when they heard it open. "I thought that would be easier all around."

Clare and Avery came in together. "Sticky buns," Avery said. "I just said to Clare we should go over to Icing and get something. You thought of it first."

"Food's comfort." Clare rubbed a gentle hand on her belly. "I fixed Beckett and the boys cheesy eggs this morning. I just needed to do something. Beckett left early, to try to get some work in."

"Owen, too."

"That makes all three of them," Hope said. "There's Justine and Willy B. Right on time."

"Nervous?" Clare linked hands with Hope.

"Yeah. We did what she asked. Now we'll tell her what we know. I should be excited, but . . ."

"It's sad," Avery said. "It's not like we expected to find him alive and well and living in Vegas, but it's sad."

"Sticky buns," Justine observed. "I made popovers." She set the plate on the island. "I've been restless all morning, and baking helped some."

"We won't go hungry," Avery decided. "We may lapse into a sugar coma, but I'll risk it."

"There's iced tea, but I'll make coffee."

"I'll do it." Carolee patted Hope's arm. "Let me take care of it."

They came in together, the three brothers, in work clothes and rough boots. Hope caught the scents of wood and varnish and paint. For some reason, it relaxed her a little.

"So," Owen began.

"I got something to say," Ryder interrupted. "To her, I guess. To everybody. I had to get my head around it," he added looking directly at Hope.

"Okay." She nodded.

"I had a dream about him last night. Billy Ryder. And don't give me any shit," he warned his brothers.

"Nobody's going to give you any shit," Beckett told him.

He thought he might have given some out if the situation had been reversed. And appreciated the restraint. "It was really vivid. Like being there."

"Being where?" Justine asked him.

"Antietam. September 17, 1862. You read about it, you see war movies, but this . . . I don't know how anybody gets through it, pulls out of it if they live through it. He was in the Union advance on Bloody Lane. It was still morning, and they'd taken heavy casualties. The kid he'd made friends with—George, blacksmith's apprentice—damn near got his head blown off. The blood was all over Billy. He was dazed, probably in shock. He knew where he was. I mean literally. He knew the Pipers, knew the land, knew the sunken road divided the farms."

Carolee stepped to him, held out a mug of coffee.

"Thanks." He looked down at it, but didn't drink. Not yet. "I could hear what he was thinking. It wasn't like reading his mind, but more like . . ."

"Being inside it?" his mother suggested.

"Yeah, I guess that's it. He started thinking about her. Eliza. She wrote to him when she couldn't get away that night they'd planned to elope. She managed to send the letter to his mother. He got it, and he wrote her back, but he wasn't able to send the letter. Didn't know, I guess, where to send it. The night before the battle, he'd written her a letter."

"He loved her," Clare said softly.

"He had a picture of her," Ryder continued, "and he took it out to look at it, thinking how he'd find her when it was over, how they'd get married, he'd build her a house, they'd have kids. She'd changed him. Opened him, is how he thought of it. Anyway, it seemed like a long time in the dream, in his head that he was lying there, wearing his friend's blood and thinking of staying alive so he could have his life with her."

"Jesus, Clare, don't cry."

"It's sad, and I'm pregnant. I can't help it."

"Tell us the rest," Hope demanded. Did no one else smell the honeysuckle? Did know one else realize Lizzy needed to hear the rest?

"They ordered another attempted advance. If you know anything about that phase of the battle, you know it took hours, the Confederate force hunkered down in the sunken road, the Union trying to break their line. And both sides took heavy losses."

Damned if he'd describe it, here in this sunny kitchen with a pregnant woman silently weeping.

"By afternoon, even though both sides brought in reinforcements, it was a goddamn slaughter. Somebody screwed up, ordered a part of the Confederate line to withdraw, and that gave the Union the gap they needed. He was part of that, of that advance once the Confederates were down to hundreds, and the Union had the high ground. You know how it was, Mom, fish in a barrel. They picked them off until bodies lay stacked up. He couldn't do it. He shot, and he killed, thinking of his friend, of his duty. Then he couldn't do it anymore. He thought of her, of his mother, his dead brother, of the blood and the waste, and he couldn't do it. He just wanted it over. He wanted her and the life they could have. And when he lowered his weapon, he was shot."

"He died there," Hope murmured.

"He fell where he stood. He could see the sky. He thought of her, he kept thinking of her, and took out her picture again. That's when he knew it was over for him. When he saw the blood, and he finally felt the pain. He thought about her right up to the end, and he thought he saw her, in his head, calling to him—sick, scared, and calling him. He said her name, and that was it."

He looked down at the coffee in his hand, this time drank deeply. "Jesus."

"He's part of you." Justine wrapped her arms around Ryder, held tight. "Of all of us. He needed someone to tell his story, someone to tell her. It breaks my heart."

"Stop that." But Ryder brushed a tear from his mother's cheek. "It's hard enough without everybody crying about it."

"No more tears." Eliza Ford stood beside Hope, and she smiled.

"Well, holy God." With Tyrone in his arms, Willy B dropped heavily on the stool beside Clare. "Beg pardon."

"You found him."

Ryder wished to God she'd chosen someone else to latch those eyes on. "He's buried a few miles outside of town, on part of what used to be his family farm. He's buried with his brothers."

"He loved his brothers, and when he learned of Joshua's death, he began to talk of joining the fight. But no, not his grave. It isn't his grave you found that matters."

She laid her hand on her heart. "His spirit. He thought of me— thank you for finding that thought, that spirit. He thought of me and I of him as this part ended. I wanted a little stone house, and a family, and every day. But most of all, I wanted my Billy. I wanted his love, and to give him mine. I have it, and I feel it. So much time since I could feel it."

She lifted her hand, turned it. "It does not fade. You found him.

Now he can find me. You are his." She turned to Hope. "You are mine. And I will never forget this gift. I have only to wait for him to come."

"There was honeysuckle near his grave," Hope said.

"My favorite. He promised we would let it grow wild near our little house. He died a soldier, but he was not born one. He died thinking of others. Thinking of me. My Billy. Love, the truest of it, never fades. I need to wait, to watch."

"Lizzy." Beckett stepped forward.

"You were the first to talk to me, to befriend me. You, all of you, helped me become again, gave me a home again. Gave me love again. He will come to me."

"Love can work miracles," Justine said when Lizzy vanished. "I'm going to believe she's right."

"She's happy." Her eyes damp, Avery leaned against Owen. "It really matters that she's happy." Then she grinned at her father, who sat stock-still, Tyrone's paws on his big shoulders, the pug's tongue lapping at his face. "What's the matter, Dad? You look like you've seen a ghost."

"Holy God," he said again, and reached for a sticky bun.

On a quick burst of watery laughter, Clare leaned over to give him and his adoring pug a hard hug.

As they left to go back to work, run errands, live the everyday, Ryder drew Hope out into The Courtyard. "I wasn't not talking to you."

"I know. I do know," she promised him. "You had a strange and difficult experience. I think it must've been like being in the war."

"Yeah, and whoever said war's hell was playing it light. It's worse."

"You needed to process it, take some time. Talking to me doesn't mean telling me everything that's on your mind."

"Okay. Maybe we can set out some guidelines sometime."

"Maybe we can."

"I've got to get back to it. Maybe you want one of those salads you like tonight."

"That would be nice."

"I'll see you later."

She watched him and his dog walk away and, smiling to herself, went back inside to her own work.

# CHAPTER TWENTY

A T JUSTINE'S REQUEST, HOPE BLOCKED OFF THE INN FOR
family on the night of MacTavish's Restaurant and Tap House's
friends and family night. For the last ten days of a sweltering August,
Avery and her crew—and anyone she could dragoon—hauled, carted,
scrubbed, and polished her new space. Often when she did her final
nightly walk-through of the inn, Hope would see the lights on across
the street, and knew Avery and Owen had yet to call it a day. Sometimes she spotted Willy B's truck parked late into the night, or stirred
when Ryder and D.A. slipped in well after she'd gone to bed.

His usual comment was: "Jesus, the Little Red Machine never runs
out of gas."

She helped when she could, hanging art or scrubbing tiles, and as
she had with the inn, saw the transformation of a neglected, unused
space into something vital and exciting and smart.

Hope spent most of the day of the event doing her favorite

thing—perfecting finishing touches—while Avery fussed with recipes, loaded in fresh produce, and held her final staff meeting.

"It's going to be good, right?" Taking a break, Avery brought Hope
a bottle of water and guzzled one of her own.

"Avery, it's going to be fabulous."

"It's going to be good." With a nod, Avery turned a circle in the
bar area. "It looks really good."

"The word's *perfect*."

The lighting struck a note between contemporary and Old World
with funky shapes and dark bronze tones. Pendants hung over the
long granite top of the mahogany bar. High-tops, low-tops, leather
sofas offered inviting seating in a room full of character and texture.
From the rehabbed wood siding to the old-style brick, the old gold
walls and sage green accents, Avery had created a space Hope imagined full of people and fun.

"It's exactly what I wanted. The fabulous Montgomery boys made
it so." Avery leaned against the doorjamb, smiled in at the restroom
where Hope had fussed, adding bud vases to the counter beside the
copper vessel sink, polishing the bronze-framed mirror. "Even the
johns are perfect."

Avery stepped back as she heard the restaurant door open.

"Sorry I couldn't get here before."

"Don't apologize," she said to Clare as she walked through. "Do
you know how pregnant you are?"

Clare rubbed her rounded belly. "Pretty pregnant." She left her
hands there as she looked around. "It doesn't look like you need me.
It looks amazing, Avery."

The dark wood floors gleamed. Lighting sparkled.

"It doesn't look like the same place. And God, something smells
good."

"I've got some soup on. Are you hungry?"

"Constantly."

"Come on back to the kitchen, have a sample."

"I will. I want to look around first." Clare walked down to the bar side, slid an arm around Hope's waist. "Wow, look at all those taps."

"Well, it is a tap house," Avery reminded her. "I'd offer you a beer, but the twins might object."

"They might. I got the thumbs-up from the doctor. I'm having a glass of wine tonight—savoring every sip—to toast your opening. Where is everyone?" Clare wondered.

"The crew will be back in . . ." Avery goggled at her watch. "Oh God, about an hour. It's later than I thought. It always seems to be."

"Everything's done." Hope reached out a hand, took Avery's, joined the three of them. "You're going over to the inn, taking a breath—and a nice bubble bath."

"I don't have time for a bubble bath."

"You do, because everything's done."

"Clare needs soup!"

"Then I'll get Clare's soup, do a quick walk-through, and lock up. You go now, so you can take that breath and bath, get dressed, look like the gorgeous proprietor of Boonsboro's fabulous new restaurant."

"And tap house."

"And," Hope said with a laugh. "Go on, Avery, take the hour. It's the last one you'll have until you shut the doors tonight."

"Okay. All right. I'll be soaking in T&O's amazing copper tub. Oh God, but maybe I should run over to Vesta first and make sure—"

"No. Go. Now." Hope pulled her to the door, opened it, shoved her out. "Bye!"

Laughing, Clare boosted herself onto one of the bar stools. "I really don't need soup. I wanted to give her something to take her mind off her nerves."

"Are you sure? I had some a little earlier. It's delicious. Roasted red pepper and tomato."

"Oh God. Well, if you insist. Just half a cup. Just a taste."

"I do insist. Sit," Hope added when Clare started to rise. "I'll bring it out."

Enjoying the sparkle of Avery's kitchen, Hope ladled soup into a cup, turned off the burner. When she brought it out, Clare sat at the bar, turned toward the room.

"Thanks. I was just thinking, back to high school. Avery and I, cheerleader cocaptains. We were friendly, but not especially close. We got close after I came back home, after Clint died. She really helped me set up the bookstore, make the transition back. And without her, I'd never have met you. And here we are."

She sampled the soup, rolled her eyes. "It's wonderful."

"Without Avery I wouldn't have met you, and I wouldn't be the keeper of the inn."

"Or in love with Ryder." Clare smiled when Hope remained silent. "It shows, at least to someone with heightened hormones."

"I thought we'd enjoy each other, then ease away amicably. Love wasn't part of the plan."

"But love looks so good on you."

"It feels good in me."

"You haven't told him."

"That's definitely not in the plans. We're fine, Clare," Hope insisted, "just as we are. I matter to him. I don't expect more."

"You should."

"It's good to be with someone when you know you matter. Not assume," she qualified, "but *know*. To be with someone, who even when you don't think you want or need it, will stand up for you. Someone who sends you flowers and buys you magic wands. I'm not going to look around the corner for what's next."

"Indulge me. If you did look, what would you hope to see?"

"The chance to make a life together. I guess I want what Eliza wanted. Love, a home, a family that comes from me and the man I love. And, of course, I want my job, good muscle tone, and a fabulous collection of shoes."

"You already have the last three, so I'm putting my hormonal mojo toward getting you the first three. Here, rub the magic babies."

With a laugh, Hope obeyed, gently rubbed Clare's belly. "They're kicking."

"They're either kicking or wrestling on top of my bladder. I'm just a little afraid of how active they're going to be when they're out and have more room."

"More soup?"

"Don't tempt me. I took the rest of the day off to help out here, and no help's needed. My mom has the boys—and she and Dad are bringing them tonight; as Harry rightfully pointed out, they're friends and family, too. Then they're having a sleepover with my parents. I'm at loose ends."

"You're also in Eve and Roarke. Go do what Avery's doing. Have a bubble bath."

"Do you know the last time I managed to sneak in a bubble bath, alone, just me? Without needing to keep an ear out for declarations of war?"

"No."

"Neither do I."

"Grab one now, and keep your phone handy. You can text an SOS if you can't get yourself and the magic babies out of the tub."

"Somehow mean and considerate at the same time. Come on, I'll help you walk through and lock up."

HOPE DIDN'T HAVE time for the indulgence of a bubble bath, but she did indulge. Ryder told her to pick the room, so she'd taken Elizabeth and Darcy for the night. Out of sentiment, she supposed, and because she thought Lizzy would enjoy the company.

"It's Avery's big night." Cozy in an inn bathrobe after her shower, Hope meticulously applied her makeup. "It's going to be great. The biggest thing in town since they opened the inn, at least in my opinion. It just looks fantastic, and tonight it's just friends and family. A kind of christening and trial run at the same time."

She glanced over as the eyeshadow palette she'd chosen lifted into the air. "Girl toys. Fun to play with. I'm going for smoky tonight, a hint of shine to go with a killer red dress and amazing shoes."

She decided there were few women alive, or otherwise, who didn't enjoy playing with makeup. To her way of thinking, those who didn't missed one of the major perks of being female.

"Clare made me think how lucky I am today, to have this place, and my friends, to have Ryder and all the Montgomerys. To have you."

She gave herself a critical study in the magnifying mirror, then stepped back for an overview. "Not bad, huh?"

She moved into the bedroom to dress, taking her time with it, enjoying the steps and stages of preparing for a big night out.

She sat to strap on the mile-high silver heels, and rose for another overview just as Ryder came in, grimy from work with a beer in his hand.

His forward motion stopped, mostly because she'd knocked the legs out from under him. The dress, in sexy siren red, clung to her curves, dipped low at the top, rose high at the hem. The long line of her legs ended in a sparkle of silver straps and needle-width spikes. She'd draped more sparkle around her neck, from her ears so she seemed to glitter and pulse in the light of the Tiffany shade.

"Nice," he said.

She winged up her eyebrows, did a slow turn, gave him a sultry look over her shoulder. "Just nice?"

"Okay, you're a fucking heartbreaker."

"I'll take that as a compliment." She smoothed the dress at her hips. "Hard day at the office?"

"Ha. Got hung up some."

"But progress?"

He had to remind himself she wanted details, then had to search for them as she sprayed on the scent that drove him just a little crazy. "Rough-ins passed this morning, and we're starting on insulation. On the exterior stone work."

"That is progress."

"Why are you dressed already?"

"I'm going over early to help out."

"I'm not wearing a suit." He said it like a warning, maybe a threat.

"Why would you?"

"Willy B's wearing one. With a vest. And a tie. I'm not."

"All right. Since I'm ready, I'm going to go over and see what I can do."

"I'd like to get ahold of you. I'd mess you up."

"You can get ahold of me later." She stepped to him, leaned—but not so far any grime transferred from his clothes to hers—and kissed him. "I'll see you over there once you're changed into not a suit, vest, and tie."

"Yeah." He saw her, he thought, even after she'd shut the door behind her. Sparkling and pulsing and more beautiful than anyone had a right to be.

❧

MUSIC STREAMED OUT of the juke, beer poured from taps, and voices filled a space empty too long. Family and friends mixed and mingled over appetizers, sat and talked, talked, talked over entrées. And lifted glasses in toast to MacT's.

Avery bustled from kitchen to dining room to bar and back, a redheaded dervish in a short green dress with a bubblegum ring bouncing from a chain around her neck.

Hope finally stopped her with a hard hug.

"It's really good," Avery told her. "Is it really good? We've got some glitches."

"It's really good, and they don't show."

"We're working them out. Candles on the tables, music, good food. Good friends."

"You hit the target, Avery, dead center. Just like you did with Vesta. You can expect to pack them in, day after day, night after night."

"We're booked solid for dinner tomorrow, and the day after. Did you see how people are stopping to look in the windows?"

"I did."

"Look, Clare and Beckett are dancing, and my dad's talking to Owen and Ryder at the bar. That's my bar, you know."

"It is indeed. And a beautiful bar it is."

"And that's my boyfriend sitting on one of my bar stools. He's so cute. I think I'm going to marry him and live happily ever after."

"I guarantee it. I'm so happy for you, Avery. So proud of you."

"Everyone who matters to me is here, right here in this place. In my place. It doesn't get better. Go, sit and have a drink. I need to check on some things."

Don't mind if I do, Hope thought and walked to the bar and Ryder. He slid off his stool, waved at it when she gave him a puzzled smile.

"Take it. Your ankles have to be crying by now."

"My ankles are steel, but thanks." She slid on.

"Give her some of that champagne you've got," he told the bartender. "You look like champagne tonight."

"Thank you. You look pretty good yourself."

"I'm no Willy B."

In his dark three-piece suit and polka-dot tie, Willy B flushed. "Oh now."

"Where's Avery?" Owen demanded.

"She went to check on something."

"She needs to sit down for five minutes, whether she knows it or not. I'll take care of it."

When Owen walked off, Willy B smiled into his beer. "He sure loves my girl." He sighed, looked around the bar. "Look what she did. My little girl. What you all did," he amended and tapped his glass to Ryder's.

"She's the machine."

"I'm going to go tell her I'm proud of her."

"Again," Ryder commented when Willy B lumbered off. "He's not especially drunk, just really happy."

"All he has to do is walk across the street to bed when he's ready, so he can get a little drunk if he wants. It's a big night for Avery. For Boonsboro. For all of us."

"Yeah." Ryder stared into her eyes. "A big one."

They stayed until midnight, then gathered at the inn for post-party replay until after one in the morning. By the time she climbed the steps for the last time that night, Hope's ankles of steel had begun to shed a few tears.

She thought of another perk of being female. Taking off heels, peeling out of a killer dress, removing every layer of makeup, and sliding into a bed mounded with pillows beside a hot, sexy man.

And when she stepped into E&D with Ryder she saw the bottle of champagne.

"Like I said, you look like champagne tonight. We could sit out on the porch awhile, have some."

She'd take off, peel out, remove and slide just a little later, Hope thought.

"That sounds good."

She went out with him, chose the wooden bench as she expected him to join her. Instead, once he'd shoved a glass in her hand, he walked to the rail, leaned on it.

No way she was joining him, she decided. She was finished standing in these shoes.

"I know it's been said—many times, many ways—but it was a really fabulous party."

"Yeah. Avery did good."

He turned back, left it at that.

He thought about this. Thought long and hard, and he'd figured it out. But now, looking at her—pulsing, sparkling, a fancy glass of fancy wine in her hand, he wondered if he'd lost his mind.

Beauty queen, city girl. Sure, she was here, she was Hope, but those things were part of her. Like the scent, those smoldering eyes, the shoes that cost more than a decent table saw.

"I hate opera. I'm not listening to opera." He didn't know why he blurted that out. It just came to mind.

"Fine. I don't like opera either."

"Yes, you do."

"No, I don't."

"You've got those opera things."

Over a sip of champagne, she gave him a puzzled frown. "What opera things?"

"Like the—the fancy binoculars?"

"The opera glasses." She laughed. "Guilty, but they're not just for opera. They're also useful for spying on sexy construction workers on hot summer days when they strip off their shirts."

His lips quirked. "Oh yeah?"

"Yeah. And for ballet, and—"

His lips flattened. "I'm not going to any ballet either."

"That's too bad for you."

"Or art films, foreign films, anything—*anything* with subtitles."

She tilted her head. "And when have I ever suggested an art film?"

"Just putting it out there, in case. Or chick flicks." With a firm nod, he swiped a hand through the air. "They're off the table."

She tilted her head the other way, considered. "I like a good romantic comedy. I'd be willing to bargain a romantic comedy for two action movies."

"Maybe. If there's partial nudity."

God, he made her laugh. He made her tremble. She took a slow, deep breath. "I hate football."

His face crumbled into the lines of a man in serious, physical pain. "Oh, man."

"However, I have no objections to a man who enjoys spending a Sunday afternoon watching football on his enormous TV or at a stadium—as long as he doesn't paint his face like some crazy person."

"Have you ever seen my face painted?"

"Just putting it out there, in case," she echoed. "I wouldn't feel obliged to drag him to the ballet, which he wouldn't like, and he shouldn't feel obliged to drag me to a football game. I like basketball."

Intrigued, he walked back, picked up the glass of champagne he'd poured himself and hadn't thought he'd actually wanted. "Yeah?"

"Yes. I like the speed and the uniforms and the drama. I don't have any serious objections to baseball. I'd need to withhold judgment until I've seen a game at a stadium."

"Minor or major league?"

"I think I should sample both before coming to any conclusions, or any definitive policies thereon."

"Okay, fair. I don't want any more pillows on the bed than what you sleep on."

She shook her head, took a slow sip, wondering if it would calm her speeding heart. "No. Absolutely no on that. You just take them off the bed at night, put them back in the morning. It takes a couple of minutes and it adds style and warmth to the bedroom. On this issue, I'm immovable."

He sat on the bench, stretched out his legs. After some thought, he figured you picked your battles, and pillows weren't that high on the list. "I don't go shopping, tagging along to haul bags or getting asked if some dress makes your ass look fat."

"Take my word as gospel on this point. You're the last person I'd want as a shopping buddy. And my ass isn't going to look fat in any dress. Write that down, etch it in your memory."

"I got it."

She let out a quiet breath. No, the champagne hadn't slowed her speeding heart, but that was fine. She liked the rush. "What are we doing, Ryder?"

"You know what we're doing."

"I'd like it spelled out if you don't mind."

"Should've figured." He had to stand again, take a moment to walk to the rail again. "Right from the first minute. You come walking in, upstairs, and it was like being hit with a lightning bolt. I didn't like it."

"Really?"

"Yeah, really. I stayed away from you."

"At least," she murmured.

"I kept my distance. Then you wanted sex."

"Oh, Ryder." She laughed, shook her head. "Well, that's true."

"So I gave you a break. It was just supposed to be sex, right?"

"Right."

"It was okay to like each other. It's better if you do. And maybe to figure each other out some, all good. But the more I figured you out, the more it wasn't just sex. I didn't much like that either."

"This has been very hard on you."

"See, that snooty tone? Why does that grab me like it does? You grab me, Hope, by the throat, by the gut, by the balls, by the heart."

Her breath caught. How foolish. How wonderful. "You said heart."

"I kept thinking it's just the way you look, because the way you look, it drops a man to his knees. But that's just a nice add-on. Really nice, but it's not the way you look. It's the way you are. Everything

kept sliding around, like it was trying to find its place. Then it clicked
in, fit. Done. You. Naked in the grass at sunrise. That was it."

"It was sooner for me," she managed, "but not very much."

"So, I'm going to tell you." He took another drink. "I've said it to
my mother, and to Carolee. My grandma, and if I'm drunk enough
I've said it to my brothers. But I've never said it to another woman.
It's not right to say what you're not sure of, or to use it to smooth
the way."

"Wait." She set her glass aside, rose to go to him. To stand with
him over Main Street and look in his eyes. "Tell me now."

"I love you. And I'm okay with it."

She laughed. Her heart sang, but she laughed and took his face in
her hands. "I love you. And I'm okay with it, too."

"I don't do poetry."

"No, Ryder, you don't do poetry. But you stand up for me. You
tell me the truth. You make me laugh, and you make me want. You
let me be and feel who I am. And you fell in love with me even when
you didn't want to."

He closed his hands over her wrists. "I'm not going to stop."

"No, don't stop."

She leaned to him, leaned on him, let that wonderful surge come,
and let her speeding heart ride on it. "I'm so happy to love you. So
happy to have you, just exactly the way you are. I'm so happy you told
me tonight, when it was about friends and family, when it was about
home."

"It used to bother me that you were perfect."

"Oh, Ryder."

"I had that wrong." He drew her back a little, to see her. "What
you are is perfect for me. So." He dug into his pocket, pulled out a
box, flipped it open.

She stared at the diamond, then at him. "You—" She didn't know how to get the words out through the stunned surprise and joy. "You bought me a ring?"

"Of course I bought you a ring." Annoyance shimmered. "What do you take me for?"

"What do I take you for?" She tried to catch her breath, couldn't. And stared down at the ring that flashed like a star in the porch lights. "Exactly what you are. Just exactly."

"I love you, so we're getting married."

She held out her hand, tapped her ring finger.

"Right." He took the ring, slid it on her finger.

"It fits," she said softly. "How did you know?"

"Measured one of your other ones."

"I'm so lucky to be marrying a handy man."

"When you do, you're moving. My wife's not living at the inn."

"Oh." Details, she thought. She was good with details and adjustments. So she wrapped her arms around him. "I bet Carolee will be happy to take over the innkeeper's apartment, shuffle the schedule. We'll work it out."

"Later," he decided.

"Later," she agreed, and lost herself in him. "It's beautiful. It's all beautiful."

She leaned her head on his shoulder, started to sigh. And her breath caught. "Ryder. Oh God, Ryder, look. There." She pointed to the other end of the porch.

They stood together in the shadows, locked in an embrace. He wore the rough clothes of a laborer, not a torn and bloody uniform. Hope saw his hand fist at the back of Lizzy's dress, as Ryder's often did with hers.

"He found her. Her Billy, he found her. They found each other. They're together now."

"Don't cry. Come on."

"I cry when I need to. Get used to it. After all this time, after all the waiting, there they are. You look like him a little. Like her Billy."

"Maybe. I don't know."

"I do. I think you showed him the way. I don't know how. It doesn't matter how." For a moment her eyes met Lizzy's. Joy into joy. "Everyone's exactly where they belong."

O N A BLOOMING EVENING IN SPRING, AVERY TWISTED HER gumball-machine ring while Clare and Hope fastened her wedding gown.

"I'm not nervous."

"Of course not," Hope said.

"Okay, a little, but just because I want to look really good."

"Believe me, you do. Turn around and look," Clare ordered.

In the bedroom of The Penthouse, Avery turned toward the big mirror. "Oh, I *do*. I really do look good."

"Gorgeous is what you look," Hope corrected. "Avery, you're gorgeous. The dress is stunning. I shouldn't have doubted your online acumen."

"It just right." Delighted with herself, Avery turned a circle so the sparkling skirt flowed with her. "It's me."

"You're glowing like a candle." Clare touched Avery's bright hair. "A flame."

"Champagne! Quick! Before I tear up and ruin the makeup Hope worked so hard on."

"For the bride, and the attendants." Hope poured. "And even for the nursing mother."

"The twins can handle it. Luke and Logan are tough."

"Look at us. The wife, the bride, and the bride-to-be." Avery lifted a glass, toasted them all. "Your turn in September," she said to Hope.

"It can't come soon enough. Which is crazy to say since I have so much left to do. But today's yours, and I can promise you everything is exactly and wonderfully perfect."

"It couldn't be otherwise. I'm marrying my boyfriend, with my two best friends beside me, my dad, the woman who's been my mom since I was a kid, my brothers. And I'm doing it in the most beautiful place I know."

"I'm going to text the photographer, have him come up. We're on a schedule," Hope reminded her.

She checked everything. The flowers, the food, the table displays. Candles, linens. Stopped long enough to help Beckett pass the chubby-cheeked twins and their three brothers to Clare's mother and Carolee. To adjust Ryder's tie, as an excuse to nuzzle his neck.

"Why don't we just do it now?" he asked her. "We're all dressed up, got a preacher coming."

"September." She lingered over a kiss. "It'll be worth the wait."

Exactly on time, she rounded up Willy B.

"Thank God." Justine patted his cheek. "He's nervous as a bride himself."

"It's my girl."

"I know it, honey. You go on and get her now."

Hope waited, fetched tissues when Willy B's eyes welled up, and gave Avery's makeup a final touch-up.

"What're you mumbling about?" she asked Clare.

"I'm praying. That I don't hear the babies cry, because if I do my milk might start up."

"Oh my God. I should've thought of earplugs." But laughing, she grabbed Clare's hand to hurry to the door.

Avery wanted an entrance, so they'd descend the stairs to The Courtyard where the guests sat, and Owen waited with his brothers.

All so handsome, she thought. All so right. In a few months she'd walk down these same steps to Ryder.

She glanced across the lot, over the white tent where Fit In Boons-Boro stood prettily in its soft blue coat, its silver trim.

She was happy to have it there, and a little sorry not to have Ryder right in back of the inn every day.

She wondered what Justine would think of next, and was grateful she'd be able to watch it evolve.

Then she squeezed Clare's hand. "Look."

On the porch facing the flower-decked arbor, Lizzy stood with her Billy.

"They're still here," Clare said quietly. "It always surprises me."

"They're happy here. For now anyway. It's their home."

And hers, she thought. Her town, her place, her home. In it she'd build a life with the man she loved.

She glanced back, blew a kiss to the bride, then walked down the steps toward the promise.

KEEP READING FOR AN EXCERPT FROM
THE FIRST BOOK IN THE INN BOONSBORO TRILOGY
BY NORA ROBERTS

## The Next Always

NOW AVAILABLE FROM PIATKUS

THE STONE WALLS STOOD AS THEY HAD FOR MORE THAN two centuries, simple, sturdy, and strong. Mined from the hills and the valleys, they rose in testament to man's inherent desire to leave his mark, to build and create.

Over those two centuries man married the stone with brick, with wood and glass, enlarging, transforming, enhancing to suit the needs, the times, the whims. Throughout, the building on the crossroads watched as the settlement became a town, as more buildings sprang up.

The dirt road became asphalt; horse and carriage gave way to cars. Fashions flickered by in the blink of an eye. Still it stood, rising on its corner of the Square, an enduring landmark in the cycle of change.

It knew war, heard the echo of gunfire, the cries of the wounded, the prayers of the fearful. It knew blood and tears, joy and fury. Birth and death.

It thrived in good times, endured the hard times. It changed hands and purpose, yet the stone walls stood.

In time, the wood of its graceful double porches began to sag. Glass broke; mortar cracked and crumbled. Some who stopped at the light on the town square might glance over to see pigeons flutter in and out of broken windows and wonder what the old building had been in its day. Then the light turned green, and they drove on.

Beckett knew.

He stood on the opposite corner of the Square, thumbs tucked into the pockets of his jeans. Thick with summer, the air held still. With the road empty, he could have crossed Main Street against the light, but he continued to wait. Opaque blue tarps draped the building from roof to street level, curtaining the front of the building. Over the winter it had served to hold the heat in for the crew. Now it helped block the beat of the sun—and the view.

But he knew—how it looked at that moment, and how it would look when the rehab was complete. After all, he'd designed it—he, his two brothers, his mother. But the blueprints bore his name as architect, his primary function as a partner in Montgomery Family Contractors.

He crossed over, his tennis shoes nearly silent on the road in the breathless hush of three a.m. He walked under the scaffolding, along the side of the building, down St. Paul, pleased to see in the glow of the streetlight how well the stone and brick had cleaned up.

It looked old—it *was* old, he thought, and that was part of its beauty and appeal. But now, for the first time in his memory, it looked tended.

He rounded the back, walked over the sunbaked dirt, through the construction rubble scattered over what would be a courtyard. Here the porches that spanned both the second and third stories ran straight and true. Custom-made pickets—designed to replicate those from old photographs of the building, and the remnants found during excavation—hung freshly primed and drying on a length of wire.

He knew his eldest brother, Ryder, in his role as head contractor, had the rails and pickets scheduled for install.

He knew because Owen, the middle of the three Montgomery brothers, plagued them all over schedules, calendars, projections, and ledgers—and kept Beckett informed of every nail hammered.

Whether he wanted to be or not.

In this case, he supposed as he dug out his key, he wanted to be— usually. The old hotel had become a family obsession.

It had him by the throat, he admitted as he opened the unfinished and temporary door to what would be the lobby. And by the heart— and hell, it had him by the balls. No other project they'd ever worked on had ever gotten its hooks in him, in all of them, like this. He suspected none ever would again.

He hit the switch, and the work light dangling from the ceiling flashed on to illuminate bare concrete floors, roughed-in walls, tools, tarps, material.

It smelled of wood and concrete dust and, faintly, of the grilled onions someone must have ordered for lunch.

He'd do a more thorough inspection of the first and second floors in the morning when he had better light. Stupid to have come over at this hour anyway, when he couldn't really see crap, and was dog-tired. But he couldn't resist it.

By the balls, he thought again, passing under a wide archway, its edges of stone still rough and exposed. Then, flipping on his flashlight, he headed toward the front and the work steps that led up.

There was something about the place in the middle of the night, when the noise of nail guns, saws, radios, and voices ended, and the shadows took over. Something not altogether quiet, not altogether still. Something that brushed fingers over the back of his neck.

Something else he couldn't resist.

He swept his light around the second floor, noted the brown-bag backing on the walls. As always, Owen's report had been accurate. Ry and his crew had the insulation completed on this level.

Though he'd intended to go straight up, he roamed here with a grin spreading over his sharply boned face, the pleasure of it lighting eyes the color of blue shadows.

"Coming along," he said into the silence in a voice gravelly from lack of sleep.

He moved through the dark, following his beam of light, a tall man with narrow hips, the long Montgomery legs, and the waving mass of brown hair with hints of chestnut that came down from the Riley—his maternal side.

He had to remind himself that if he kept poking around he'd have to get up before he got to bed, so he climbed up to the third floor.

"Now that's what I'm talking about." Pure delight scattered thoughts of sleep as he traced a finger down the taped seam of freshly hung drywall.

He played his light over the holes cut out for electric, moved into what would be the innkeeper's apartment, and noted the same for plumbing in the kitchen and bath. He spent more time wandering through what would be their most elaborate suite, nodding approval at the floating wall dividing the generous space in the bath.

"You're a frigging genius, Beck. Now, for God's sake, go home."

But giddy with fatigue and anticipation, he took one more good look before he made his way down the steps.

He heard it as he reached the second floor. A kind of humming— and distinctly female. As the sound reached him, so did the scent. Honeysuckle, sweet and wild and ripe with summer.

His belly did a little dance, but he held the flashlight steady as he swept it down the hall into unfinished guest rooms. He shook his head as both sound and scent drifted away.

"I know you're here." He spoke clearly, and his voice echoed back to him. "And I guess you've been here for a while. We're bringing her back, and then some. She deserves it. I hope to hell you like it when she's done because, well, that's the way it's going to be."

He waited a minute or two, fanciful enough—or tired enough—to imagine whoever, or whatever, inhabited the place settled on a wait-and-see mode.

"Anyway." He shrugged. "We're giving her the best we've got, and we're pretty damn good."

He walked down, noted the work light no longer shone. Beckett turned it on again, switched it back off with another shrug. It wouldn't be the first time the current resident had messed with one of them.

"Good night," he called out, then locked up.

This time he didn't wait for the light, but crossed diagonally. Vesta Pizzeria and Family Restaurant spread over another corner of the Square, with his apartment and office above. He walked down the sloping sidewalk to the back parking lot, grabbed his bag from the cab of his truck. Deciding he'd murder anyone who called him before eight a.m., Beckett unlocked the stairwell, then climbed past the restaurant level to his door.

He didn't bother with the light, but moved by memory and the backwash of streetlights through the apartment. He stripped by the bed, letting the clothes drop.

He flopped facedown on the mattress, and fell asleep thinking of honeysuckle.

THE CELL PHONE he'd left in his jeans pocket went off at six fifty-five.

"Son of a bitch."

He crawled out of bed, over the floor, dug his phone out of the pocket. Realized he was holding his wallet up to his ear when nobody answered.

"Shit."

Dropped the wallet, fumbled out the phone.

"What the hell do you want?"

"Good morning to you, too," Owen responded. "I'm walking out of Sheetz, with coffee and donuts. They've got a new clerk on the morning shift. She's pretty hot."

"I'll kill you with a hammer."

"Then you won't get any coffee and donuts. I'm on my way to the site. Ry should be there already. Morning meeting."

"That's at ten."

"Didn't you read the text I sent you?"

"Which one? I'm gone two days and you sent me a million freaking texts."

"The one that told you we rescheduled for seven fifteen. Put some pants on," Owen suggested and hung up.

"Hell."

He grabbed a two-minute shower, and put some pants on.

The clouds that rolled in overnight had managed to lock the heat in, so stepping outside was like swimming fully dressed through a warm river.

He heard the thump of nail guns, the jingle of music, the whine of saws as he crossed the street. From inside, somebody laughed like a lunatic.

He turned the corner of the building as Owen pulled his truck into the parking lot behind the projected courtyard. The truck gleamed from a recent wash, and the silver toolboxes on the sides of the bed sparkled.

Owen stepped out. Jeans, a white T-shirt tucked into his belt— and on the belt the damn phone that did everything but kiss him good night (and Beckett wasn't taking bets against that)—marginally scuffed work boots. His bark brown hair sat tidily on his head. He'd obviously had time to shave his pretty face, Beckett thought resentfully.

He shot Beckett a grin, and Beckett imagined the eyes behind those bronze lenses were cheerful and alert.

"Give me the damn coffee."

Owen took a tall go-cup, marked with a *B*, from its slot in the tray.

"I didn't get in till three." Beckett took the first, deep, lifesaving gulp.

"Why?"

"I didn't get out of Richmond until close to ten, then I hit a parking lot on 95. And don't, just do *not* tell me I should've checked the traffic report before getting on. Give me a fucking donut."

Owen opened the enormous box, and the smell of yeast, sugar, and fat oozed into the thick air. Beckett grabbed a jelly, wolfed half of it, washed it down with more coffee.

"Pickets are going to look good," Owen said in his easy way. "They're going to be worth the time and money." He cocked his head toward the truck on the other side of his. "Drywall's up on the third floor. They're going to get the second coat of mud on today. Roofers ran out of copper, so they're going to fall a little behind schedule on that, but they're working on the slate until the material comes in."

"I can hear that," Beckett commented as the stone saws shrilled.

Owen continued the updates as they crossed to the lobby door, and the coffee woke up Beckett's brain.

The noise level spiked, but now that Beckett had some sugar and caffeine in his system, it sounded like music. He exchanged greetings with a couple of the crew hanging insulation, then followed Owen through the side arch and into what would be the laundry, and currently served as an on-site office.

Ryder stood scowling down at blueprints spread over a table of plywood on sawhorses. Dumbass, his homely and purehearted mutt—and constant companion—sprawled snoring at his feet.

Until a whiff of donut had his eyes popping open, his scruffy tail thumping. Beckett broke off a bite of donut, tossed it, and the dog nipped it neatly out of the air.

D.A. saw no logical purpose in the fetching of sticks or balls. He concentrated his skills on fielding food of any kind.

"If you're going to ask for another change, I'll kill you instead of Owen."

Ryder only grunted, held out a hand for coffee. "We need to move this panel box, then we can box in this space here, use it for second-floor utility."

Beckett took another donut, considered as Ryder ran through a handful of other changes.

Little tweaks, Beckett thought, that wouldn't hurt and would probably improve. Ryder was, after all, the one of them who lived most intimately with the building. But when Ryder moved to eliminating the coffered dining room ceiling—a thin bone of contention between them—Beckett dug in.

"It goes in, just as on the plans. It makes a statement."

"It doesn't need to make a statement."

"Every room in this place is going to make a statement. The dining room makes one with—among other things, a coffered ceiling. It suits the room, plays off the panels we're making for the side of the windows. The depth of the windows, the ceiling, the arch of stone on the back wall."

"Pain in the ass." Ryder scanned the donuts, opted for a cinnamon twist. He didn't so much as glance toward the madly thumping tail as he tore off the end, flipped it into the air.

D.A.'s teeth snapped together as he caught it.

"How'd it go down in Richmond?"

"The next time I volunteer to design and help build a covered deck for a friend, knock me unconscious."

"Always a pleasure." Ryder grinned around the donut. His hair, a deep dense brown that edged toward black, sprang out from under his paint-stained MFC gimme cap. His eyebrows lifted over eyes of gold-flecked green. "I thought you were mostly doing it to get into Drew's sister's pants."

"It was part of the motivation."

"How'd that go for you?"

"She hooked up with somebody a couple weeks ago, a detail nobody bothered to pass on to me. I never even saw her. So I'm bunked down in Drew's spare room trying to pretend I can't hear him and Jen fighting every damn night, and listening to him complain how she's making his life hell every damn day."

He drained the coffee. "The deck looks good though."

"Now that you're back I could use some help on the built-ins for the library," Owen told him.

"I've got some catching up to do, but I can give you some time after noon."

"That'll work." Owen handed him a file. "Mom's been down to Bast's," he said, speaking of the furniture store down the street. "Copies of what she's after—with dimensions, and the room they're for. She wants you to draw it up."

"I just did the last batch before I went to Drew's. How fast can she shop?"

"She's meeting Aunt Carolee there tomorrow. They're talking fabrics, so she wants to see if and how what she's got going fits ASAP. You're the one who took off a couple days hoping to get laid," Owen reminded him.

"Struck out, too."

"Shut up, Ry." Beckett tucked the file under his arm. "I'd better get started."

"Don't you want to go up, take a look?"

"I did a walk-through last night."

"At three in the morning?" Owen asked.

"Yeah, at three in the morning. It's looking good."

One of the crew stuck his head in. "Hey, Beck. Ry, the drywaller's got a question up in five."

"Be there in a minute." Ryder pulled a handwritten list off his clipboard, passed it to Owen. "Materials. Go on and order. I want to get the front porch framed in."

"I'll take care of it. Do you need me around here this morning?"

"We've got a few million pickets to prime, a mile or two of insulation to hang, and we're decking the second-story porch, front. What do you think?"

"I think I'll get my tool belt after I order this material."

"I'll swing back through before I head out to the shop this afternoon," Beckett told them, then got out before he ended up with a nail gun in his hand.

❧

AT HOME, HE stuck a mug under his coffee machine, checked the level of the water and beans. While it chomped the beans, he went through the mail Owen had stacked on the kitchen counter. Owen had also left sticky notes, Beckett thought with a shake of his head, listing the times he'd watered the porch and houseplants. Though he hadn't asked Owen—or anyone—to deal with those little chores while he'd been gone, it didn't surprise him to find them done.

If you were dealing with a flat tire or a nuclear holocaust, you could depend on Owen.

Beckett dumped the junk mail in the recycle bin, took what mail needed attention and the coffee through to his office.

He liked the space, which he'd designed himself when the Montgomery family bought the building a few years before. He had the old desk—a flea market find he'd refinished—facing Main Street. Sitting there, he could study the inn.

He had land just outside of town, and plans for a house he'd designed, barely started, and kept fiddling with. But other projects always bumped it down the line. He couldn't see the hurry, in any case. He was happy enough with his Main Street perch over Vesta. Plus it added the convenience of calling down if he wanted a slice while he worked, or just going downstairs if he wanted food and company.

He could walk to the bank, the barber, to Crawford's if he wanted a hot breakfast or a burger, to the bookstore, the post office. He knew his neighbors, the merchants, the rhythm in Boonsboro. No, no reason to hurry.

He glanced at the file Owen had given him. It was tempting to start right there, see what his mother and aunt had come up with. But he had other work to clear up first.

He spent the next hour paying bills, updating other projects, answering emails he'd neglected when in Richmond.

He checked Ryder's job schedule. Owen insisted they each have an updated copy every week, even though they saw or spoke to each other all the damn time. Mostly on schedule, which, considering the scope of the project, equaled a not-so-minor miracle.

He glanced at his thick white binder, filled with cut sheets, computer copies, schematics—all arranged by room—of the heating and air-conditioning system, the sprinkler system, every tub, toilet, sink, faucet, the lighting, tile patterns, appliances—and the furniture and accessories already selected and approved.

It would be thicker before they were done, so he'd better see what his mother had her eye on. He opened the file, spread out the cut sheets. On each, his mother listed the room the piece was intended for by initials. He knew Ryder and the crew still worked by the numbers they'd assigned to the guest rooms and suites, but he knew J&R—second floor, rear, and one of the two with private entrances and fireplaces—stood for Jane and Rochester.

His mother's concept, and one he liked a lot, had been to name the rooms for romantic couples in literature—with happy endings.

She'd done so for all but the front-facing suite she'd decided to dub the Penthouse.

He studied the bed she wanted, and decided the wooden canopy style would've fit nicely into Thornfield Hall. Then he grinned at the curvy sofa, the fainting couch she'd noted should stand at the foot of the bed.

She'd picked out a dresser, but had listed the alternative of a secretary with drawers. More unique, he decided, more interesting.

And she apparently had her mind made up about a bed for Westley and Buttercup—their second suite, rear—as she'd written THIS IS IT!! in all caps on the sheet.

He scanned the other sheets; she'd been busy. Then turned to his computer.

He spent the next two hours with CAD, arranging, adjusting, angling. From time to time, he opened the binder, refreshed himself on the feel and layout of the baths, or took another look at the electrical, the cable for the flat screens in each bedroom.

When he was satisfied, he sent his mother the file, with copies to his brothers, and gave her the maximum dimensions for any night tables, occasional chairs.

He wanted a break, and more coffee. Iced coffee, he decided. Iced cappuccino, even better. No reason not to walk down to Turn The Page and get one. They had good coffee at the bookstore, and he'd stretch his legs a little on the short walk down Main.

He ignored the fact that the coffee machine he'd indulged himself in could make cappuccino—and that he had ice. And he told himself he took the time to shave because it was too damn hot for the scruff.

He went out, headed down Main, stopped outside of Sherry's Beauty Salon to talk to Dick while the barber took a break.

"How's it coming?"

"We've got drywall going in," Beckett told him.

"Yeah, I helped them unload some."

"We're going to have to put you on the payroll."

Dick grinned, jerked a chin at the inn. "I like watching it come back."

"Me, too. See you later."

He walked on, and up the short steps to the covered porch of the bookstore, and through the door to a jangle of bells. He lifted a hand in salute to Laurie as the bookseller rang up a sale for a customer. While he waited he wandered to the front-facing stand of bestsellers and new arrivals. He took down the latest John Sandford in paperback—how had he missed that one?—scanned the write-up inside, kept it as he strolled around the stacks.

The shop had an easy, relaxed walk-around feel with its rooms flowing into one another, with the curve of the creaky steps to the second-floor office and storerooms. Trinkets, cards, a few local crafts, some of this, a little of that—and, most of all, books and more books filled shelves, tables, cases in a way that encouraged just browsing around.

Another old building, it had seen war, change, the lean and the fat. Now with its soft colors and old wood floors, it managed to hold on to the sense of the town house it had once been.

It always smelled, to him, of books and women, which made sense since the owner had a fully female staff of full- and part-timers.

He found a just-released Walter Mosley and picked that up as well. Then glancing toward the stairs to the second-floor office, Beckett strolled through the open doorway to the back section of the store. He heard voices, but realized quickly they came from a little girl and a woman she called Mommy.

Clare had boys—three boys now, he thought. Maybe she wasn't even in today, or not coming in until later. Besides, he'd come for coffee, not to see Clare Murphy. Clare Brewster, he reminded himself. She'd been Clare Brewster for ten years, so he ought to be used to it.

Clare Murphy Brewster, he mused, mother of three, bookstore proprietor. Just an old high school friend who'd come home after an Iraqi sniper shattered her life and left her a widow.

He hadn't come to see her, except in passing if she happened to be around. He'd have no business making a *point* to see the widow of a boy he'd gone to school with, had liked, had envied.

"Sorry for the wait. How's it going, Beck?"

"What?" He tuned back in, turned to Laurie as the door jingled behind the customers. "Oh, no problem. Found some books."

"Imagine that," she said, and smiled at him.

"I know, what are the odds? I hope they're as good for me getting an iced cappuccino."

"I can hook you up. Iced everything's the order of the day this summer." Her honey brown hair scooped up with a clip against the heat, she gestured to the cups. "Large?"

"You bet."

"How's the inn coming along?"

"It's moving." He walked to the counter as she turned to the espresso machine.

Pretty little thing, Beckett mused. She'd worked for Clare since the beginning, shuffling work and school. Five years, maybe six? Could it be that long already?

"People ask us all the time," she told him as she worked. "When, when, when, what, how. And especially when you're going to take down that tarp so we can all see for ourselves."

"And spoil the big reveal?"

"It's killing me."

With the conversation, the noise of the machine, he didn't hear her, but sensed her. He looked over as she came down the curve of the steps, one hand trailing along the banister.

When his heart jumped, he thought, Oh well. But then, Clare had been making his heart jump since he'd been sixteen.

"Hi, Beck. I thought I heard you down here."

She smiled, and his heart stopped jumping to fall flat.